Ark for the Uncalled

VLADIMIR MAXIMOV

Ark for the Uncalled

Quartet Books
London Melbourne New York

I dedicate this book to my wife, Tatyana.

First published in English by
Quartet Books Limited 1984
A member of the Namara Group
27/29 Goodge Street, London W1P 1FD

Translated from the Russian *Kovcheg dlya Nezvanykh* by Julian Graffy

British Library Cataloguing in Publication Data

Maximov, Vladimir
  Ark for the uncalled.
  I. Title   II. Kovcheg dlya nezvanykh. *English*
  891.73'44[F]   PG3483.2.K8
  ISBN 0-7043-2455-5

Typeset by M C Typeset, Chatham, Kent
Printed and bound in Great Britain
by Mackays of Chatham Ltd, Kent

Main Characters in
Ark for the Uncalled:

On the Train:
Fyodor Tikhonovich Samokhin (Fedya, Fedenka, Fedyok) – peasant from
the village of Sychovka, region of Tula.
Tikhon Samokhin – his father.
Agrafena Samokhina – his grandmother.
Nikolai Ovsyannikov (Kolya) – peasant from neighbouring village of
Kondrovo.
Klavdiya Ovsyannikova – his wife.
Lyubov Nikolayevna Ovsyannikova (Lyuba, Lyubka, Lyubanya) – their
daughter.
Sergei Tyagunov – locomotive mechanic from nearby town of Uzlovsk.
Natalya Tyagunova – his wife.
Alimzhan Batyev – Tatar, from Uzlovsk.
Pavel Ivanovich Mozgovoy (Pasha, Pashenka, Pavlusha) – the leader of
the convoy.

In the Kremlin:
Iosif Vissarionovich Stalin.
Lavrenty Pavlovich Beria – head of Soviet secret police.
Aleksandr Poskryobyshev – Stalin's private secretary.
Ilya Nikanorovich Zolotarev (Ilyusha) – peasant from Sychovka who is
making a career in the Soviet bureaucracy.
Kira Slutskaya – Jewish actress.
Sergei Vladimirovich Simansky – Russian Orthodox Patriarch.
Pyotr Nikolayevich Krasnov – Cossack general, fought on the side of the
Germans in the Second World War.
Nikolai Nikolayevich Krasnov – his grandson.
Andrei Grigorevich Shkuro – Cossack chief, fought on the side of the
Germans in the Second World War.
Sergo Kavtaradze – friend of Stalin's youth.

At the Railway-Sidings:
Misha Bogat – Secretary for organizational work in the district committee
of the Young Communist League.
Alimushkin – NKVD lieutenant.
Lyampe – NKVD major.

Ivan Osipovich Khokhlushkin (Vanya) – leader of construction brigade.
Petrunya Babushkin, Semyon Blokhin, Yasha Khvorostinin, Foma
    Polynkov, Andryukha (Andreika) Shishigin, Little Ivan Zuyev, Big
    Ivan Zuyev – members of the brigade.
Mariya (Masha) – woman who lives with the brigade.

At the Objective:
Viktor Nikolayevich Pashin – major.
Polina Vasilevna Demidova (Polya) – doctor.
Gubin – driver.
Nikolai Nosov – regular soldier.
Leonid Petrovich Lyalin (Lyonya) – mechanic.
Vladimir Konashevich (Vovchik) – pilot.

At Baikal:
Pyotr Yevseich Shilov – Zolotarev's driver.
Ivan Zagladin – member of Khokhlushkin's brigade, in administrative
    exile.

On Sakhalin and the Kuriles:
Matvei Zagladin – member of Khokhlushkin's brigade, working as a
    herdsman on the island of Matua.
Prikhodko – head of the civil authorities on Sakhalin.
Yarygin – head of the political section of the regional civil authorities.
Ponomarev – head of the civil authorities on the Kuriles.
Krasyuk – his deputy for political affairs.
Pekarev – head of personnel for the Kuriles.

The names in brackets are the affectionate diminutive forms by which
Russians habitually address each other.

'For many are called, but few are chosen'
Matthew 22:14.

Chapter One

1

Through waking, through sleeping, through the veil of night, across the time of times and again across half of time, cleaving the darkness of nights and the lightness of days, two voices stream, drift, fall upon the sinful earth:
  'Have you been there again?'
  'I have.'
  'And have you come again to intercede for them?'
  'I have.'
  'Are you not tired of doing so?'
  'No.'
  'But they have betrayed you again and cursed your very name!'
  'That is of no importance.'
  'You are incorrigible.'
  'I am of your line.'
  'What do you ask for this time?'
  'Still the same thing.'
  'They have long forgotten who they are; they care for nothing except their insatiable flesh; they can no longer reach their goal.'
  'They will reach it. Blindly, but they will reach it. Only you must help them one last time.'
  'As you wish, but do not come back again with this request . . .'
  And starry silence re-forms over the whole vault of the earth, over Russia, over the village of Sychovka, near Tula.

2

In fact it was a village only in name. Of almost forty homesteads, at best five or six lived off the earth, and those half-heartedly. This loosening of ties with the land had begun as early as the end of the last century, when, by the will of the fates, the first branch-line of the Syzran–Vyazma railway was laid through this district, and the local poor moved off in search of a merry life and an easy kopeck.

1

And then things went downhill faster and faster: 1905, the Stolypin Reforms, the First World War, the fierce Civil War, and the Three Great Famines, with the Second World War as a bonus – all of them cruelly weeded out Sychovka, depriving it finally of its basis in the black earth.

Few survived these fatal trials, and those who did spawned a hollow tribe who from miserable childhood on were more accustomed to beggary and theft than to peasant labour or a village trade. And so by our time Sychovka was famous only for having gifted to the region and humanity three doughty horse-thieves (who were none the less beaten to death), two district policemen and a man who almost became a People's Commissar, but disappeared somewhere on the long camp trail between Vladivostok and Nagaev Bay.

The busy and noisy epoch encircled the village ever more tightly with seasonal work: the blue pyramids of mine waste-heaps rose up along the whole horizon, the open-work planks of bore-holes began to loom in the nearby gullies, there was a smell of burnt clay over a brickworks, which had appeared as if by magic above a weir, and the old road to the kingdom of the railway became ever wider and more trampled. People fled the land as in famine, or elemental disaster, as though punished by God. The earth became a burden for man, his misfortune and his curse. It imposed duties and gave nothing in return except cares, taxes and daily fear. Man grew fretful and morose.

Finally, of those who remained close to the land, one was a blacksmith, one a bee-keeper, and the rest are best not spoken of: war-widows with a brood of their own and other people's children. They were all registered as members of the neighbouring Collective Farm in Kondrovo, where they made up a special Sychovka brigade, which was about as useful, it has to be said, as last summer's rain.

In the destructive bustle of its mad existence, the village didn't even notice when during high water the banks of the weir burst and the swirling water swept away its peaceful cemetery (in those years the young of Sychovka died elsewhere and the old people and the sudden victims of the First Great Famine were buried in their own kitchen-gardens). And when at last the village came to its senses, it was neither struck dumb nor plunged into despair, but obediently began to carry its dead to the graveyard at Sviridovo, five versts away. As it lost its link to the earth, so the village forgot its own past.

The only signs of peasant life – the chain linking them to the past and recalling their ancient condition – were the dumb animals: the hens, the geese, the ducks, the piglets, and, more rarely, the cattle. The uncertainty of their life forced the villagers to hold on to this necessary economic support for the time being. But the presence of these immemorial beasts in the unstable, arbitrary life of the village only made the decay all around seem more poignant.

By our day, the fragile vessels of their five-walled huts, roofed in straw or tarred felt, were advancing without rudder or sail through the murky waters of stagnant Russia, neither recalling the past nor guessing the future, out of sight of shore or hope, with a drunken yearning in their eyes and bitterness in their hearts, and no one there, neither a single person nor a single living creature, could have answered the question: Where to and what for?

3

'Get going!' As he got into the cart, the father didn't even turn his head in the direction of the hut. With his streaming wall-eye he just stared into space somewhere above his son's head and said: 'Why make a fuss? I never want to see it again!'

Fyodor sensed, guessed that his father's heart was aching, but that he didn't want to let on; he wanted to keep the Samokhin self-control, didn't want to indulge himself, and so the brief parting with the house he was born in seemed to him even more heart-rending. 'Why don't we stay here? Why go anywhere else?' he said, and with sudden fury he jerked the reins. 'Where the hell are we going anyway?'

For all his life, as long as he remembered, Fyodor had wanted to rush off, anywhere, just to get away from this God-forsaken hole, this abject poverty, this endless, coarse drunkenness. It was precisely for this reason that he had left school years ago for the trade academy, and then gone to the front as a volunteer; but wherever fate cast him he would inevitably return here, to this achingly cold expanse, to the smells of rotten straw and dung in the snow, to the smoke of the stoves in the mornings. During long nights spent far away he dreamed of the mowing by the yellow water of the little Sychovka river, the modest little gatherings outside the village, the endless winter evenings on the warm stove. Waking up in the dark, he was seized by a bitter-sweet yearning.

And now, on his way to distant parts, to the back of beyond, to the Kurile Islands, unimaginably far away, Fyodor was convinced that it would not be that long before he would be drawn to come back here, and that though he would curse the day he was born, he would nevertheless return.

The decision to try his luck far away once again was made as soon as he read the announcement that they were looking for men. As usual the recruitment bureau promised mountains of gold in the future, and these promises were accompanied by generous travelling expenses. At that time Fyodor had recently been demobbed and had spent some time unemployed, in search of sure and steady work. At the front, he had worked as a driver and learnt how to operate a field-radio, so he knew his own worth.

The recruiting agent cast a quick glance at his papers. Without even asking him any questions, he nodded: 'Go to the medical commission, and then fill in these forms . . .'

The whole family got up: as an exception, his father, his mother and his ancient grandmother were put down as dependants (his qualifications had clearly impressed the recruiting agent greatly). At first his mother wasn't eager to go off who knew where, abandoning her own house and a small but steady supply of food, but his short-tempered father quickly knocked sense into her, and his grandmother didn't care whether she was lying down or on the move – she even seemed to perk up at the prospect of the journey. And so, at last, they set off.

They left during a slushy spring in which everything lost any sharpness of contour and was submerged in a brittle, icy dankness, which made parting particularly melancholy. In this sea of drizzle and slush even the cart seemed like a boat, sailing into the unknown.

At the turning for Uzlovsk, Fyodor could stand it no longer. He turned round and suddenly found himself panting for breath: he seemed to have his heart in his mouth and a burning sensation like a red-hot coal inside him: 'Lord, will I ever return?'

In Uzlovsk, Fyodor returned the horse he'd borrowed to the commune stables, found lodging for the night for the old folk, and himself went off in search of a bar, where in the company of the local alcoholics he drank himself to oblivion. In his lucid moments he poured out his heart to his chance drinking-companion, invalided in the last war, who was ready, in exchange for free drinks, to agree with everything he said: 'You've obviously fought yourself . . . That means that as an injured war hero you have the right to live anywhere you like . . . Even Leningrad, even Sochi . . . Aren't I right?'

'Of course.'

'So why did you come back?'

Fyodor's hospitality had made the invalid quick-witted: 'Well, it's my home town, when all's said and done. People are right when they say "East, West, home's best".'

'You're right. But the devil sends me bobbing round the world like, if you'll pardon the expression, a turd round an ice-hole, or rolls me on like a rolling stone. People these days have feeble souls, with no attachment to anything, only good for scooping out to make jelly . . . I grew up here. I've buried lots of people here. I've got drunk at more christenings than I care to remember. So what attracts me to the Kurile Islands, tell me that, old mate.'

His 'old mate' was clearly ready to go along with anything he said, as long as the drinks kept appearing: 'You've hit the nail on the head, lad, it's crystal clear. With a head like yours you'll go a long way.'

'I don't know about that,' said Fyodor, feeling better and better disposed towards his companion, 'but I have got three trades, and my war record's pretty good. I got six medals and the least of them was "For Valour".'

'You can tell an eagle by its flight.' The invalid wouldn't let up. An insuperable thirst wrapped his rabbit eyes in celestial brightness. 'There aren't many like you around these days . . .'

The conversation went on like this until the bar closed, by which time the group around their table had reached half the size of a small company, with everyone ready to hang on the words of his benefactor till the cock crew, if necessary, not forgetting meanwhile to order himself a succession of drinks at his expense, and snacks to go with them. The invalid disappeared unnoticed somewhere in the middle of Fyodor's story about his childhood and youth, but there were new listeners for his epic of life at the front.

'The battalion commander says to me: we've got to, Fedya, we've got to. So I say to him, well if we've got to, we've got to, we'll do it as well as we can, you can rely on me. So off we went, the three of us, my two trusty mates and me. We were inseparable – into fire and water, wherever you like . . .'

The whispers of admiration around him carried Fyodor along, and no force in the world, except the police, could have stopped him.

Then everything became a blur: faces, people, conversations. Everything was swimming round him, and he too was swimming somewhere, with no idea how he'd got out into the street. The frosty early spring night sobered Fyodor up a bit. He walked slowly through the silent town, plunged into almost total darkness, and as he gradually shook off his drunkenness his soul began to regain consciousness, and with it awareness of the world around him. Suddenly he sensed the hidden warmth of the houses behind their fences, felt the ringing crunch of the soft ice under his boots, saw the starry sky above his head: the earth seemed like an enormous ship, sailing off somewhere through the night to shores as yet unknown. And an elation he had never experienced before coursed through his veins: 'Lord, brothers, we should just live and live in this beauty, but we spend all our lives cutting one another's throats!'

And it was Night, and Man was in that Night, and with them was He who preserved them unto His Day.

4

In Moscow, the heated goods wagon they had travelled in was shunted off to the goods station at Mitkovo while they waited for the whole train to be formed up. The station was huddled between two old blocks in an old part of the town. On one side was a brewery and the boxes of a few workers' houses, while on the other was a quiet street lined with poplars, where detached wooden houses alternated with good old stone ones from before the Revolution. Fyodor knew this street well. His distant relatives, the Samsonovs, lived here. He had been mobilized with Aleksei Mikhailych, the head of the family, and went off to the front in the same troop train. Samsonov was a serious fellow, who had spent seven years in the camps of Kolyma for links with Trotskyites. He died on the way to the front, before Fyodor's very eyes, and this gave Fyodor a permanent sense of guilt before his relatives: as if he had survived at his kinsman's expense. So that now when he passed through Moscow he never visited them. He had heard that they lived in abject poverty, on bread and water. Aleksei Mikhailych had left two children, and his wife Fedosya, an educated woman from Uzlovsk who was very interested in clothes and completely incompetent, would have been lost without Samsonov's sister Mariya, whom she had taken into the family from the village as a nurse in better times, and who had remained with them. It was now she who ran the house, if those almost bare fifteen square metres in a communal flat that resounded with drunken shouts could be called a house.

But now something impelled Fyodor, something – though he himself could not yet have said exactly what – forced him to go there, to that quiet street under the poplars, into that unprepossessing yard between two houses, that dark dirty corridor of the noisy, box-like flat, and to knock at the grubby door of his distant relatives.

A fragile-looking woman opened the door. Though obviously not old she looked prematurely aged, and as she watched him with dull, expressionless, seemingly tear-stained eyes, she asked, with equal lack of expression: 'Who do you want?'

'Why you, Fedosya Savelevna, how are you?' And sensing the fear about to appear on her listless face, he calmed her down: 'Your relative, from Sychovka, Samokhin's son, Fyodor.'

And seeing the immediate expression of warmth and life on her face, Fyodor realized how much this woman must have had to endure, to be so glad to see a man who was not really even her relative, or at least one of the most distant kind.

'Come in, come in!' she said, bustling around. 'I thought even our relatives had forgotten us . . . Of course it's not the time to do much visiting . . . Let's at least have some tea. Are you here for long?'

'No, we're just passing through. I've signed up for the Kurile Islands. Our train is forming up at your station.'

Fedosya began to dart about the room. She hit her wide-eyed son over the head – 'Quiet, you!'; she picked up the tea-pot and then a tiny, already opened bottle of vodka; then she decided to peel some potatoes, and from her frenzied behaviour it was obvious that even twelve years of living without her husband had taught her nothing at all. 'Oh you town women,' Fyodor thought with melancholy pity, 'you're all the same.'

'It's a shame Marusya's on the first shift today – she'd have been so pleased to see you!' Bustling about incompetently, she kept talking and talking, as if she were trying to ward off some secret dark thought. 'She's my only helper. I'd be lost without her! At least we've managed to get the little girl a place in a nursery, or I don't know what we'd have done with her. But as for him,' she gave a contemptuous nod in the direction of the boy, who looked with hidden expectation at the guest with the medals and badges all over his chest, 'he's got completely out of hand, I can't do anything with him. If his father was here he'd knock some sense into him . . .'

It was only then that it dawned on Fyodor with dizzying clarity: she kept talking and talking and rushing around the room to no purpose because she was hoping that he had brought news of her husband, hoping for a miracle to bring her spiritual comfort!

7

But what could he tell her? How at the halfway point, somewhere near Sukhinichi, Messerschmitts had suddenly bombed them in open country, and their commanding officers had been the first to run for their lives, while the untrained and leaderless soldiery of the first wave of conscripts had rushed after them? Or how her husband was the only one not to lose his head, and had given the order to split up and make way gradually to a nearby wood? Or how, staying back till everyone else had got away, he'd looked round to make sure nobody was left behind, and had then been caught by the final dive of a Messerschmitt just as he was reaching the trees?

Fyodor had buried him himself with his Sychovka mates, and he even thought he remembered the grave, but so much had happened after that to the area around Smolensk, and he himself had been so pummelled and battered in the four appalling years that followed, that it didn't ever occur to him to go and look for the hastily dug grave.

No, Fyodor could not have told her about this, he dared not. Instead, he just said: 'It's lively kids like him who turn into real men, Fedosya Savelevna.' And immediately he started preparing to leave, afraid that he would not be able to control himself after all, and would tell her without intending to.

'I'd better be going, Fedosya Savelevna, or they might leave without me.'

She realized something, sensed something. She looked completely crushed, and the last ray of light slowly left her dull eyes.

'What a shame . . . You haven't even had a proper cup of tea. But of course, if you must . . . it's a long journey . . .'

As he got up, he could not resist stuffing a hundred-rouble note, folded in four, in a gap in the chair, which he pushed up against the table.

'Goodbye, Fedosya Savelevna, don't think ill of me.'

'Good heavens, no! . . .', she answered almost wordlessly.

And so he left. Moscow was dazzling as the snow dripped from the roofs in the sun. Sparrows like jumping crotchets pecked out their innocent music in the tangled net of the budding poplars. Perfidious cats screwed up their eyes in the sunlight, sensing easy prey. Little boys played oblivious noisy games of hopscotch and tag on the pavements. The world was floating in a sunny haze towards those same unknown banks. Life went on.

A slight melancholy from his meeting with Fedosya Samsonova still gnawed at Fyodor, but in his twenty-five years he had seen so many deaths, and had himself been more than once only a hair's breadth away from it, that his sadness at the death long ago of Aleksei Mikhailovych, whom he had ardently respected from that day on, eventually gave way to a sharp sense of belonging to the exuberant world all around him.

Fyodor strode on, not noticing the puddles, with a light gaiety in his supple young body, and a joyous certainty that he still had a long time to live, that he was about to start on a long journey with the promise of new experiences, and that, at last, this would be the making of him. He would not return to Sychovka empty-handed: 'Courage, Fedya: death or glory, we can show the world what we're made of!'

5

Tikhon Samokhin was what the villagers called a 'nervy' man; put more simply he was a petty tyrant. That was how he'd lost his eye: one day he had refused to give way to a neighbour's bull. He put the fear of God into his wife, and even his mother, an old woman of some character, was afraid of her son's moods. Tikhon had one weakness: his son. Either because he had had no other children, or because of the sentimentality common to all cruel people, he forgave Fyodor everything – and not only forgave him, but approved all his inclinations and caprices from his earliest years. Yet miracles do happen: the lad did not turn out the way such children usually do – he didn't turn out spoilt, he didn't tyrannize his family, but grew into the village favourite, an obliging lad who could say no to no one.

And so now, when Fyodor appeared at the door of the wagon, the old man, busy resoling his mother's felt boot with a useless piece of rubber, immediately grinned at him: 'Not bad weather today, eh, Fedya?' And he winked conspiratorially with his one eye. 'Had a good time, have you? Spring fever?'

'No, Dad, I went to see Samsonova, Aleksei Mikhailych's wife. You must remember Fedosya Savelevna.'

And seeing that his son had not been hanging about in bars, but like a responsible fellow had been visiting relatives – admittedly distant ones, whom Tikhon had not forgiven their earlier arrogance, but relatives all the same – the old man completely softened and even felt a certain sympathy for Fedosya himself: 'Of course! She was a smart woman, I remember her well. Her father was a train-driver, a barrel-chested fellow, and her husband almost became a People's Commissar, only they cut him down a bit, but he was a fine figure of a man too.'

'Stop the jokes, Dad', Fyodor snapped angrily. 'The woman's at her wits' end. All she has is two mouths to feed. Thank God Maruska helps her or they'd be done for.'

The old man agreed to this as well, immediately adapting to the new tone.

'Take no notice of me, Fedya, I didn't mean anything. I feel sorry for the woman myself, alone with two kids, with no support from anyone, no way out. It's very hard.' But a stubborn malice, eating him up, still came to the surface. 'Only I don't think Klavka Andreeva had it any easier, when the likes of Alyoshka Samsonov drove her off to Siberia with her kids wearing little more than their underwear. All she had was a cow and a horse and she was slaving away without her husband.'

'You're right, Tikhon Sevastyanich,' came the voice of Nikolai Ovsyannikov from the upper bunk opposite. Usually a taciturn and reliable fellow, he came from the neighbouring village of Kondrovo. 'And it wasn't just Klavka! What about Venka Agureev? Or Semyon Lakiryov? Or Gavrushkin from Torbeyevo? Don't you remember how they took him, as if he was a madman, and kept banging him over the head with a pistol-butt? One bloke in glasses was particularly vicious: he looked really puny, all skin and bone, but he made noise enough for three: "Hit the kulak bastards", he kept shouting. What a swine. It makes me wild even thinking about him.'

Suddenly he fell silent, clearly realizing his anger had made him say too much. Ovsyannikov was a peasant who had been battered, crushed and trundled off: battered by the Civil War, crushed by the famine during Collectivization, and then trundled around the camps for illegally mowing a meadow in the grove at Kondrovo. Luckily for him the Second World War wiped his slate clean. He came home covered in medals as far as his belt, or else he'd have had no peace till his dying day, and he wouldn't have been allowed to sign up for the Kuriles.

Ovsyannikov was on the way out there with his wife Klavdiya – continually pursed lips in a browless, evil face – and their only daughter Lyuba, a quiet seventeen-year-old blonde, pregnant by some fine young fellow who'd been passing through, as she later admitted to her parents. As a rule, this family communicated only in whispers and tried to keep its distance from the others, either because of their daughter or simply by force of habit.

The wagon as a whole was divided into four parts, four pens, four so far separate, enclosed worlds: two on each side, one above and one below, with a sturdy ladder between them. The Samokhins had the lower berth to the left. The Ovsyannikovs had the upper one on the right. They were the only real peasants here. The other two families came from Uzlovsk.

Opposite the Samokhins was a young couple called the Tyagunovs. Sergei was a mechanic at the locomotive depot, and Natalya a ledger-clerk at the station accounts department: bright, lively, with a brick-red fringe from ear to ear. She spent her time rushing here and there getting supplies for the journey, never omitting to dart a devilish look in Fyodor's direction.

Above the Samokhins were the large, boisterous family of the Uzlovsk Tatar Alimzhan Batyev, known, of course, as Baty. All day long up there one could hear shouts, tears, laughter, a babble of various noisy voices.

This red box on wheels, this iron ship which had seen so many sights in its time, was now to be their home and their fortress for the long journey to the Great Ocean or, as it is also called, the Pacific.

When Fyodor thought about it, he felt both joy and alarm. The war had jolted him around in heated wagons and Pullmans of all kinds and conditions. It was one thing to travel for a day or two in the company of your mates: that was pure pleasure – you could get to know them and they could get to know you. It was something else entirely with a family in each corner, one of them with an entire brood. 'It's like a damned menagerie,' he laughed to himself. 'You don't know whether to laugh or cry!'

Fyodor got up to go out and have a smoke, but when he reached the door it opened wide in front of him as if by magic and he saw a high-cheekboned face with a network of tanned wrinkles and a mouth full of gold teeth that grinned from ear to ear: 'Hallo, lads! How's life? How are things?'

'Life's all right,' Fyodor answered for everyone: for some reason he'd taken an immediate liking to the fellow with the false teeth, 'but things are pretty awful.'

'I see you're a witty fellow' – the man's grin grew even wider. 'If you like I'll appoint you entertainment officer for the whole trip.'

'And who might you be?' Fyodor did not like being put down.

'That's no way to speak to a superior, soldier.' The man went on smiling, but a coldness had crept into his grey eyes. 'But if you're really interested, I'm the leader of the convoy, Mozgovoy'; and after a pause he added, 'Pavel Ivanovich.'

With two agile movements (clearly he was used to this), the newcomer was in the wagon; he lightly pushed Fyodor to one side,

11

as if he was an inanimate object. Then he stood in the middle of the wagon, and with the confident glance of a man who knows he is in charge, he said: 'Attention! Listen to my orders!' He really did stand in the middle of the wagon as if it was the captain's bridge. 'Drink is categorically forbidden, likewise fighting. When the train stops, remain within the station bounds. As for the other activity, keep it within reason. Anyone who breaks the rules gets put off the train. Is that understood?'

In his slightly unwieldy body, tightly wrapped up in a worn-out short greatcoat with side pockets, in his way of holding himself, in his short, imperious movements, one sensed a man who knew his own worth and that of the life he'd lived.

Instinctively, in their guts, the peasants understood: the boss! And expressing the general mood, Alimzhan replied smartly from the upper bunk: 'Yes, comrade chief!'

He gave another gold-toothed smile, pushed his semi-military cap to the back of his head and concluded: 'Well, that's fine then. At the double, they're just going to couple the engine on and we'll be off.' And suddenly he disappeared with a final order: 'Steady!'

Ovsyannikov was the first to break the silence. 'He's a serious fellow. He'll be a strict taskmaster! He's obviously done this kind of thing before.'

'We ate talkers like him for breakfast,' snapped Fyodor, irritated by his own humiliation.

'In that case you'll probably be going hungry, Fedya,' Tikhon egged on his son. 'The man's an oak!'

'Don't bang your heads while you're bowing!' snapped Fyodor, more from self-esteem than anything else; when all was said and done, Mozgovoy was quite a good fellow. 'Haven't you suffered enough yet?'

Natalya Tyagunova had the last brief, encouraging word: 'Gird your loins, lads. That fellow won't leave you much time for any mischief!'

And as if in confirmation of her words, the long whistle of the engine came through the slightly open door, the wagon jerked forward and, slowly gathering speed, it moved off into the expanse that lay open before it.

Having a smoke in the doorway, Fyodor watched the landscape drift by. From the time when, as a very young man, he had first left home, a feeling had gradually welled up in him like water through sand, until it filled him completely: it was a feeling of the definitive loss of everything that was now passing by; every house, every tree, every pointsman at every level-crossing, the level-crossing itself, even the whiffs of bluish dusk gathering through the pines over the suburban dachas. 'Can I really be leaving for ever? Will I never . . .' thought Fyodor, and his heart sank and ached.

The further they went, the more flat and wooded the landscape became. At first it seemed the same stretch of Central Russia in the evening haze of late spring, but gradually, almost imperceptibly, things around him were changing, as if the dusty panes had suddenly been wiped with a damp cloth: the distant landscape became sharper and fresher.

How could Fyodor then have guessed that their train had made a sharp turn to the East!

Chapter Two

1

The burning stings of grains of sand stuck into every pore of their skins. Their bodies resounded brittly and painfully, as if woven out of a fiery, porous mass. Their lips, the roofs of their mouths, their throats, seemed to form a single, hastily smelted trumpet; they exuded hoarse and burning pain. But the people, the multitude of people, stretched out along many horizons, kept walking and walking through this sand, and none of them knew where this truly mad journey would end.

The kingdom of sand had become the cradle, the dwelling of these people. Their life flourished and disintegrated according to its unstable but pitiless laws. In this kingdom, as in any other, people miraculously found each other, and from their love children were born into the world. They had hardly learnt to walk before they too moved on, side by side with the others; further and further. In the end a generation survived which, born in motion, thought that this motion was the meaning of its existence. They had no one they could ask, they did not turn to the graves, and those who walked in front and knew everything were so far away that even a bird would have to fly many days and nights on end to catch up with them.

But if someone could imagine Him who walked at their head, he would have seen a tall Old Man with the deeply sunken eyes of a basilisk and a bitter furrow at his firm lips. He was ageless, as old as Time, or perhaps older. He walked leaning on an elm staff, hardly looking where he went, seemingly at random, paying no attention either to goal or to easy terrain. Some secret but precise knowledge *led his intentions and actions. He* knew *not only where and when they would stop, but even what was being done behind his back – that he also* knew. *He knew but he did not turn round; only, with the passing of years, the bitter furrow at his firm mouth became ever more bitter, and his steps, despite everything, more steadfast and rapid.*

At his side, half a step behind him, like his shadow all these years, was a still virile man whose easy stride displayed his lively mind and inquiring character. He trusted the Old Man implicitly, trusted his hill-dweller's wisdom, his lofty mission and his communion with the Scroll of Time. He still remembered the day when they had left the land of Egypt: the morning reflected in the mirror of a reservoir, the pestilential silence of the narrow, clay-walled streets, and the fiery breeze from the desert. Then he was little more than a boy; the girls did not even lower their eyes as he passed, and the tiny children invited him to join in their games; but so many years had gone by since then and so much had happened that he might long since, in his own opinion, have become a grandfather or even a great-grandfather. But dedicating his life to the Old Man he had stopped thinking of women, and the flesh no longer troubled him.

He would have considered himself a happy man, had he not begun in recent times to notice strange and frightening things. Or more precisely one strange thing: suddenly he had begun to think from time to time that he had passed this way before. He was so staggeringly sure of this that he felt an almost irresistible urge to close his eyes, to shake off the hallucination and never return to this enticing temptation. But the terrible fata morgana *recurred ever more frequently, plunging him into despair and spiritual confusion.*

Yet on one occasion he was unable to hold out; the resemblance was just too mirror-like: the scarcely noticeable protuberance of a clay ruin, covered in thorny undergrowth. Suddenly he thought he must slowly be going mad. The ruin was eroded at the edges and so the middle of it formed an uneven but distinctive cone, exactly like the one he had seen long before. The white shadow of madness touched his head. Do not punish me, Lord! Do not deprive me of my reason!

At dead of night, when the sleep of oblivion had settled on the horizons of horizons and the last embers were burning out under the ashes of the evening bonfires, he silently crawled towards the Old Man and quietly complained: 'Forgive me, rabbi, but I think I am going mad.'

'Speak.'

'I have the feeling that I have already seen the places we passed through today. Either it is an abyss, or a temptation. Rid me of this delusion if you can.'

'Forget about this.'

'But I am afraid, rabbi!'

'Will you find it easier if I tell you that you are right?'

'Have pity on me, rabbi!'

'Do you want pity or truth?'

'Will I have the strength to bear this truth?'

15

'You know everything already, and you are in the hands of the Lord.'

'But why, why, rabbi? Why do we pave our path with graves so many years?'

'But do you not hear the cries of the new-born?'

'So that tomorrow they can be buried? Why?'

'So that when we have buried our slaves we can emerge as free men, and forget about slavery for ever. If you are not ready to go further, remain here and return to dust in ease and thoughtlessness.'

'I am with you, rabbi . . .'

And as if awoken by his answer, the sand under their feet trembled and began to move, and there came from the very bowels of the earth a long and threatening rumbling, reminding them of the fragility and vainness of earth's stability.

2

The damp poplars, on which the first leaves had appeared, exuded morning drizzle under the window. Seen through them, the nearby houses looked particularly myopic and forlorn. The dull sky over the town, flecked by short flights of sparrows, promised a miserable day. The three enormous windows let in a steady draught of cold air: they had hastily turned the local secondary school into a central administrative bureau, which was why Zolotarev's office still looked stubbornly like an ordinary class-room. Neither the ornate chandelier, nor the heavy carpets, nor the clumsy mahogany furniture could give dignity or isolation to a space which seemed specifically created for draughts and bustle.

After the comfortable, well-heated offices with their curtains and *portières* to keep out the sounds in the Berlin suburb of Karlshorst, where Zolotarev had successively run several sections in the Economic Directorate of the headquarters of the Soviet Military Administration in Germany, he found it difficult to get used to the morose desolation of the walls of his homeland, which he had almost forgotten during those years.

The assignment took him unawares. Even a day before he could not have imagined that his fate would take such a sharp and inconceivable turn. There had long been talk in Berlin of an impending visit from 'the boss himself', but this was probably why hardly anyone took the rumour seriously. People even teased each other – cautiously, they would not have dared anything more explicit – with announcements of the safe arrival of the big boss, but when he finally did arrive unexpectedly everyone kept quietly to their office burrows, expecting judgement and punishment. The sinister reputation of the visitor, who acted as overseer of the organs of internal affairs and state security at the highest level, contributed strongly to this unease. Those who had ever had even chance dealings with him remembered their meetings without particular enthusiasm.

Zolotarev waited like the others. He had long since learnt the saving rule of any service: they may call for you and they may not, but in any case wait patiently; be on the alert, ready and fully armed. He had meticulously gone through in his mind any possible oversights in his department, had gathered the most important papers in a special stamped file which he kept for solemn occasions, had decided how he would speak and behave: 'I don't think I've forgotten anything,' he concluded. 'Lord, spare me this trial! Let this cup pass from me!'

But 'this cup' did not pass from him. Next day, towards evening, the internal telephone on his desk cooed out its command: 'Jump to it, Zolotarev!' In the threatening half-whisper of the adjutant of the Directorate Commander, he sensed an oddly encouraging note. 'At the double! Report!'

He cast a quick glance down (was his uniform in order?), ran his left hand lightly through his hair (was it tidy?), took the stamped file in his right hand (following chancellery instructions!), rushed silently along the corridor and a minute later, no more, he was already opening the leather-covered door of the Directorate Commander.

The tall man in civilian clothes at the general's enormous desk did not even raise his eyes to look at him. He listened to his regulation report with the same indifference, not taking his eyes off the papers, which he seemed to be not so much reading as studying page by page, as if he was trying to get to the sense that was hidden not in the text itself but behind it. As he jerkily turned the pages the lenses of his pince-nez reflected his impatience, and his browless effeminate face winced with occasional irritation. Still not raising his head from the papers, he suddenly disconcerted Zolotarev with a question: 'Do you like fishing?'

'I do, comrade Marshal of the Soviet . . .'

'My name is Lavrenty Pavlovich.' He raised his eyes to look at Zolotarev for the first time. Behind their magnifying lenses they looked especially piercing. 'It's easier and shorter.' A scarcely noticeable Georgian accent only emphasized the indolent imperiousness of his tone. 'It's good that you like fishing. I

17

appreciate it when a man likes his work. Here's the job I have for you. Will you go as head of the central administration to the fishing grounds in the Far East?'

'I am ready to carry out any task which the party or the government entrusts to me!' A warm wave of elation and gratitude enveloped Zolotarev. 'Dear Lavrenty Pavlovich . . .'

'Enough, enough,' the latter lazily waved his puffy palm. 'I believe you.' He got up slowly, moved aside the file full of papers (it was only then that a sudden insight told Zolotarev that this was his personal dossier), left his desk and, hands behind his back, began to waddle around the office. 'But you must realize, Zolotarev, that the main thing is not the fish. We are entrusting to you an important political mission of extreme delicacy. Our valiant soldiers have liberated lands that are immemorially Russian from the Japanese aggressors: Southern Sakhalin and the Kurile Islands. Your task is to consolidate that success. We shall give you money, men and material, but you must give us firm Soviet power in these new lands. Is that clear?'

'Yes, sir, comrade . . . Lavrenty Pavlovich!'

'Do you know what a Bolshevik is, Zolotarev?' The man stopped directly opposite him, staring straight at him, and went on, without waiting for an answer. 'A Bolshevik sets himself a goal, screws up his eyes and then moves forward towards it. He sees nothing around him, only his goal, and he walks towards it.' The marshal in civilian clothes demonstrated how to screw up your eyes and how to move forward. 'Is that clear?'

'Yes sir, dear Lavrenty Pavlovich . . .'

But the man had already turned his back on him: 'You may go.'

Three days later Zolotarev was settling into his new office in Moscow, on Verkhnekrasnoselskaya Street. Having learnt from his earliest days in the bureaucracy the golden rule that 'the bosses know best', he gave no thought to how the choice had fallen precisely on him. Now he was full of an exhilarating sense of his own power over enormous territories and tens of thousands of people. The mere awareness that one word from him could bring all these lands, all these masses to life, and set them in motion, aroused a wave of arrogant enthusiasm in him. 'Good on our lads,' he almost sang to himself, 'we'll show them what we're made of!'

Zolotarev was leafing mechanically through the lists of recruits he had been given to sign, looking desultorily through the dense columns of figures and names, when his attention was suddenly drawn to one particular name in the typewritten list: 'Samokhin, Fyodor Tikhonovich, born 1919. Place of birth,

Sychovka, district of Uzlovsk, province of Tula'.

There could be no mistake. There could not be another Sychovka, also in the district of Uzlovsk, also in Tula province. And there had been only one Samokhin family in the village. And Zolotarev had not forgotten their son, the ringleader of the local lads. 'Just my orphan's luck,' he complained angrily, sensing his recent elation disappear instantaneously. 'All I need to start off with is people from my own village!'

Usually Zolotarev tried not to think of Sychovka and its inhabitants. Almost everything he wanted to forget about was linked with his native village. His father had abandoned the land as a young man and gone to the Syzran–Vyazma railway as a fireman. His wages were quite good for the time and by the standards of the village, but he brought less than half of them home and so they ate bread only every other day, and sometimes less often. Quiet and amenable by nature, he became irrational in his cups, and then everyone without distinction felt the sharp edge of his tongue: his wife, his son, his father-in-law and mother-in-law. The morning after he would sigh, berate himself, even look in at the church, but on pay day the whole thing would start all over again. So his family was considered one of the poorest in the village, which caused his son not a few insults and black eyes: only really lazy boys failed to tease or beat him.

This long nightmare came to a sudden and dramatic end: drunk again, his father fell under a shunting locomotive, and through the efforts of the railway management Zolotarev was sent to the boarding school for railwaymen's children with a full allowance.

There, with the enthusiasm of a convert, he plunged into public activity in which, as the son of an extremely poor proletarian, he rapidly began to thrive. At the outbreak of war, Zolotarev was already secretary of the Uzlovsk regional committee of the Komsomol, but, even though he was well protected by his position and his power, he still tried if possible to avoid his native village. He wanted to forget, to eradicate the memory of the oppressive nightmare of his Sychovka past, but like rust in grain it occasionally came stubbornly back into his mind.

When Zolotarev had first sat down at a desk, had felt the reassuring stability of the chair beneath him, had breathed in the senselessly busy atmosphere of an office, he had suddenly realized with jubilation that at last he had found salvation. Here, where authority depended not on fists or on an ability to hold your liquor but on a subtle skill at keeping quiet when necessary and speaking out when necessary, he finally felt in his element, and from then on nothing, short of a second Flood, could have dislodged him from the position he occupied. And he began a surreptitious life-and-death struggle for every inch of his place in the sun, elbowing those near him aside and sometimes stepping over them until, rapidly exchanging each chair for a better one, he reached a seat in the *nomenklatura*. And there he put down firm roots.

For the same reason, Zolotarev was still unmarried; he was afraid that the bustle of family life would cause him to miss the chance of climbing another step of the career ladder. The women in his life could be quickly counted, and not one of them had left a remotely lasting mark or echo. Only once had he given way to a heady delusion, let his heart soften, and cravenly betrayed the rule he had set himself once and for all; and this had almost cost him if not his life, then at least his career.

His memory was turning to a tiny fragment of the distant past when suddenly the internal telephone rang: Zolotarev was being summoned to the Minister.

From the emphatic significance with which the Minister got up to meet him, Zolotarev guessed that this would be a long conversation.

'Good evening, comrade Zolotarev, sit down.' The bulldog chin of the Minister was tensely expectant: the solemn pause that followed was long enough to emphasize the importance of the moment. 'Today,' he looked at his watch, 'at exactly twenty-one hours, you and I will be received,' the Minister's voice turned to a solemn rasp, 'by comrade Stalin. I trust you understand,' his short straight neck grew stiffer still, 'what that means.'

For a moment the news scorched his throat; then the hot wave rose to his head. He knew only too well what that meant. The school he had had to pass through in his years working in the party apparatus and the security organs had cooled his earlier youthful ardour to a significant degree, leaving just a mixture of fear and admiration before a man who had reached the position where it was no longer necessary either to fear rivals or to seek anyone's friendship. His earlier blind enthusiasm had now become a conscious and convenient mask which made it possible for him to swim freely in the uncertain waters of the sea of the *nomenklatura*, a sea in which words did not have the direct sense they had in the real world. Here they were only passwords, symbols, landmarks. You had to be on the alert at all times; you had to be two people: speaker and listener, capable of correcting yourself, of stopping yourself in time. A superfluous sound, a redundant note, a carelessly turned phrase brought death or oblivion in their wake.

And the whole lacy web of these subtle signals rose in an intricate spiral to a single point, a single man, and was controlled from there skilfully and pitilessly. But there was no way back for those whom fate had favoured with a miraculous ascent through its deadly labyrinths to contact with the point where all threads met. Each of them became that palpitating glow-worm which shone just as long as the shadow of this point did not fall on it. Therefore the coming audience did not promise Zolotarev only rainbows: the heights that were opening were vertiginous, but the abyss below them was deeper still.

'Such an honour, comrade Zolotarev, is not accorded to everyone.' Once again the Minister had adopted a lofty tone, but he could not sustain it; he softened, a childish smile spread across his face like a fleshy mouth-organ, revealing his tobacco-stained teeth. 'And we too have not been forgotten. That means we too are valued. Because otherwise we, as Commissars for front-line soldiers, are treated by the Council of Ministers as stepsons, last in every queue; all we get is the knocks, and not a word of gratitude. The war is over, and now we are on the move again. The people have got down to real work, they've got to be fed. If comrade Stalin has called us, there must be a reason.' The Minister stared at him expectantly. 'He's also thinking about the young people, the young cadres. He's far-sighted, he's preparing worthy replacements for old fellows like us . . .'

The Minister was clearly flattering Zolotarev, who was aware of the real reasons for this fawning and therefore treated him as an equal, though without ever stepping beyond the bounds of his subordinate rank; experience told him that things were safer that way. The department which had sent him here, and those in charge of that department, to all intents and purposes held all the threads of the state machine in their hands and had total control of it, reacting instantaneously and harshly to the slightest deviation from the norms, principles and directives approved by those in authority and accepted by all. A man attached by this department to any cell of the government machine became a sort of unofficial source of power in it, ready when necessary to replace the existing source of power. And if the Minister vibrated servilely in his conversation with him, it was because in his own time he too had replaced his predecessor in similar circumstances, and he knew full well how things had turned out for him.

'Well,' the Minister looked at his watch and got up, his massive body instantly at the ready. He took a deep breath of air as if he was about to dive into water. 'It's time.'

Through the car windows, Moscow flowed dismally past in freezing drizzle. Even the gaudy patches of posters and banners, bleached by the rain, brought no gaiety to its sullen dampness through which a human stream, totally preoccupied, moved from place to place. Zolotarev, like almost all provincials, had no love of the capital, but he was constantly drawn to it because it held possibilities the realization of which would allow him to look down disdainfully at his village past, and which would at the same time be a reward, a prize, a compensation for all the insults and humiliations he had suffered on the way up. Leaning back against the seat and listening to the Minister with half an ear, Zolotarev noted with proud satisfaction all the fawning notes in the voice of his companion, and also the good quality of his clothes, and the respect with which the policemen on point duty saluted as they passed. 'This is the life,' he grinned to himself. 'If my old dead Dad could see me now!'

'They say,' the Minister was becoming more and more confiding, 'there are major changes coming. The excitement of battle has gone to the heads of some of our generals. They've started taking themselves for Napoleons, giving themselves airs, losing touch with reality.' Expecting equal frankness from his listener, he even turned slightly in his direction. 'Dizzy with success, you might say. We need general reconstruction. You can't fulfil the plan just by cheering it – we need a different style of leadership. We need to bring forward some young men. The old ones have become stale – they're worn out.' Sensing no response from his companion, the Minister stopped short, and without the slightest embarrassment he changed the subject. 'The Kuriles are now our most vulnerable spot. We must . . .'

The pass system at the Kremlin functioned with the irreproachable precision of a well-maintained automatic. Once they had passed the Spasskiye gates and stopped at the government entrance, the control and pass system of the internal guard began to pay them the minutest attention. The checking of documents began in the hall, and then it was repeated on every landing of every staircase, every passage or turn, until they reached a long corridor, lined on both sides, at a distance of a few paces, by rows of security officers, calm and still as statues. As they passed, each of them slightly opened his stony lips and said: 'Slow down, comrades . . . Slow down, comrades . . . Slow down, comrades . . . Slow down . . .'

And this almost friendly warning only made his heart more tense and constricted.

The man who got up to meet them in the outer office was small, sallow, thin, with a sharply receding hairline.

'Good evening, comrades.' His deeply sunken eyes, the colour of melted snow, bored into them inquiringly. 'Comrade Stalin will see you now. I warn you: ask no questions, answer only when you are spoken to, do not interrupt, do not enter into discussion. Is that clear, comrades?' Without waiting for an answer he glided silently from behind the desk, made his airy way to the door of the study, disappeared behind it and in an instant returned, as if by magic, and told them to come in. 'Comrade Stalin will see you now.'

Stalin was sitting at a desk in the depths of his study writing, shielding his eyes with his palm as if from sunlight. He made no sound nor gesture in response to their appearance but went on writing, while they stood huddled by the door waiting for a nod or a word, all their hungry attention on him. It had begun to seem as if the ominous silence would never end, when at last he put down his pen, took his hand away from his brow, took a cigarette from an open packet of 'Northern Palmyra's, carefully rolled it between his fingers for a long time, lit it, and only then got up and left the desk. He turned out to be a bent but still vigorous old man in a marshal's suit, the trousers of which were for some reason stuck into foppish handmade felt boots.

'The Kuriles,' he said in measured tones, without even the slightest preamble, walking slowly round the study, 'are our Far Eastern underbelly.' The words had obviously pleased him. 'That's exactly it, our underbelly. Our outpost on enemy territory.' Again he repeated approvingly, 'our main Far Eastern outpost. And we should never forget that these are immemorially Russian lands, ceded to the Japanese after a lost Tsarist war.' His Caucasian accent, which people talked about so much, seemed to emphasize the weight of what he said. 'The development of our fishing industry in the Kurile Islands is not only and not so much an economic aim as it is a political aim. Your directorate, comrade Zolotarev, is now playing the role of our plenipotentiary in these territories. You, therefore, comrade Zolotarev' – at this point he raised his heavy, sclerotically veined eyes at his vistors for the first time – 'are our ambassador in the Kuriles, or, if you wish, our Soviet Governor-General.' It was obvious that this comparison had amused him, and he passed between them, rubbing his hands in satisfaction. 'Lavrenty Pavlovich recommended you to me as a competent and promising worker.' Suddenly he stopped to one side of them, half-turned towards them, and gave a quick glance at

23

the Minister. 'What do you think, what's your opinion, comrade Minister?'

The Minister instantaneously shrivelled up, almost choking in his suppliant eagerness to agree: 'Precisely so, comrade Stalin! Comrade Zolotarev is a rising young specialist with great experience in leading men.' He felt there might be some hidden trick in the leader's question, so he hurried to anticipate events. 'I consider that comrade Zolotarev will justify every confidence the party and the government have in him, wherever he may be sent.'

The leader turned his back on them and again walked along the study, obviously considering the matter to be closed.

'The Japanese militarists, with the help of their friends from across the ocean, will undoubtedly try in the future to lay claim to the Kurile Islands. Vigilance, vigilance, and more vigilance – that is our basic line in the liberated areas . . .'

Zolotarev had earlier heard it mentioned that the leader was red-haired, slightly pockmarked and had long arms: but now, face to face with the man, he forced himself not to notice this, tried to commit to memory other features, other details, that were important for him and his future. He was confident that his fate would take a sharp and inexorable shift from this very day: in his rise through the hierarchy he had entered the home straight, where any false moves could be fatal.

Stalin struck Zolotarev as a man constantly listening for something, constantly waiting for something to happen; he seemed preoccupied and his conversation expressed only an external link with his surroundings. It was as if he used words to fence in, protect, barricade what was happening inside him from any penetration or outside interference. The hollowness and for-tuitousness of these words seemed to assure him of the reliability of his continuous self-defence.

'In the words of the Russian proverb: there's a time for work and a time for play.' Stalin decisively stubbed out his cigarette in the ash-tray. 'Let's watch a film, comrades. An excellent film with the famous actor Charlie Chaplin.' He gestured to them to follow him. 'Comrade Stalin teaches us that in our country,' without concealing his mocking tone he threw open the side door, 'everyone has the right to work, rest and education.'

It was widely known that such an invitation from Stalin to watch a film was a sign of his particular attention, and so Zolotarev immediately assumed a dignified air and grew bolder.

Almost on tiptoe they walked past Stalin through the open doors one by one, and found themselves in a small hall with a screen covering the whole back wall and individual little tables, each with its own chair. The same laconic man from the outer office met them, nodding to each of them where they should sit: 'Attention, comrades,' he instructed them in a rapid whisper. 'Do not turn round, or talk among yourselves, or get up without permission.'

And he melted away, disappeared into sudden darkness. Somewhere behind their backs two voices, one with a note of command, the other servile, exchanged a few indecipherable phrases. Then the screen was lit up, to reveal a funny little man in a clumsy suit and a bowler hat, carrying a cane. Every minute he got himself into the most unexpected comic situations. Zolotarev had seen all the man's films several times before the war, and had been convulsed with laughter; but only now, in this little hall, sensing behind his back the presence of a force before the face of which things, events and people seemed reduced to microscopic proportions, did he suddenly see that there was not in fact anything particularly amusing about them, that the eccentric little man on the screen was anything but happy, and that the vertiginous carousel of his misfortunes hid some logic that was beyond the control of mortal man . . .

The light went on and simultaneously the man from the outer office appeared, with another rapid whisper in their ears: 'Comrades, please follow me. Do not address comrade Stalin. Do not turn round.'

In single file they followed him to the exit. Stalin was sitting at a little table near the door shielding his eyes with his palm, as if from the sun, just as when they had first seen him. When Zolotarev, who was last in line, walked past, he slightly parted his fingers as if wanting to check something about his visitor once more. With a sudden heart-stopping realization, Zolotarev noticed that his eyes were wet with tears.

'Well, well,' Zolotarev said to himself as he walked on, 'everyone has his troubles. You are heavy, crown of Monomakh. . .'

On the way back the Minister was crushed and silent, and only when he got out of the car at his own door did he mutter: 'The instructions of our leader, comrade Zolotarev, are our guide in our actions.' Evidently resigned to his fate, he had nevertheless decided to do everything he could to postpone the inevitable. 'Tomorrow you must arrange your trip to the Islands. Spend as long as you like, the new set-up needs to be carefully studied and analysed. And incidentally, on the way there you can look in on

25

our Baikal fisheries, see how production is going, it may be useful to you in the Kuriles. I shall sign the order in the morning. Till tomorrow.'

He slammed the door shut and with a heavy gait, as if suddenly old, he walked across the pavement towards the entrance to his house.

'He's for the knacker's yard,' Zolotarev concluded with sympathy. 'All of us are geese, fatted for table!'

3

Zolotarev had to get rid of the burden that was overwhelming him as soon as possible, to unbosom himself, to tell someone everything that had happened to him that evening. He had not yet managed to make any friends in Moscow and, to tell the truth, he had not been in any hurry to do so; it was not a time for frankness and he had no relatives in the capital. Therefore, after leaving his boss, he asked the driver to take him to Preobrazhensky Square, to the only private address he had in his address book: 6 Korolenko Street, Flat No. 11, Kira Slutskaya.

He had met Kira in Potsdam when she came there with a concert brigade. They happened to sit next to each other at a dinner which the town commandant had arranged in honour of the visiting Muscovites. They had drunk a lot, fooled around and danced, and then he had taken her back to his place. After that single night they had begun to write to each other, though with no sense of mutual obligation. He confided in her the details of his life after the war; she replied, in her regular schoolgirl's handwriting, with news of the people who hung around the Moscow theatre and literary worlds, related with amusing and malicious precision. Her letters were written in the slightly condescending tone of an elder sister, though they were the same age, but this only amused him; from the lofty position he occupied it struck him as childish naïveté. Kira was not married; she admitted to considering marriage just too much bother for an actress. She lived alone, her parents having disappeared during the Leningrad blockade, and the effect of this precocious independence and solitude was evident in her trenchantly expressed ideas and categorical judgements.

One day, after he had moved to Moscow, Zolotarev had telephoned her but she had not been in, and then, getting caught up in the hectic preparations for his departure, he had never been able to find the time to try to get in touch with her again; so that now, on his way to her flat, he was again afraid that he would not find her at home, or, worse still, would find her in but not alone, especially since he was visiting her unannounced.

Zolotarev found the number he was looking for with some difficulty in the dark of the cold corridor. Then he spent a long time, burning his fingers, lighting matches, looking for Kira's name against the array of bell-buttons for the various occupants, and rang for even longer before he heard her hasty steps approaching the door.

'Come in.' She showed no surprise on seeing him, as if they had seen each other the day before. 'How are you? Only don't talk too loud, the neighbours are asleep.' That was her way of talking, in staccato phrases. 'This way.'

He was in such a hurry, so eager to unburden himself, that even before he had taken off his coat he blurted out: 'I've just come from comrade Stalin!'

'Really?' she answered laconically, busying herself at the stove. 'And what did he have to say?'

But Kira's reserve did not cool his ardour. Eagerly, losing his thread, jumping from one line of his story to another, he told her what had happened in enormous detail, not, of course, omitting the tears he had noticed in Stalin's eyes. When he eventually fell silent Kira was still standing with her back to him, bent over a kettle on the stove. The small room, with its single window, was grey and almost empty. A table, a characterless cupboard, a humpbacked armchair with a decrepit fringe, an ottoman, a few photographs on the yellowing walls did little to soften its impersonal coldness. It seemed as if its occupant had hastily and arbitrarily placed a few chance objects around the room and then immediately forgotten about them: just another individual cabin, indistinguishable from thousands of others in the fragile ark of the Moscow flood.

'Brilliant staging,' she responded without turning round. 'Classic Stanislavsky.'

'What?' At first he could not understand what she was on about, and when he did, he got angry. 'Do you realize . . .'

'I realize, I realize, my dear, and I've no intention of committing suicide.' She turned, came up to him and, calming him down, ruffled his hair. 'It's just that great events must be well staged, Ilya. Great men have a penchant for the theatrical gesture – it's their artistic nature.'

'I suppose you meet great people every day.'

'No, but I have a friend who is very close to one of the high-ups.'

Zolotarev was immediately on his guard: he had heard a lot about the theatrical interests of his bosses.

'You too, perhaps?'

'I wouldn't get very far along that path,' she said in a matter-of-fact tone, as if she was talking about something obvious. 'I'm a Jew, hadn't you noticed? You Russians aren't very keen on Jewish women at the moment.'

The news was more depressing than alarming. Until then he had never had occasion to consider the problem seriously. It simply had not existed for him. Zolotarev met Jews mainly at work. In most cases the only things that distinguished them from their colleagues were competence, a capacity to adapt to circumstances and the ease with which they got on with people. But his advance through the hierarchy had been so cloudless and rapid that he had never felt any envy of their talents. And though vague rumours had reached him of an official change of course in relation to Jews, he had not paid particular attention to them: 'That's how it is today, but tomorrow it'll be different!'

'Rubbish!' He got up and pulled her towards him. 'Put it out of your head – it's not important. I'm not asking to see your passport. How d'you know I'm not a Tatar?'

And suddenly he felt as if he'd scalded himself: he saw so much timid thankfulness, so much grateful supplication in her eyes that he could not endure it and, afraid of his own weakness, he turned away. That night it was as if he saw Kira properly for the first time: she combined the early maturity of a woman with the trusting naïveté of an adolescent, a combination emphasized by her boyish haircut and the soft, almost childish oval of her face. When, dozing off, she closed her eyes, the expression of pleading and gratitude on her face became even more unbearably disarming.

'You know,' she said, coming to and leaning against him, 'there are supposed to be terrible earthquakes on the Kuriles.'

'There probably are,' he agreed unthinkingly. 'After all, it's near Japan.' And he rubbed his forehead against hers. 'But why should you worry, it's about as far from Moscow as the moon.'

'What do you know!' She pressed closer against him. 'In winter we had tremors here.'

'What tremors? It was all just talk!'

'It's still terrifying.'

'Sleep, you idiot, I'm here.'

'I am asleep . . .'

In the morning he didn't try to wake her; he got himself ready quietly and left her a note as he went out: 'I am in a position to know. Don't worry. Love.' And only out in the street did he realize in amazement that this was the first time he'd left a woman a note.

The sky above Moscow was completely cloudless, it promised to be a sunny day, and as he walked through the deserted capital Zolotarev had no doubt that from now on his fate was in his own hands, that the trip to the Kuriles would be the beginning of a further advance, and that the most important part of his allotted span was only just beginning.

At midday a military aeroplane soared over the Moscow outskirts, carrying Zolotarev out East.

Chapter Three

1

The train advanced in jerks, neither quickly nor slowly, sometimes passing rapidly through large towns and stations, sometimes spending days cooped up in shabby sidings. The cool spring seemed to crawl along with them, neither waning nor really developing: the thaw in Siberia comes slowly. And only when they were on the outskirts of Omsk, when they saw the full dazzling width of the Ob stretched before them, did the sun finally reach its full strength and begin to stay with them from morning till night.

The train gathered speed, covering big distances in large spurts, losing time only at junctions, where occasionally it was held up for as long as three days.

They approached Novosibirsk at night, but did not enter the town; the convoy was delayed at a supply depot.

Early on, around dawn, Mozgovoy appeared in the wagon, as usual like a fiery steed: all his veins throbbing, his bones constantly in motion, his imperious eye squinting. Standing in the middle of the wagon with his feet wide apart and his rough hands behind his back, he shouted his orders: 'Good morning, honest public. Listen to my instructions: men, collect your rations, the fourth warehouse next to the pump-house; women, take your mops, it's spring-cleaning day. Clean the deck, scrub it till it's spotless, I'll check it with my handkerchief. Let me know when you've finished. See you later!'

Turning on his heels, he disappeared through the doorway and went to do his voice exercises further along the convoy . . .

The first one to come to was Natalya Tyagunova. Shaking her shock of red hair after him, she said, more approvingly than in reproach: 'The pockmarked devil, you'd think he'd hitched us to a cart the way he drives us on. There's no holding him in check, damn him!' She jumped briskly down from the bunk and gave a proprietorial look round the wagon, hands on hips. 'Come on, girls, roll your sleeves up! He's right, why should we rot in dirt, we're people, aren't we? You, Lyubka, you take it easy.' She

30

made Ovsyannikov's daughter, who had tried to get up and help her, sit down. 'We'll manage without you – you'll do better looking after Granny Samokhin. Take her out to lie in the fresh air.' She was even sterner with the men. 'That's enough lying around, lads, you'll get pains in your backsides. Go and queue for the grub or there'll be nothing for you to eat tonight.' Pushing the men towards the exit, she took a rag into her purposeful hands. 'Enjoy your walk, and don't come back empty-handed . . .'

On the way to the warehouse, Fyodor couldn't help offering Tyagunov a little innocently mocking sympathy: 'I see you can't get up to much with a wife like that, Seryoga. She's clearly got a pretty heavy hand!'

'She's right, though, Fedyok,' Sergei's face lit up proudly, and he winked at Fyodor. 'She's like a brick wall, she'll get you through anything, it's not worth trifling with her! And she's educated, not like you and me, we're pig ignorant, we can hardly count to ten . . . You have to have a head on your shoulders!'

'Of course, we in our felt boots are not to be compared with you in your galoshes,' muttered Ovsyannikov darkly, walking along behind them with the Tatar. 'We're not good enough, eating with the animals, washing in the dew, but we still reached Berlin. We didn't get lost with our village ignorance.'

Alimzhan laughed peaceably, clicking his tongue condescendingly at his companions and their Slav obtuseness: 'What's all this talk? God gives you your wife and you take whoever you get – there aren't any others. You live, you make children . . .'

By the time they reached the storehouse an unruly queue had formed, mostly of familiar faces, people they had glimpsed on the journey. The conversations were the same ones they had already had on the crowded train, but had not remembered.

'If we go on at this speed, lads, by the time we reach these islands it'll be time to go on leave,' one of their neighbours from Torbeevka, a short but stout fellow with a quiff of flaxen hair sticking out of his cap, grinned in greeting. 'We'll just keep going out and coming back: we'll arrive, stick our leave papers in our belts and go home: once round the bars, we'll drink away our money and enlist again. And then we'll get our pensions, not a bad life, eh?'

'You should be so lucky!' said a voice from the queue. 'We won't be getting much leave out there. All I want is to leave those Kuriles on two legs. They say there's some disaster there every year: apparently all the earth out there is unstable, whole islands disappear under water.'

And so they started.

'Yes, lads, it's good money, but it's not easy getting it.'

'Yes, it's there all right, but you sweat blood for it. Only it's very tempting – everyone wants to earn good money.'

'However much you earn, you can't take it with you.'

'You should have thought of that earlier, lads. You've drunk away all your travelling expenses, now you'll have to work to earn more.'

'Well, it's no use crying over spilt milk. We'll just have to get on with it.'

The man at the scales in the warehouse, a Greek with a big nose in a short leather jacket, looked at them with his peat-coloured swindler's eyes, rolling the words off his puffy lips: 'Gogolev, Ivan Semyonich, family of four.' He carelessly threw bread, flour, margarine, potatoes on to the scales, one after the other. 'What are you huffing and puffing about, Gogolev? Think I'm giving you short weight?' His swarthy fingers flew over the weights. 'One potato more or less, what difference does it make to you or me? On the other hand, you've got quality goods, no trickery. Take it before I change my mind. I'm a kind fellow.' And shrugging off all possible protests, he rushed on: 'Next!'

The queue was nearly dealt with but the men, laden with their supplies, were in no hurry to go back to their places in the convoy; most of them were stretched out towards the station as markers for the stragglers, enticed by the hospitable bustle around the local bars: their souls thirsted for the elation of drink and for songs.

'Lads, are we mad or something?' Sergei Tyagunov said with sudden vehemence, moving off in the same direction. 'Why should we lag behind the others? We're no stupider than they are.'

'Why not, after all?' said Ovsyannikov, squinting at Fyodor. 'The women are obviously all hard at it. Let's go and have a heart-to-heart – they won't miss us.'

Alimzhan again clicked his tongue, nodding approvingly: 'What's all this talk, I said . . . Let's go!'

They went the rest of the way in silence, even with a certain solemnity, as if preparing themselves for some ritual or an act upon which their immediate future depended.

When they entered the bar they saw that it was already full; in the atmosphere of smoke and damp beer fumes the waitress's voice seemed to ring out from somewhere under the floor: 'Don't all crowd around, lads. There's enough for everyone. You'll all get the chance to get a skinful – you've got the whole day ahead of you. They've found their way here, the clumsy oafs, now you won't get them out of here till they're out of their heads. Drink what I've poured you, or I won't give you any at all!'

They found themselves somewhere to sit, thanks to the efforts of Tyagunov. In the noisy crush of the bar he was like a fish in water: unceremoniously he dispersed a noisy group in a corner, cleared a place at a table, dived into the crush in front of the bar, and soon came back with two mugs of beer in each hand and a bottle of vodka under his arm: 'Take these for me, lads, only we'll have to drink the vodka out of one glass.' He took a thick tumbler out of his pocket. 'Do as you like – I'm certainly not squeamish. I shan't catch anything. Whoever is brave enough can go first . . .'

The more they drank the more the world around them fell away, the surrounding voices seemed to disperse and go quiet. They were left alone in the space they had cleared and with a conversation which they alone understood. Their drunkenness carried them beyond the smoke and stench of the beer-house into another world, another space, where the spirit of big-heartedness, eternal friendship and instant mutual comprehension reigned unalloyed. Mountain heights rose so close to them that it seemed that in less than an hour they would grow airy wings which would carry them beyond this sinful world, with its towns and villages, its light and its darkness, its Trans-Siberian railway and its Kurile chain. Lord, how much repose lies in wait for a suffering soul at the bottom of a glass tumbler, if only, of course, it is full of intoxicating liquid!

Among the succession of toasts and vows of eternal friendship, when it was already time to go back, Fyodor suddenly distinguished in the fug the sharply defined face of Tyagunov: 'Brothers,' his lips trembled with excitement, whispering the words syllable by syllable, 'the hare is scratching about, but I've got him in my sights.' He bent down swiftly and with a single movement raised above the table a lad of no more than twenty, pale with terror, holding him by the collar of his greasy padded jacket. 'Snooping about in our sacks, you bastard!' He looked round in impatient triumph. 'A thief, lads, stealing from working men.' The people around him melted away watchfully, forming a circle, and Tyagunov threw the lad into this circle on to the damp floor covered in spittle. Aiming at the bridge of his nose, he gave him the first kick with the heel of his boot. 'Take that, you bastard!'

What had happened to Sergei's usual gentleness? Suddenly his whole body was distorted with mindless fury, which spread to those around him and evoked a similar response in them. And so, as soon as the first blood appeared under Tyagunov's boot, the crowd instantly rushed at the lad lying on the floor as if someone was urging them on, and covered him from view.

'Aargh . . . aargh . . . aargh! . . .'

Fyodor would have rushed into the mêlée to try to stop them, calm them down, put an end to this bloody violence, but the enormous hands of Ovsyannikov grabbed his arms like pincers and carried him outside by force.

'You fool, can't you see? Those people have gone mad,' he remonstrated with Fyodor, dragging him away from the hubbub of the beer-house. 'Anyone who tries to stop them will be beaten to pulp, innocent or guilty. It's nothing to do with us, Fedyok. Let the police sort them out – that's what they're paid for.'

From behind them they heard the thin voice of Alimzhan, raised in entreaty: 'What are you doing, lads? It's against the law. What a trouble there'll be. Maybe you should take him to the police. The law must . . .'

'You can't talk like a normal person to our lads. Not on your life!' said Ovsyannikov as they walked away. 'They'll cut each other's throats for a kopeck, and if they can do it in a crowd, ten against one, then that's even better. All they want is to take it out on someone. We're working off our malice, Fedyok. They've got the people white-hot, they don't let us breathe, so we take our revenge on each other. Don't get worked up about things like that, Fedya, else they'll trample you underfoot . . .'

When they returned, they saw that the daily life of the convoy had been completely transferred into the open air. Between the railway line and the forest alongside it, from the head Pullman to the back of the train, smoke rose over family stoves and bonfires. The smells of their simple meals spread through the area, mixing with the strong smell of charcoal, tar and black oil wafting from the station.

'Sit down, Fedyok, you look exhausted,' his father said as he tried to get a fire going under their dinner-pot placed on a small trivet. 'Your mother will fix you something to eat, I'll heat it up for you.'

Fyodor dropped the knapsacks of supplies, fell heavily down on the warm turf at the side of the line and said, speaking with difficulty: 'Don't bother, Dad. Leave it. I've got something on my mind. I don't feel like eating, my stomach's churning.'

And he stretched out exhausted on the grass, and closed his eyes.

2

Towards evening, as the dusk came on, Mozgovoy appeared at
their wagon acompanied by the surly head of the railway police:
'Listen here, good citizens!' He looked older and his eyes had lost
their usual steady expression. He seemed hunted as he darted
glances from side to side. 'Tyagunov has been arrested for murder,
and Batyev too as an accomplice. The families must decide
whether to go on or stay here and wait for the trial. If you're
staying, take your things out of the train, and if you want to go on,
go with the sergeant now. He'll take down your evidence, that's
the rules.'

The sergeant opened his squeamishly pursed lips as if deciding
whether to speak, but changed his mind, yawned lazily into his fist
and turned away.

In the silence that reigned, Natalya was the first to speak: 'I
shan't go on without my husband.' She shook her red hair as usual.
'I don't care what he's done, he's my husband.' And walking
towards the wagon, she grabbed hold of the door-handle: 'It won't
take long to gather our stuff . . . you could fit it all into a cripple's
begging bag.'

No sooner had Natalya disappeared into the wagon than the
Tatar clan were also set in motion. The Batyevs quickly gathered
all the dishes they had taken out for dinner into a heap and then
silently, not looking at anyone, they filed off to get their things.
For a long time afterwards Fyodor dreamed of this bright May
midday, the gold light of Natalya's hair, and through the
brightness the silent file of the Batyev children. 'Lord, save us and
have mercy on us.'

'What the fuck did they do that for?' Mozgovoy swore angrily,
for some reason addressing his remarks only to Fyodor. 'Didn't I
tell you not to drink? Now they'll have to starve to death felling
wood, if they're not shot . . .'

But Fyodor stood turned to stone, seeing nothing, hearing
nothing of what happened after that.

The sky was studded with stars when Ovsyannikov sat down
beside him at the fire and took out his tobacco pouch.

'Can I sit here?'

'There's lots of space.'

'D'you want a smoke?'

'No thanks.'

'Are you feeling awful?'

'It happens.'

The fire was going out, the flame was disappearing, a light layer of white ash was settling on the dying embers. The darkness around was getting thicker and more impenetrable, cutting them off from their surroundings with a viscous wall.

Ovsyannikov stared continuously into the fire, smoking his roll-your-own cigarette, occasionally spitting into the fire: 'My life's been on the way down for a long time, Fedya.' The reflections of the dying fire danced in his eyes, which stared unseeingly forward. 'I've seen all kinds of things in my life: begging and prisons and the war as well. I should sit at home now, do my peasant work, tell tales, look after my grandchildren. What makes me seek my fortune at my age, roam halfway round the world to no purpose? Of course it's mainly for the girl, when all's said and done. They'd never have let the poor thing alone in the village, they'd have kept on mocking her, they'd have been the death of her. We can always see the mote in someone else's eye.' His voice suddenly softened and trembled. 'Don't be taken in by her quietness. She's got quite a character, and she sinned out of trust, I imagine, or out of pity for some good-for-nothing.' He threw his cigarette end into the fire, watched the coals consume it, spat one last time and began to get up. 'The Russian peasant has taken off into distant lands to seek his fortune, but he'd have done better to stay at home and look after his own land, which is abandoned to weeds and neglect.' And he walked off into the night, tall, clumsy and slow. 'It's time to get some sleep, Fedya, good night . . .'

The sound of his footsteps died away in the darkness, leaving Fyodor alone with his thoughts in the pitch-black silence around him. 'What a day!' he thought in anguish, leaning back against the warm grass. 'You wouldn't wish it on your worst enemy!'

The low cloudy sky sailed past him, casting a spell on him without his noticing it, and soon he began to feel as if he too was sailing with it into night, into the darkness, into the unknown.

3

When Fyodor went back to the wagon, several pairs of eyes looked at him inquiringly and expectantly: no one there had even taken a nap before he came in. In the shimmering, unsteady light of the wick lamp the familiar faces swam out to meet him as if they still hoped that he would remove their burden, greet them with news that would bring them relief. But Fyodor had nothing to tell them and no good news; he just sighed heavily, and without looking at them he lay down on his bunk.

'You should eat something, Fedya,' his mother said quietly. 'You've been going around all day on an empty stomach, you haven't touched a thing. Why do you torture yourself? We're simple people, the laws aren't written by us and we shouldn't get ideas.'

Fyodor didn't reply. He stretched out beside his father, but he was clearly not fated to sleep that night: suddenly the door rolled back and in the doorway in the moonlight they saw the confident face of Mozgovoy with a can half the size of a bucket in his hands.

'Get up, lads! Night alert! All hands on deck! Don't stint on the food, you women – the men are going to drink.' He spoke quickly, impetuously, as if he was afraid of being interrupted. 'It's first-rate brew – my mother got it ready for Mayday, and she used pure treacle, no half-measures.' He put the can down noisily on the cold stove, and started windmilling around it. 'Hurry up, lads, or it'll dry out. It'll all evaporate up the stove flues, and then you'll be sorry.' Pouring the brew into the mugs they held out towards him, he continued to rush about feverishly. 'Drink, lads, don't be shy, I've already had a skinful of it; if there isn't enough we'll get some more, it's no trouble.'

But however much he tried, however much he attempted to provoke his fellows into enthusiasm, the planned drinking-bout came to nothing. The shadows of their recent companions still floated in the confined space of the wagon, and their unseen presence impeded their words and movements. Each of them felt at least a little bit responsible for what had happened, as if he himself had almost got into trouble but had saved his skin at someone else's expense. And so the nocturnal meal looked more like a wake than a drinking-bout or a friendly libation.

It was only towards the very end, when the sun was rising in the doorway and it was getting light, that a clearly drunken Ovsyanni-kov made the first response to Mozgovoy's loquacity: 'What a life we have now! It's all a mess, whatever happens turns out wrong. There's no way out, you escape one yoke and they harness you into another. What a miserable life!' His pale eyes looked tense and glassy in his drunken anguish. 'I remember at the front: they made me a sapper, though the only things I'd ever blown up were fish in Khitrovo. So I'd be fixing a fuse to an anti-tank mine and a sinful thought would come into my head: if only you could invent a bomb that would reduce the whole earth to rubble.

I was so sick of this convict's life!'

Tikhon, squinting inquiringly at Mozgovoy, cautiously agreed: 'What can you say, we've had more than our fill of trouble, enough for our grandsons and great-grandsons. Only why should we complain? We earned it, we thought it up ourselves, no one else did.' He looked defiantly at his son with his one eye, grinned and added mockingly, 'Old fools like us, it's all we're used to. We get what we deserve and there's no way out of it, but why the hell our sons should want to live in this same shit, that I'll never understand . . .'

'You're talking a lot of rubbish, Dad, your tongue's out of control,' Fyodor snapped without conviction. 'You've had your feast, so now my head's got to ache. You should have some conscience, and not work off your hangover on someone else!' But suddenly realizing that he had gone a bit too far, he softened. 'You've just seen what tricks they play on us, Dad. One, two, and you're locked up!'

This turn in the conversation was clearly not to Mozgovoy's liking; he poured the rest of the brew into the mugs and tried to steer the conversation into calmer waters: 'In my opinion, lads, whatever happens is for the best. They'll give our mates five years at the most for complicity – kids' stuff, hardly worth bothering about. They'll scarcely notice it before they're standing outside with their things – only they'll be a bit wiser. One zek, as they say, is worth two ordinary men.' He turned to Fyodor in search of support. 'Am I right, soldier?'

But Fyodor was no longer listening. Everything was spinning round him in a colourful carousel, and in this carousel he suddenly distinguished the quiet face of Lyuba. Leaning against the door-post, she stared distantly at him with her wide-open eyes, and this long glance softened and calmed his soul even more. 'And who on earth was it made her like that?' he thought, astounded by joy. 'She shines without fire!'

4

A girl, a young girl, almost a child, was running along the dewy grass, holding ragged slippers in her hand and waving them in time with her running. She was running with her head well back and screwing up her eyes in the sun. Her calm, freckled face was flushed with the effort, her flaxen hair stretched out behind her like a train, and her floral cotton dress flapped against her legs. She ran so freely and lightly that she seemed to be floating on air, illuminated by cloudless grace; around her field and wood were languid in the light of the May sun, the wide river stretched out muffled in haze, and the railway, smelling of smoke, resounded with hootings and clankings. But the girl, the little girl, the half-child was unconcerned. Now she had eyes only for herself; she concentrated on what was secretly ripening within her, growing and, like a flight through the firmament, moving stubbornly towards the light.

Lyuba, Lyubanya, Lyubov Nikolayevna!

Chapter Four

1

He was tormented by the infirmities of old age. They had stolen up on him suddenly, unawares. Only yesterday, it seemed, he had had nothing to complain about: he got up around midday alert and ready to spend the next sixteen hours in an exhausting vortex of meetings, committees, telephone conversations. He never faltered in his certainty that he was destined to live a long time, and the many current legends about incredible Caucasian longevity only confirmed this belief. He scrupulously collected information about longevity throughout the world, and obsequious scribblers, knowing his partiality for this, published similar information almost every day. Every discovery in this area became the object of his careful study. And when one ex-nurse, who had been one of the girls who hung around them in the underground (whom, incidentally, he had always rather disliked for their exalted loquacity), proved the miraculous effect of soda-baths on the rejuvenation of the organism, he commanded that she be invested with every imaginable order and prize.

But one morning he woke up with palpitations. His head was spinning nauseatingly, he felt a throbbing and tingling in his fingertips. Throughout the day he had a thumping pain in his temples and his feet were frozen stiff. From then on ailments never left him. Either for no reason at all his sight would be defective, or, at the most inappropriate moment, his arms and legs would go numb, or, on occasions, he had only to turn round clumsily for his whole back and neck to succumb to cramp. Neither soda-baths according to the recipe of the ex-nurse – who had by now, with his patronage, steam-rollered her way into the Academy of Medicine – nor moderation in drinking and smoking was of any use, nor the exercises that he did furtively on waking without letting on to his servants. He watched himself disintegrating.

He disliked and feared doctors. It was not that he was afraid of the possibility of a plot, of machinations, of evil intent: let his defeated enemy console himself with such ideas, all the more so since he himself encouraged such versions so as to make political capital out of them when necessary. Moreover, in the harsh battle for hegemony he had long since managed to disarm his immediate entourage. Medicine sickened him with the danger of constant incursions into his secret life. In the hands of a clever adversary every failing, every flaw, every infirmity could become a weapon against him; and besides, he himself was not over-anxious to be particularly well-informed on this account; ignorance was simpler. Once long ago, in the 1920s, he had trusted some bearded neuropathologist who had made an idiotic diagnosis which had got into the foreign press; he had then had to sort out the mess with the help of the GPU, after which, to be on the safe side, he had got rid of those who had sorted it out for him. He also despised doctors for their ineradicable fastidiousness, which had almost caused the failure of several extremely important political machinations. He was firmly convinced that it was better to dispense with their services, sticking to a tried and tested rule: never to let anyone get closer to him than was absolutely necessary.

During the years of party in-fighting he had mastered the saving rule of distance, according to which even his close entourage had always to remain remote enough for their leader to be seen globally, without flaws or weaknesses, precisely the way he felt he should be seen by others. But he had also learnt that men tend to get used to their situation rapidly; in time their eyes become keener, their ears sharper, the play of light and shade more clearly noted in their minds. Therefore, at regular intervals, he was constrained to make a scrupulous weeding out of the space around him, so as to fill the vacuum this created straight away with new shoots, free of the burden of history and experience.

Take, for example, Zolotarev himself, fished out by the ubiquitous Lavrenty in the still waters of his diocese: the cunning devil, he knew how to please his master! One was immediately well disposed towards the fellow: tall, fair-haired, maladroit, with respectful elation in his cornflower eyes. Not a living creature, but a blank sheet of paper; write on him whatever your soul desires, then rub it out and write something else as the need of the day dictates. By comparison with this new fellow, the old Minister looked like a sweaty hog in a white undercollar. The time had come to get rid of these fat, constantly breathless bonzes; they had reached that fatal stage beyond which they became dangerously accustomed to power, dangerously self-confident, with a consequent dulling of the sense of the distance that separated him from them, and the threat of breakdown in the established order of their relationship with him. The victorious war, with its inevitable frankness and the weakening of day-to-day controls, had given birth in a few people to illusions, vain expectations and unrealizable hopes. The structure of the apparatus was in need of radical renovation. The condemned men must be replaced by men like Zolotarev, free of clan prejudice and excessive aspirations, not men but clay, from which he could mould whatever he might wish. It was only with them – if fate would give him twenty or thirty more years – these strapping lads with the obedient elation in their cornflower eyes, that he would eventually bring the world to its knees.

But he had made himself a rule that there should be no hurry. Let this Zolotarev come up against a few problems working independently for a while on those God-forsaken Kurile Islands, get a taste for running his own ship, far away from his office fortress; if he succeeded, the lad could be tried on the next rung of the ladder. If he didn't trip up he could continue his ascent, up to the very point where the fatal day would dawn for him too.

These thoughts about the Kuriles led him into abstraction. After all, he thought, they were somewhere at the back of beyond, where, in Lavrenty's sinister joke, no prisoner had ever set foot: even on the map they just looked like a barely noticeable sprinkling of brown spray in the blue expanse of ocean. Suddenly, not for the first time, the real world left him: he observed himself from the outside, and was amazed at how small and defenceless he was in the huge and furious world. Suddenly he wanted to be somewhere far, far away, on those Kuriles, for example, where he could burrow into some hole and sit there in the warm, seeing and hearing nothing of what went on around.

And let some lonely traveller, an exhausted wretch just like him, knock at his warm burrow (just like the one he'd had in his Kureika exile) and say: 'Let me in, man, it's arduous being alone.'

'Come in,' he would reply cheerfully, 'we can live amicably cheek by jowl, it's merrier when there are two.'

The traveller would come in and ask: 'Who are you, man, and what is your name?'

And then (generally he kept this for the end), with his habitual modest dignity, he would answer, quietly and simply: 'Stalin.'

'I wonder,' he grinned to himself, 'would he have apoplexy straight away, or a little later?'

He even screwed up his eyes in anticipation of this pleasure, but at the same time his memory obligingly recalled his recent conversation with the team of China experts, who among other things had remarked upon the frequency of seismic tremors on the sea-bed in those parts, and this immediately brought him back to reality, to the pressing affairs of the fast-dying day.

Before the hectic day was over, he still had to sign a new list of eliminations. The document lay on his desk waiting for his final decision. He had confirmed many such lists in the past ten years and had never felt the slightest regret about them. In his position the equation was as simple as breathing: either you got them, or they got you; there was no other way and therefore no point in thinking about it. But this time in the neat column of names there was a woman who came from his region, a distant relative. To tell the truth she was a very distant relative indeed – who, in Georgia, is not related to whom? – but he was linked with this woman, now probably very old, by a half-forgotten encounter which now floated back out of oblivion.

How old was she then? Sixteen? Seventeen? Eighteen? Recently his memory for events and facts, once so sharp, had started to deceive him. Year by year its failures became greater and longer. This infuriated and tormented him. He tried to note down the fragments of the past which occasionally came into his head, so as to use them to reconstruct the whole story later, but this seemingly trustworthy method failed, and all that was left was to come to terms with the inevitable consequences of age.

But that August morning in old Tiflis, when he was rushing here and there through the secret labyrinth of the streets of Navtlugi, trying to shake off the police, was so sharply etched in his memory that it might have happened yesterday.

For the first time since the Great Hold-up, the police were at his heels that day. The noose encircling him was being squeezed tighter and tighter, ready to close at any moment. As he was approaching the lines of the horse-tram, where the police cordon lay in wait, a young girl darted out between him and the cops, an airy creature framed in something white and blue.

Of course she understood in an instant exactly what was going on. She stopped and stared at him with her enormous eyes that filled half her face and were full of fright, elation and determination. Her sudden appearance caused momentary confusion among the cops, and that was what saved him. He slipped unhindered between them and a passing tram, and disappeared on the other side of the street into a labyrinth of courtyards and passages.

But it was not gratitude that caused him to vacillate now: both before and after her many people had helped him, and this had not

43

saved them from the fate prepared for them. It was this moment of elation, terror and determination: for the first time a young girl, a young woman from one of the most respected Georgian families, the beautiful Natella Amiradzhibi, known to all Tiflis, had looked at him with such an unfeigned readiness for anything. And though afterwards he was afraid to admit it even to himself it was precisely then, on that August morning, in the brief moment of their meeting face to face, that he had definitively found confidence in himself, in his star, in his prophetic destiny.

For many years she had avoided the fate of others; he had instinctively protected her as a pledge, a guarantee, a promise of the fate in store for him, but this time her turn had come. With the passing years her tongue had begun to wag too freely – evidently the effect of age – her presumption had swelled out of all measure, and this might throw a shadow on his biography, cast in letters of bronze. The woman must be got rid of so as to right the situation.

He had always treated women with a mixture of caution and disdain. This had been evident even in his childhood, in his parents' house, where his quiet mother always deferred unprotestingly to his constantly drunken father. As always, thoughts of his mother robbed him of equilibrium, and everything which had vaguely tormented him, had suffocated him from his adolescence on, had sometimes deprived him of sleep, now gushed over him again with a searing inner bitterness.

As long as he remembered – at school, in the seminary, then in the underground and in the battle for power – it had been his torment and his curse, his Gethsemane, his Passion and his Golgotha. He had attempted to escape this spiritually desiccating hallucination in his two unsuccessful marriages, in passing debauchery, sometimes in drunkenness, in orgies of investigation against his erstwhile friends, but still it followed him tenaciously, overcoming oblivion and time. In the end he locked his mother up within the four walls of a luxurious Tiflis mansion and tried to forget about her, not even attending her funeral, but even after this the memory did not leave him. And the higher he rose, the more immovable his power became, the more insupportable was this burden of the past. In his childhood he had managed to escape it through fighting, in his youth through prayer, in his mature years by serving in the Okhrana, but nothing was able to suffocate within him the vengeful whisper of memory: 'You are the son of the town strumpet, who bore you of her rich neighbour, Revaz Ignatoshvili, to avenge herself on her drunken husband; you are a bastard and your mother is a whore!'

'Damn you,' he tried angrily to shrug off the vision. 'I don't want to think about you, go away!'

He knew almost for certain that it was a lie, that his mother, up to her eyes in day-to-day work, simply did not have time for herself and her own interests, and that the slander was most likely set in motion by some drunken layabout during a squabble with his father at table in a village restaurant, but he could never persuade himself fully of this, and perhaps he did not want to.

One by one he had eliminated everyone who might have known of this or even heard rumours of it, but each of them, feeling a presentiment of disaster, had managed to pass on this pebble destined for him into other hands. And the past, like a boomerang, came back to him time and time again.

Moreover, his little friend from Baku (it was precisely in Baku, on the boards of the central prison, that he had confided in him – oh, foolish youth! – that he had been riskily frank with him: who knew then how things would turn out?), his Baku friend was still around, still walking the parquet, the deceitful lenses of his glasses still flashing light in all directions. He was still there, drinking-companion of his senile orgies, his Malyuta, his *éminence grise*, whom he had drawn close to him at the outbreak of war for his experience as a torturer and his servile forgetfulness. He was waiting for his hour to come, the flattering raven, waiting for the appropriate moment to peck out his eye, whatever the proverb might say, keeping in reserve, at the very bottom of his dark soul, this trump card against him. Only the man had not yet been born who was capable of outdoing him in the art of patient waiting; one German had tried, a competent fellow who could knock spots off the others, but in the end his plans too had come to nothing; and this vixen in the pince-nez would also fail. However much she tried, she would survive precisely as long as he had need of her. And as if in confirmation of his new decision he went to the desk, his new boots squeaking, and without sitting down appended his signature in the corner of the sheet with a flourish and pressed the bell.

A feeble creature with a face of parchment appeared at the door almost immediately, and in obedience to the scarcely perceptible movement of his brows rushed silently to the desk, but stopped expectantly midway, his whole appearance simultaneously exuding devoted competence and a consciousness of the significance of the moment.

Oh, how he scorned them all: both those who surrounded him and those who had disappeared long ago, and this gnome with the

45

expression of canine zeal on his little parchment face! Both together and separately they represented that easily malleable part of the human tribe which for all their malleability, and perhaps precisely because of it, turned out to be capable of any vileness, if it would bring them an inexhaustible supply of food and personal security. The human cost of the process of natural selection: he fished them out at random from their faceless fellows, used them adroitly and then, with neither hesitation nor regret, swept them back into oblivion.

In the list on the desk was the name of the wife of the gnome standing in front of him in the semi-military suit. The man did not yet know what had happened, Lavrenty having brought him the document without going through the secretariat; and so, observing the devoted air of his assistant, he could not help maliciously muttering to himself: 'If you like sleigh-rides, you'll have to learn to like pulling the sleigh.'

He silently placed the ratified list at the edge of the desk. His shadowy assistant rushed forward, picked it up and, receiving wordless permission, sped from the room as silently as he had entered: the incarnation of tact, speed and dutiful obedience.

He did not even need to exercise his imagination to be certain what would now happen on the other side of the door, but this no longer concerned him; those who had crossed the boundary of the circle of which he was the centre would have to learn to pay. To pay every day and any price: their self-esteem, their dear ones and, if need be, their life. So let this one pay too, all the more so since for his master too this document represented another loss, albeit a less significant one.

Many years of practice had given him the capacity to evaluate new situations instantaneously, and to assimilate them just as quickly, coming to terms with the details as they went on. But what had just happened still troubled him slightly.

The enormous door, covered on the outside in expensive leather, opened slowly and in the doorway he saw his assistant on all fours with the list he had just confirmed in his teeth. Still on all fours, whimpering like a dog, he crossed the room and, stopping an arm's length away, rose to his knees, exuding loyalty and supplication.

But this evoked nothing in his soul but morose squeamishness. He could not stand blatant weakness in people, considering every external manifestation of it a sign of internal degeneration.

'The son of a bitch, he feels pity for his wife,' he thought with cruel anger, 'but the fact that his wife is ready to sell herself to any foreign intelligence service is of no concern to him!'

With a negligent movement he took the document, cast a rapid glance at the neat column of names and then stuck it back in his secretary's mouth.

The rest did not interest him.

He turned to the window, excluding his assistant from the sphere of his consciousness and memory. When the man had gone he stretched in satisfaction, undid the collar of his marshal's uniform (to which he had never become accustomed after the ample cut of his field-jackets), got up and, slightly trailing his left leg, walked slowly to the side door, behind which was his bedroom with its old iron bed covered in a rough soldier's blanket.

He had trouble getting to sleep. For some reason he remembered the earthquakes on the Kuriles, and he immediately decided to summon the Muscovite seismographers to give him a detailed report on the problem.

2

For a while it had been his rule to write down the day's events. At first these notes were confined to a rapid record of meetings, conversations, the facts and news he had learnt; but then, gradually, they had started to accrete details, asides, footnotes, progressively taking on the form of a regular diary.

Once, rereading what he had written, he was convinced that everything he had written here was clearly expanding into something of an internal monologue or a confession, something too frank to fall into the hands of historians. His cynicism never crossed the limit beyond which it might hold some hidden threat to him. The influence of his seminary education remained: somewhere in the innermost depths of his soul he could not manage to shake off the fear of possible punishment. But though conscious of the explosive danger of his activity he still could not renounce it, and even became more and more attached to it, finding an especial, almost narcotic, pleasure in it.

He noted down everything: thoughts, phrases, expressions which had struck him as well-turned; conversations, situations, memories, singling out those he would never have dared to speak out loud. He wrote with passion, with ease, without restraint, mercilessly eliminating the words it was his habit to use in his official activities. For the first time since, long ago, at the insistent urging of Ilya Chavchavadze, he had abandoned his youthful

47

versifying, he was in thrall to an irresistible urge to write.

And although not a single living soul could enter his quarters or his study with impunity, at the end of each day he would carefully put the manuscript away in the safe he had had fitted into the bedroom wall above his head, where he kept his most secret documents: the archive of Nechaev, consisting of several exercise books sewn together, and the parting letter of his second wife. There in the wall above the bedhead they seemed safer.

But the more the manuscript grew, the more his spiritual unease increased. His head was filled with the most fantastic alarms about its possible disappearance: during one of his brief absences or an illness, as a result of a chance fire or deliberate arson, while he was asleep or unconscious, or had had a stroke, when the notes could be if not stolen then at least photographed, as happened in a number of detective films he had seen. His most recurrent nightmare was of being struck by sudden paralysis and lying helpless, motionless, watching some traitor, possibly one of his closest advisers, empty the secret safe before his very eyes, an insolently mocking smile on his face. It was that provocatively mocking smile on the scoundrel's face which particularly infuriated him, driving him to distraction.

Today this obsessive vision had racked him since morning. He tried to escape the torment by aimlessly walking around his study, by making telephone calls, even by reading official documents; but the tenacious *fata morgana* once again would not leave him, and continued to dry out his soul.

By the end of the day the torment became almost unbearable. And at that point he finally decided to have recourse to the measure he had been refusing to take all day, never having allowed himself to trust anyone fully. But before summoning his assistant for an enforced conversation he switched on the tape-recorder: the agreement must be recorded, just in case.

He appeared at the door almost the moment the bell rang, standing at alert attention, as ever, his document file held at his side as clear proof of his constant readiness.

'Iosif Vissarionovich,' he whispered almost inaudibly from the doorway. 'At your service.'

'Well, my wise fellow,' getting down to business he was still anguished by doubt, dragging his feet, taking aim, 'listen to me carefully. I've got a certain something in there,' he gave a slight nod in the direction of the adjoining room. 'D'you understand?'

The man's eyes became instantly alert, the Adam's apple in his thin neck throbbed convulsively, his body tensed and straightened: the assistant seemed to be getting ready to soar at the slightest sign.

'I understand, comrade Stalin.' The words no longer sounded, but flew weightlessly from his lips. 'I am at your service.'

'If anything happens, destroy it.' Once he had said the main thing, Stalin relaxed and leaned back against his armchair. 'Do you understand? You have the key, guard it with your life. Don't give it to Lavrenty or anyone else. If anything happens, burn everything immediately.' This time the assistant's silence was more eloquent than any words: the agreement had been made, the two parties were equally aware of the importance of the moment. 'What's that you have there?'

'You asked for information about the Kuriles, Iosif Vissarionovich.' His assistant was still trembling, taking in what he had just heard. His hand shook slightly as he held out the file.

He had indeed, after his recent conversation with the Sinologists and Far Eastern specialists, demanded a brief summary of the most important information on this question, because he did not like details, which prevented him from taking in issues as a whole without beating about the bush. He had even given an order for the maximum reduction of the general encyclopaedia, considering the Brokgaus and Efron too burdensome to assimilate.

Now, as he read the note prepared for him, he was only the more convinced that he had been right to do so. What had taken two full hours of hypotheses, statistics and proofs was expressed here with lapidary precision on a half-sheet of vellum:

TSUNAMI – waves rising on the surface of the ocean as a result of subterranean earthquakes. They move at a speed of 400–500 kilometres an hour. The waves reach a height of 15–30 metres on coastal cliffs and in narrow estuaries. If they hit a low shore they can reach far inland, causing great devastation. *Tsunami* is observed most frequently along the shores of the Pacific ocean.

'Fine, what else?'

'Svetlana Iosifovna telephoned.' The assistant was already backing towards the door. 'When can she see you?'

The mention of his daughter again upset him, reminding him of a succession of daily unpleasantnesses. In his own way he loved that angular girl with the constant shadow of a smile on her long face. He spoiled her in so far as he knew how, and followed her development from afar, but to his irritation, the older she grew the more she resembled her mother: spiritually unstable, too gregarious, at heart profoundly stubborn. In addition he had recently sensed that she was hiding some extremely significant part of her life from him, which he found particularly unacceptable. 'It would be better,' he complained, 'if she just played the merchant, like her brother. At least we would then know where we stand!'

And then this inexplicable attraction to Jews! According to Lavrenty's reports, whole crowds of them swarmed around her. She chose her friends and her escorts from among them, spent her free time with them; her first admirer had been a Jew who had had to be disposed of with the help of Lavrenty. The second one had likewise been the cause of some trouble, though she had learnt nothing from it, only becoming a little more tearful.

He had particular accounts to settle with that race. In his youth he had paid little attention to them, accepting them as an inevitable evil or as the irritating price of any risky enterprise. But as the years passed, his attitude to them had changed markedly. The higher he rose, the more often he had to encounter them, every time irritated by the arrogant disdain he sensed in them. In the end he hated everything about them: their habit of dishing out quotations apropos of anything and nothing, their attention to trivial details, their self-assurance – even their carelessness about dress, which bordered on slovenliness. He could never forgive them their ironical smiles during his speeches, their insolent interruptions from the hall, their meaningful laughter behind his back. The very memory of this reduced him to a seething rage. 'Miserable chatterers, mangy bastards!' He shook inwardly.

He recalled a phrase of Radek's many years ago: 'Stalin and I are not in agreement about the agrarian question: I want to see him lying in his grave, and he wants to see me in mine.'

'Chatterer! Lousy Talmudist! He tried to outwit Stalin himself! Only the man has not yet been born who has managed to do that! Go and study the agrarian question in hell, bastard theoretician!'

It had never occurred to these Marxist phrasemakers that besides the science of verbal skirmishing which made them drunk as wood-grouse there also existed the far more politically important science of commanding, ruling, holding power; and that in that science he, unlike them, was like a fish in water, and each of them by comparison was just a blind puppy. In full accordance with his screenplay, they ended by strangling each other with their own hands.

But even those who remained and served him not out of fear but out of devotion continued to irritate him by their zeal, their servile elasticity, their glutinous hospitality. Mekhlis, for example: a bustling chatterbox, ready for anything. And whatever did his daughter see in that busily empty race? . . .

'Is that all?'

'Yes, Iosif Vissarionovich.'

'There'll be time.' He washed his hands of it, and condescendingly consoled his assistant. 'Why are you walking around like a drowned man? Can't you forget your wife? Your wife is rubbish, an enemy, a traitor. Don't we have enough real Soviet women? You'll have a wife, I guarantee it. Leave me . . .'

Returning to his interrupted deliberations he thought once again, as he had so many times these last few days, about Zolotarev. 'It's men like him I should advance, not those useless theoretician-chatterers.' He remembered the frank adoration with which the cornflower eyes of that fair-haired lad had devoured him. 'I should get rid of those mangy phrasemakers along with fat hogs like the Minister of Fisheries. This blue-eyed Tulan is far more reliable. If he sorts out the Kuriles, I'll make him the Minister.'

As the evening passed he began to succumb to fatigue: his age was telling on him. He closed his eyes in exhaustion and for no reason at all he recalled an evening in Baku prison before his second escape.

He had spent all that day, he remembered, playing a frenzied game of cards with the head of the cell, a local thief. He was in luck, his eyes were dizzy from a succession of trumps, he was beating the bank time after time; and when in the end his companions were completely cleaned out, one of them, Samed Bagirov, a notorious local bank-robber, venting his fury, turned to him in frank mockery: 'Tell me, Soso, is it true that you're an Ossetian Jew? With the luck you have . . .'

The bold fellow paid dearly later for a joke made in anger; but then, on that stuffy evening, under the crossfire investigation of several pairs of eyes, it took not a little effort and restraint to control himself and not throw himself on the man who had insulted him.

Even now, in leaden half-sleep, subconsciously aware of the unreality of the chance vision, he almost suffocated from rage at the very memory of it . . .

'Tell me, Soso, is it true that you're an Ossetian Jew? With the luck you have . . .'

With this detestable mockery in his mind, he fell asleep till the following midday.

'Well, have you come to? Recovered your spirits?' He raised his heavy lids to his assistant; the man stood before him, as ever, slightly to one side of the desk, looking at him with servile readiness. 'You thought the party would abandon you in your hour of need, but the party has not forgotten about you. As you see, the party has found you a real Soviet woman, a comrade, a friend. Live with her now and rejoice; one like her will not betray you, will not deceive you, and, most important of all, she knows how to hold her tongue.' He did not even attempt to conceal his mockery. 'She'll be well paid for it. Are you satisfied?'

'Thank you, dear Iosif Vissarionovich. Your word is law for me.' Evidently agitated, he shuffled from foot to foot, swallowing convulsively. He seemed to lower his eyes, but then he opened them again in fright. 'I am a soldier of the party, your soldier, comrade Stalin.'

He knew for sure what was happening now in the soul of the parchment statue standing in front of him: he had adored his arrested wife, as had been reported to Stalin long ago with all sorts of spicy details; sinner that he was, he had a weakness for spicy details. But this only increased his conviction of the rightness of the decision he had taken and already put into practice. 'Get rid of the woman from the cart and the mare has it easier,' he could not restrain his malicious joy, 'or else we'll always be lost among skirts. She's not the first and she won't be the last!'

Suddenly he remembered his first marriage, and as usual in these cases he felt a brief twinge of faintness. This had been the first and, as it turned out, the last time he had succumbed to weakness. 'Why ever did I have to meet you, to my misfortune?' At that moment, with spiritual anguish, he despised himself. 'Why do you dog my heels, Keke?'

It was so improbably long ago that from his present lofty position and from the present time it seemed to be a hallucination. He could not now even have said with confidence whether he had loved her. Those times had left in him, in his soul, in his consciousness, not the image of an individual person or event but rather the sharp sense of irredeemable loss. All that remained of Keke herself in his memory was a reflection of the conciliatoriness she radiated, and the words of the song which she usually sang before going to sleep.

Along with her the first and last attachment of his life had disappeared; after that his heart had gone deaf for ever, he had been turned to stone. Even memories of that period aroused in him only dull fury. He had not been able to stand the son of the marriage, whose very existence recalled the past; and he had therefore sacrificed him without regret when faced with a choice between politics and fatherhood.

Even at her funeral he had sworn to eliminate everything that might prevent him from becoming the master of his own destiny. He recalled that on meeting his namesake and childhood friend Soso Iramishvili – whom a party split had by then made his political enemy, a Menshevik (though even by then he was profoundly indifferent to both groups) – he had defined his position in this way: 'You know, Soso, she was the only one who could still manage to soften me. Now I feel no pity for anyone. My heart is made of stone.'

All this flashed past him in an instant and, raging at himself for his passing weakness, he barked somewhere in the direction of the desk in front of him, and then to the side of it, to the window: 'Well, what else is it? . . . Only be brief.'

'You ordered me to find the original of the Gorky poem with your annotation in the museum.' With respectful caution the assistant put the manuscript, yellowing with age, on the edge of the desk. 'Here it is, Iosif Vissarionovich.'

Oh, this idiotic story. Once, during one of his meals at Gorky's place on Nikitskaya Street, where the lachrymose novelist was boring his guests out of their skulls with his narrative poem about a girl whose young man is spared by death as a reward for her fidelity, he had flattered the capricious but temporarily indispensable old man by scrawling straight on his manuscript: 'Here is something which is stronger than Goethe's *Faust*. Love conquers death.' He had forgotten it almost as soon as he had written it; one had to write all sorts of rubbish for the day-to-day good of the cause! But then, during one of those 'stag-nights' which for old pre-war time's sake he occasionally arranged in his dacha, Lyoshka Tolstoy, now dead, in a pause between two dirty stories (he knew how to please his benefactor, the titled flatterer!) had related the curious case of a certain perspicacious literary scholar who had cooked up and defended a doctoral dissertation on the absence of a comma between the words 'something' and 'which' in his inscription. The cunning bastard had proved, by means of references to the classics and excursions into the secrets of linguistic semantics, that the 'great leader of all times and all peoples' had, by omitting this unfortunate comma, effected a revolution in modern punctuation. He had soon forgotten about it, but a few days ago, signing a resolution for the erection of a memorial to some wretched 'classic writer', he remembered it and ordered them to find him the original. Good God, how many of them had there been in recent years, these servile schemers, ready to sell their soul to the devil in exchange for a lucrative job in his entourage!

'All right, leave it.' He frowned in disgust. 'What else?'

'The Patriarch is in the outer office, Iosif Vissarionovich,' the man struck an understanding pose. 'You arranged to see him at 2.30. It is now precisely 2.25' (he cast a quick glance at his watch to confirm this).

'Call him in.' But then he changed his mind. 'No, hold on, I'll go.' He rose with an effort and moved towards the door, again trailing his game leg. 'It can't be helped, the mountain will go to Mahommed, if it has to.' He imperiously opened the door, stepped into the lobby, pushed another door in front of him and, stepping back into his study, gestured expansively.

'Please, Eminence!'

Let the crafty Pole appreciate his ability to forget, his benevolence! Before sanctioning the placing of the mitre of all the Russias on the head of this monk from the backwoods, he had carefully studied the dossier of citizen Sergei Vladimirovich Simansky, former noble, date of birth 1877, place of birth St Petersburg, priest, without occupation. After concluding with relief that the aforementioned citizen had committed enough sins against the state to be sentenced to death three times over and then to a good dozen twenty-five-year stretches in the camps, he gave his agreement. He preferred to have to deal with hardened sinners; he knew what to expect of them and they were easier to manage.

The Patriarch rustled past him respectfully in his new satin cassock, made a few steps into the study and stopped uncertainly, half-turning to the ruler: 'Good day, comrade Stalin!' He gave due emphasis to the word 'comrade'. 'Where shall I sit?'

'Nearer, nearer, Eminence.' He raised his eyebrows to his assistant as a sign that he should leave, and the man disappeared in an instant. Then he threw his arms round his visitor's waist in a half-embrace and led him to the desk, where he drew back the nearest chair for him. 'Please, Your Eminence.' And only after he had helped the Patriarch to sit down did he walk round him and fall into an armchair with a jocular groan. 'We're getting old, Your Eminence, we're getting old.'

'What are you saying, comrade Stalin, what are you saying?' the Patriarch rushed to intervene. 'You must live and prosper a long time yet for the good of the motherland and the people. The Russian church prays for you every day!'

'Oh priest, priest, you're no better than the others,' he grinned lazily to himself. 'You neither fear nor disdain the ways of the ungodly, you son of a bitch. You console yourself that your cunning is for the sake of the church, for the sake of your flock, that the Lord will forgive your transgressions in this world in His name. You think that your church is still standing on a rock, but it has been standing on sand for a long time; when I want to, I shall puff and no trace will remain, cassocked Pole, whose throat should have been cut properly long ago!'

But aloud he said, with frank lassitude, as if shrugging off tiresome flattery: 'It comes to us all, Your Eminence, it comes to us all.' And immediately, almost without pausing, 'You would do better to tell me of your needs, Eminence, and we shall try to help you as far as is possible.'

Of course, he knew in advance what matters would be raised. His secretariat prepared him detailed information before every meeting. He enjoyed amazing his interlocutors with his professional competence. So he hardly listened to the Patriarch, merely noting the unexpected details which might come in handy at the end, when the need would arise to dazzle his visitor with his famous memory.

He looked with detachment at the slightly puffy, apoplectically shiny face of his visitor, and for some reason he tried to imagine himself in his place, mentally tried on the brand-new satin cassock with the gold pectoral cross in the middle, the white cowl, the amber rosary beads on his wrist. 'If my dead mother could see me in that mantle!' The very idea of it amused him. 'What a joy that would have been for the old girl; it was all she dreamed about!'

In his soul he often chafed at his seminary past, but sometimes, during moments of total and inescapable solitude, he would be suddenly overwhelmed by an inexplicable, suffocating melancholy, which made his heart ache and his feet turn to ice, and the emaciated face of Father Sandro, who taught Church Slavonic in their seminary, would rise from oblivion, a bony finger raised in reproach: 'You will burn in the fires of hell for your pride, Dzhugashvili, you mark my words! . . .'

Perhaps that was why he occasionally indulged his whim of inviting the Patriarch for tea and abstract discussion. Today's encounter seemed all the more appropriate since he happened to have a minor problem to discuss with the priest. Studying the Kuriles these last few days he had suddenly, to his own amazement, hit upon the idea of creating an Orthodox parish there; it seemed to him that without this final flourish the structure of the new power on the islands would lack a definite base. The matter could be arranged by a single telephone call to the appropriate department, but he had nevertheless decided to use it as a pretext for a personal meeting. Now, however, listening with half an ear to the insinuating jeremiads of his visitor, he already regretted it.

'Certainly, Eminence, I shall sort it out.' Once again he did not hesitate to rise, to walk round the desk and begin the whole ceremony in reverse, from the desk to the door. 'We should meet more frequently, Eminence, more frequently. But as our old Russian proverb says, "I'd be happy to go to heaven, but my sins won't let me." Work, work, work, my head is spinning, I have no time to catch my breath.' When they had reached the door and he held it open for the Patriarch, he touched his forehead lightly with his fingertips as if he had remembered something: 'Oh yes, Eminence, I almost forgot: I wanted to ask you to create a parish on the Kuriles. We are sending people there now, with their whole families. We must think of the old folk – you wouldn't get them into a cinema for all the tea in China, they are so firm in their faith. It wouldn't be a bad thing to humour them . . .'

Taken by surprise, the Patriarch was lost for words, but he soon recovered himself and said with a slight respectful bow: 'As you wish, comrade Stalin.' And already with greater boldness, with frank gratitude, he added, 'I thank you, Iosif Vissarionovich.'

When his visitor had left, he was immediately plunged into gloom. He felt heavy and frowned. 'That priest can go to hell, he's just a waste of my time!' Back at his desk he spent a long time looking into space, trying to assemble the day's events, but failing to concentrate he picked up the manuscript brought from the museum with a swift movement, dipped his pen in the inkwell and inserted an extravagant comma before the word 'which'.

Chapter Five
Zolotarev's Dream

1

It turned out that Zolotarev was not the only passenger on the aeroplane. There were also three tipsy pilots who, judging by their conversation, were on their way to new positions after their first post-war leave.

One of them, a captain with a delicate, almost girlish face, was regaling his companions with radiant memories, looking around with eyes full of blissful excitement.

'She was a pure gypsy, nineteen years old, amazing figure – she could do anything. I can't imagine where she learnt it. She showed me things you wouldn't believe.' He even closed his eyes, overcome with emotion. 'She said her mother's a thief, goes around stealing from shops, and that she herself has been living off men since she was fifteen, but when she took her clothes off, she was something to look at! Oh, Rita, Rita, I'll never forget you as long as I live! . . .'

Soon Zolotarev began to feel drowsy: the excitements of the day before and a night without sleep were having their effect. And in his semi-conscious state his thoughts went back to that far-off spring of 1936 in all its frighteningly clear detail . . .

2

The district committee of the Young Communist League, where he worked as a vocational instructor with young people from the countryside, was housed in a wooden outbuilding in the courtyard of the headquarters of the local railway division. From morning till late at night the cramped box of a building, subdivided into several narrow cubicles, was shaken by ringing telephones, knocks at the door and people shouting at each other. The bosses summoned people to see them without undue ceremony, just by knocking on the dividing walls. A casual, matey atmosphere still prevailed; the higher officials, already run to fat, instinctively tried to prolong what seemed to them a reckless youth, but time was having its effect: the telephone calls were becoming shorter, the knocks on the door more muffled, the voices of the visitors more respectful.

When one day the secretary for organizational work, Misha Bogat, knocked on his wall to summon him as usual, he did not attach particular significance to it: just another summons, part of the daily bustle; but no sooner had he entered Bogat's next-door cubicle than he realized that a long and difficult conversation was in store.

At Bogat's side, leaning negligently on his desk, sat a gloomy-looking fellow with black hair wearing an NKVD lieutenant's uniform. He was enviably handsome: a lock of his jet-black hair fell over his eyes, he had a finely chiselled, slightly aquiline nose, a dimple in his sharp, clean-shaven chin; but behind his bright, seemingly made-to-order features one sensed a certain ingrained malice, which put one on guard with him instinctively as soon as one saw him. It was as if he had once got into a fury about something and never since managed to relent or calm down.

'Let me introduce you. This is comrade Alimushkin, from the Organs.' Bogat was doing his best to seem calm and matter-of-fact as if this was just an ordinary meeting, just an ordinary conversation, but he was not succeeding. His voice had gone hoarse, and his moist eyes darted about behind his glasses like animals at bay: the very appearance of such a visitor in the district committee offices boded a veiled threat. 'The comrade has business to discuss with you. I'll tell you in advance, Zolotarev, the district committee is in favour. I'll leave you to it then.' He got up indecisively, evidently expecting his visitor to protest, but the man did not bat an eyelid, leaving Bogat himself to extricate himself from the predicament as best he could. 'Make yourselves at home, I have to go to the executive committee anyway . . .'

As he walked from the desk to the door, Misha's anyway puny figure seemed to shrivel even further, and when he reached the threshold and turned towards them for the last time before leaving he looked quite pitiable: in his semi-military field-jacket, which seemed to stick out on him in all directions, and with his tousled hair, he looked like a puppy on a lead which has been chased into a corner. With a look of doom on his dejected face, he disappeared.

'My business with you is of a military nature, Zolotarev.' The visitor grinned morosely, either at the departing Bogat or perhaps in anticipation of the conversation that lay ahead. 'You are an experienced worker, you have a fine sense of discrimination, you know how to work with people – we think you will cope. Do you know the number seventeen railway-sidings? . . .'

Only now, looking at the visitor, Zolotarev realized that he had already come across him, or rather that sombre grin of his, somewhere in the kaleidoscope of the various district committee lobbies. However hard he tried to remember the details, all he could think of was that grin, which each time had chilled him and made his heart miss a beat. As he listened to the fellow, Zolotarev tried not to miss a single detail: in his position the slightest thing could turn out to be either fatal or fortunate, depending on the circumstances . . .

'. . . There's a construction brigade working there now, quite a crowd of them. There isn't much to choose between them, none of them up to much, a load of thieves and vagabonds. They've never had anything heavier than a pack of cards in their hands, winter or summer. Real drop-outs, in short. Twelve rogues and there's a woman there as well. As for her, she's not to be trifled with either, she's been through fire and water, she's been evicted from the town, and been had up for seduction of a minor. Their team leader is a crackpot, a "man of principles" by the name of Ivan Khokhlushkin. He used to go round the local villages working as a carpenter. He's bright enough, only he's not right in the head, and his tongue wags. He keeps ranting about universal justice, he's got those blockheads all worked up. They've got a commune going – they share everything, including the woman apparently. It smells of an organization, with a tendency towards counter-revolution; it's time to break it up. We're thinking of sending you there for political education work, like when Furmanov was sent to Chapaev, and if they don't come to their senses good and proper we'll liquidate them as socially dangerous elements. Do you understand?'

'When do I start?'

'We'll go there now, there's no point hanging about. You can get your things later, it's not very far . . .'

Soon the district committee jeep was carrying them through the flat, treeless countryside along the River Oka in the direction of Elets. The last snow had only just disappeared from the fields and the bare earth was steaming with relief, exuding the warmth it had stored up all winter. Grey wisps of smoke rose from the stoves over the occasional islands of myopic villages, and through it the green patches of roofs from which the snow had melted were dimly visible. Dishevelled jackdaws hopped with great concentration along the swollen posts of the fences along the way, surveying their plunder as it came back to life all around. The windy spring was freeing the world from the icy carapace of winter.

Sitting opposite Zolotarev, the lieutenant gave him instructions, his devilish eyes boring gloomily into him.

'Keep your eyes skinned, brother. Don't miss a trick. Any trifling detail could turn out to be a crucial clue in an affair like this. We've heard on the grapevine that a tramp goes to see them; he seems to be the half-brother of their cranky leader. He keeps quietly propagandizing universal brotherhood and equality. All in all it's a mixture of anarchy and religious claptrap, and it's time to put a stop to their little racket, only we'll have to act firmly.' He took a cigarette case from his breast pocket, took out a cigarette and, rolling it between his fingers, turned away for the first time. 'By the way, I know that martyr bastard of theirs like my own five fingers. We were at school together, he was a clever fellow, always near the top of the class. If we were doing arithmetic you'd have just started your calculations and he'd have the answer written out – everyone copied from him. And he's a real talker. He tells you the world is made of milk and honey and you just sit there and drink it all in. He could have gone a long way, if he hadn't got the devil knows what foolish ideas into his head.' The jeep suddenly slowed down and they were thrown against each other. In that moment of involuntary closeness Zolotarev was scorched by a spark of concealed mockery somewhere in the depths of those burning eyes. 'Only we weren't born yesterday either – we know how to screw people's heads back on, and if he doesn't come to his senses he'll have only himself to blame.' The jeep turned smoothly into a short dead-end track and stopped up against the buffer of a goods wagon. 'Out you get, Zolotarev, we're there . . . And keep your ear to the ground.'

After the stifling closeness of the jeep's tiny cabin, he caught his breath in the cold air of early spring. The track ran along a thin belt of trees, petering out at a tiny pond, or rather a hollow at the side of the path full of thawed snow. Beyond it, through the bluish haze on the near horizon, loomed the slag-heaps of the local mines. A damp silence reigned all around, broken only by the harsh cawing of jackdaws.

'Here it is, their rotten lair.' They walked past a row of three four-axle wagons that had been turned into living quarters. 'They've dug themselves in, couldn't be better. It won't be easy to smoke them out, but we've dealt with worse cases. We'll find a cure for them too . . .'

At the very end of the track a woman appeared, moving slowly up the slope carrying a tin bath full of wrung-out washing. And the nearer she got, the more distinct her features, the swifter became the throbbing in Zolotarev's throat. There was hardly anything special about her timidly shapeless, drained face except for a fiery red lock of hair which hung from under her headscarf and gave her a distinctive attraction.

'Good day.' Stopping a few steps away from them, she gave a slight bow: the words were pronounced quietly, simply, without defiance. 'Have you come to see Ivan Osipovich?' Without waiting for an answer she put down the tin bath at the top of the path and added, 'Go in and warm yourself in the wagon. I'll just run and find him on the tracks – he's not far away, he'll be here in a minute.'

As she passed, she glanced at them mechanically and this fleeting, almost unseeing glance nearly made Zolotarev choke. 'Who'd have believed it!' the words spun dizzyingly round his brain. 'Who'd have believed it!'

'Look at the tart,' Alimushkin snorted, his appraising glance following her down the path. 'She looks as meek as pie, but still waters run deep: she's got two convictions behind her, not counting the times she's been bound over.' He spat furiously to one side, nodding authoritatively to Zolotarev. 'Let's go to the stove, komsomolets. Why the hell should we stand out here in this freezing wind?'

In the meagre furnishing of the wagon a woman's attentive hand had clearly been at work: everything was scraped scrupulously clean, every object, every small thing was in its own strictly defined place, and even the gauze curtains at the windows embroidered with little crosses, as well as another curtain which separated off the corner of the wagon from the rest of the compartment, looked smart. An iron stove, on which there stood a cast-iron pot covered with a piece of woollen cloth, was still giving off a bit of heat. There was a smell of washing, of frugal cooking, of burnt-out coal.

'Sit down, Zolotarev, have a smoke,' he said, as if he owned the place. He took off his cap and casually flung it on to a folding table at his side. 'Standing up won't make you any the wiser.' The trestle bench fixed to the table creaked under the strain of his weight. 'Whatever you see or hear, take it all in, but don't note anything down. Keep it all in your head – it's safer that way. Call in to see me twice a week to make your report. It isn't very far . . .'

There was a confident knock at the door, and at the same time a slightly muffled but equally confident voice called out, 'May I come in?' And then a figure appeared on the threshold, letting in the cold air of the dying day: 'Good evening.'

You could have taken him for anyone you liked: an office worker, an engineer, a teacher changed into a threadbare uniform, but surely not a railway workman. Everything about him – his youthful, slightly emaciated face framed in blond hair, his slightly stooped body, his respectful yet independent manner – all this betokened an inclination more towards intellectual endeavour than manual work. And only his calloused, rust-ingrained hands showed him to be a man long engaged in hard physical work.

'Sit down, my host, be our guest.' Zolotarev's companion was clearly trying to ingratiate himself with his former comrade, although attempting at the same time to maintain an authoritative tone. 'I've brought you a commissar to help you, Ivan. You're getting a bit tangled up here on your own without any political instruction. Let me introduce you: Ilya Nikanorych Zolotarev. He's no slouch, he's an experienced comrade. There aren't that many of them about these days, and the authorities are concerned about you. I'm sure you'll get on like a house on fire.' He shifted uneasily on the bench and kept looking meaningfully at Zolotarev. 'An alliance of communists and non-party workers, you might call it.'

Khokhlushkin sat down slowly on the bench with his back to the table, between the lieutenant and Zolotarev. He carefully laid his mittens at his side, clasped his rough hands round his knees and began to speak in measured tones, savouring every word.

'Thank you. A good man will always come in handy. We're a bit cramped for living space, of course, but as they say, the more the merrier. We'll find room for him here and I'll move in with the lads, which will be even handier for me. So make yourself at home my friend, don't be shy. Only you'll have to eat from the communal pot. We're all brothers here. Well, what news from Uzlovaya, Dmitry Vlasych?'

Alimushkin's account consisted of well-chewed town rumours about who else had been arrested, who had been moved to new jobs where, what gossip there was at the depot and the divisional railway headquarters. Zolotarev listened to him with half an ear while his cautiously expectant gaze kept moving back to the door. Soon the silence which reigned outside was broken by the sound of voices, distant at first but growing ever nearer. Then a sound cut through the animated chatter, somewhere right near them, just outside the wagon door it seemed, and he found himself panting for breath at the woman's teasing laugh: 'Are the workers all worn out? I'll get you something to eat in a minute. You'll have to take pot luck with what God and the warehouse had on offer. There isn't much fat in it, but it's filling.'

Instead of answering, someone's husky tenor burst into a jaunty, provocative song:

'Up on the hill there's a truck,
They're mending its brakes
Nothing but grain fields up there
And men with rakes.

Come on, Masha, bring on your goodies, I could eat a horse!'

Immediately the door opened noiselessly and her laughing face appeared: 'Don't mind me, I'm going to get in your way a bit.' She was already busy at the stove. 'I've got to feed the lads. They're starving.'

Alimushkin glanced at her out of the corner of his eye with undisguised suspicion. Then he got up. 'Let's go and get some air, Ivan. You can talk better outside – there are fewer ears listening.'

'All right, if that's how it is.' Khokhlushkin followed his visitor slowly out of the wagon. 'If you want to talk outside, we'll talk outside.'

'Oh you men!' she nodded after them. 'You can't say anything simple. Everything is full of hints and double meanings.'

Busy with the dishes and the stove, she didn't look at him. 'I've got no time for your conversations. We're simple people, we've got enough troubles of our own. Only why do they keep pestering Ivan Osipych, coming out here, offering to educate him as if he was a schoolboy who didn't know anything about life?' She suddenly drew herself up sharply and spoke with radiant animation and vigour. 'It wouldn't be a bad idea for them to come and learn from him and bow down in gratitude to him and thank God for bringing them face to face with a man like him.' She fell silent again, piled up the dishes on top of the pot, picked the whole lot up carefully from underneath and turned to Zolotarev as she made her way to the door.

'Could I ask you to open the door for me?'

With the same throbbing in his throat, he rushed to open it. Convulsively he pulled it towards him, let her pass and followed her outside.

'My name is Ilya Nikanorovich,' he called after her. 'Call me Ilya.'

'I'm Mariya,' the words came from the nearby shadows to the muffled sound of footsteps fading into the distance. 'Call Ivan

Osipovich, it's time for supper.'

The evening promised to be starless and overcast. A heavy drizzle was falling over nearby fields. No light filtered through the ridge of trees beside the railway track, which had become a dense black wall. And only the dull gleam of the little pond at the bottom of the slope gave a touch of brightness in the dank thick shadows of twilight.

Zolotarev made his way mechanically along the little path, beside the ridge of trees, down towards the pond. As it came into view he vaguely made out two fingers silhouetted against the surface, leaning towards each other, talking confidentially.

'Oh, Vanya, Vanya,' Alimushkin's voice had lost all trace of anger and insistence. Its tone was pleading, fawning. 'Why on earth did you fill your head with these crazy ideas? Some commune you've set up, one and a half tramps and as many beggars! However much you feed them they'll still have their eyes on the woods. You could pay them a hundred times over, share everything you've got with them, and they'd never be satisfied. It's like throwing it down a well! And all the time they're laughing at you on the sly. Just look at the clothes you wear, the food you eat, you're all skin and bone!'

'It's enough for me.' His voice was calm, clear, unwavering in the thickening darkness. 'My mother's got her pension and I don't have any other relatives, so why should I save it up? You can't take it with you. If you spend your life thinking about filling your stomach, there's not much point in living.'

'You may lose your head, Ivan. You'll get yourself into a lot of trouble and it'll be too late.' A note of anger was coming back into his voice. 'Oh, Vanya, Vanya, if I had your brains, I'd take the bull by the horns. With your intelligence and a file like you've got you should join the People's Commissariat and take charge of thousands of people. There's such a lot of flotsam and jetsam floating around up there these days that anyone who's not too lazy can make it, God help us. Just give me the word and I'll make sure you have the green light all the way. I'll get you a clear run.'

'You go on about flotsam and jetsam, but what am I supposed to do there?' Ivan did not even disagree, he just kept reaffirming thoughts which he seemed to have sorted out and talked through long ago. 'I wouldn't make much of a boss, you know, I have trouble enough with the dozen I've got here. And anyway, what good would a post like that bring me, just a lot of bother to very little purpose. Everything in this life has its limits, bosses too, and then what? Not everything is in our hands, as it turns out.'

'You're talking some sort of rubbish, Ivan.' Alimushkin's former ill-humour was taking a firm hold on him again and bearing him on. 'These days you get a least a ten-year stretch with exile to follow for that kind of religious nonsense. I suppose you know that, you blockhead. If you're so clever and not afraid of the devil himself, go and tell people all this enemy drivel at a public meeting: tell them how you want to establish universal equality on a basis of sectarian ravings. Maybe they'll listen to you, what do you think?'

'He who needs to will hear for himself,' Khokhlushkin remarked, just as calm and straightforward. 'Why should I go disturbing people's peace of mind to no purpose? In time they'll come to their senses themselves. Life did not begin today, nor will it end tomorrow.'

The shorter of the shadows suddenly broke in two and immediately disappeared from the slate-grey surface of the gleaming pond.

'All right then, Ivan, live your own way,' Alimushkin's voice floated towards Zolotarev. 'I shan't give you any more advice. Carry on with your whims. But remember, you'll only have yourself to blame '

'I've really got mixed up in something here,' Zolotarev thought perplexedly as he turned back towards the living quarters. 'I must remember I'll be walking on pretty thin ice. I could fall in myself unless I'm careful.'

3

The damp changeable weather lasted a few days longer, and then more or less settled down into a mixture of warm showers and sunny intervals. Zolotarev whiled away his days making wall-newspapers and collecting quotations from newspapers and pamphlets for the political instruction he was conducting. At times he even forgot about the real reason for his presence in the place; his activities seemed a natural extension of his feverish work at the district committee. Gradually life at the railway-sidings became ordinary, normal, routine.

His relationship with Mariya was rather tense and uncertain. She was obviously avoiding him and hardly spoke to him at all except for the minimum number of words needed in the daily routine. In the evenings, when she had finished the daily chores, she retreated behind her curtain and stayed there noiselessly till the following morning.

His heart beating feverishly, Zolotarev would watch as her frail figure moved back and forth, silhouetted against the gauze curtain in the lamplight. He felt faint as she undressed, combed out her hair and lay down. And her every movement was reflected against the spotless gauze curtain like a figure in a silent film. Afterwards, in the darkness, he would lie listening to her irregular breathing for a long time, in expectation of something unthinkable, and quite unable to get to sleep. 'If only it would warm up,' he sighed as he tossed about feverishly, 'then at least I could sleep outside!'

By the end of the week Zolotarev could stand it no longer, and when the light went out behind her gauze curtain he summoned up his courage in the darkness and spoke to her: 'Listen, Mariya, here we are living under the same roof, and we haven't yet said a real word to each other.'

'You're here to represent the authorities, Ilya Nikanorych,' the quiet voice replied from the darkness. 'What kind of conversation could you and I have?'

'What kind of an authority am I? I'm just a pen-pusher at the District Committee Office.'

'You're still not one of us. You don't walk about carrying a pickaxe.'

'I go where I'm sent – it's my job to obey orders. Here today, gone tomorrow. I'm a long way from being one of the bosses.'

'We're a long way further, we live for the day and by the day. We're at work from morning till night, so we don't have much time for chin-wagging!'

'And so your youth will slip by. Life is short!'

'I was young once, but that's all past,' she sighed distractedly. 'I frittered it all away having a good time.'

'How can you say that, Mariya? Your whole life is ahead of you.' He was making tentative, fumbling overtures.

'I know better than you about my own life. All I want now is to live out my days at Ivan Osipovich's side, and nothing more.'

'Have you fallen in love with him or something?' Zolotarev was suddenly on the alert, his ears pricked up. 'How do things stand between you?'

'What are you saying, Ilya Nikanorych?' Immediately her voice became warmer, rich and melodious. 'Why would he want me? He can find himself much better! And anyway, he doesn't think about things like that! He spends more and more time thinking of others. He never has time for himself – he always puts himself last. I'd go to the ends of the earth with my eyes closed for him. I'd wash his feet and drink the water. There's nobody else like him. People have become completely wild, ready to cut each other's throats. Look at the rabble he's got gathered here – they were all as bad as each other, in and out of the police station, but Ivan Osipovich has managed to get through to them. They've become people. Everyone around here knows him. They come from all the villages for his counsel and you should see the number that come from the town. He has a kind word for everyone, and what else does a man need now?' And as if coming to a firm conclusion, she said: 'There are no people like him around any more, none at all!'

Every word she spoke fell like a stone upon him, making the dark burden of the anguish that filled him more and more unbearable. He felt as if a single agonizing red-hot string of pain was being stretched taut right through him, through his body, through his heart, through his soul, its sound searing his throat unbearably. Zolotarev had never experienced such torment before, such a sense of being suffocated. A part of him that could never be replaced had broken off with groans of pain like a baby from an umbilical cord. And as he drifted into feverish sleep he concluded in despair, 'The ball is over!'

4

Unlike most of the municipal institutions, the NKVD district department was plunged into imposing silence, broken only by the tapping of a single typewriter behind a door marked 'Reception'. It turned out that Zolotarev was expected: a taciturn woman with moustache-like down on her upper lip slightly raised her sleepy eyes from her antique 'Underwood', got up and nodded to him to follow her.

'Come in, come in, komsomolets!' Alimushkin greeted him as if all he had been doing was sitting waiting for him to appear. 'Let's go and see the chief straight away. He wants to talk to you.' And then he turned with an obsequious laugh to the woman. 'Get us some tea, will you, Vera my love!' Then he winked at Zolotarev. 'Did you see that one? In the Civil War she tore officers to ribbons during interrogations. She was famous all along the Syzran–Vyazma railway. Now she's living out her days as section head with us.' Suddenly he assumed a dignified air and, knocking respectfully but energetically at the door padded in oilcloth, pulled it lightly towards him. 'Go in.'

The room was large and almost empty – a desk, a few chairs

along a bare wall, a stool fixed to the floor just by the door, a portrait of Dzerzhinsky above the desk. The man who raised his close-cropped head to meet them was thick-set, almost square, with two pips on the epaulettes of his linen military shirt and the order of the Red Banner on his plump chest: 'Is this your remarkable young man, comrade Alimushkin?' He spoke slowly, correctly, with obvious effort, betraying his non-Russian origin. 'Let's listen to your remarkable young man, comrade Ali-mushkin.'

Standing to one side, slightly behind Zolotarev, the lieutenant nudged him encouragingly: 'Give your report, komsomolets, don't be shy!'

Zolotarev knew what was expected of him, and if this had happened at another time and in another situation he would not have hesitated long over what line to take. But now, instead of plunging recklessly in as usual, he was momentarily silent and frozen, as if he were about to dive into a pool of icy water.

True, this hesitation lasted only exactly long enough for him to take a deep breath of air. Then the words began to pour out, without a hitch, as if he were reading from a crib. He sang for them like a well-drilled nightingale, guessing what they wanted as he went along, needing no prompting or hints: he burned his bridges, cast his soul upon the four winds. He bade himself a final goodbye, he had no more regrets now and no reason to repent. He might as well be hanged for a sheep as for a lamb!

According to his report, Soviet power did not exist at the railway-sidings; an underground organization was being formed, beyond all doubt. If this enemy conspiracy was not broken up immediately, those involved might soon progress to open acts of terrorism.

'I see.' The major gave a strong push against the desk with his hands and his chair slid back against the wall behind him. 'What is your opinion, comrade Alimushkin?'

The lieutenant's face darkened for a moment and then he stood to attention, like a borzoi straining at the leash, and spoke in a hoarse whisper: 'He must be taken.' And he repeated more quietly, more hoarsely than ever: 'He must be taken immediately.'

With another effort the major turned his chair sideways and glided round the desk, ending up almost in the middle of the office. Only then did Zolotarev realize why he sat there like a Buddha: the armchair was an invalid chair which he worked manually. The lower part of his body, from the waist down, was carefully covered in some sort of rug or blanket.

'So you think we should arrest him, comrade Alimushkin?' His tenacious gaze bored into them inquiringly, distrustingly, while he rubbed together his plump hands, covered in a mass of black hairs. 'What do you think, is he a Stundist?'

'Not at all, comrade Lyampe!' Alimushkin had clearly not understood his boss, but was evidently trying not to show it. 'He's just muddying the waters. He's a trouble-maker. I've known this Khokhlushkin since I was a boy – he's always been the same.'

'I see.' As he looked at them the major kept rubbing his hands, as if trying to wash them clean of something corrosive. 'It's never too late to arrest someone, comrade Alimushkin. We must reflect, weigh things up. I've looked at his file. He comes from a proletarian family of very poor peasant stock. What will the political effect be?'

'You can't cover every eventuality, comrade Lyampe.' Alimushkin was once again shifting from one foot to the other. 'We should break them up without delay or else it'll go further and get out of control.' A thinly veiled threat had crept into his tense voice. This little arriviste knew for certain that if anything went wrong neither his medals nor his merits would save his boss: bigger shots than him were being disposed of these days. 'Our vigilance is getting slack, comrade Lyampe.'

'Maybe he really is a Stundist?' The major showed no reaction to the threat in the lieutenant's tone but continued to appraise his audience with mistrust, lost in his thoughts. 'Or a sectarian – I've met a lot of them.' He lowered his wide forehead and went on, talking more to himself than to them. 'My father was a Stundist, my grandfather was a Stundist, I grew up among Stundists. They were just simple people, but they stood up for justice and equality. They understood these things in their own way, but they didn't yet know the genius of Marx, the genius of Lenin. They believed in their hearts that everything must be just. Perhaps your Khokhlushkin is one of them?' He suddenly turned on them again, staring questioningly at Zolotarev. 'Perhaps our remarkable young man will think again, weigh his words? Perhaps the question can still be resolved directly inside the collective?'

This time Zolotarev spoke out straight away with confident directness and no hesitation: 'It's useless, comrade Lyampe. The collective has completely degenerated. Extreme measures are essential.'

'If that's the case,' his chin set harshly and the light finally left his eyes, 'go and make out the documents, and I shall sign them.' With an effort he rubbed his hands again and turned away, apparently leaving them to get on with things. 'Let him answer according to the law.' The wheelchair swung sharply round and moved back to the desk. 'And while you're about it, finish the case of those two from Bobrik-Donskoi. We must find out who is behind them. The station-master and the storekeeper can't have been working on their own – you can sense there's an experienced hand at work. You may go.'

When they had left the room Alimushkin put an arm round Zolotarev's shoulders and hugged him for an instant, then nudged him forward.

'Now we have a free hand.' Beckoning Zolotarev into his office, he sighed with excitement, in anticipation of prey. 'Old Lyampe has strange ideas and loves to make speeches, as if the Civil War was still just around the corner. To hear him talk you'd think all enemies went around wearing their gold epaulettes, while all the rest behaved like brothers and sisters. But these days the enemy is hidden all over the place, lying in wait to attack you in your own home.' He almost pushed him into the office and followed him in, nodding to him to sit at the desk. 'Sit down and write. Just the way you described it to Lyampe, word for word.' But even when he had sat down at the desk opposite Zolotarev, he still could not calm down. ' "According to the law?" The will of the international proletariat – that is our law! But what could you expect of a German anyway! He doesn't have the slightest idea about Mother Russia.'

The mustachioed woman whom Zolotarev had met before came in without knocking, holding a tray on which there were two tumblers of watery tea. Without a word she put the tray down on the edge of the desk and, not glancing at either of them, silently left the room.

A whiff of some intangible threat had entered the room along with the woman, but instead of disappearing when she left it seemed to settle into the walls, the furniture, the papers and even, it seemed, his soul, biding its time. Zolotarev's hand suddenly refused to obey him, his head went blank and empty, his eyes stopped focusing. The words fitted neatly into rows, phrase continued to follow on phrase, the exposition retained its logical sequence, but that element of conscience-easing self-abnegation which had made him so eloquent in Lyampe's study was now absent. 'If only I could get this all over and done with as soon as possible,' he concluded wretchedly. 'I can't take any more of it!'

'That's it.' Zolotarev pushed what he had written over to Alimushkin. 'See what you think of it. I think I've got it all down.'

The lieutenant spent a long time reading and rereading it, sighing and frowning involuntarily. Then, looking at him mockingly, he said: 'Well, you'll never be Lev Tolstoy, brother, but it'll probably do. We've got what's necessary. We'll get permission and we'll take them, along with those two old foxes from Bobrik-Donskoi.' Without getting up he held out his hand across the desk and winked approvingly. 'I'll make sure you get your bonus. You'd better go now, we'll meet again soon . . .'

In the corridor Zolotarev bumped into Misha Bogat. Blinking at him with the eyes of a trapped animal, Bogat muttered almost inaudibly and with great difficulty: 'They've asked to see me. They say it's urgent. They call everything urgent, I don't have to tell you.' He walked on with faltering steps into the uneasy shadows of the corridor and whispered, 'Drop in at the district committee. We'll have a chat.'

The door into the reception room was now wide open, and as he walked past Zolotarev felt a motionless, frankly questioning glance trained on him from behind the battered 'Underwood'. 'What an old witch,' he thought, and a chill passed through him. 'I shouldn't be surprised if she's put the evil eye on me!'

5

Late the next afternoon Petrunya Babushkin looked into the wagon. He had a big head and a slightly bulbous potato-nose, and Zolotarev had long ago noted his particular diligence at political education classes.

'It's pay day, Ilya Nikanorych.' His piercingly blue eyes shone with geniality. 'The lads are celebrating and they want you to come along. It would be a sin to refuse, so please do come . . .'

The night promised to be warm and clear. The surrounding countryside was coloured by the crimson of the dying day. The still air was full of the scents of fruit and flowers. Only the occasional hoots of steam-engines from somewhere beyond the smouldering horizon pierced the hushed silence of evening. The world was getting ready for sleep.

The table had been set outside, in front of the row of wagons, to take advantage of the good weather. They were already waiting for Zolotarev and immediately cleared a place for him on the bench directly opposite Khokhlushkin. From the beginning to the end of the meal, Ilya had a suspicion that Khokhlushkin had more or less guessed what fate was in store for him, if he was not absolutely certain: the team leader sat in silence, with downcast eyes, his heavy arms folded. It was only after their glasses had been filled that he parted his resolutely closed lips: 'Well, may it not be the last, please God!' He was gazing somewhere straight ahead of him, across the table, but right through Zolotarev, as if he was speaking not to him but to some inaccessible companion.

'And if there are to be no more, then let us not bear grudges against each other. We have lived together in truth and in conscience. We have never harmed anyone. We have earned our bread ourselves. If one of you holds something against me in his heart, let him speak now before all, or it will be too late. It is better to speak out face to face than to mutter behind each other's backs.' His eyes suddenly narrowed, fastening meaningfully on Zolotarev. 'His soul will be easier . . .'

As they stared straight at each other, Zolotarev looked closely at Ivan for the first time. He was thin to the point of emaciation and had fine big bones. His long face, with its bushy eyebrows and sharp chin, denoted firmness of spirit and strength of character. Khokhlushkin seemed to have worked out once and for all an idea which had possessed him. Having come firmly to believe in it he lived by it constantly, never racked by doubts, never deflected from his course.

'Our people here can read and write, Ivan Osipovich.' Zolotarev tried to make a joke, but it came out rather sourly. 'If they have any complaints they can write to the wall-newspaper.'

'You think so?' Khokhlushkin was holding a loaf of bread to his chest and cutting off large hunks, peasant fashion. 'We can never tell what is passing through another man's soul. Sometimes a man can't even answer for himself, let alone others. But I know that my conscience is clear. I have not robbed or killed or committed evil. I have neither done nor prepared evil deeds against the government. We did not bring them to power, and it is not for us to remove them from power. Only I feel in my heart that I shall not be long with you.' Again a distant, preoccupied expression came into his eyes. 'But please God, it will pass us by.'

A silent angel passed over the table, and then everyone started talking at once, interrupting each other, rushing to have their say. But soon Semyon Blokhin's piercing tenor made itself heard above the general hubbub. He was the live-wire of the brigade, with a steady supply of jokes on his smiling lips.

'We're with you to a man, Ivan,' he said quickly, occasionally looking anxiously at Zolotarev. 'All for one, and one for all. Where the needle goes, the thread will follow.' He shook his curly, prematurely balding head. 'God will not forsake us and the swine will not eat us!'

'We live in peace, we do harm to no one,' Yasha Khvorostinin backed him up with a scowl from the far end of the table, flashing an angry, mistrustful glance at Zolotarev. 'If people don't like it here, they're free to leave.' Yasha's broad-cheek-boned, heavily pockmarked face looked dark and tense. 'Good riddance to them. Don't you worry, Ivan, I give you my oath of loyalty.'

Ivan looked at him with a grateful smile, but admonished him indulgently: 'Make no oaths, Yasha, make no oaths, anything can happen. They might put you through so much that you'll disown your own mother.'

And Zolotarev suddenly felt himself to be the focus of the expectant hostility of the entire group. He was thrown into confusion, conscious of how pitiful and useless were the justifications that came into his mind. He even tried to pretend that he had not noticed anything, but at that agonizing moment he heard the long hooting of the duty jeep from somewhere deep in the distant shadows of sunset. It drew nearer and soon the dark, round shape of the jeep itself appeared at the signals of the railway-sidings. It slowed down sharply and turned smoothly into the side-track.

'They've saved my skin,' Zolotarev panted with relief, and almost ran down to the sidings. 'There's nothing this lot can do now.'

The last thing he saw as he got up was the distracted expression on the face of Mariya. Throughout the conversation he had been aware of her moving about behind Khokhlushkin. Apart from anything else he was struck by her look of total, almost inescapable doom. 'Damn you, you madwoman,' he cursed, as the earth scorched his feet. 'Why did you have to come along to complicate things?'

From some distance away Zolotarev made out Alimushkin's lock of hair through the open window of the jeep's cabin. Behind him he could dimly see a few men wearing uniform caps.

'Listen here, Zolotarev,' Alimushkin was shaking with excitement. 'We're off to Bobrik-Donskoi now, to settle the hash of that pair down at the station. We're going to carry out a search, it'll take half the night, but we'll be back here before morning. Be on the alert. We're going to arrest your bastard saint. When we come back, the mechanic will give the signal. Get him up yourself, and don't wake the others. We don't want any panic. Our job demands a certain skill – we want it all sewn up, if you follow me. Go on now.' And turning away, he gave an order from the dark of the cabin. 'Step on it, Shinkaryov!'

The jeep moved off smoothly, getting up speed as it disappeared into the thickening darkness. Soon all that could be seen were the tiny pin-points of the brake-lights . . .

By the time he had returned, the meal was already over and the things had been cleared away. Only the ex-trackman, Filya Kalinin, sat there dozing, his tousled head slumped forward in his hands. He was fond of the bottle, but otherwise he was a simple and obliging fellow. And for a brief moment Zolotarev felt a stirring of frank envy of this serene oblivion. 'If only I could lie down this minute and let all of them go to hell!'

But at that moment the sound of muffled voices floated up the slope to him and brought him down to earth. Filled once again with determination, he walked in the direction of the voices, no longer racked by alarm or doubt. 'What's happening to me?' he raged against himself. 'I'm behaving like an old woman, by God!'

As he came to the end of the track, a shadowy figure emerged from the dark mass of trees and barred Zolotarev's path.

'Listen, Ilya Nikanorych.' He made out the scanty beard of Foma Polynkov, who usually exasperated him with trick questions. 'They say you can get a medal for denouncing the right people. I imagine there's no shortage of offers these days. The mint'll get choked up churning them out – it'll have to drive them off by the trainload.' His almost toothless mouth opened in a frankly mocking grin, and Zolotarev caught the whiff of alcohol. 'What's up, Ilya Nikanorych, afraid you won't get yours?'

'Get out of my way, Foma.' Zolotarev did not recognize his own voice. His temples were throbbing with fury. 'Or I shan't be responsible. I'll break every bone in your body.'

Fuming, he moved off into the night. The shadowy figure disappeared behind his back, giving a brief chuckle.

'You don't like being rubbed up the wrong way, Ilya Nikanorych, but I don't have anything else to offer you . . .'

The little pond down at the foot of the slope shone with an oily gleam. Every detail of the night was reflected on its tiny surface: the sky, with its scattering of stars; the lacy foliage of the trees round its edges; a swarm of midges over the water. In the motionless stillness he could distinctly hear the profitable labour of nature and soil: the grass was pushing through the warm soil as fast as it could, eager to breathe the still air; the trees flexed their gnarled joints in sleepy languor; and waking from the slumber of day, insect and warm-blooded beast emerged from every burrow and crack, crawling and darting here and there. In the secret pulsation of the night he sensed its own evident rhythm and order.

As he approached the water, Zolotarev slowed his pace warily. To one side of the lake he caught a glimpse of someone's long head in a gap between the trees.

'. . . We'll all quit at once. The world's a big place, there's enough room for all of us. Manual labourers can always find work.' It was only from the lazy drawl that Zolotarev recognized Andryukha Shishigin, who was known in the brigade as a taciturn fellow with his head firmly screwed on his shoulders. 'No one will refuse, they'll have to kill us all before we leave you now.'

'What are you thinking of, Andreika? Use your brains, they'll start pinning sabotage on me as well.' In Khokhlushkin's admonishing tone there was an element of melancholy indifference. 'What is to be will be.' He had evidently heard Zolotarev's footsteps, for he added quickly, 'Go, Andreika. It will soon be light. I'll stay here a while.'

The silhouette disappeared from the gap between the trees and the bushes along the band of trees rustled. Then the night was plunged into silent expectation, leaving Zolotarev alone with Ivan. He sat in a grassy clearing among the fir-trees at the edge of the pond, his sharp chin resting on knees drawn tightly together.

'Can't you sleep?' As he settled down beside him, Zolotarev could hardly contain his trembling excitement. 'You should go and lie down, Ivan Osipych. Morning is wiser than evening, they say.' He said the first thing that came into his head, talking non-stop, as if he was trying to cast a spell on himself, or something within him. 'Stop worrying your head, there's nothing you can do about it. Don't worry, everything comes right in the end.'

But for the first time since they had met Khokhlushkin interrupted him before he had finished, speaking quietly but with stubborn insistence: 'Why don't you leave me alone, Ilya Nikanorych? What are you looking for?' His face, dim and pale in the darkness, was racked with anguish. 'I have no guilt upon my soul, and if I do I shall answer for it myself, I shall not blame anyone else. I have lived in justice since my early years and I shall die a just man. So don't follow me around, Ilya Nikanorych, don't try and keep watch on me. I'm not a wild beast, I shan't run away . . . there is nowhere to run . . .'

And there was such agony, such pain in his voice that Zolotarev could not find words to answer him. He got up and dragged himself off through the still night to the saving warmth of the wagons.

For a second it suddenly seemed to dawn on him that he had

seen all this before sometime, in some unknown past: the sultry night with the stars shining through the leaves, the timid shadows among the trees and the grief-stricken man on the rustling grass. 'The visions you see!' With an effort of will he shook off the delusion. 'It's like a dream!'

Only when he was back inside the dark wagon did he come to his senses a little. He lay down without undressing, but sleep was already out of the question. He listened attentively to Mariya's uneven breathing. 'If only she doesn't wake up,' he willed, despondent and apprehensive. 'She'll scream the place down.' When the abrupt honk of the horn brought him to his feet the windows were already lit by the blue-grey dawn. The objects in the wagon were barely visible in the dark, and the mark of nocturnal torpor and desolation still lay upon them. 'Well, keep your fingers crossed!' He tried to tiptoe stealthily to the door. 'I can knock off work today, and it'll all be out of my hands!'

But just as he reached the stove Mariya emerged from behind the hitherto motionless corner curtain, fully dressed as if ready to leave.

'What's going to happen now, Ilya Nikanorych?' Her face was deathly pale, her lips were trembling slowly. 'Where are you taking him?'

'It's no concern of ours, Mariya,' he said, trying cautiously to move her aside. 'The authorities know best; they give the orders and we carry them out.'

But she would not budge. She stared at him with swollen eyes, her hands clasped beseechingly on her breast: 'So that means if you're following orders a sin is not a sin? Dear Ilya Nikanorych, tell me, whose day has he darkened, whom has he ever offended?' Her knees buckled and she sank slowly at his feet. 'Ilya Nikanorych, I'll pray to God for you if you tell me. I'll be your slave till the day I die, I'll be a mat under your feet. You can trample all over me whenever you want to, only save the poor fellow. He's innocent – he has never transgressed either in his mind or even in his dreams, believe me.' Getting no answer from him, she clutched at his boots and pressed her cheek against them. 'I know that you like me, I'll do anything you say, only please save Ivan Osipych! I beg you in the name of Christ the Lord!'

The blood rushed to his head and for a moment he trembled. His resolve weakened, and against his will his hand reached down to the lock of golden hair which had come free of her headscarf; but at that very moment he heard another hoot of the horn, this time longer, more insistent. Cursing his momentary feebleness in the depths of his soul, he finally shook himself free of her arms, jerked open the door and with a single bound leaped from the wagon and rushed headlong towards the sidings.

On the way he almost knocked over Petrunya Babushkin, who immediately started running alongside him and, straining to keep up, whispered ardently in his ear: 'Ilya Nikanorych, please don't get the wrong idea. We're not mixed up in this, we're just simple people! There weren't any particular links between us. Vanka went his way and I went mine. I had nothing to do with what he was up to.'

Quickening his pace, Zolotarev spat, he felt such loathing.

'Leave me alone, you police spy, you'll have plenty of time to shit yourself elsewhere, damn you.'

'Don't take offence, Ilya Nikanorych.' Babushkin immediately slowed down, and stopped. 'What can you expect of us yokels?'

Zolotarev was to remember this morning and this running conversation for a long time. More than once he would have to make a choice between, as they say, friendship and duty, and invariably on such occasions he would envy the simple ease with which Petrunya Babushkin had that day renounced the brigade leader whom he had seemed openly to idolize . . .

'Oh, komsomolets, you missed the fun.' Alimushkin was hurrying to meet him, accompanied by a young rifleman from the militarized railway guard. 'You can congratulate me, we've got all the eggs in the basket. Now go and take a look round; before you know it they'll be raising the roof.'

Zolotarev turned and almost fainted with shock: practically the whole brigade had turned out and was keeping a watchful eye on the arrival of the uninvited guests. Khokhlushkin was clearly standing apart from the others, as if to emphasize that they had no connection with him and with what was about to happen. On either side of him, leaning against the panelling of the carriage, were his namesakes, the Zuyev brothers: Big Ivan and Little Ivan. And though there was little between them either in height or in build – they were born only a few minutes apart – these nicknames had stuck to them in the brigade, helping those around them to distinguish them. Always ready for a scrap or a fight, the brothers stuck like glue to each other and their chief.

'That's the way things are, Ivan,' Alimushkin stood square in front of him, talking with staccato briskness. 'We're taking you to the District Department. They'll sort things out there. Don't make a fuss, it's useless.' He turned to the rifleman and nodded. 'Take him away.'

The young man, his fair-skinned face a mass of freckles from ear to ear, clapped his hand clumsily on Ivan's shoulder: 'Let's go, citizen.'

Khokhlushkin obediently stepped forward, but at that moment something unexpected happened: Little Ivan suddenly turned out to be holding an axe. No one had noticed where or when he had managed to find it, and he had already raised it over the head of the dumbstruck rifleman when the brigade leader forestalled him.

'Stop it, Vanyok.' He thrust himself between them. 'It won't do any good – there'll only be more bloodshed. I'd rather you told my mother not to upset herself, that I shan't be away long. And look after Mariya or she'll go to pieces.' And he stepped forward again. 'Let's go, soldier! There's no point in standing around.'

Alimushkin was still shaking with mad fury. He was noticeably irritated at the way things had turned out and his fingers were tapping on the clip of his holster. But in a moment he regained control and, turning after Khokhlushkin, he managed to shout a threat at Little Ivan: 'I haven't finished with you, kulak brute! We'll talk elsewhere, and you'll be saying your prayers!' He then called to Zolotarev. 'Hurry up! There's no time to chew the cud. Run!'

The inside of the jeep was hot and filled with cigarette smoke. A second rifleman was keeping an eye on two other men, evidently the ones from Bobrik-Donskoi: one was a grey-whiskered old man with hairs sticking out of his ears; the other a young fellow of about thirty, in a railwayman's cap, who flashed his gold teeth in a cheery grin as they got in.

The jeep gave a third hoot of its horn, juddered off and gathered speed as it glided past the sidings. Instinctively Zolotarev looked back along the track. He sighed and caught his breath so that he almost choked. Mariya was running alongside the jeep, her lips parted in a shriek. Gradually she fell further and further behind and the jeep, rattling past the signals, came out on to the open road. The face of the running figure became smaller and smaller until the lock of red hair tumbling from beneath her headscarf became a tiny smudge in the hazy blue of the road which snaked away into the distance.

'Look at that,' the one with the gold teeth grinned again, nodding at the window. 'The girl's really in a state.'

He darted a mischievous glance at Khokhlushkin. 'She's yours, is she, brigade leader?' The latter sat silently in a corner, his head held back, his eyes closed in weariness. 'You're famous, you are, brother, They say you've mastered all sorts of knowledge, that neither plague nor sores can affect you, that you can make soup out of an axe, and you're getting people to live in a commune. Well, whether you carry out miracles or not, you're in for it now with our red brother until he's "carried out the verdict". And no fine words will help you.' Getting no answer, he turned to his companion. 'Listen, Nikitych, cranks are ten-a-penny these days. They're all falling over themselves to be put to death. They want to be martyrs. At least you and I have our memories – we lived life to the full. But as for these poor calves, what the hell are they being taken in for?'

But the old man did not reply either. He merely spat gloomily and malevolently from time to time at his feet . . .

As they approached Uzlovaya there was a sudden downpour with claps of thunder and jagged flashes of lightning. For the last few kilometres the jeep seemed to be swimming through a curtain of water through which the line of buildings outside the town stretched like ghosts. When finally the first box-like huts of the station loomed indistinctly through the whirling rain and the jeep slowed down, Alimushkin leant over to Zolotarev with a business-like air: 'All right, komsomolets, go straight over to your district committee.' He had noticeably softened after his recent harsh behaviour. 'We've left something for you there with Bogat.' Then he winked in elucidation. 'I have a rule: one good turn deserves another.' And he nudged him towards the door. 'Out you get, komsomolets . . .'

Before climbing out into the rain Zolotarev stole a look into the corner, in the direction of the brigade leader. He was sitting with his head still slumped back, but his eyes were now wide open as if he was staring at something straight in front of him inaccessible to the ordinary eye. For a brief moment their glances met, but to Zolotarev's astonishment there was neither reproach nor condemnation in his eyes, only anguish – deep, lasting, desiccating anguish. With that Zolotarev stepped out into the downpour, into the town, into the new day.

Misha met Zolotarev without particular joy, but he was immediately emphatically respectful, even affectionate.

'Don't sit down.' He started rummaging through the desk drawer. 'This won't take a minute. You'll be off in a brace of shakes. Here!' Taking care not to meet his gaze, he held out an envelope. 'I was instructed to give you this in person, on the orders of comrade Lyampe himself.' Misha scratched his stubbly chin thoughtfully, trying to gaze somewhere beyond him, and sighed dreamily. 'You're off to Sochi, Ilya, where the Black Sea enchants the eye. Some people have all the luck!' Then he got up quickly, and without offering his hand he sent him on his way. 'You've earned it – take your reward and good luck to you . . .'

Zolotarev left the district committee building with a bitter after-taste from what turned out to be his last meeting with Misha. He could not get rid of the feeling that Bogat knew far more about him than was necessary for his job, and unease gnawed at his soul. 'He was the one who got me into it, and now he's turning up his nose, the lousy four-eyed creep!'

After the rain, the town look cleaner and more spacious. Everything around – the roads, the houses, the trees, the electricity wires – was steaming and glistening in the brightness of the freshly washed morning. The crazy water mixed with muddy sand was coursing headlong along the gutters. Aroused by the downpour, the birds were twittering away ecstatically, the noise mingling with the bellowing and bleating of animals in the yards and the hooting of engines at the station. All the signs were that the day would turn out bright and fine.

On his way home Zolotarev could stand it no longer and he opened the envelope, already guessing what it contained. Inside there were three hundred roubles and a chit for a whole month at the coast. For a short while he mechanically read and reread the text of the ticket made out in his name, and all the events of the previous night were suddenly concentrated in this rectangle of soft cardboard: the brief supper, the watching at the pool, the tears of Mariya, the denial of Petrunya, the arrest. His fingers suddenly went weak and the paper slipped out of his hand, fell into the stream of rainwater at his feet and then, becoming slowly sodden, floated away along the gutter and soon disappeared from view.

On that day, for the first and last time in his life, he went out and got blind drunk.

Zolotarev was woken up by a warning tap on his shoulder: the shyly smiling face of the captain, a man he knew, was leaning over him: 'You'll sleep through it all, dear comrade. We're about to land! See how beautiful it all is down there!'

The plane shook as it lost height, and out of the nearby window Zolotarev saw a brilliant expanse of blue, getting rapidly wider, framed by a strip of the rusty-green brushwood of the taiga. The stretch of water beneath the plane's wing sparkled and got larger and larger until it filled the whole window, and as he woke up fully Zolotarev realized with relief: Baikal!

Chapter Six

1

Somewhere near Irkutsk the convoy was suddenly shunted into a siding, and after they had waited a few hours Fyodor went into the front carriage to ask Mozgovoy when they would move on. The station was absolutely tiny, with three sidings and a single station building, right next to the signal-box.

Dusk was settling over the station and over the taiga. The air was stuffy, full of the buzzing of mosquitoes. The forest along both sides of the track stretched into the distance like a trellis, even and dense. Seen close up, not through the window of a speeding carriage, the forest seemed to Fyodor even thicker and denser.

'How immense the forest is here,' he caught his breath involuntarily. 'It probably stretches a thousand versts. There's enough wood to build over the whole of Russia, not like our little woods with their single pine-tree.'

Mozgovoy met him gloomily. He clearly wasn't in the mood for guests.

'Hallo, soldier, I haven't seen you for some time. Give me some good news. They're all bringing me the shit.'

Only then did Fyodor realize the state Mozgovoy was in. He had had a good skinful of what must have been fairly lethal wine, and was consequently melancholy or, more precisely, raging against the whole world.

'I came to ask when we'd be leaving,' Fyodor assured him peaceably, 'but since you're not in the mood, I'll go.'

The conciliatory tone of his visitor calmed Mozgovoy down, and his harsh face softened.

'All right, soldier, come in and sit down. Only what can I tell you? Plant a stake and it sometimes goes on standing, but as for a whole convoy, God alone knows. Oh, these people, these people, what's the hurry?' He was in the mood to philosophize. 'You know, as wise people in Nagaev used to say, the longer you sit, the less time there'll be left to go. Why don't you just sit down with me instead and we'll pour ourselves a little drink to make our souls feel easier! . . . Hey, Mother, get the soldier and me something, you know what!'

To Fyodor's surprise an old woman, thin as a rake, appeared from a dark corner of the carriage, her face as harsh as Mozgovoy's: 'Hallo.' (Her voice turned out to be much more soft and mellifluous than her features had implied, even affectionate.) 'There's no reason why I shouldn't get the guest a drink, only you, Pasha, have probably had enough. It's not that I grudge you it, but you'll just go around with a sore head tomorrow.'

'All right, Mother,' he shrugged it off good-naturedly, 'let's have what we've got on the table. I'll take that chance!' And then, turning to Fyodor, he went on, 'She's been hanging on my heels since I was a young lad. If it wasn't for her, I'd have definitely perished over nothing at all. I certainly wouldn't have survived all my punishment camps. How many tears she's cried, how many bribes she's slipped the stinking guards so as to oil the palms of those beasts of prey and get her Pashka out of the hands of the grim reaper, I've lost count. I was laid low with scurvy, the bed-bugs in the huts covered my whole hide in bites, I didn't have a single bone left unbroken after the terrible beatings, but she got me out of it, didn't leave me to the reaper.' He jerked Fyodor towards him by the collar of his field-shirt and said, 'That's what a mother is, do you understand?' In the light of the kerosene lamp, you could see under the striped sailor's vest that his muscular body, covered in tattoos, growths and scars, really did seem cruelly battered. 'Don't spend a long time at it, Mother! My soul is panting!'

'It's ready, Pavlusha, it's ready.' She hurried out of her corner with a wide board in her hands instead of a tray. 'You praised me so, Pasha, that I'm quite ashamed before our guest.' She spread out the food neatly and deferentially before them. 'I've already seen all your family. You're obviously thrifty people – you can tell at a glance. Well, eat up, lads, and I'll sit over there in the twilight. I've still got a lot of sewing to do . . .'

'D'you see?' Mozgovoy nodded as his mother moved away. 'She's a bit odd. All her life she's been beaten over the head, but still she comes out offering hospitality. Did you ever see such people? Well, come on, soldier, let's get one down us. To our meeting, as they say, and many of them . . .'

Fyodor had seen and heard a good deal in his short life. He'd supped four full years of war, which is also no joke. Blood and shit, he'd seen a bit of everything, but what he learnt that night from his drunken host was enough for four lives of a hundred and fifty years each. Sometimes he wondered whether the drink wasn't making Mozgovoy pile it on a bit, so incredible and implausible did his whole story seem . . .

'. . . D'you remember the song, soldier?: "The flame beats on the cramped little stove", something like that. Only in my dug-out in the Kolyma punishment camp there was no stove. We made fires on the ground if we managed to steal something, and if we didn't we warmed ourselves with our own stench. We'd get up at 6.00, and lights out at 10.00, and no days off or holidays. You got your ration in the morning, though I'd hardly call it a ration, more like a piece of frozen clay, and outside it's minus fifty degrees centigrade. If you don't make your norm, there'll be no ration. We dug for gold with our pickaxes like men possessed, and all the time there was a blue haze in our eyes. Only when my teeth fell out like peas from a pod, I lay down in my dug-out and they could have shot me – I wouldn't go out again! . . . Pour me another glass of this rot-gut, soldier . . .' He downed his drink in one and again he grinned at Fyodor, revealing a set of metal false teeth. 'If you refused to go out in those days there was only one punishment: you were shot. But I didn't care any more; if they shot me, they shot me! So I lay there like a louse in the frost, waiting to die – I couldn't have got up if I'd wanted to. The guards didn't ask what I was up to, the guards know their job. They dragged me out of the dug-out by force and took me to the guard-room. All around the guard-room there were crowds of officers and all of them were standing to attention, and in the middle, sitting smoking on a little stool, is a puny little runt in a colonel's coat. You could have knocked him down just by looking at him. My soul started off for heaven, soldier, you couldn't see its heels. I realized: Nikishev! It's all up with me, I thought. Nikishev is completely merciless – he doesn't care who he strikes down. He even used to kill his own men on the spot – he was famous for it throughout Kolyma, he had spoken to Stalin himself the way you and I are talking now. And though I had never set eyes on him, I immediately knew it was him. Oh soldier, soldier, may you never see such a vile rotten louse, even in your nightmares!' Mozgovoy looked straight ahead abstractedly, as if he was going through it all again. 'The soldiers of the guard were holding me on both sides to stop me falling down, and Nikishev, the mangy cur, came up to me and asked me, all sweetness, "You're ill, are you?" I kept silent – I didn't give a fuck about his little games, and anyway I didn't have the strength to move my tongue. "I do have one medicine for him," he said, "only it's a bitter one." He turned to me, "Aren't you afraid?" I opened my trap for the first time – it made no difference now. "No, citizen commander," I said, "I've lost the habit." I watched him, he was smiling, he liked my answer. "D'you want to go as a brigade leader to a group of politicals?" And I said in the same tone, "What, without my teeth?" I paid dear for that little joke, soldier. I didn't notice him thump me, and when I realized it was too late. "Take him to the infirmary," he said, "let him lie there for a while. I need lads like him. You can tell at a glance he's a sailor." And ever since then there's been no end to it, I rush around doing his bidding, the son of a bitch. May he rot in hell for what he did to a regular sailor! I spent a month shirking in the infirmary. They patched me up a bit, and then they took me back to the guard-house again and gave me some prisoner's clothes for the journey. "Change into these. We've got to take you to the chief. Wrap yourself up warmish. It's a long way!" "So where do they need me now?" I ask. "Yours not to reason why," they answer. "Kit yourself out and then stand still and keep mum!" As you know, I'm not that keen on arguing, so I get dressed, taking deep breaths all the time. They put me in this low officers' sledge as if I was some boss, and take me straight across the taiga for my political mission. I remember it as if it was yesterday. There are three tarpaulins covered in snow above the shore, and a bit further on some sort of barn, or stables, and three huts for the guards. "Get out," they say, "you're expected." So they take me into the officers' hut and what do I see? Nikishev himself is sitting there, swilling cognac, eating dried prunes, his tunic unbuttoned. "Sit down, brigadier," he says, "we'll have a chat." And he pours me half a mug of brandy. "Drink, brigadier," he says, "I've got things to tell you." So I down it in one and my head starts spinning, I'm so out of practice, and he starts: "I've read your file," he says, "very interesting file," he says. "It's the only one I've got, citizen commander," I say, "I haven't earned any others yet." "Born in the Kuban, eh?" he asks, "a Cossack, are you?" "That's right, citizen commander," I say, "from the Cossack village in Platnir-ovskoye." "And what, have you got family there?" he says. "What family?" I say. "All my family died in the famine, citizen commander. Only my old mother survived – she's living some-where near here." "You remember the famine, do you?" he says, looking at me like a cat at a mouse. "You haven't forgotten it?" "How could I ever forget it?" I say, "I shan't forget it as long as I live, and I'll tell others about it. Even the flies croaked." "If that's the case," he says, "come with me. I'll give you a little political education lesson!" So he throws his colonel's kaftan on his shoulders, picks up his sheepskin hat, and off he goes out of the hut. He makes straight for the barn and I go after him, and guards rush up from all sides waiting for orders. We rush into this barn, Nikishev shouts out the order, without turning round. "Bring 'em here, the sons of bitches." The convoy guards slip him a little stool – they know their job, the crawlers. "We're going to give you what you might call a political agitation lesson with visual aids." So they drag up these two zeks. They are both thin as rakes. Believe me, brother, I've seen people about to croak, I've been two spits from croaking myself, but I've never seen anyone like that pair. They were just rotting skin and bone. So they put them in front of him and they stand there waving like spiders' webs in the breeze, you could have stuck your finger through 'em. One of them has a bit of black beard – he seems like a Jew – the other one looks like one of our lads: snub nose, frog eyes. Their faces are completely empty. They've both had it with life, I reckon. So my Nikishev nods to the guards to scram, and then he turns to the zeks and says to them, all sweet like, "Pleased to meet you," he says "ex-members of the central committee, sirs, what good news have you, anything to delight the ear of the party and government?" So our living corpses stand there in silence, staring straight ahead of them, and go on waving. "Swallowed your tongues, have you?" Nikishev starts getting a bit angry. "Or have you forgotten how to talk? What about you, Isaiah," he says to the Jew, "you were running propaganda throughout the Caucasus, you were a really big wheel, you sang like a nightingale, you brought all the free Cossacks down to the common denominator, you made all our mother Kuban a *kolkhoz* granary, you cleaned out all the peasant corn-bins, there was nothing you wouldn't have sacrificed for the motherland – yourself, the people, you were very enthusiastic about your work. And all with the aid of your trusty Ivan Alekseich." At this the snub-nosed, frog-eyed Russian looks down at his feet. "You'd got in some practice in the Civil War, though, hadn't you, Ivan Alekseich? Denikin's officers will remember your caresses for years in the Paris cabarets, and your own people in the Kuban won't forget in a hurry how you and Isya led them to the happy future with a revolver. Our great leader didn't give you a medal for nothing now, did he, eh? . . . eh?" The old goners stand there – they've even stopped swaying – waiting for their time to come. And then he turns to me; his eyes are white with rage, his thin lips are blue. "Learnt your political education lesson, brigadier?" he says, undoing his holster under his coat. "I entrust to you, brigadier," he says, "my fighting arm. Show us on a live

target what they taught you in the navy. I take full responsibility."
I don't know what happened to me then, brother. I didn't know
what I was up to. I had this white haze in my eyes, remembering
the way the town poor wandered through the Cossack villages,
when all you could hear was the groans of people dying and the
wailing of the women over their babies' cradles; I remembered the
tiny kids crawling on all fours through the stubble looking for last
year's rotten stumps to eat, and all my grown-up relatives croaking
side by side on the cold stove, the stench of carrion spreading right
through the yard, as if the plague had got them . . . I couldn't see a
thing. Suddenly, soldier, I pulled the trigger, and emptied the
whole barrel into them. Then I fell down myself, whether for lack
of air or because of the brandy I don't know, and all I could hear
was Nikishev standing over me whispering, "D'you understand
what's what now, brigadier? Go and find your brigade and don't
forget who you're dealing with. They're all tarred with the same
brush, the sons of bitches. They've shed more blood than you have
sweat, and now you're in charge of them . . ." So off I went,
brother, and it's been up and up ever since . . . Bring us another
one, Mother, I feel bad anyway!'

Mozgovoy poured himself a full glass, downed it in one and
instantly slumped over the table in the sleep of the dead.

The old woman walked slowly out of her corner, stood quietly
over him for a while, rocking backwards and forwards in her grief,
then said: "He always torments himself so, and what for? He's not
as bad as the others. He still can't forget he was once a mechanic
on a steamship. They arrested him for negligence, and once he was
in prison, I don't have to tell you, anything can happen. That's the
sort of place it is.' She sighed, and bowed slightly to Fyodor.
'Don't be too hard on him, if something's not right. The morning
knows best, they say. Good night.'

At that moment Fyodor sensed that she was convinced not only
of the bitter rightness of her son's behaviour, but also that Fyodor
shared this conviction, because he could not do otherwise.

Fyodor went out into the night, feeling neither drunk nor even
heavy. He was overwhelmed by furious rage. Again and again the
minutest details of what he had just heard ribboned through his
mind. He tried to imagine himself in Mozgovoy's place, to imagine
how he would have behaved, but most of all he was tortured by a
sense of general hopelessness.

'We crush each other,' Fyodor fumed, 'then we change places
and start all over again. The result is everything always goes
wrong. And you can't see an end to the carousel!'

Night was stuffy, dense and impenetrable over the little halt, and more impenetrable still was the same strip of taiga which loomed along the side of the railway line; and were it not for the pulsating life of the convoy as he made his way along it, the world might have seemed deafened for ever by its own cries of pain.

As he opened the door of his own wagon Fyodor heard someone's breathing beside him.

'Who's there?'

'It's me, Fyodor Tikhonych.' He recognized the voice of Lyuba Ovsyannikova. 'The men are making such a din, my head's spinning.'

'What are you standing outside the wagon for, you ninny? Why don't you walk along the train? There aren't any wolves here and no one'll eat you.'

And as he spoke Fyodor felt his soul soften with pity. For as long as he could remember, strange as it might seem, he had always treated women as if they were younger than himself, whatever age they actually were. This had clearly started in his family, where his father, in his constant tyranny of his mother and grandmother, implicitly gave him the right to feel pity for them or to show them his boyish sympathy. More than once, during the four long years of a war which favoured quick friendships, Fyodor had had the chance to cure himself of this crankiness, but either out of natural inclination or for some other reason he had not managed to overcome this innate weakness.

Fyodor had been casting shy looks at Lyuba since the start of the journey. She exuded a kind of astonishing spiritual calm which made everyone around her feel calmer and simpler in her presence. She treated her girlish misfortune peacefully and equably, and responded to the reproaches which rained down on her from her mother from morning till night with a silent smile. Fyodor liked her precocious independence and her inconspicuous but firm capacity to hold her own among others, not to mention the constant care she took about her appearance. More than once along the way he had mentally noted that Lyuba would surely make someone a good wife.

'If you like I'll walk with you while the others are still asleep,' he suggested to Lyuba with his habitual condescension. 'Don't be afraid, I shan't eat you.'

'But I'm not afraid of you, Fyodor Tikhonych, I'll go anywhere you like, blindfold if you want.'

And she said this with such winning simplicity, with such confidence in him, that he could not resist and drew her to him gratefully and carefully, as if she were a child, and immediately heard her heart palpitating against his chest.

2

The next morning Mozgovoy entered the carriage stone-cold sober, as laconic of word and gesture as ever.

'Morning, soldier. This is how things are. I've had a word with the station-master: we're stuck in this hole till kingdom come unless we get a good push from someone in authority. So this is what I'm going to do. Pin on all your medals and we'll take the first train to Irkutsk. We'll act as a team. You can flash your medals at them and I'll sweet-talk them. The station-master here is an understanding sort of fellow and he'll stop a goods train for us. Get the picture? . . . '

Soon they were shaking along in the brake-van of an empty coal-train, carrying them off in the direction of Irkutsk. The sun was getting stronger, and in its blinding light the thinning strip of taiga reflected all the colours of the rainbow. And what had frightened them by its monotonous impenetrability when seen from the ground, at a distance of a few paces, now amazed them by the variety of its relief and vegetation as they stood high on the footplate of the brake-van as it climbed a steep embankment. Slightly rusty conifers gave way to the bright multicoloured glades of meadows; the sabre-flashes of the bends of little rivers to the round glassy surface of lakes; the orphaned nakedness of clearings to the smoking tar of full-grown pine-forests. Then as they entered the town itself something so immense and so luminous flashed into sight through the sparse trees that Fyodor involuntarily screwed up his eyes as he realized, more with his heart than with his reason: Baikal!

Irkutsk met them with the sleepy silence of its calm streets. The heat had driven all signs of life under the rescuing shade of awnings, offices, myopic five-walled huts. More than half the town was made of wood and the fume of a heat haze rose from it. The asphalt in the centre of the town had melted under their feet.

Mozgovoy dragged Fyodor tirelessly round the various administrative offices, pushing him forward and droning out: 'Look at it from our point of view, comrades. The convoys are rushing to the work front on an extremely important government mission: the exploitation of lands liberated from the Japanese expansionists. Every day costs a fortune! There's no possibility of further delay. I

88

beg you to take charge!'

They spent some time being sent on from one office to another and then a third, and then on again, being refused everywhere, until in the end, in the regional Party Committee Office, a cheery fellow wearing a Buryat *tyubiteika* and exhausted by the heat suggested: 'I'll give you the latitude and longitude of it. Only careful not to betray me. Are you receiving me?'

Mozgovoy took on a knowing air: 'Loud and clear.'

'Your boss, central board commander Zolotarev, is in town today. Go over to see him. One way or another he's in direct contact with the Boss himself. Are you receiving me?'

'Where?' Mozgovoy croaked in a loud whisper.

'Maybe you'd like me to drive him round to your train as well?' he chuckled lazily. 'That's it, over and out . . . '

It was almost lunchtime and they stopped at the nearest eating place, where over a couple of beers Mozgovoy outlined to Fyodor his further plan of campaign: 'We'll have to hook this one with a different fly. You won't impress him with medals – he's got a sackful of his own. I've got a different bait for him. They say he comes from Tula, which is where half the convoy hails from, not to mention you. We'll chuck in the bait – he'll probably bite. Who doesn't want to be an eagle before his own people? I'll keep you in reserve. You may come in handy later.'

'We've still got to find him.' Fyodor tried to cool his companion's ardour. 'The hen's on the nest, but where the egg is . . .'

'Finding him's no problem. You call this a town? More like a village and a half. The main thing is getting him to take the bait. It doesn't always work.' Suddenly he gave Fyodor a strange look, as if examining him from a distance.

'Maybe Zolotarev is from the same village as you are, soldier. You never know your luck.'

Fyodor shrugged the idea off: 'Half the people in Uzlovaya are called Zolotarev, they're two-a-penny.'

Why, after all, should Mozgovoy know or even guess that Fyodor not only remembered the family of Ilya Zolotarev very well, but that he could even recount many things about his present commander that he himself had probably long since forgotten or at least tried to forget! The enclosed little world of the village usually retains the shames and glories of its inhabitants in its collective memory for a long time, especially if they have got on in life. And therefore Zolotarev, who had long since got used to soaring like an eagle, was in no hurry to display his new plumage in his own village, preferring whenever possible to give it a wide berth; and no one there was very keen on seeing him either.

'You can always try your luck, brother,' Fyodor mentally encouraged his companion, 'but it's a long shot!' But aloud he said: 'You know how to talk to the high-ups, so the ball's in your court.'

Before setting the plan in motion, Mozgovoy rehearsed their roles again: 'You've got to cover the rear, soldier. Watch me and learn – it might come in handy in your old age. The first place we go is the Fish Board. That's his diocese, so they should know, but on the way we'll call in and buy some scent. Women are very important in matters like these. Forward, march, soldier! Hand to the wheel!'

Three moves – the information bureau, the chemist's, the regional Fish Board headquarters – and they took up an initial position near the director's office. Mozgovoy gave Fyodor a sign to stay there, and himself went into the office.

Fyodor was wandering aimlessly along the corridor waiting for Mozgovoy to return when suddenly a bald gnome with glasses on his raspberry-coloured bulbous nose appeared before him.

'Are you from out there, comrade?'

'Sort of,' said Fyodor in confusion.

'I'm Kunov, special correspondent of the branch newspaper,' the gnome introduced himself, busily opening an enormous notepad which half hid him from view. 'What's new out there?'

'Things seem . . . all right . . .'

'You mean, everything's wonderful?' The spectacled gnome had something crablike about him: clinging, tenacious, evil. 'What about something more specific?'

Fyodor completely lost his head.

'All in all . . . you might say . . . all sorts of things . . .'

'And even more specifically?'

Fyodor shrugged his shoulders and sighed.

'That is no answer, comrade.'

And who knows how it may have ended if at that moment Mozgovoy had not emerged triumphantly from the outer office to get him off the hook: 'Forward, soldier!' He dragged Fyodor after him, dismissing the gnome with a single eloquent gesture. 'Go away, comrade! Affairs of state.' As he walked towards the exit, he explained. 'He's dug in, in the district committee hotel. They'll never let us in there. We'll have to catch our carp by phone. To the post-office!'

But Zolotarev had gone out. They had to keep phoning back,

and kill time between calls at the nearest beer-stall.

'Our bosses, soldier, don't have norms to fill each day,' Mozgovoy explained, enjoying blowing the foam off his beer. 'They're so busy drinking and living it up, they don't have time to go out into the world. Only simple folk like you and me, we don't mind waiting anywhere, in prison or drinking beer. Am I right, soldier, or am I not?'

And it was only sometime in the middle of the night that Mozgovoy flashed a victorious grin that revealed all his metal teeth from the telephone box, and gave Fyodor a peremptory wink: 'Come here, soldier!'

He was not put through immediately. He was cross-questioned minutely and at length as to who he was, why he was phoning so late and what was his business, to which Mozgovoy, the cunning old fox, kept stubbornly giving the same answer: a matter of national importance. In the end the battle of two obstinate bureaucratic wills concluded with an absolute victory for Mozgovoy: Zolotarev himself picked up the phone.

'Comrade Zolotarev?' He was inspired. 'This is the plenipotentiary of your central board, Mozgovoy, speaking . . . I said Mozgovoy, Pavel Ivanovich! I am accompanying a convoy of workers to Vladivostok, en route for the Kuriles. Most of them are from Tula! From Uzlovaya! . . . Uzlovsk lads! The convoy,' at this point he winked again at Fyodor, this time conspiratorially, 'has been held up for nearly five days at siding No. 42. I'm asking for your immediate intervention to cut through this bureaucratic red tape and put a stop to this outright sabotage. The fulfilment of a state mission is under threat. I decline all responsibility for its failures . . . Yes, at your command, comrade central board commander! Yes . . . yes . . . I am ready to fulfil any task . . . yes . . . yes, comrade central board commander!'

Delicately, as if it was something very fragile, the plenipotentiary replaced the receiver and left the telephone box, not attempting to hide his self-satisfaction. He slapped Fyodor patronizingly on the shoulder: 'And you didn't believe me! You live and learn, soldier, and you'll still die a fool. Did you see how you have to break down men like him? That's the way to do it, all right! The carp didn't dangle very long . . . '

They were in luck. They even managed to look in at the station restaurant before it closed, and Mozgovoy, pouring various kinds of liquor down Fyodor, swore to him: 'Stick with me, soldier, and you won't go wrong. I'll lead you wherever you like and get you through. In Vladivostok I'll put you and your family on the first steamer. What d'you want to sit around wasting your money in the town for? If you arrive on the first steamer, you'll be in demand. You can choose where you want to work yourself. I'm telling you, soldier, it's a gold-mine, the Kuriles!'

They shambled round the sidings at the goods station, looking for a train going in their direction. Then Mozgovoy tried to sweet-talk the crew into letting them make the trip in the locomotive with them – they weren't keen on spending the night in the cold brake-van – and finally he talked them into it, though it was against the rules. And soon the noisy locomotive was carrying them through the starlit darkness over earth, over taiga, over time, into the whistling tunnel of space.

Fyodor crouched against the shaking wall of the tender, watching the flames playing in the stove, thinking about himself, and Lyuba, and the land with the smoky name of Kuriles, and perhaps, for the first time in years, his soul felt light and at ease.

3

No one played the pipe at their head, no one lured them after him, no one tried to talk them into it. They went of their own accord and surged forward close-packed, thrown against each other, their shining foreheads hitting the backs of those in front. An aboriginal instinct led them, a presentiment, a fear rooted in their blood which once aroused never leaves the body alone, forcing it to tremble at its own existence. There were so many of them that it seemed as if the whole coast was covered in the cold ashy colour of lava, and that this lava flowed down soundlessly into the sea, leaving not even foam behind it. The day was getting towards evening, but they kept on and on moving, and their name was legion of legions and the sea closed indifferently over them as if they had been sand or seaweed. And when, in the end, their mad flight was accomplished, the earth became a little cleaner and it became a little easier to breathe. But in the morning, as soon as the sun had risen, the whole thing began again.

Chapter Seven

1

He was met at the aerodrome by the second secretary of the district committee, a lively chatterer in a civilian raincoat over his semi-military uniform, who drove him past the town straight to the nearest fish-farm.

'There's pressure from above for us to mechanize the fishing,' he complained to Zolotarev on the way, 'but they give us no credits. So once again you have to scrape the money together from the local budget. We just about manage, of course, but we have our own holes to mend as well. We've only just got through the war, we're putting patches on patches, but never get the chance to do it properly. The land is coming to, thawing out a bit, but there's a great deal more ploughing to do before we reach full capacity . . .'

The fields began as soon as they left the town, punctuated by patches of woodland. The road began to rise gradually, the landscape thinned out, narrowed, the glades and clearings became sparser and more forlorn, and soon the car, groaning heart-rendingly at the bends, was looping its way through solid taiga. As they climbed the sky ahead became higher and more distant, hooked on to the black spikes of pines and larches.

'Even a year ago it was impassable here,' explained his voluble companion. 'It was a wall of cedars, with only bears for miles around; now it's very different, even quite reasonable. You just need tyres and petrol and you can go right round Baikal. It may not be asphalt, but you can drive on it.'

'So reconstruction is proceeding?' Zolotarev responded absent-ly, looking avidly at the road as it snaked off ahead of them. 'That's good. It's time for the country to get back on its feet.'

'Every cloud has a silver lining,' the secretary grinned morosely, and immediately explained: 'We wouldn't have got it done ourselves – it's too grand a plan for the likes of us – but fortunately the MVD helped us out with a contingent. They never run short of men.'

'Are there lots of them here?'

'It's going on all over the place: stone-breaking, tree-felling, road-building, a bit of everything. But it's all to our advantage. The region's coming to life.' He turned to him inquiringly: 'D'you want to take a look?'

The proposal took Zolotarev by surprise. Working in a department which had power over all the branches of the state prison-camp network, he had never, strange as it might seem, seen a live camp inmate. To him it was all just something that got expressed through figures, summaries, geographical names, and was defined in his world by the impersonal words 'them,' 'with them', 'to them'. Even those of them whom he had known personally or met earlier sped from his memory the moment they fell into the oblivion of the barracks, dissolving instantly into a faceless 'there'. In the institution where he worked the subject of the camps was not explicitly forbidden, but it was not done to speak of it, like speaking of death in a house where someone has just died. It was considered a sign of bad taste, a challenge to those around you, if not an act of provocation.

'Well, we could have a look, I suppose,' he said, succumbing to the temptation. 'But we mustn't delay. I'm very pressed for time.'

'It's only a couple of minutes away,' his driver said, cheering up noticeably at the prospect. He slowed down, and the taiga beyond the windscreen took shape and spread around them. 'It'll soon be time to have a bite to eat anyway. If we go down a bit, there's a stone-breaking camp by the river. There's an old man just outside the zone who's living in controlled liberty – he looks after the bees and earns a living by supplying fish for the officers' table. He won't refuse us either. A quick-witted old fellow, he is. He won't piss in the wind. You won't regret it,' he concluded, without waiting for an answer, and turned down the first side path.

Rocking from wheel to wheel, the car jolted its way through the steaming darkness of the pine-forest, its enormous trees reaching up to a ribbon of bluish-white sky ahead. Lazily, seemingly against its will, the forest let them through. The marks of wheels could hardly be seen on the thickly overgrown track, and sometimes Zolotarev felt that they were not moving but going down to the bottom, slowly sinking in the rusty-green spider's web of the taiga.

The abyss that surrounded them on all sides was not remotely like the well-trodden copses he remembered from his childhood, or the lacy thickets the war had taken him through. In this disordered tangle of trees and grasses without odour or nuance there was some scarcely perceptible menace, which made his soul feel more orphaned and ill at ease with every passing minute. 'One step to the side and you're done for, clearly,' he shuddered. 'You'd never find your way out again.'

At first, through the thinning trees of the thicket, they saw a distant strip of water. Then, when they reached the edge, they discovered a wide path which cut sheer into the rocky bank. Finally the car drew to a halt, almost leaning over the ribbed edge of the ravine.

'We're here,' the driver said, switching off the engine and turning to his passengers. 'You can see everything from here. It's like the royal box.'

And indeed, from the high cliff, sheer above the lake, they really could see in all directions. Ahead, as far as the eye could see, a mirror of water stretched like a polished table, blending on the horizon with the dazzling blue of the sky, and with a wall of pine-timbers at the shores to the side.

'Take a look, down there on the left, in the cleft,' said the district committee secretary, for some reason lowering his voice. 'That's their camp.'

Looking down in the direction in which he had nodded, Zolotarev was dumbstruck: at the foot of the high, hideously chewed cliff a large group of men were rushing around, stripped to the waist, surrounded by observation towers linked by barbed wire. 'So that's what it looks like,' he muttered, panting for breath. 'Who'd have believed it?'

Looking at this battle between cliff and men, Zolotarev suddenly and with great clarity imagined himself working among them, and he shuddered. For in that fatal game of chance in which he was participating everything might turn out completely differently for him, and then toiling behind barbed wire would be the best thing he could hope for. He could not know why this cup had passed him by, but because it had done so he began to feel an arrogant awareness of belonging to some charmed circle, to a race of victors, so to speak, to those who ruled rather than those who were ruled. And with a cheerful sense of relief, Zolotarev turned to his companions: 'Well, where is your old fellow?'

'Just nearby, in a little wood,' the driver said quickly, savouring the prospect of a good meal. 'He'll give us first-class hospitality!'

They crossed a little clearing and then made their way along a barely visible path through thick undergrowth and came out to a house, or rather a hut, a cabin, with a single window and a flat roof. The cabin glimmered in front of them among the pine-trees, beckoning them with its neat, well-cared-for look.

'Not bad for a convict,' Zolotarev joked, shaking his head. 'He's

95

got himself a real dacha, the old dodderer.'

Alarmed, the driver hastened to explain: 'You should see the way the old fellow works. He does enough for three men. All the supplies depend on him. If it wasn't for him, the whole thing'd collapse. Apart from him it's all town riff-raff and politicals, and it's well known that lot don't know the meaning of work!'

The possibility that he might be deprived of a free meal had clearly cut him to the quick, and in his anxiety he had not noticed that he had gone beyond the bounds allowed a subordinate, something his direct superior did not delay in pointing out to him: 'Enough chatting, Shilov! You'd do better to go on ahead and warn the old man, so he'll be ready for us . . .'

But the man was already coming out to meet them from his large hives. He was not wearing protective netting, just a sort of beret or peakless cap pulled down over his eyes. As he approached, he bowed slightly, but without a word.

'He never opens his mouth,' explained Shilov. 'Apparently there's a sect of that kind, but he's harmless.'

Still not saying a word, the old man invited them into the house and, with a bustle he was obviously used to, laid his simple dishes before the important guests: a basin of slightly salted white fish, honey from his hives, blackberries in a large glass jar, a quarter-bottle of mead, and some cedar nuts to help pass the time pleasantly. But there was so much generous resignation, so much readiness to be of service in everything the man did for his self-invited visitors, that Zolotarev was dumbfounded.

Watching him now, watching his bustling movements, his servility, Zolotarev suddenly caught himself thinking that some-where, at some time, he had met this man. In fact, the man was not as old as he had at first seemed. It was probably only his greying beard and his premature wrinkles that made him look old: behind them was a strong-looking peasant of around forty, no more. Staring into this face and gradually removing from it, layer by layer, the dense shadows of time, Zolotarev finally re-established the whole image of a man whom he of course knew, knew only too well. And his heart sank.

As if continuing in his waking moments the dream he had had recently on the plane, fate had caught him here, in this prison cabin, in the person of this man who had disappeared with his brother on the night of the arrest: Ivan Zagladin.

'The dream comes true.' He swallowed the searing bitterness that rose to his throat. 'Now wait for it!'

But the man just went on silently moving around his guests,

serving them food, occasionally looking in Zolotarev's direction, yet whenever their eyes met he immediately looked away.

To reveal himself by either a word or a glance would have been the equivalent of death for Zolotarev: people disappeared into oblivion for far more innocent relationships. But the man himself, seemingly out of innate timidity, did not appear at all eager to reveal his links with a Muscovite boss. Nevertheless, to insure himself against any possible chance development, Zolotarev hurried up his companions, who had been preparing to take a little rest: 'It's time, comrades.' He stood up and turned towards the door. 'We've got a long way to go and I've got very little time, as you well know.'

On his way out Zolotarev felt their resentful glances on his back, but he did not care: their malice could not hurt him; they weren't important enough. Once outside he turned round, and above the heads of his companions, who followed him disconsolately, he again caught the glance of Ivan as he watched from the threshold of the hut, and understood beyond question that Ivan had recognized him, that he remembered and bore no grudge.

On the way, Zolotarev asked Shilov, as if by chance, 'What was your old crank arrested for?'

'I suppose for being a sectarian.' The man had still not got over his irritation about his interrupted meal. 'They don't arrest you for nothing!'

All the rest of the way Zolotarev didn't say a word. He seemed to have lost all interest in their little trip. Vague presentiments of some irreversible and terrible change in his life had entered his heart for the first time, arousing a profound, almost physical aversion to everything that surrounded him.

2

Afterwards Zolotarev lost himself in a dizzying succession of meetings, committees and tours of inspection. He succumbed to the usual excitement of his work, but in his rare moments of complete solitude, especially at night, the chimeras of his past returned to suffocate him and, panic-stricken, he would seek any sort of activity to occupy his mind. But whatever happened, dark forebodings did not leave Zolotarev, and without realizing it himself he attempted in all sorts of ways to postpone his departure for the Islands. He was regularly afflicted by the same insistent dream: water, a great deal of water, and he himself in the water, as if in an aquarium. Zolotarev tried to shake off the mad hallucination but it always returned, despite the bustle that reigned all around, and sometimes it reduced him to a state of quiet fury.

Time passed, and days became weeks. The sultry summer moved towards its peak, but Zolotarev still delayed, looping around Baikal, inspecting the most out-of-the-way fish-farms. Moscow put no pressure on him, the Minister evidently being satisfied with such a turn of events – the less noise from his potential successor the better. The Kuriles themselves, it is true, were becoming anxious – inquiry after inquiry about him came to Irkutsk, but that did not count – they could wait!

And when eventually his procrastination had become too obvious to those around him and it was no longer possible to delay his departure any further, he asked Shilov to drive him off somewhere, anywhere, wherever he liked.

They set off in the early morning and wandered along the roads at the side of the lake almost till midday; sometimes Baikal disappeared from view, sometimes it reappeared as if beckoning him, luring him to its cool shores.

'It's time to get a bite to eat, Ilya Nikanorych,' Shilov observed, nodding at the clock on the dashboard. 'There's a fish-guard lives nearby. He's an honest fellow and understands the way things are. D'you have any objection?'

'You decide. Only within measure.' In a few weeks of round trips Zolotarev had got used to the transparently consumerist vocabulary of his temporary driver: when Shilov spoke of an 'honest fellow' who 'understood the way things were,' he was referring to the degree of his readiness to show hospitality, nothing more.

'The jug knows its measure, Ilya Nikanorych,' the driver replied cheerfully, immediately turning off towards the beach, 'and never pours beyond it.'

The treeless slope led gently down to the water, or rather to the water-reeds, a mass of which stretched far into the lake. Soon the rutted track turned sharply off from under their wheels and led along parallel to the lake, but the car juddered over hummocks until it reached a little reed hut constructed at high-water mark.

'The way some people live!' Shilov chuckled as he got out of the car. 'While I spend my whole life at the wheel breathing shitty petrol fumes! Sergeich! . . .'

At first nobody answered. The silence was broken only by a sprinkle of shrieking birds, but then a faded, semi-military cap appeared among the reeds and moved towards them.

'Pyotr Yevseich, greetings!' The prow of the boat appeared in a narrow gap among the reeds, and then a tall fellow covered in oilskins from head to foot, standing in the boat wielding a pole. 'Haven't seen you out here for ages!'

'I've brought you a visitor from Moscow.' Shilov took the bull by the horns: 'What can you offer us?'

The fellow took off his oilskin cap respectfully, revealing a large, prematurely balding head of flaxen hair.

'For a good man something can always be found, Pyotr Yevseich.' The fellow was scrutinizing Zolotarev with unfeigned curiosity. 'But why are we sweating in this heat – a little bit of breeze would be handy.' He motioned to them to get into the boat. 'The weather's just right for it. Sit yourselves down. It's very close by . . .'

The narrow passage through the reeds gradually widened into a sort of regular winding corridor. In the vegetation on each side of the boat they could hear the secret life of the lake: a fish flashed by in search of food, mallards exchanged their heart-rending calls, a bird of prey silently stalked its victim from the sky. And everything exuded the power and plenitude of the animal world.

The fellow raised his pole out of the water, picked up the oars and, as if sympathizing with the Muscovite guest for his present state, he began to talk: 'The land is rich around here, no question, you can get anything you take a fancy to. It's a real life here . . . my brother, for example, doesn't step on to dry land till it's almost winter – he just lives in the reeds. He's almost grown scales . . . He gets covered in mud and picks his teeth with a bird's feather. You'll see for yourself soon – it's not far now . . .'

The boat ran into a new band of reeds, the man picked up his pole again and, manoeuvring adroitly through the vegetation, he led it through to a small watery clearing hidden from sight on all sides, where there was a solidly rigged raft with a sort of cabin or little hut on top of it.

Another man emerged from this hut, the very image of the boatman only slightly older, slightly larger-boned, slightly more thickset, and with an expression of undisguised irritation on his unshaven face.

'What now?'

'I've brought you a visitor, Sanyok,' said the boatman with a noticeably ingratiating tone. 'He's from Moscow, not less.'

'Well.'

'It's not right next door, you know.'

'Well.'

'We ought to show the man some hospitality.'

'Well.'

'Well, that's it.'

'Well.'

'Well, you should have said so!'

'Well.'

Every time he said the word 'well' he gave it a different meaning, so that one had the impression of listening to a real dialogue, a discussion, a conversation. 'Yes, brother,' Zolotarev thought with sympathy as he looked around, 'you live in such a backwater that you would forget how to speak.'

Throughout the lengthy meal the hermit did not say another word, and only when they were leaving, as he clumsily shook the hand Zolotarev had proffered, did he force himself to announce in great embarrassment: 'If ever you're in the area . . . My brother and I are always happy . . . In short, don't hesitate . . . You never know . . .'

On the way back the boatman sighed, groaned and explained to them confidentially about his brother: 'Before the war he was considered the merriest fellow in the whole area. There wasn't a single party where he didn't play his accordion. But when he came back from the front he was crushed: that's it, he said, I've seen enough of everything, I don't want anything else, I wish I was blind! He became very pensive. Maybe it was shell-shock, or maybe something else. Fortunately he got himself fixed up in the fish-guard, and spends all day and all night in the reeds. He never sees anyone . . .'

On the way back to Irkutsk Shilov, cautiously testing his boss's mood, also had a tale to tell: 'We've got quite a number of cranks like that Sashka around here. Every little corner has its own wild man, you might say. Still, as they say, it's cranks that make the world go round. But things are different in Irkutsk, Ilya Nikanorych. You've seen for yourself the work that's going on in our region, the people we're producing! Give us time and people will be talking about the men of Irkutsk . . .'

Zolotarev was only half-listening, silently giving the district committee driver his head at last. By now he was indifferent to the driver's pitiful babble; inside he was already in other latitudes, in another world: the subterranean rumble of the Kurile chain was gradually overwhelming him, and would remain in him now till the end.

Freeing himself mentally from his surroundings, Zolotarev

attempted to establish those few key points in his life at which he might have turned back at a dangerous moment, but however much he examined the past, everything always turned around a single point: Kira. Feeling an instinctive need to establish at least an illusory foothold in preparation for what was to come, Zolotarev was consumed by a desire to telephone her immediately he got back to remind her of his existence, to hear her say something, even something trivial, which would nevertheless commit them both. Obsessed with this thought, he left Shilov at the entrance of the district committee hotel.

When, in the foyer, they told him that people from his home town were trying to get him by telephone on a matter of 'national importance', he just frowned with irritation: 'It's the oldest trick in the book.'

'Fine, it can wait,' Zolotarev answered indifferently. 'Get me Moscow instead! Here's the number . . .'

But the call from his so-called 'fellow-townsmen' caught him before he had managed to reach his room. Zolotarev would have ignored it, but feeling pity for the agonies of the switchboard-operator, engaged in helpless single combat with his regular caller, he picked up the phone: 'Yes?'

From the incoherently assertive explanation of a man who was clearly drunk, but who called himself the plenipotentiary of the central board, he understood that a convoy of men from his own region of Uzlovaya had been held up for nearly five days outside Irkutsk, that they had been told to expect to remain there for a so far unspecified time, and that his immediate intervention was therefore required. The man stressed particularly assiduously that they were from 'his part of the country,' something he found especially unpleasant.

At any other time Zolotarev would not have failed to put the pushy caller in his place, but now, anticipating the conversation with Kira, he could not wait to get rid of him as soon and as simply as possible.

'Go back to your convoy,' he ordered, and hastily interrupted the caller's attempts to prolong the conversation. 'I repeat, go back to your convoy. You will leave tomorrow. That is all.'

The telephone rang again as soon as Zolotarev had put down the receiver, and what was even more surprising, Kira herself answered. He suddenly realized that he was nervous.

'Hallo, it's Ilya.'

'What's happened, Zolotarev? Where are you?'

'In Irkutsk.'

101

'So what's happened, Zolotarev?'

'I just decided to call.'

'Unlikely, Zolotarev. You? Phoning me? From Irkutsk? Unlikely.'

'But true.'

'You're getting old, Zolotarev.'

'What gives you that idea?'

'You're becoming sentimental.'

'Can we talk seriously?'

'For as long as you like, but how long will you cope with it?'

'Kira, calm down.'

'Fine, I'm listening, Zolotarev.'

'How are you getting on?'

'Is that all? . . .'

They went on like this for about ten minutes longer, and it was
only after their hurried goodbye that he conceded bitterly that it
would have been better if he had not telephoned at all.

For a long time, he could not get to sleep. Never before had he
felt his own solitude, his isolation from everybody else, so sharply,
so palpably. It had turned out that there remained on this earth
not a single living soul who might have desired or wished to see
him for the sake of seeing him – not on business, not out of
self-interest or ulterior motive. A void yawned all around him, full
of the phantoms and ruins of past encounters, still-born
friendships, failed connections: he would leave, disappear, turn
into dust and ashes – without a trace and unremembered. And the
most bitter realization of all for Zolotarev was that he had chosen
this destiny himself, that he had long since lost both strength and
desire to change his life in any way, and that tomorrow morning he
would get up and move further down the same path without any
regret.

'I'll have to shake those railway engineers up a bit tomorrow,'
he decided as he finally sank into sleep. 'It's quite scandalous!'

3

*Good day, my beloved brother Matvei! In these first lines of my
letter I am glad to inform you that thanks to your prayers and the
grace of God, I am well, as I hope you are also. I sincerely hope that
you passed your journey calmly and in good health. The summer
here has turned out hot, and the dryness all around is a real scourge.
My life flows on from day to day in labour and prayer; the end of*

my sentence will soon be here, but will they let me leave? All is in the hands of the Omnipotent; if they keep me here, then it is His will that I should carry this cross further as I have carried it thus far. But in my cross there is also the spiritual joy of helping my neighbours suffering in prison, which I do each day as far as I am able. Torturers of all ranks and callings do, it is true, persecute me, but did not Our Lord foretell it? Ivan Osipych, our master, ordered us 'to render unto Caesar the things that are Caesar's' and Christ himself had mercy on his torturer, so there is no shame in our doing likewise, sinners that we are. There are all sorts among them; some of them even show signs of conscience or pity to the prisoners, and some even wish to open up their hearts, but as you know I have long since made a vow not to waste my soul in vain words. In silence you can hear much; such abysses, such mountain heights are opened up within people that I am afraid to write of it. The other day I was visited by men from the district authorities, and with them (you will not believe this) was Ilya Zolotarev, the destroyer of Ivan Osipych. He has become an important boss; the others dance attendance on him. I recognized him immediately, for he has not changed, only put on a little weight. While they were eating, he continually tried to avoid my gaze; he had recognized me too, it seems. It is not for us to judge him, brother; his conscience is his judge, and if he turns away his eyes, then it is still alive in him, it throbs inside him, torturing him to death. There are many such men now, whom sin pins down but does not crush; they live, they sin, they suffer, they rise again from the ashes, for they have not killed their living soul; it survives and rises again to God. Our duty as pastors, brother, is to assist in this a little; not for nothing does Scripture say: 'Bless those that curse you and pray for those that persecute you.' I write this, brother, since judging by their conversation at table Ilya is on his way to your parts to bring justice and order. Therefore, should fate bring you together, do not harbour enmity towards him in your heart, in the name of Our Lord and the words of our master, Ivan Osipych. It is clear that his hour is coming anyway. There is a deathly anguish in his eyes, blackness pervades his face, and the odour of sulphur rises from him. It is not for us sinners to sprinkle salt on his soul. The man who brings you this letter is worthy of trust; he was released yesterday and is travelling to your islands to try his luck. I remain for ever your younger brother, Ivan. Christ be with you.'

Chapter Eight

1

'I do not know why I have been allowed this small indulgence, but since it has happened, I should like, dear grandson, to bid you goodbye. Today is the fourth of June 1945; remember that date. I am convinced that this is our last meeting. I do not think that you will be implicated in my case; you are too young for that, and you have no past. I am convinced that you will survive, that you still have your whole life ahead of you, and that you will return and see our people, but I already have one foot in the other world: if they do not kill me, I shall die myself, without their help. I regret only that this has happened to us so unexpectedly and clumsily. I expected everything except treachery, a base betrayal of the word of an officer. If you survive, describe everything that you see and hear, describe whom you meet, without embellishment, without exaggeration, but also without abusing the good. Above all, do not lie! Tell only the truth, even if it is not to certain people's taste; bitter truth is better than sweet lies. Our emigration has spent too long in blind self-congratulation, self-consolation, self-deception. We were always terrified of looking the truth in the face, of admitting our errors and our mistakes; we always overestimated our strength and underestimated our enemy. If it were possible to start again, all would be different. But clearly, and this is the will of divine Providence, we are to end our days here. You, the young, must make your own conclusions from our mistakes. We shall not win an easy victory over the Communists; in the struggle against them we need other methods, other words, another approach. We have spent too long sitting in foreign cafés breaking our spears in pointless internecine squabbles; it is time to understand that the source of our errors lies in our divisions. Look around you, grandson, but for God's sake do not write anything down. Besides, they will not let you write anything; they are not that kind of people. But even if you do get the opportunity, do not use it; write neither the smallest note nor record; use only your head as notebook and camera. Forget nothing; everything here is extraordinarily important, every detail,

however trivial. Remember your via crucis *from Lienz to the present day. The world must learn the truth, what has happened and what is yet to happen, from the treachery and the betrayal to the very end.*

And for God's sake do not imagine that you are a great thinker or a writer; do not make profound conclusions, or hasty assessments, do not rush to condemn. Let the reader do this for you. Do not aspire to formal precision, to stylistic elegance; that is given to few. Just be Nikolai Krasnov, chronicler of your own fate. Simplicity, sincerity, kindness to those who have fallen will be your best counsellors. In my time, as you know, I have written many books, which have not been at all to the taste of our present masters. My works have been translated into seventeen languages. By the way, even today, at the first interrogation, they asked me where I got my material and my characters and do I have any other works, published or unpublished, and where are they. Of course they got nothing from me, but you should know and remember that your grandmother, Lidiya Fyodorovna, has the manuscript of the tale 'The Ruinous Caucasus'. I have dedicated it to our young people in Russia. If you get out of here alive, grandson, publish this book in my memory. Much may yet happen to you on your Golgotha, but whatever happens, flee the sin of hatred of your own country, your own people, as you would flee fiery Gehenna. Russia and the Russian people are not guilty of what has befallen them. At that time they were betrayed by everyone: both their own leaders, and the allies. At first, those who stood between the throne and the popular masses; and then even those whom honour required to aid them in their misfortunes. And how could I, after all that, have trusted the former allies a second time! For they hate Russia with a ferocious hatred – for her youth, her strength, her magnanimity. But these gentlemen are deceiving themselves, if they hope to strangle her with the hands of the Bolsheviks. Russia was and will be. Not as before in boyar costume, in sermyaga *and* lapti, *but she will rise again in all her power and beauty; God will not allow it to be otherwise! You can exterminate a million people, but others will come to replace them; the people will not die and everything will change when the time comes. For Stalin and his cronies will not live for ever; they too will die and new people will come, and with them changes. The resurrection of Russia will not happen suddenly, in a brief moment; such an enormous body cannot be healed instantaneously, but in the end she will nevertheless take heart and again rise on to her powerful legs. It is a shame that I shall not live to see that day. Do you remember, grandson, our meetings with the soldiers in*

Judenburg? They were good and sincere fellows. This is the real Russia, my boy, and I accuse them of nothing. Their fathers knew not what they did. But now let us say goodbye, grandson. It was not given to me to have direct descendants, but all the Krasnovs are as close to me as if they were my own flesh and blood. Unfortunately I have nothing to bless you with, neither cross nor icon; they have taken everything from me. Let me at least make the sign of the cross over you in the name of the Lord; may He protect you. Farewell, grandson! Bear me no ill; preserve the name of Krasnov. It is not a great name, not a rich name, but it brings many obligations. Farewell!'

2

He closed the file marked 'Top Secret. MGB Investigation Department' on the report of the meeting Pyotr Krasnov had had with his grandson Nikolai exactly a year ago. The rest did not interest him, the details of the investigation being a matter of indifference to him. Let the lawyers rummage through them – that was how they earned their bread.

'What a fine-spirited blockhead,' he exclaimed with involuntary rage. 'A Manilov in general's epaulettes! He confused the dressing-room of a prison bath-house with his wife's boudoir! He confessed everything. He told the whole story – everything he later denied during the investigation. The self-styled fighter would have done better sitting at home playing patience.'

The ex-general was of purely academic interest to him. At first he could not understand, he just could not fathom why the hell a career soldier, a prolific writer, an émigré, dragged into politics against his will, could have embraced such a doomed enterprise. And only now, after he had read the note, did everything become clear. It turned out that the senile old dodderer had calculated on their struggle ending in a draw: he would finally manage to give the Bolsheviks a bloody nose and then go and hide under the hospitable wing of their allies. He was a real goose – there was no getting away from it. Monsieur the ataman clearly had a short memory if he trusted the gentlemanly assurances of his English colleagues: as if a 'word of honour' counted for anything in grand politics; as if he himself had not given such a 'word' to Dybenko in Gatchina! They felt no embarrassment, his English colleagues, about delivering up to reprisal even the member of the Order of the Bath, Andrei Shkuro, a person who according to their 'humanitarian' laws should have been untouchable. Thank God he had studied the 'gentlemanly behaviour' of his 'allies' through his own experience. During four years of war they had more than once left him to the mercy of fate while imperturbably seeking to become friends with him again as soon as the fortune of war turned to the Eastern Front. They were nothing but a vile race of market traders in dinner-jackets whose aplomb soon evaporated in conversation with the victors. In its foulness this political rabble was capable of transgressing all divine and human commandments if its own cowardice did not prevent it. Now, however, with his tanks on the Elbe, he just had to raise his voice and they would deliver him not only Shkuro and Krasnov, but even their own king if only they could live out their days in the illusory conviction that they were free. The ataman's calculations had not worked this time – he'd got it all wrong! Old age had clearly had its effect; his mind had become addled, confident of the judgement and the gratitude of future generations: civilization was crumbling, but he still worried his head over the chronicles. He wanted to get into the annals and had found himself a Pimen, a babe on whose lips the milk had not yet dried. Where he was going it would not be a question of not getting permission to write; he would not even be allowed to sneeze out of turn. By the time his grandfather had been strung up the grandson himself would be croaking some-where near Kolyma; you couldn't hang them together, after all – he was too young to hang on the same gallows as a general. It was too much of an honour for him!

Of the whole group of Cossack generals and officers handed over to him by the English, he himself had been interested only in these two – Krasnov and Shkuro. He had never even heard of the others, except perhaps for Sultan Kilech Girei. He had gleaned some information about them from the lapidary biographies in their files and enriched it through his own intuition, which he always found to be unerring.

The younger Krasnovs did not even count for him. (They had followed their grandfather through family inertia or, to use their own term, family tradition!) Domanov and Golovko had not existed for him before (straightforward deserters, thistles in the corn that had not been weeded out in the thirties – the sweep should have been wider then, the strokes deeper!); neither did Sultan Girei occupy him long (he knew Caucasian rancour from his own experience – can the leopard change his spots?); von Pannwitz was immediately placed in the category of war criminals (once a Prussian always a Prussian; a junker's soul aspires to an officer's death, but his beautiful dream bursts!). And so, having removed only the two Nikolai Krasnovs, father and son (too small fry!) into a separate list, he condemned all of them to the same punishment: death by hanging! It was necessary to do this as a warning to the allies and as a lesson to the emigration, who had taken leave of their senses and had to learn that there were things they could not get away with.

That left two more – Solomakhin and Vasilev. And if in the first case everything was more or less straightforward – the head of the general staff, second in command in the army hierarchy, he considered himself bound to share responsibility with his commander – the second was much more complicated. Once again, as with the case of Pyotr Krasnov, a number of questions arose to put him on his guard. Why did a staff officer, promoted with great speed to the rank of general, try so stubbornly and implausibly to convince the investigators that he was the initiator, creator and inspiration of the whole affair in general and the military alliance with the Germans in particular? Why, scornful of proof, did he take all the guilt upon himself and protect his accomplices? Why, in short, was he so eagerly rushing at the noose?

He did not believe in any altruistic motives, leaving such fantasies to priests and novelists, and he therefore asked for a detailed file on Vasilev to be drawn up immediately, including materials gathered by operatives abroad, but the information brought from there shed not a jot of light on the case.

Vasilev had left a young and by all accounts beloved wife in Paris, a son, by now seven years old, whom he idolized, and a relatively secure position. He had settled easily into the unfamiliar environment, spoke three languages, was a good car mechanic (at one time he had even driven a taxi), was good with money and at clerical work (he had worked for several years as the secretary of a colourful wheeler-dealer of Russian extraction by the name of Ginzburg) and was accepted in foreign political circles: not a single flaw, not a single hint that would explain his later conduct.

In the end he limited himself, as he often did in such situations, to leaving time to solve this conundrum, commuting the desperate general's capital punishment to camp, taking care at the same time, so as not to arouse any doubt or misunderstanding among his subordinates, to make the same change in the case of Solomakhin, as if making a distinction between the degree of guilt of staff officers and those at the front line who had participated directly in the combat. Let these gentlemen-strategists from the rear get some air into their dried-out brains cutting wood in our Soviet forests, he seemed to be saying.

And although he had decided on the fate of the prisoners at the very beginning, they continued to come back into his mind – or more precisely the first two of them, Krasnov and Shkuro. In the almost thirty years that had elapsed since life had thrown them together on different sides on the same barricade, which had decided who was going to rule and who was to grieve over the past in European cafés, fate had not been kind to them; but even now, years and years later, the image of these men, eroded by time, had a powerful effect on him, arousing in him vague images, echoes, memories of that rapturous time when the world, collapsing in blood and cries, had seemed so malleable and simple. Without realizing it, he was already looking at them through the eyes of those around him now, who judged the past through the stream of novels and films about the Civil War. Whether he wished it or not, he and they had ended up on the same page of history, only with different fortunes, in different roles and hypostases, but now they could not escape this indissoluble closeness.

He was eager to look at them, to convince himself of their real concrete existence, to try through this optical self-delusion to remove the temporal barriers and find himself face to face with his own past. He resisted this debilitating temptation for a long time, but one day he could stand it no longer. He telephoned Beria: 'Listen, I want to see them.'

'Any time, Soso.'

'But I don't want them to know about it.'

'Whatever you say, Soso.'

'The day after tomorrow, at midnight.'

'Where, Soso?'

'Do it like last time.'

'I shall bring them, Soso.'

'That is all . . .'

From time to time Beria arranged such meetings for him here, in the next room, in the small cinema. Under cover of night, the prisoners were secretly brought here and left alone, convinced that they were in some other section of the Lubyanka.

He watched them from the projection-room window, vengefully exultant at his own invulnerability and the spectacle of the spiritual death-throes of his defeated enemy. The last time Vlasov had been brought here with his chief-of-staff. The scene had been so distressing that even he, who had thought himself used to everything, felt slightly sick at the very thought of it. It is true that on that occasion, unlike with the Cossack chief, the investigators had received instructions from above not to be squeamish: they had used the whole arsenal of physical interrogation methods.

Both atamans were to be brought here today. Waiting for the appointed time he picked up the file of current developments, opened it and began to read. At the very top was the sentence the military procurators planned to pass on the senior Japanese officers captured in Manchuria. He waded through a morass of bizarre and unpronounceable names and titles and hieroglyphic signatures. His eyes ran quickly over all this to rest on the final recommendation. As usual, insuring themselves against any eventualities, the wily procurators had proposed the supreme sentence against all of them in defence of society, but left variations to his magnanimous whim. They had learnt their lesson, the sons of bitches!

Reading about the Far East reminded him of his April meeting with the 'fishermen', at which he had made a note of the broad-shouldered sturdy fellow with the light of devotion in his cornflower eyes, and he immediately recalled that he had long been meaning to ask for a detailed general survey of that region.

He pressed the button and, looking down at the desk in the certainty that his assistant was already standing, servilely expectant, in the doorway, he said: 'Get me some sensible information on Sakhalin and the Kuriles immediately; make it simple and short, no waffle. I'll read it when I go to bed.' Then, still looking down at his desk, he held out the file with the suggested sentences. 'Send this back. They say the Japanese have long been interested in Siberia; we'll give them a chance to study it first-hand, in the taiga. That is all.'

And he returned to his papers.

3

At exactly two minutes to midnight, the direct telephone link cooed softly, even tenderly.

'Ready, Soso,' Beria announced laconically. 'When do you want us to start?'

'I'm on my way.'

He got up slowly, went out of the side door into a windowless corridor and, at the far end, pushed upon a little door in the wall. Here, in the darkened box of the projection-room, Beria was already waiting for him.

'Can we begin, Soso?'

'Go ahead.'

The first to be let into the room was Shkuro. Small, almost frail, in a uniform of which almost all the seams had split, he walked feverishly around between the little tables, glancing about with a look of stupefaction on his face, contantly pushing back the lock of slightly greying blond hair that made him look younger than he was. There was something provocatively boyish about him which when you first saw him made it difficult to be certain of his actual age.

When Krasnov suddenly appeared at the back of the hall, he rushed to meet him: 'Pyotr Nikolaich, my dear fellow! How glad I am to see you!' Convulsively he fell upon the tall old man, his shaggy curls against his chest. 'How are you?' Then he stepped back, still holding Krasnov's hands. 'How do you feel?' As he rained questions on him, Shkuro looked anxiously and concernedly at him, as if looking for confirmation of some secret hunches. 'You don't by any chance know why we've been brought here?'

'Hallo, hallo, Andrei Grigorich, my dear fellow!' The old man clearly had difficulty staying on his feet. His ragged uniform hung on him as if he were a wax figure. 'They told me that they were going to confront us with some secret bits of documentary film.' He shrugged contemptuously. 'But nobody says precisely what it is. I have lived my life openly – everything I have done and thought is documented in my books. Neither have you, I think, ever been a cloak-and-dagger knight, but, as you well know, they have their own rules.' Limping heavily, he moved towards an armchair. 'Let's sit down, Andrei Grigorich, my dear fellow, there's nothing to be gained by staying on our feet, and anyway I don't think my feet will support me.' With Shkuro's help the general settled at a table, sticking a stiff leg out slightly into the gangway. 'That's better . . . '

Sitting at the window of the projection-room, he noticed the scarlet stripe on Krasnov's shabby uniform trousers and suddenly recalled the exhibition of entries in the competition for a new uniform before the reintroduction of officer grades and epaulettes into the army. Lord, the things they came up with! The second-rate designers surpassed themselves in provincial fantasy: in their striving to out-fop each other they brought into the St George Hall, which had been cleared of chairs for the day, such a mass of iridescent lumber that after examining this peacock realm all he could do was to raise his hands in horror. He remembered that he had then made them bring a full set of uniforms of the Tsarist army and, looking quickly over the selection of officers' uniforms with their six buttons on each side, he had ordered them to cut off one button, leaving everything else exactly as it was, so that people who saw it would not feel embarrassed to describe it to their friends and their descendants!

But the conversation in the hall was continuing in the same vein: 'I am not afraid of death, Pyotr Nikolaich,' Shkuro was insisting hotly; 'you might say that I have spent my whole life in her embrace. All that I regret is having to die not in battle but in some cellar or prison yard!'

'Oh, Andrei Grigorich, Andrei Grigorich,' Krasnov shook his tired head reproachfully, 'does it really matter where you die, as long as your conscience is clear?'

'Pyotr Nikolaich, you are a European, a writer, an intellectual – the whole of humanity is your home; but I am a Cossack, a peasant: a May night in Tikhoretskaya is dearer to me than the material prosperity of humanity. When I remember the smell of the steppe in May, my heart is torn apart!'

'Don't say it, Andrei Grigorich, don't say it,' the old man said in a trembling voice. 'For I too am a Don ataman. I also have a Cossack heart which has not forgotten the bread of its fathers. Only why torment yourself to no purpose, Andrei Grigorich? You cannot change anything. You and I will have to meet our Maker soon. You should calm down, prepare your soul, pray . . .'

Listening attentively to this conversation, he involuntarily asked himself whether there was anywhere in the world a man to whom he would be so ready, should he chance to meet him in such a deathly encounter, to speak frankly and openly, to reveal his soul. Going through dozens of names and faces in his mind, he was finally forced to admit, with a bitterness that gnawed at his heart, that there was no one.

As for the man who was now sitting behind his back and who, linked to him through shared blood and a shared secret, was, it would seem, prepared to follow him through fire and water, he would trust him with the secrets neither of his heart nor even of a single scheme. He knew only too well that the man would sell and betray him the first time he got the chance, without even a wink from behind his pince-nez.

'Thank the Lord that we have been allowed to meet before we die. Now I can die more easily, Pyotr Nikolaich.'

'I too, Andrei Grigorich, I too. I loved and valued you greatly, you know that.'

'My dear fellow, Pyotr Nikolaich!'

'I shall pray for you, my dear friend . . .'

The performance was becoming unbearable. He rose and,

hiding his annoyance, shouted out an order in the darkness to the man behind his back with peremptory rudeness: 'Give these gentlemen the pleasure of looking at their penates one last time before they die. Organize the judicial spectacle somewhere in the Caucasus.'

'Wherever you say, Soso.'

'Choose yourself.' But before leaving the room he thought for a moment and as he walked down the corridor he added, without turning round, 'Best of all in Pyatigorsk . . . '

When he got back to his study, he found a file with a neat vellum label: 'Sakhalin and the Kurile Islands: a general survey'.

He soon became imersed in this official reading matter, and without realizing it he cut himself off from the world.

4

1 *Geographical Situation* The distance from Sakhalin to Moscow by sea and rail via Vladivostok is 10,417 kilometres. The difference in time between Moscow and Sakhalin is eight hours. The distance from the northernmost point of the island, Cape Elizaveta, to the southernmost, Cape Crillon, is 948 kilometres. At its widest point the island is 160 kilometres across, being on average about 100 kilometres across. At its narrowest point in the south it is only 27 kilometres across. Sakhalin is separated from the mainland by the Tatar and Nevelsky straits, the estuary of the Amur river and the Gulf of Sakhalin. The straits separate the Sea of Okhotsk from the Sea of Japan. Off the south-west coast of Sakhalin is the small rocky island of Moneron. Just off the coast on the Sea of Okhotsk side is Seal Island. Slightly to the south of Sakhalin, stretching from south-west to north-east, are the Kurile Islands. From their southernmost point, the straits of Kunashiri, which separate the Kurile chain from Japan, to the northernmost island of Shumshu is a distance of 1,200 kilometres. The Kurile chain is the upper part of a volcanic ridge which rises to a height of 1,000–2,000 metres above sea-level, and which reaches a depth of more than 10,000 metres below sea-level. There are 39 active volcanoes on the Kurile Islands. The highest of them is Mount Alaid, which is 2,339 metres high. From the southernmost point of Sakhalin, Cape Crillon, to the Japanese island of Hokkaido is a distance of 40 kilometres at the narrowest point, and the distance from the island of Kunashiri to Hokkaido is only 17.5 kilometres. Sakhalin, the 56 islands of the Kurile archipelago, Moneron and Seal Island can all be combined into a single administrative territorial unit. The area of this region is 87,100 square kilometres, which is three times that of

Belgium, twice that of Switzerland, and larger than Austria or Ireland.

'Ireland . . . Ireland . . . Holland . . . Finland . . . Kurland . . .
–land . . . –land . . .' This syllable skidded round his sleepy brain
like a cracked record, until with a convulsive effort of will he
caught on to the irritating sound and finally came to.

2 *Nature and Climate* A considerable part of the territory is occupied by
mountains. The West-Sakhalin and East-Sakhalin ranges stretch for
hundreds of kilometres from north to south. They reach a height of 1,609
metres. The surface of the island is gashed by a dense network of about
1,000 mountain rivers, which are small and shallow with the exception of
the Tymi, the Poronaya and the Lyutogi. The total length of these rivers is
almost 22,000 kilometres. They are fast-flowing and full of rapids, with a
large number of waterfalls. The highest waterfall is the Ilya Muromets,
which is 140 metres high. There are 7,000 lakes on the islands (including
Sakhalin). They cover a total area of tens of thousands of hectares. In the
north the lakes are generally shallow, with low, marshy banks. Along the
north-east coast is a chain of lagoons, separated from the sea by sandy
dunes. The water in these lagoons is quite salty and the vegetation along
their banks is poor. In the flood-plains of the rivers are many oxbow lakes
which are the habitat of valuable animals, the musk-rat and the otter. In
spring and autumn thousands of migrant ducks, geese and swans gather on
the lakes. Hot springs are found on the Kurile Islands in the craters of
extinct volcanoes. The soil is generally poor, containing few nutritive
elements: turfy meadow soils in the valleys, brown forest soil and
mountain-forest soil on the hills, mountain slopes, spurs, alluvial terraces
and watersheds. Sakhalin and the Kuriles are in the moderate monsoon
zone, though the climate here is far harsher than in other parts of the
moderate zone. Because they stretch from north to south their range of
temperatures is very great. In the central part the average annual air
temperature is −1.5° and in the south +2.2°. In January the temperature
ranges in the north of the island from −16° to −24°, in the south from −8°
to −18°. The warmest month is August, when the average temperature
ranges in the north from +12° to +17° and in the south from +16° to +18°.
The coldest regions are Poronaisk, Tymovsk, and Okhinsk. In winter the
temperature can reach −40° or −50°. But in summer the air temperature
in these regions can be as high as +35°. Winter is snowy and long. Spring
is slow and cold, with late snowfalls and fogs. Summer is relatively short,
rainy and cool, due to the ice which at this time of the year is being carried
south by the current from the Sea of Okhotsk along the east coast of the
island. Autumn is sunny and generally warm. The climate is greatly
affected by the enormous expanses of sea surrounding the islands, the

cold Okhotsk current which flows along the east coast of Sakhalin, and the warm Tsushima current which reaches the south-west coast of the island, and also by the mountainous terrain of the place and the nearness of the Asian mainland. Despite the fact that the Kurile Islands are situated between the latitudes of Kiev and Sochi, the climate here, especially in the northern part, is remarkable for its harshness and extreme variability. The decisive cause of this is the situation of the Kurile archipelago between the Sea of Okhotsk and the Pacific Ocean, and also the closeness of the cold Oyashio current. The predominant wind direction changes twice a year when the centres of atmospheric pressure change. In winter currents of cold air from the mainland move towards the ocean, causing a predominance of northerly and north-westerly winds over Sakhalin and the Kuriles, and sharp frosts. In summer currents of cool air move in the opposite direction, from the ocean to the mainland, and, as they pass over the islands, bring much precipitation, and therefore the summer here is cool and damp. The annual total of precipitation in Sakhalin and the Kuriles reaches 1,000 millimetres and more.

Suddenly his head started spinning, as had happened relatively often recently.

The text began to swim before his eyes and merge into a flowing mass. Used to this phenomenon, he closed his eyes, as was his habit, and attempted to relax through total inactivity. As always in such cases a chain of half-forgotten visions rose from the secret backwaters of his memory.

He thought of a winter night at Kureika: the lace of ice on the square of the tiny window, the reflections of the flames of the stove fluttering on the walls, and on a bench near the door the clumsy figure of the gendarme, one of the local half-breeds, who had seen the flames and called in. He did not visit very often, dropping in occasionally on his way along the river bank, more from boredom than professional duty. He spoke slowly, as if with effort, but always provocatively: 'You're a strange fellow, my lad. You sit around all day as morosely as our brother the Chaldon, with no amusements and no friends. Your little brothers in Turukhansk are droning on day and night without pausing for breath – they never let each other get a word in. They've talked over the whole of Russia, what should become of Mother Russia, because as far as they are concerned our mother cannot do without them.' Pretending to have a coughing fit, the visitor hid an ironic smile in his fist. 'But when it comes to the women, I hear you've got your wits about you more – you even managed to put a bun in one's oven, though that doesn't take so much brains . . .'

Even in his semi-conscious state he winced involuntarily: he could not recall that soft young girl with the sleepy eyes in her flat face without a squeamish shudder. She came to clean up for him from time to time: a bachelor exile on six roubles of public money a month could easily afford the five kopecks a day she charged. And one day, ceding with indolent docility to his masculine weakness, she lay down with him, after which she began visiting of her own accord, did his cleaning for nothing, since she was 'his woman,' and soon became pregnant.

The son of this liaison, the spit and image of his father, was now a very tiny cog in his father's wheel, working somewhere between the radio committee and the central propaganda service, and thank God had the wit not to remind him of his existence.

If only he could have known then what fate had in store for him, how many errors and how much shame he might have avoided, how much pointless embarrassment at his own humiliating maladroitness!

But the past stuck to him stubbornly, reminding him that he was mortal, that he was just like everyone else, that all around there was vanity and pointlessness. And all this caused him anguish and torment.

3 *Natural Resources* On the islands of Sakhalin region one finds in close proximity fields of oil, natural gas, and hard coal, peat-bogs, limestone, sands rich in gold and titanomagnetite, soil rich in iron ore, chrome, manganese, copper, silver, cinnabar and graphite, volcanic sulphur, pumice, marble, precious metals and various other useful minerals. Coal is one of the most important raw materials of the region. The total reserves of coal on the islands have been estimated at 12.4 milliard tonnes, 52% of which are brown coal. The majority of these reserves is at a depth of under 300 metres and can be mined by the open-cast method. The local coals are various in their composition. In addition to coking coals there is lean coal, rich coal, long-burning and gas coal. They are characterized by high calorific capacity – about 8–9,000 calories. Certain coals have a high percentage of bitumen, which makes it possible to manufacture them into combustible liquid. The greatest natural wealth of the island is in oil and gas. It is so far the only region of the Soviet Far East which has considerable known reserves of these crucial raw materials. Scientists estimate reserves of oil on the islands at hundreds of millions of tonnes, of gas at several trillion cubic metres. About 60,000 square kilometres of the region's territory promise worthwhile prospecting for oil and gas. The main oil-fields are in the north-east of Sakhalin: Ekhabi, Katangli, Kolendo, Sabo, Tungor, and others. Many of them contain both oil and

gas. Sakhalin oil is unique in its qualities: it is light, low in sulphur and paraffin, contains a high quantity of valuable light oil products and can, like the gas, serve as a good raw material for the chemical industry. The region is rich in peat-beds, which cover an area of about 410,000 hectares; the known reserves of raw peat are over 4 milliard cubic metres. Prospecting for new fields will make it possible to double or treble these figures. In general the peat produces little ash, about 3–6%; the technical conditions for exploitation are favourable. Among the useful metallic minerals, gold is found in quantities sufficient for industry. Deposits are found in the hills of eastern Sakhalin, in the valleys of the Langeri, Iuleika, and Derbishev rivers and their tributaries. Gold content is as high as in the majority of the Far East fields and chemical purity is higher. Gold prospecting should be worthwhile in the north-west part of Sakhalin, the upper Tym and Poronai rivers. On the Kurile Islands discoveries have been made of titanomagnetite-bearing sands, and of ores of copper, lead and zinc, with traces of rare elements like indium, gallium and tallium; there are also indications of platinum, mercury and other metals. Useful non-metallic minerals include virgin sulphur, natural cement and building materials. Large reserves of sulphur ores with a relatively high sulphur content have been discovered on the Kuriles. A base for the development of a cement industry is offered by the limestone reserves around Gomon, estimated at 50 million tonnes. Building materials consist of different kinds of stone, clay, sands, deposits of gravel and shingle, pumice. Near the oil deposits there are asphalt lakes. There are a large number of subterranean freshwater, thermal and mineral springs. These can serve as the source of a centralized drinking-water system and also for technical purposes; they can be used for heating small settlements and towns, for growing vegetables in hot-houses and in the open.

4 *Flora* The region's trees include larch, polar birch, fir, wild vine, dwarf cedar and cork trees. The western coasts of the islands are far richer in vegetation than those on the east; they support palm-leaved groundsel, Kamchatka bead-ruby and Sakhalin buckwheat, which reaches a height of 3–4 metres. In the north of the island there are dwarf alder, mosses, lichens and knotted larches with broken crowns. In the south one encounters vegetation typical of the central regions of the country or even the subtropics: oak, ash, kalopanax, aralia, wild berries, including combined beds of blackcurrant and raspberry. On Sakhalin and the Kuriles there are a considerable number of rare species of plant, vestiges of the ancient flora, including eleutherococcus, dimorphandreae, Wright viburnum, magnolia, Sakhalin spruce, yew, and Siebold's walnut. The total flora of the region comprises 1,400 different kinds of plants. Many of them have healing properties. The main plant wealth of Sakhalin is its

forests. They cover over 43,000 square metres, or more than half the entire territory of the island. They contain more than 200 kinds of trees, bushes and lianas. The most widespread trees are spruce and fir, consisting of Yeddo spruce and Sakhalin fir. In the north one finds Dahurian larch. There are large areas of white and Erman's birch. The total reserves of wood are almost 650 million cubic metres, or about one and a half times that of the neighbouring Far Eastern regions. The average annual increase is about two cubic metres per hectare. This high-quality taiga wood is useful for building, and for the paper and woodworking industries, and can produce plywood, furniture and other necessary materials.

5 *Fauna* Of the 296 species of mammal registered in the Soviet Union, more than 80 are found on the Islands. Animals valuable for their fur live in the taiga: otter, squirrel, fox, ermine. On the high wooded ridges, with their steep cliffs and rocky outcrops, one can find sable in numbers offering potential for exploitation. There are also polar hare, brown bear, northern deer and musk deer. On Sakhalin and the Kurile Islands there are over 300 species of bird. On some of the islands there are noisy nesting-grounds of cormorants, gulls, and guillemots. Partridge, hazel-grouse, wood-grouse, geese and ducks exist in quantities offering potential for exploitation. In the offshore waters of the Sea of Japan, the Sea of Okhotsk and the Pacific Ocean there are fur-seals, ringed-seals and grey-seals; up to fifteen species of whale are encountered including the blue, the Greenland, the finback, the sei, the dolphin, the swallow and the white. The Sakhalin-Kurile basin is a major fishing-ground. Up to 90% of the annual catch is made up of herring, plaice, hump-backed salmon, dog-salmon, Korean cod, Pacific saury, mackerel, cod, saffron cod, rasp, halibut, crab, squid, scallops, fur-seal, ringed-seal, grey-seal, and water plants such as laminaricae and ahnfeltia. There are also important supplies of smelt, sea-trout, rudd, bull heads and various other species of fish.

Again he stopped reading, succumbing to tiredness. The happy days when he was capable of sitting at his desk for eighteen hours a day without moving and then getting down to work again after a short sleep in the anteroom were long gone.

Now, and more frequently with every passing year, by the end of the working day he would be overwhelmed by physical weakness, and without realizing it he would periodically switch off from the world around him and succumb to vague visions and chimeras.

'Species of fish . . . species of fish . . . species of fish . . . ' The words were imprinted on his sinking brain, but before his eyes he saw winter Moscow in the first virginal flurry of snow and protective darkness.

The fine snow crunched under his boots, a light frost pinched his ears, the darkness around seemed so crystalline that if he only closed his eyes he might imagine that (for the first time for so long) he was wandering all alone around the town, with neither guard nor companion. But the two straight ranks of soldiers' boots at each side of him indicated the direction and the purpose of his steps.

He was already outside the Novodevichy itself when he lifted his head and, glancing along the line of soldiers at his side, suddenly met the gaze of a tall lance-corporal, standing outside the monastery gates at the end of the file. The corporal looked straight at him with wooden devotion (just like that Tulan of Lavrenty's had done recently) but for a fraction of a second this official devotion was pierced by a charge of such searing hatred that he could not stand it, and for the first time in many years he turned away first.

Then as he sat on a low bench near the tombstone, his head pensively downcast, his thoughts were transported far from the grave, far beyond the boundaries of the cemetery into this world which encircled him in a fatal noose of hatred, which the unfortunate lance-corporal had involuntarily unleashed on him. 'For what?' he asked himself. 'After all I'm not doing it for myself, I'm doing it for them!'

But a voice hidden somewhere in the innermost recesses of his soul stubbornly contradicted him: 'for yourself!'

And so the walk back between two rows of soldiers through the sleeping town from his wife's grave to the Borovitsky gates of the Kremlin was as arduous and breathless as a mountain climb . . .

6   *History* Russia began the exploration of Sakhalin and the Kurile Islands at a time when other countries knew nothing of their existence, or at least had only a very vague idea of it. When Russian explorers came to the area there were no state institutions and the sparse native population lived in scattered areas. It has now been established that the Russians first heard of Sakhalin in the 1640s. Geographical descriptions and maps of the time indicate that there was no real awareness of Sakhalin or the Amur estuary either in Europe or in Asia. Between 1639 and 1641 a detachment of Cossacks, under Ivan Moskvitin, reached the lower Amur. An analysis of the documents has made it possible to establish for certain that in the winter of 1639–40 on the Ulya river (on the coast of the sea of Okhotsk)

local Evens first informed the Russians of the existence of 'islands of the Guiliak horde'. The penetration by I. Yu. Moskvitin and V.D. Poyarkov to the coast of the Pacific Ocean was one of the major geographical discoveries of the seventeenth century. A major contribution to the study and opening up of the Far Eastern lands was made by the brave Russian explorer Yerofei Pavlovich Khabarov. He left Yakutsk in 1649 at the head of a detachment of Cossacks and 'trappers', and spent five years travelling through and studying the Amur basin. Cossacks under the command of Ivan Nagiba, sent off in 1652 to make contact with Khabarov, failed to find him and emerged on to the estuary of the Amur and the gulf of Sakhalin. They both confirmed the information provided by Moskvitin's and Poyarkov's detachments, and provided new data about the island. Soon after that Sakhalin began to appear as an island on several maps of Siberia. Almost at the same time the Kurile Islands were discovered and exploration began. The autochthonous Ainu-Kurile inhabitants were completely independent. In the language of the Ainu, 'kur' means 'man', and the name of the islands comes from this. A major stage in the study of the Kurile Islands was the expedition by the Cossack pyatidesyatnik Vladimir Atlasov in 1697. In 1711 Kamchatka Cossacks, led by Danila Antsiferov and Ivan Kozyrevsky, reached the island in canoes and small boats opposite Kamchadalga Ness. Peter the Great elaborated a special plan for the study and colonization of the newly discovered Far Eastern lands. Following his orders, the first naval expedition to the Kuriles was organized under Evreinov and Luzhin (1719–22).

In 1799, on the initiative of Grigory Shelikhov, a major Russo-American commerce and trading company was set up, and it managed the Russian possessions in the Pacific from Alaska to Japan, including the Aleuts, the Kuriles and Sakhalin, until 1867. In December 1786 Catherine II published a decree setting up the first Russian round-the-world expedition, which was ordered to 'reaffirm our rule in the lands discovered by Russian sailors' and gave instructions that they should 'circumnavigate the large island situated opposite the estuary of the Amur, by the name of Sagalin Anga Gata, describe its coasts, gulfs and harbours as well as the estuary of the Amur and, keeping as close as possible to the island itself, observe the state of its inhabitants, the quality of the land and forests and the fruit of its industry'. The expedition took place in 1803. It was headed by Ivan Kruzenshtern, whose ship approached Sakhalin on 14 May 1805 and cast anchor in Aniva bay. Kruzenshtern made a detailed study of the island, made contact with the Ainu inhabitants and gave them presents. In summer of that same year members of his expedition described and made maps of the entire eastern and north-western coasts of Sakhalin, and also of fourteen islands in the Kurile chain. This was the first-ever map to give a correct general outline of the chain. G.I. Nevelsky explored the eastern, northern and north-western coasts of Sakhalin, and the Amur channel, and established that the estuary was navigable for sea-going vessels. Between Cape Lazarev on the mainland and Cape Pogibi on Sakhalin he discovered a navigable strait which now bears his name. 'Sakhalin is an island, the estuary of the Amur can be approached by sea-going vessels from either north or south.' The same year Nevelsky left Ayan on a transport ship, the Okhotsk, approached Happiness Bay and established winter quarters on its coast, which he named Petrovskoe. He then founded a military post on the estuary of the Amur river, which he called Nikolaevsk. In 1853 the surveyor D.I. Orlov, on the instructions of Nevelsky, founded the first Russian military post on the islands at Ilinsky. Early in the second half of the nineteenth century the international situation in the Pacific Ocean changed radically. Russia was interested in the establishment of good neighbourly relations with Japan, which was in direct proximity to her eastern borders. On 22 January 1855, in the town of Shimoda, the first Russo–Japanese treaty was signed. According to this treaty the majority of the Kuriles remained Russian (the border was fixed between the islands of Uruppu and Etorofu) and Sakhalin remained undivided. The treaty of Shimoda was the beginning of a process establishing diplomatic relations between Russia and Japan. On 25 April 1875 the treaty of St Petersburg was signed, according to which Japan accepted Russian claims to the whole of Sakhalin and received in exchange all the Kurile Islands. In 1905 the Japanese landed at Sakhalin. For the capture of the islands the Japanese government had detailed troops, large in number for that time: 12 battalions, a squadron and a detachment of machine-gunners, totalling 14,000 men and 18 artillery pieces. The assault party landed on 40 ships. In the very first days of the war, completely outnumbered, the governor of Sakhalin, General Lyapunov, surrendered with his entire chief of staff. On 23 August 1905 the Russian government signed the Treaty of Portsmouth, according to which the southern part of Sakhalin was ceded to the Japanese. This situation remained until the liberation of these regions by the Soviet army.

'A good springboard,' he concluded, thinking again of Zolo-tarev. 'There's scope to show what one is capable of.' And glancing at the clock in the corner, he began to get up. 'That's enough for today.'

Outside he could see the pitch-black June night in this Year of Our Lord 1946.

Chapter Nine

1

In the May sky, rocking smoothly at the height of a bird's flight, a horse was floating. In its rough cage, quickly knocked together out of fresh slabs, it seemed from below to soar quite naturally above the earth like a creature from another as yet unknown world, so calmly and majestically did its flickering eyes shine through the wide chinks between the planks.

The horse floated, rocking, in the May sky, and all around, almost from the edge of the sea to the very highest of the surrounding jagged cliffs, a many-tiered town stretched out long and noisily, with a forest of masts and hoists almost all the way along its foot.

Evidently the coast had once inclined heavily in this part of Asia, and the ocean had surged into the coastal hills, filling every hollow, every cranny, every indentation in the surrounding mainland. Since then the steep horseshoe of the bay had formed an intricate lace of lagoons, small islands and creeks. And over it all, from dawn till dusk, there hung a grey or blue haze, depending on the weather, a mirage, a *fata morgana*.

Though Fyodor had seen many countries and towns, he might have had difficulty naming a place that was richer and more spacious, if it were not for a barely palpable sense of alarm, or rather, caution, in the atmosphere. Here a man felt as if he was perpetually in someone's sights, in an invisible trap, a noose, a pen. It was as if there, at the last signal-box before the town, an invisible curtain fell down behind every arrival, separating the world irremediably into two halves.

Fyodor might have spent a long time seeking the source, the reason for this sensation, if the reality of it had not itself become apparent.

The pier where the one hundred and fifty families had gathered with their belongings waiting for embarkation suddenly came almost imperceptibly to life, only to return to a now uneasy calm: it was as if a snail, having emerged only slightly, had rushed back to conceal its fear in the reliable chasm of its shell. But even when hidden, fear continued to cast anxious glances in the direction from which a faceless grey-black column, surrounded by silent dogs and guards, was turning out of the port gates in the direction of a neighbouring pier: faster, faster, faster! In their silent half-trot there was a hint of frightened menace, which made you pant dizzily for breath as your heart felt the play of icy draughts.

Like an accordion the column first spread out along the shore, only to huddle up blackly by the nearby pier.

'Sit!'

Bending and hunching sharply, the dense mass quickly sank until, tamed, it had settled down into a black ribbon against the grey of the pier and the blue of the sea. Their ragged clothes were black, their faces were black and even the smell they exuded seemed to Fyodor to be black.

In this huddle of almost indistinguishable faces Fyodor could see nothing remotely remarkable. On the long journey from Moscow to Vladivostok he had encountered such groups many times: either through the barbed-wire-covered skylight of a wagon of a passing goods train; or a whole crowd of them seen from the train in a glade in the taiga (you hardly had time to look at them properly before they disappeared from view); or seen up close and in detail as they squatted at the side of the rails waiting for someone or something. They had become less noticeable, merged in the general picture, a part of the scenery, a landmark of the journey, a feature of everyday life.

But now an irresistible force suddenly drew him towards them, these sullen glances, these blank faces, this bitter dirty smell. It was as in a dream, where any resistance only reinforces the attraction to what is imminent and inescapable. What would be would be!

Fyodor strode towards this faceless black mass, and suddenly his head started slowly spinning and his ears noisily and hotly ringing: a single face emerged clearly from the black mass in front of him and took shape. It did not look so different from the others, with its hungrily sunken eyes, the coarse stubble on its wan cheeks and its long gaze which looked not so much outside as within itself.

But even if this face had changed still more, Fyodor would have recognized it among thousands: his platoon commander! Aleksandr Aleksandrovich, in short San Sanych, with his constant smile from ear to ear, his habit of adding 'right' to almost every word and his desperate, almost feverish recklessness . . .

How could Fyodor forget the fatal battles in the Pinsk marshes!

123

Even now the very thought of it made him shiver, as if he had relived in a single moment the frozen darkness of that snowy winter of 1943. They had been hemmed in among frozen tussocks without the slightest hope of getting out, of getting warm or even having a rest. For days they had warmed the frozen marsh with their own bodies while his bosom buddy, the platoon commander San Sanych, whispered rakish heat into his half-frozen ear, laughing hoarsely: 'Ekh, Fedka, what you and I need now is two birds to warm us up a bit – that would stoke our fires! And why are you so frozen anyway, Fedka? What kind of blood have you got in your veins? I can piss warmer than it. Move about, move about, you son of a bitch, what are you doing, settling down for the night? There's no point going numb yet, brother – we've got a whole war ahead of us, and the high command owes us two weeks' rations, if not more. There must be a wagonload of virgins still in your village – if you turn your toes up now you'll regret it in the other world . . .'

And carried away by the commander's feverish banter, his warm numbness was transported into a sultry summer day in his village, and the bells on the hillsides rang in his ear . . .

'When I was a little girl
I ate no coconutty,
now these coconutties
beat me on the botty.'

The verse was stupid and he had no idea where it had come from, but it went round and round in his head like a constantly repeated gramophone record.

The sound broke off as suddenly as it had started and immediately, like an instantaneous passage from night to day, pitch-black hell was unleashed; it was as if the marshes around had themselves reared of their own accord, and waking from their frosty hibernation had begun a dance of death. Fyodor had never experienced such an artillery barrage in the entire war. They fired at them at almost point-blank range, without mercy or respite. A crimson light flashed and was extinguished before their eyes and invincible terror brought a cold dampness to their palms: raging fear gradually thawed out their bodies. Fyodor knew this state: in three years at the front he had already got used to this desperate languor, when initial confusion gives way suddenly to a heavy, fiery heart-blackening hatred.

In the momentary illumination of an explosion, Fyodor caught

124

sight of the solemn, firm expression on the face of his commander, without his usual smile, and sensed rather than heard him say laconically: 'Forward!'

Fyodor's body became light as charcoal, almost weightless, he seemed not to jump but to soar over the frozen tussocks, and they rushed deliriously forward through this erupting hell, through its black flames and rank fumes in search of illusory but longed-for safety.

'Hurrah-ah -ah -ah!'

When he fell, he felt neither pain nor the fall itself; he was just covered in darkness and the raucous pant of his commander rang from end to end of that darkness: ' "Fyodor walked from the hills; a sack on his back . . ." There's more shit in you, brother, than there is in a cow . . . Lean on me, I'll get you out of it, I'm a carthorse . . . I've got a charmed life, brother, neither water nor fire can get me . . .'

Fyodor floated with his own darkness, listened to the familiar voice, thinking with vague irritation, 'What are you going on about, you don't come from the country, you're just pretend-ing . . .'

He did not know much for certain, of course (San Sanych wore his heart on his sleeve, but did not let anyone into it), but he guessed that his commander was not the simple fellow he made himself out to be, and that he had as good an idea as a general of what was going on, if not better. He was far too free and easy when he spoke to his superiors (a little condescendingly, with a slight smirk which an outsider would probably miss); he read books that were far too clever for his rank, and thought far too precocious thoughts in between his smiles and jokes. 'Oh, San Sanych, San Sanych,' Fyodor often thought pityingly to himself, 'you'll end up losing your head. You're taking someone else's burden on your shoulders!'

Therefore when, after being in hospital, he rejoined his section in Western Prussia and learnt of the commander's arrest, Fyodor was not surprised, although for a long time he grieved bitterly over him: 'So much for your charmed life! It turns out the old folk are right: you can't renounce poverty and you can't renounce prison. What a fellow we've lost over nothing at all!'

All this flashed through his mind in a moment, plunging him into bitter despair and settling on his soul. He could not resist it; he walked over to his former commander: 'Listen, lieutenant . . . San Sanych, don't you recognize me?'

The man did not even blink. He just shrivelled back a bit,

125

continuing to look straight ahead and into himself, but the convoy guard was already bearing down on Fyodor, his submachine-gun at the ready: 'All right, back off! This is your first warning, you fucker!'

'Brother,' Fyodor said hastily, 'listen, it's my platoon commander – we were at the front together. You must have fought yourself, let me have a word with him.'

The mocking greenish eyes stared unflinchingly at Fyodor, as if they did not even see him: 'Your lieutenants are standing to attention now felling trees and twirling wolves' tails. Get back, I said!'

Fyodor could feel himself suffocating. A familiar white jaw-parting fury blinded him. Bullishly oblivious, he marched towards the guard: 'You lousy scum guard, you rearguard louse, go on, pull the trigger, you bastard, or can you only do it in the back?' Fyodor thought he was shrieking at the top of his voice, but in fact he was almost whispering. 'How come I never saw you at the front, you Vologda rabble? You obviously didn't have time – too busy shooting people here? Go on then, shoot me, try it, or d'you only have the courage for going to shit in the yard? . . .'

Who knows how this would have ended? (badly, probably! a few nearby sheepdogs, whimpering in anticipation, were tugging the leads out of the hands of their masters, and the green-eyed man, getting bolder, had decisively slipped the safety-catch), but at the moment when the inevitable seemed about to happen, a loud voice resounded from the other end of the pier: 'Up!'

The seemingly numb black monster of the column instantaneously came to life, undulated and straightened out. The tail of the column was still swaying into place when its head was already disappearing in a narrow chain up the ladder of a lend-lease ship, to the shouts of the guards and the whines of the dogs.

'You're in luck,' the guard shouted in relief as he joined the column. 'I'd have had you dancing on the end of my muzzle.' And then to the prisoners he added, 'Right, you fascists, get in line!'

Fyodor looked at his commander with a final despairing hope but he made not the slightest gesture in response: he got up with all the others and stood looking at his feet, his back slightly hunched. Slowly the column moved off, inching forward, and with it the ex-commander, who soon merged into it, black and indistinguishable as ash in tatters of burnt paper. 'Oh what a life we lead,' Fyodor ground his teeth with feeling, 'to ruin a man like that!'

'Why do you go asking for trouble, you son of a bitch!' Fyodor's father rushed at him, blindly blinking the tears from his good eye. 'Lads like you are quickly brought to their senses these days. Even marshals have to lick the boots of that lot. You should think about what you're doing . . .'

But Fyodor's soul was so bitter and miserable at that moment that he could not control himself, and he interrupted his father, perhaps for the first time in his life: 'Get lost, Dad. I'm fed up to the back teeth with the lot of you.'

The old man immediately understood what torment his son was going through and walked away, silent and self-effacing.

But in the May sky, at the height of a bird's flight, still rocking smoothly, the horse floated, and the sadness in its exhausted eyes flowed down in blessing on to the people and the earth.

2

Through the porthole the water rose like a wall, occasionally revealing a little part of the low, grey sky. The cargo hold had been only slightly adapted to carry passengers and was rocking at almost 90°. The vessel's planking creaked and groaned like an eggshell in somebody's strong but careful hands. At times it seemed as if the sides would not hold and the boat would crack along the seams, collapsing under the pressure. Someone was groaning, someone else cursing, yet another vomiting down below, under the planks, often and violently. Things had gone mad and come to life, pinning men in nooks and corners. And in this mixture of creaks, groans and oaths, some crank was managing to strum a balalaika with drunken imperturbability:

'I went to a soldier's girl to spend the night
But I was in no hurry.
I'm the finest fellow in Sychovka,
And I wear an embroidered shirt.'

The balalaika-player seemed unconcerned about what was happening all around him. It was as if he had never left his native village, and had found himself among all this crush through a drunken error.

'The finest fellow in Sychovka,
And I wear an embroidered shirt . . .'

Fyodor sat at his grandmother's feet, holding on to her to try to protect her from the rolling as much as possible. Holding her hands as usual on top of a colourful quilted blanket, she looked straight ahead with her sharp, drily flashing eyes, and her bloodless lips trembled convulsively. She was talking to herself about something known only to her. What was she thinking of here, at the end of her life, thousands of versts from her native village, at the edge of her conceivable world, the young Tulan girl, now nearly eighty? Through the web of furrows that almost eighty autumns had traced across her thin face, through the blue mist of fever, through the shroud of blindness, she was discovering something constant and definitive, the simple secrets of fate, the childlike truths of vain human endeavour, the total decay of human life: jackdaws glistening on the sparkling loam after the plough; rancid smoke in spring over the snow-flurry of apple-trees in bloom; the suffocating tickle of dry hay during haymaking in the distant fields; and her skirt sticky with congealed blood after the first oblivion of childbirth. Shadows, ghosts, visions of the past called her to a place from which there is no return. Emerging from ashes, what will you return to?

Her heavy, calloused, quite unfeminine hands shook regularly, as if she kept touching something sharp or hot. As long as Fyodor remembered, all his conscious life, his grandmother's spade-like palms had always been a secure reference point at home, a sign of warmth, a family guarantee of their work and their lineage. The past unfurled before him like a set of coloured photographs: grandmother putting a pot of steaming potatoes on the table; or in the cow-shed, fork in hand, up to her ankles in manure, well-built, laughing, in a light open jacket, her kerchief fallen on her shoulders; damp washing spread out on a stone at the side of the river, a grey morning mist over the water, and in this mist grandmother's hands moving smoothly like two large dark brown blades; her rough strong fingers sorting through the yellowing papers in her soft tin treasure-box for who knew which time: her husband's burial certificate, two or three letters, faceless photographs taken thirty years before; himself in the old woman's arms shrieking in pain from the nettles after she found him that hot day among the raspberries: 'Don't steal them, you crook! Ask granny, she'll give you some!' Lord, when was it? Did it even happen? Vanity! vanity! vanity!

The bloodless lips of the old woman kept moving and moving, saying the words that only she could hear, but her torment gradually got through to Fyodor and at last he understood: 'I want

128

to live a bit longer, Lord, I don't feel I've lived at all, it's as if I've only just been born this morning and now I have to die the very same day. How have I angered you, Lord? Leave me for another year at least. What difference can it make to you, but for me, an old woman, all my joy is in looking at the wide world. Since the day I was born I've been nowhere, I spent my whole miserable life in my own village, bent over the soil, up to my ankles in dung. I went to bed at dusk and got up at dawn. I remember when I was only eighteen . . .'

'Is there something I can do, Gran?' Fyodor tried to get through to her. 'Tell me, Gran . . .'

'Lord,' she neither heard nor saw him, 'do not be angry with me in my old age . . . am I guilty to want to live just a little bit longer? For what will they say in the village, that she went off in her old age, and that God punished her, but I went because of the children, because of my grandson . . . how could I live out my days on my own with no one to give me a glass of water before I die . . . what have I done to merit such a fate? . . .'

'Granny.'

'Lord, forgive me in my wretchedness. I blame myself, but I cannot stop it – the evil one has got hold of me . . .'

'Gra . . .'

'Lord, it's as if I was still in my crib in mother's hut . . .'

She stopped in exhaustion and at the same time the rocking calmed, becoming more regular. Her face became softer, smoother, took on a brighter, earthy colour. Her narrow forehead became covered in cold sweat, her nose sharpened and went blue. She was still breathing, still warmed by living flesh, but the spirit of life was already parting from her and no force in the world could now have stopped this parting.

Fyodor shook his father, who, exhausted by the rocking of the boat, was dozing on the floor, among the baggage, leaning against the knees of his wife, who was also nodding drowsily, half-asleep. 'Dad . . . listen, Dad, look after gran, I think she's taking a nap.' His father just had the strength to nod in agreement before he sank back into feeble exhaustion.

Fyodor made his way to the exit through an almost impassable pile of baggage of all kinds and stretched-out bodies. The whole mass was rolling about, groaning, cursing, weeping. In this hell, Fyodor caught sight of someone's open chess-board, jumping like a yellow bird in the surrounding bedlam. The board was so incongruous, so absurd here that for the first time Fyodor himself felt queasy.

And in a distant corner someone's drunken tenor voice continued to insist, to the balalaika, that he was none other than 'the finest lad in Sychovka, and I wear an embroidered shirt'.

Only when he got out on deck was Fyodor able to take in a deep breath of fresh, damp air. He looked about and his heart sank: the sea all around was roaring and rising up, and in its seemingly senseless dance he felt some purposeful force. It was difficult to imagine what this force might be and where it was leading, but the dark profundity he sensed in it promised the voyager mountain heights and immense abysses. It was like dreams in childhood, after an illness, when you sometimes find yourself standing in such darkness, by such fiery caves, that you want, oh how you want to touch them, but you're afraid even to stretch out your hand.

Here, beating against the bars of cages screwed to the deck, there were all sorts of animals – hens, ducks, geese, sheep, cows, horses. In a covered cow-pen, there was even a cage with two rabbits. The almost human torment and suffering of this realm filled his heart with aching pity. In the damp wind the familiar smell of dung and animal sweat was particularly strong. Farewell, Sychovka, but remember – I shall return! If only he knew when!

Fyodor was about to stretch his hand into the cow's cage to stroke her anxious calf, the mirror image of its mother, to feel its tenderness and warmth under his fingers, even to calm it down a little, but suddenly he was given a peremptory push on the elbow.

'What are you doing here?'

Fyodor turned round, but under the tarpaulin cloak he could distinguish nothing but a greying beard.

'What about you?'

'I'm guarding these.'

'Why guard them? No one will steal them.'

'They won't steal them, but I have to make sure they don't get washed overboard by accident.'

'What're you going to do, hold them down?'

'I can't hold them down, but if something happens I can call for help and we'll save the rest.'

'Where do you come from?'

'From near Ozherelye. Why are you asking me questions? Where's your documents?'

'Have you gone blind, Dad, can't you see my documents?' and Fyodor glanced at the 'iconostasis' over the right pocket of his field-shirt. 'I squashed lice in trenches for four years to get this "document".'

'There's a lot of you wandering around here with documents like that till the first official finds them.' But he softened. 'Have you got a smoke?'

'Here, take a couple.' Fyodor expansively threw him a packet of 'Belomor'.

The old peasant smirked contentedly, took a cigarette and threw back his cape to reveal a large head in an old soldier's cap. The face underneath it turned out to be not at all old, with blue eyes and a slightly porous nose. Carefully rolling the cigarette between his fingers, making sure not to lose a single shred of tobacco, he sniffed it at length and with obvious pleasure from all angles till finally, with no less pleasure, he lit up from Fyodor's German booty lighter: 'Once the president of the village Soviet gave me one, but this is the next one since then.' He bared his strong yellow teeth in a blissful smile. 'The way some people live; what chance is there for ignorant folk like us!'

'I see from your cap that you were at the front.' Fyodor wanted to get a conversation, any conversation going, so as not to have to go back down into the stench and curses; even the balalaika there, with its idiot refrain, now made him feel only anger. 'Who were you with?'

'No,' the man answered serenely and willingly. 'I've got an ulcer, had it since childhood. Ever since I was a kid I had a weak stomach, and when all that started, the collective farms and the famines, the bread and water and the weeds, I got really weak.' The conversation seemed to have ground to a halt before it had really got started, but suddenly the man began to talk with energy. 'When everything started brewing, in '17, I was still a lad. I got married soon after, and I minded my own business, causing no trouble to anyone. My wife was nothing extraordinary. You couldn't say she was a great beauty, and she wasn't particularly hard-working, but she wasn't lazy, just average. Only I loved her a great deal, I couldn't live without her, she's got a hold on me, sinner that I am, as if we'd been forged together by the blacksmith: you couldn't hack us apart with a pickaxe and you couldn't prize us apart with a chisel. That's the way it is now, but then we lived like everyone else: we worked the land, we ate bread when there was some, we had children. Our village was small – a sparrow could hop from end to end without pausing for breath – eighteen families, that's all there was to it, all living in little huts, not a single proper five-walled one. There wasn't even a church, the only thing that made it a village was the name. But we were people, like everyone else. So what kind of fate is it that makes men unable to live in peace in the wide world?' He even raised his

131

hands to heaven, or tried to – it was very difficult in his narrow tarpaulin cloak. 'So things got going in '17 and it's been the same ever since. And then our lousy little village began its golden age – it passed through with its scythe, or rather its bludgeon. A pretty sight! In the very first famine this group, this band, if you can call it that, this little band came to the village – eight pig snouts, specially selected, shouting "Give us bread!" And where were we supposed to get it from – we'd have had to give birth to it! Every hut had someone dead or dying. They gave me a shaking too, the sinners. They gave me a good shaking.' He lingered over the word 'good', as if preparing for a jump, his slightly flattened nostrils flaring furiously. 'I'll never forget it . . . But why did they do it, the eight of them, I'm not made of iron . . . So that's where I got my ulcer. You can have it for nothing if you like – I'm not greedy . . .'

And off he went, without pulling up his cloak, along the sloping deck, as if into a frontal attack.

'Too much talking will get you into trouble one day,' Fyodor told himself angrily. 'A chatterer is a gift to spies!'

And he also walked off, but in the other direction, down into hell, into the fumes, the oaths and the tears, and the balalaika's idiot ravings, and a new, as yet unknown anxiety powerfully invaded his soul.

3

His father said: 'It's no good – you might as well get out. What's the point of going on digging? It's just rock. Lord forgive me, the earth round here is rubbish.'

There was indeed a very shallow earth covering. Fyodor had dug only to his waist and it was already stone – and what stone, flint! But as for the smell and colour of it, Fyodor had been in many parts of the world, yet he'd never known anything like it, it was more like peat, but with a different consistency and colour – black, slightly tinged with blue, with the smell of a stove long after it has gone out.

He and his father lowered granny into the soil, straightened up and stood there silently, as if appraising their work. But if that is what they thought, it was only an impression; simply in this brief moment they were parting with something which would never return: with the call of someone's ashes, with the shadow of someone's joy, with the warmth of winter evenings, the smell of fresh-baked bread, the acrid smoke of distant Sychovka; but is it possible to spell out everything a man thinks about at such a moment?

Her coffin, the coffin of this aged girl, knocked together quickly from anything that came to hand, looked all at sea in the miserable grave, like a child's boat in melted snow, and no one was pointing it in the right direction any more and there was no longer anywhere for it to stop. Lord, what is it then? Fate, destiny, predestination that a Sychovka peasant, daughter of thirty generations of peasants, should give up her soul to God on land that was recently Japanese, with neither cross nor confession. Lord, have mercy on her!

His mother was not crying, not even wailing as tradition demanded. She just looked dully in front of her, with such utter despair in her eyes that everything around seemed old and withered.

'All right, that's enough,' his father barked, squinting at his wife out of the corner of his eye. 'Fill in the hole, it's where we'll all end.' And he started the job himself, with swift, unceremonious movements, with a sort of incomprehensible frenzy. 'She lived her life.'

Together they quickly covered the coffin, smoothed out the grave and even edged the little mound with turf. Then his father pulled out of a nearby hillock some wild plant with a blistered stem and dug it in at the head of the grave. Only after that did he clean off his clothes, calm down and say softly, 'Well, all done just like other honest folk.'

He was deeply moved as he looked at his work and became quite radiant. 'We too know what's what.' Again he cast a glance at his wife. 'Come on, mother, there's no point standing here. You'll never cry enough tears.'

She got up and turned towards the settlement, moving like a machine, and he followed her, trying not to intrude on her grief, and yet at the same time to show her by his whole demeanour that he, her husband, was at her side and also 'knew what's what' and, if need be, would show it.

To an outsider his behaviour might have seemed a little absurd, but Fyodor knew for certain that his father loved his silent wife, loved her madly, though he had clearly not said two words of endearment to her in his entire life, had always kept her in fear and trembling, showing her who was master; and therefore, looking at them now, Fyodor was overcome by a tenderness for them both that brought a lump to his throat. 'God gave me these parents, they're completely inseparable, the old devils!'

The life that was ahead of him seemed mysterious and alluring. Although four years in the carousel of war had got him used to sharp shifts of fate, this sudden move from one part of the world to another made him wonder whether he was dreaming and none of this was really happening: 'Bloody hell, what possessed me to come the devil knows where? But there's nothing for it now, I'll have to make the best of it!'

There was a slight smell of rotting fish and tarred ropes coming from the ocean. There was scarcely a ripple on the water, which stretched smoothly to the horizon, and its sparkling surface breathed silently, evaporating in a pale lilac haze. This is the way it must have looked to the man who called it 'Pacific'.

They went to the canteen for the wake. They found an empty table with some difficulty, and his mother took the plate of *kutia* she had prepared out of its cloth: 'Let us remember, for the sake of Christ, his servant Agrafena,' she crossed herself slowly. 'May the earth be like down to her, may she rest in peace.'

'I made it for the housewarming, but we'll have to drink it at the wake.' His father furtively removed a bottle of home-brewed vodka from his padded jacket, taking out the stopper, wrapped in a rag, with his teeth. 'We should call someone over. It's not right to have a wake without a single guest – we're Christian people after all.'

Fyodor looked round mechanically, and to his surprise met the gaze of his interlocutor on the deck of the ship, who was sitting alone at an empty table, looking understandingly at them.

'Hallo, old fellow,' Fyodor nodded. 'Bring up a chair, you can be our guest. Our grandmother has just died and we're having a wake.'

At first they remembered her in silence, but after the third drink the village home-brew had its effect and their tongues were loosened.

'So she was called Agrafena?' The guest started on a safe topic, as if getting his bearings. 'Who'd have imagined it, to live her whole life in the village and then go off to the Kuriles to die. Our Mother Russia is on the move, off beyond the distant hills, and where she'll stop, God alone knows. There isn't even any soil on these Kuriles, mark you, just stone, and that's standing on a fire and might blow up at any time. Listen, can you hear it?' Somewhere far away there was a dull, muffled rumble which even made the fragile box of the canteen shake slightly. 'That's it, all right. They say some big noise is coming from Moscow to put us all in order. Unfortunately the heavenly bureaucrats have got their own big noise so they won't listen to his orders. We Russians should sit at home on the stove and not go wandering backwards and forwards all over the world.' He got up decisively. 'Right, I must be off. Thanks for the hospitality and Christ be with you. If you feel like it, call in and see me. I've got myself a dug-out down there nice and close to the Japanese. Just ask for Matvei Zagladin, they'll show you where.'

And off he went, tall, grave, confident in himself.

'Clearly a man of ancient stock,' Tikhon watched him leave. 'He knows his own worth. Men like him used to become bishops, or merchants, it's clear from the start that he knows what's what. I remember . . .'

His father's reminiscences would probably drag on for some time and Fyodor was in a great hurry; he had to see the personnel chief without fail.

'Finish it up without me. I've got to go and get my papers sorted out, and then I'll go to the military bureau and register. See you later . . .'

4

There was no room to move in the personnel bureau. People sat, stood, came in, went out, and a thick fug of tobacco smoke rose to the ceiling. Voices, scores of voices, floated and drowned in this smoke like disembodied fish.

Someone next to Fyodor, long unshaven and with broad brows under his fur hat, was monotonously complaining to no one in particular: 'They drive us off God knows where and there's no arrangements. They gave us a room for five, so they say, but there isn't room for two to turn around – it's more like a passageway than a room and the rain drips in, in every corner. And as for the grub, I'm sick to death of their fish – it's got lots of vitamins, they say, it's good for you, they say, but these vitamins are no good to me – they just mean I've got to keep going out in the yard. A meal without gruel is no meal at all as far as I'm concerned. In Moscow they told us it was the land of milk and honey . . .'

Behind a narrow partition which separated the bureau head's study from the waiting-room, he heard a falsetto voice squeaking furiously: 'What kind of a bloody welder are you? You've spent almost a year welding a handle on a bucket! And anyway what the hell do I want welders for – I need fishermen! And don't you stick your red card under my nose! I've got a whole drawer full of them

– I can hang them on the Christmas tree. The repair works are full of people like you. You signed up as a jack of all trades, so go and work on the nets. That's it . . . Next!'

After languishing for the rest of the afternoon in this pointless bustle Fyodor finally got into the office, where he found himself face to face with a hunchback of about fifty with rumpled hair and wire-framed glasses, through which eyes that pierced with constant malice looked at him inquiringly.

'Do you have your contract with you?' He grabbed the papers Fyodor held out to him and, with hardly a glance at them, stretched his hairy hand towards a pile of files on a shelf at his side. Like a magician finding a marked card, he nimbly pulled out the necessary folder. 'Right. Let's take a look.' He leafed through it rapidly, and immediately softened approvingly. 'I'll tell you straight, Samokhin, Fyodor Tikhonovich, you've got a beauty of a personal file.' He looked with open admiration at Fyodor. 'With a file like that you could join the party now. I'll write the recommendation myself. We need people like you, Samokhin. Eagles like you are hard to find – most of the people we get here these days are riff-raff, rabble, tramps on the lookout for easy money: you can't leave a turd unguarded – they'll steal it and sell it for drink. And besides, the border's nearby. You have to keep an eye open – you never know what they might get up to when they're drunk. We need a man for the post launch – it's a responsible position. Japanese waters are only a few miles away, so you have to have your wits about you. We need a tried and trusted cadre. I see you were in the military police, and you've also been a driver – all the cards are in your hands. The mechanism isn't very subtle, but the lads in the repair yard will show you how it works. Agreed?' And clearly noticing that Fyodor was still vacillating, he added hastily: 'Right, run to the medical post – it's on the other side of the barracks. Get yourself a medical certificate and then you can have your documents dealt with. That's all. Next! . . .'

He did not have to stand around at the medical post. The door, which gave straight on to the street, was wide open. Fyodor knocked at the door-frame for form's sake, went in, opened his mouth and almost choked on his words. A woman was standing in a white doctor's coat at an open medicine cabinet, and looking at him as if she had long been confident that he would come.

'Polina Vasilevna . . . Polina . . . Polya . . .'

And he felt the scent of that noisy, damp autumn of 1941 when after he had been shell-shocked for the first time, in the retreat from Bryansk, he was lying in a Moscow hospital bed waiting to be discharged and to return to the front. The days passed monotonously and dully outside the window, with occasional sharp frosts and damp foggy evenings. Through the rusty conifers of the hospital grounds there were patches of sky heavy with rain-clouds which filed languidly past, their shaggy manes snagging in the treetops, and the damp-flattened land stretched dully to the distant horizon.

Frustrated at his inactivity, Fyodor played draughts frenziedly from morning till night with his neighbour, Yasha Kupernik, a gunner-radio-operator, bandaged up in a cocoon with gaps for eyes and mouth in his faceless gauze. The days passed, heavy and grey as the weather, and it seemed as if there would never be an end to this hospital tedium.

The stuffy monotony had no effect on Yasha. Quite the contrary, with every passing day he seemed more lively and energetic. What Fyodor liked in him was his inexhaustible capacity for buffoonery, behind which from time to time, like rust on shining tin, he sensed a secret grief. It was as if Yasha was feverishly trying to soothe a chronic and already unappeasable pain with a torrent, an avalanche of words.

'My parents thought I was a *Wunderkind*,' his eyes shone damply under the bandages, bewitching his neighbour with the tracery of his nervous banter, 'just because when I was five I could thump out "Where have you been, little siskin?' on the piano with one finger. And can you imagine, they dragged me off to the capital of our motherland, to Oistrakh himself. It terrifies me to think of what happened there: papa shouting, mama crying, Oistrakh tearing his hair out: all he needs is another *Wunderkind*! And, with my Jewish luck, I ended up entering the famous Conservatoire itself, may it crumble to the ground, and I almost finished my course, but luckily the war intervened. Now, thank God,' he lightly banged his two stumps together in their plaster casts, and through the gaps in his face bandages Fyodor saw a brief flash of despair, 'my sufferings are at an end, unless they can teach me how to play the drums without drumsticks . . .'

This almost hysterical despair oppressed Fyodor more heavily every day with a sense of vague guilt. He gradually began to feel ashamed of his light shell-shock, of his hearty appetite, even of his hands that the war had not maimed. It seemed to him that by getting away so lightly he had somehow robbed Yasha, and all the lads like Yasha, and that he was now living at their expense, on the sacrifice of their bread and their health. And though his head ached so much when he woke up that he felt sick, Fyodor was tormented by a desire to get out of here as soon as possible, whatever hell-hole he was sent to. He was already beginning to lose hope when early one evening he was summoned to the duty doctor's office, where a tall, prematurely balding major got up to meet him.

'Samokhin? Fyodor Tikhonovich? Born in '19?' Without looking at him, the major jerkily leafed through the file, licking his yellowed fingers from time to time. 'Member of the Komsomol? Of peasant origin? Village of Sychovka, region of Tula? Unmarried? Gone through the baptism of fire? Right.' Here he looked at Fyodor for the first time. His gaze was long and motionless, as if he was looking not at his surroundings but inside himself. 'All right, Samokhin, your file is in order – your proletarian bones will stick in the throat of any enemy. We're taking you to an objective of extreme importance, we are showing great trust in you. You must understand that, the matter is top secret – as the saying goes, "eat your mushroom soup and keep mum . . ." Is that clear?'

'Yes.' Fyodor did not know whether to laugh or cry: the opportunity to escape the hospital walls at last was like a birthday present, but at the same time working in a department that was spoken about in hushed voices and with anxious glances over the shoulder made him far from happy. 'A soldier must obey.'

The major grunted approvingly, closed the file, looked in his direction and repeated the formula: '08.00 hours tomorrow, at reception. Your papers you will get from me. Is that clear? Carry on.'

The next morning a battered one-and-a-half ton truck, rocking from wheel to wheel, drove him through the copses beyond Moscow towards his destination. The miserable late autumn was damp and muddy. The leafless thickets, with their piercingly bright bunches of rowan berries, were covered in a sticky mould-like drizzle. The occasional glades stretched like endless troughs under the wheels, and at times it seemed as if the truck was not driving but swimming through the sky, which had tumbled on to the earth.

Fyodor languished in the back of the van among the sacks and cases, smoking, cursing softly at the bumps, dozing lightly: he had to keep getting up, jumping down into the mud at the side of the road, shoving the slabs they carried for the purpose under the wheels and then helping the major to lean against the back and ease the unwieldy truck out of some new rut it had sunk into.

The driver, a lanky sergeant-major with his fur hat down over his ears and his new pea-jacket wide open, swore morosely from the footboard, flashing his metal teeth at them: 'Fucking technology! Scrap-iron on wheels, that's what this bugger is. It's no good for driving, you might try cracking nuts with it, though it probably wouldn't be any fucking good at that! The tyres are completely bald, how many times have I asked for new ones? Fuck it, they don't take a blind bit of notice, and they call it the fucking Organs! . . .'

'That's enough, Gubin! Talk like that can get you before a tribunal.' Standing up to the ankles in mud, the major even tried to stamp his foot to give his words greater authority, but his voice held no trace of either will or insistence, merely tiredness – total, profound, chronic tiredness. 'You are a Chekist, Gubin! Aren't you ashamed?'

By nightfall they began to encounter the patrols of the battle outposts. As they drove on these became more frequent, looming from the half-darkness in the most unexpected places: they were clearly near to the front. The major had hasty whispered exchanges with the sentries and the truck drove on: into forest, into bad weather, into the night.

When at last their headlights picked out of the ink-black night a plank-wood house with firmly closed shutters, Fyodor no longer felt like either standing or moving: night had fallen on him with all its soporific power. Everything that happened after this – the sounds, the gestures, the movements – seemed to be happening outside of him, apart from him, above the weight of sleepiness he bore within him. He carried this burden through slush and darkness into a room dimly illuminated by a kerosene lamp, where he was met by a broad-shouldered fellow with a strong, pock-marked face, wearing an open field-shirt.

'You look exhausted, soldier!' The fellow was rushing round the table laying out their simple meal: pure spirit, bread, pickles. 'Have a quick drink, and you can fall out. I was beginning to get depressed here, sitting on my own all the time, with no one to talk to. Although it's not the kind of place you can get bored,' he winked meaningfully.

To the sound of his cosy chatter Fyodor soon fell asleep, finally defeated by the alcohol. And he dreamed of a hot summer in his village, with the little blue petals of the cornflowers in the almost brown rye, with the crazy zigzags of the dusty rut that crossed it. Along this rut, his mother was rushing to meet him, hardly touching the ground, and the dust raised by her bare feet rose in a little light cloud: 'Drink some water, Fedenka, or a little cold kvas! Fedenka! . . .' And her voice enveloped him in blue serenity.

139

And the dream came true: Fyodor awoke illuminated by such blinding bliss that he wanted to screw up his eyes and lie there motionless for a long time until he had forgotten the awfulness of the previous day and his sombre memories. Outside the sun was at the height of its generous power. The horizon which had looked so desolate yesterday was transfigured with colour and motion. The sky stretched up to the heights in new-washed festive blue. A white tracery of mist, in which the half-dead leaves hovered like bright fish in an aquarium, black and gold, illuminated by smoky drips of water, lay over the nearby wood.

'It seems you've brought the good weather, soldier.' The fellow from the previous day was standing in the doorway, a pile of firewood in his arms, his uniform buttons all done up, his belt fastened, his whole strong, pockmarked face shining. 'We were getting really depressed with all this damp, we thought it would go on raining till the snows came.' Nimbly, he lit a fire, and the flames soon began dancing gaily. 'We'll have a cup of tea to clear our heads and we can go and report to the authorities. Our major only looks severe; in fact he's a reasonable sort of fellow.'

He laid the table just as nimbly and neatly, brewed the tea, poured it into mugs and then watered it down with hot water. He then sat down opposite Fyodor. It was obvious that he was sincerely pleased to have someone working with him, that he enjoyed the role of generous host and that all in all someone to talk or listen to was a long-awaited present for him. 'Yes, I can see, you must be sick to death of sitting here on your own, brother,' Fyodor thought as he watched and listened attentively, 'to fall so greedily on me with your chatter.'

'To get things clear, I'm called Nikolai, Nikolai Nosov.' He was obviously in seventh heaven as he sipped the tea from his mug. 'I was also sent here from hospital; I got my lot in a bombing-raid near Kiev – a splinter lodged in the small of my back. It aches when it rains, otherwise it's all right. Everyone here's got something wrong with them – with some it's the body, others the head. In a word, an invalid and a half, and a woman for good measure. Only the woman, I'll tell you now, is a real firebrand – she can knock the two of us out with one tit, a woman with character, and no mistake. She's a doctor, you'll see for yourself. The plane mechanic is a real fruit – bonkers, it's true, but harmless. Then there's the major, and that's the whole team. When we need fliers they bring them from the village, five versts from here – there's a squadron there.'

'And when do you need them?' Fyodor tried a cautious inquiry.

'What goes on here?'

It was as if the man had just been waiting for this sign of curiosity: his face lit up with joy and he leaned confidentially towards Fyodor, putting aside his mug as he rushed to explain: 'Of course you and I are just the small fry, just ordinary soldiers. We pick up our guns and stand around on guard, but mark my words, brother, what's going on here is top secret stuff. We're sending agents behind enemy lines, get it? Most of them are no older than you and me, but they jabber away in German as well as they do in Russian. The major here gives them their final run-through and Polina Vasilevna, the doctor, checks their health; you're not going to send a sick man on such a mission. The one bad thing,' he sighed with regret and got up, 'is that we all live in such secrecy, each one of us hiding in his hole, we never talk at all, unless something comes up to do with work. Occasionally you can get a word or two out of the mechanic, when he's sober, but that's once in a blue moon. You and I will live in this hovel together while the big-wigs are over there in the big house,' he nodded out of the window. The fellow was already standing impatiently in the doorway in full uniform. 'Time to see the boss, soldier!' And, as they went out, 'What's your name, then?'

Beyond the few trees that grew outside the hut there stretched a long, carefully mown clearing surrounded by thick undergrowth behind which there was a dark wide band of woodland. The path first led over to the clearing and then across it and the undergrowth into the wood itself, and up to a building that looked like a dacha, fitted up on all sides with a whole collection of extensions and outbuildings.

'Go in, he doesn't bite,' Nosov nudged him towards the house. 'As you go in, it's the door on the left. I'll wait here and have a smoke. The main thing is to keep quiet – let him drone on a bit. He likes that, but eventually he gets tired of it. Good luck!'

After the blinding light of the glade, it was pitch-dark inside. Fyodor groped his way to the door he needed, and knocked. For a time there was no response. Then a dull voice said: 'Come in.' The major was sitting with his greatcoat round his shoulders, looking somewhere straight through Fyodor. With a languid gesture, he interrupted Fyodor's attempt to report according to regulations.

'That's enough. Sit down.' And immediately, without any expression on his face, drily, as if by rote, his glance sinking deeper and deeper within himself with every word: 'The Organs, Samokhin, are the vengeful sword of the Revolution, the eyes and ears of our party. The internal enemy is now active at our rear in

141

concert with the external enemy; the achievements of the Great October are under threat. The international hydra has taken it into its head to reimpose a tsar, merchants and capitalists on our working class and our toiling peasants. In a word,' he concluded matter-of-factly, and for some reason he nodded at the portrait of Dzerzhinsky hanging solitarily above his head, 'keep your eyes peeled. Everything that happens here is a military secret. Whatever you see or hear, forget it immediately. Put it out of your head. Any loose talk, and you'll be up before the tribunal and the heaviest sentence is death by shooting. Is that clear? As for your duties, Nosov will fill you in. Go and see the doctor now, the door opposite. You'd better have an examination for form's sake. Carry on.'

Even before he saw her, more precisely from the moment Nosov had mentioned her, he had felt a mixture of vague alarm and certainty that something unexpected was about to happen. And as soon as he did see her, his presentiment became stronger and turned into reality: a tall woman of about thirty, with a build appropriate to her height, watched him with a look of mocking authority on her strongly but pleasantly modelled face. Her dark hair, held in a bun high on her head, covered her stubbornly borne head like a crown.

'Strong as an ox,' she smiled, removing the stethoscope from his chest. 'You can get dressed. You'll live for years, soldier, you'll live to be a hundred, unless you die on the way. You're obviously from the country.' Her mocking tone was not offensive, on the contrary it was very engaging and made him want to talk. 'Where do you come from, what region?'

'Tula.' Involuntarily he had been infected by her tone. 'We're known as samovar-makers.'

A wave went through her whole body and her face shone confidently, revealing two childish dimples on her cheeks and another on her chin: 'All right, you may go, samovar-maker. Serve the Soviet Union. You're a bit too young to be visiting doctors, but call in to see me if you see the light. You could die of boredom here, as God's my witness.'

She ran her hand across his close-shaven head indulgently, as if he were a child. And this mechanical gesture aroused such a hot wave of childlike gratitude in him that he rushed headlong from the room, afraid of bursting into tears.

Nosov rushed to meet him, dancing impatiently about; the lad was obviously bursting with curiosity: 'Well?' He nodded in the direction of the house. 'A fine pair, a ram and a cow, eh? They deserve each other. They're like cat and dog, but they don't show it. There's something between them from long ago, from before the war I think – some row.'

Screwing up his eyes with their pale lashes, he looked inquiringly at Fyodor.

'I bet she asked you over. Don't get involved – you'll get your wings burnt. There have been lots of others here before you and they've all ended up at the front in no time at all. Our major's a hard master, he gives you a soft bed and a harsh awakening. Let's go and see the mechanic instead – it's more fun with him, even if he is completely off his head . . .'

They went round the house, crossed the terrace and went through a back door to a shaky staircase which led them to an attic full of piles of summer lumber. The whole mass of broken furniture, dusty rags and cobwebs had an air of decay and desolation.

'Leonid Petrovich,' Nosov called cautiously, winking conspiratorially at his companion, 'are you asleep?'

In the far corner, to the right of the only window, there was a screech of straining springs, and a tousled faceless head appeared in the shade of the window. Gradually getting used to the half-darkness, Fyodor distinguished swollen or perhaps just flabby lips in the dark patch of this head, framed in a week's stubble, and above them a potato-nose and the sunken fireflies of the man's eyes. Even before he spoke, Fyodor caught a strong whiff of alcohol.

'Oh, it's you Nikolai, come over here.' The head disappeared into the darkness and again the springs screeched heavily. 'I think there's a bit left – we'll polish it off.'

When Fyodor's eyes had completely got used to the dusty darkness he made out an old backless settee in the corner under the window, covered haphazardly with an army blanket. On it there sat a very drunken man with a half-empty bottle in his hand.

'Is this the next one?' The lips parted in the stubble in a sombre grin. 'One more experiment, you might say. Well, we'll see, we'll see if you're up to it, dear comrade.' From somewhere beneath him he rescued a battered mug. 'But meanwhile, sit down, dear comrade. We'll water your arrival, so to speak. This is the only mug, so you'll have to get used to taking turns.'

Though there was very little drink it went to their heads slightly, but without loosening their tongues. Of their drunken circle only the mechanic shone abstractedly with visions of times past: 'I remember, in Gori the lads jumped from the bridge,' but clearly, having remembered vividly how the lads had jumped from the bridge in Gori, he considered the subject exhausted, and fell silent until visited by another memory. 'When I saw her there for the first time, in Krasnodar . . .'

Whom he saw when in Krasnodar, his listeners would have to guess. Eventually the mechanic slumped, leaned back against the settee, and a wave of blissful sleep spread across his stubbly face: he was probably remembering another joyful scene from the past, one which had no need of outside witnesses.

On the way back Nosov complained unmaliciously to Fyodor: 'See what a crowd they are? Imagine it, this is the fourth month I've been dithering about here and I can't see an end to it. But I have to admit working here's an easy number: stoke three fires and keep an eye on the engine, there it is, under camouflage at the side of the little haystack.' Fyodor looked in the direction he pointed: at the other end of the clearing, on the edge of the wood, a solitary crop-sprayer stood under camouflage netting. 'They bring food from the village and do our washing there too; in a word, you can sleep away your days – you can survive it. Why should I go off back to the front? I'm no longer enough of a fool. You do the tour of inspection a couple of times tonight, then you can sleep in as long as you like. Tomorrow it'll be my turn . . . Only who are we supposed to be guarding it from – there's cordon after cordon for miles around.'

Late that evening, Fyodor went out to do his first tour. The autumn darkness was getting denser and thicker, the air was getting colder. From time to time a star broke away from the frozen firmament somewhere, spiralled across the sky and disappeared into the nocturnal blackness. All around there was a sense of peace, the profundity of life and restful calm. It seemed inconceivable that somewhere close by there was the front in what was perhaps the major war of the century.

'Just your luck to end up here, Fedya,' he thought, going over the day's events in his mind. 'Take care you don't lose your head!'

5

A period of bright weather set in, with early frosts, thaws in the midday sun and chilly fogs in the evening. Fyodor's duties really did turn out to be very simple. At dawn he would grab a quick bite to eat and set off for the woods, where he chopped up dead trees for firewood, loaded it up and lit two fires in the big house, one for

144

the major and one for the lady doctor. Then he would go and doze away the time till lunch at his guard-post. While Fyodor was busy with his duties, the major and the doctor were both still asleep. Then he was asleep. By the time he woke up, they were both already shut away in their own part of the house, and therefore after two days at the objective he hadn't really seen them properly, let alone had the chance to talk. In the evenings, as he made his tour, Fyodor spent some time looking through the doctor's lighted window, but however much he cajoled himself, he could not bring himself to go in.

'She's out of your league, Fedya,' he insisted, resisting the temptation to look into the beckoning abyss, 'all she'll do is make fun of you.'

On the morning of the third day, returning from the woods, he bumped into a black-haired lad, little more than a boy, in a sporty suit and canvas shoes without socks, at the porch of the big house. The boy greeted him busily and ran down the steps, concentrating on his morning exercises. 'Your PT won't help you,' Fyodor grinned, looking at his puny, even feeble body. 'You'd do better asking your mother to give birth to you again.'

For once the major was in his office. The mechanic was there too, this time clean-shaven and wearing a worn-out but elegant leather jacket, under which he had a brand-new field-shirt with sergeant's triangles on its blue tabs.

'Listen, Samokhin.' For the first time the major looked at him with intelligent appraisal. 'From now on you're getting instructions from Lyalin. Every word of his is your command. From now on we're in a state of total military alert at the objective. Is that clear? Carry on.'

On the way the mechanic frowned, his face bearing evident traces of hangover. He spoke jerkily, angrily.

'He's off his head, the old fart. Help me fill up this old petrol can,' he nodded in the direction of the plane, 'and that'll be the end of your total military alert, dear comrade. You can leave the rest to me.' Pottering indolently about near the plane, he went on swearing and grumbling quietly. 'It's not just a case of being afraid to cross enemy lines in it. I'm almost frightened to breathe in it in case it falls to pieces. Konashevich is crazy, that's why he flies it. He'd even fly in a sewing-machine. They've found themselves a fool and they're making use of him. Go on, soldier, don't get under my feet. Why don't you go and have a drink with Nikolai – you'll be more use there.'

'I've been given an order, so I'm getting under your feet,'

Fyodor replied, offended. 'There are lots of orders and only me to take them.'

The mechanic turned round to face him, frowned guiltily, and said quietly, sadly, as if for his edification: 'You have to understand a fellow when he's hung-over, soldier. A man in such a state is not himself, a man in such a state soars in rebellious spheres, his spirit thirsts for destruction . . . Listen!' He suddenly started: not far away, in the middle of the forest, they heard the spluttering of an engine. 'Another coffin on wheels taking Konashevich to the slaughter.'

The truck which Fyodor already knew emerged on the road which led from the woods. It coughed its way to a halt in front of the porch of the guard-post. A man dressed in leather from head to foot jumped out and rushed towards them across the field.

When he was still some distance away, he began to wave his pilot's helmet over his head. 'Lyonya!' he shouted, 'Don't worry, it'll get up, the plywood is very light! Hallo, Lyonya!'

The appearance of the visitor had a startling effect on the mechanic: his eyes lit up, he straightened his back, and some vestige of colour came to his sunken cheeks.

'With you in it, Vovchik, it'll fly even without the plywood. Good to see you!' Lyalin rushed to meet him, they embraced, and still embracing, began to slap each other clumsily. 'We'll warm it up a couple of times, and it'll go like a dream – we've managed it with worse.'

'You and I haven't had a drink for ages, Lyonya,' the visitor chuckled contentedly. 'When I get back we'll get stuck in – we'll get drunk as lords!'

'Completely plastered!'

'Out of our skulls!'

'Totally legless!'

'Paralytic!'

'Pissed as newts!'

It obviously wasn't the first time they had played this game, which seemed to have a special significance known just to the two of them, which only made them fall about with laughter even more.

'Till we start seeing little green snakes.'

'Crawling green snakes!'

Then the three of them sat in the guard-post, whiling away the time drinking tea, while Konashevich generously entertained them with his amusing banter: 'The lads in the regiment are pissing hot water: we've got some new machines. The old ones are being sent

to the Turkish border. Maybe we're really going to start fighting at
last. So far we seem to have been playing to lose – only burying
people. And what people! Ace cadres being turned into fertilizer –
it makes your heart bleed!' Suddenly he darkened and his face
grew cruel. 'Your lot are off their heads too. Where do they think
they're sending these kids? They should still be playing soldiers.
They're taking first-year students – all they have time to teach
them is *ein, zwei, drei, Hände hoch*! It's like shooting peas at a wall
to see if one of them will grow. Well, it won't!' His face became
distorted. 'They'll shoot them all, like partridges!'

Nosov appeared noisily at the porch, his whole bearing
exuding zealous readiness: 'Comrade lieutenant, the major wants
to see you.'

The lieutenant grinned as he got up unwillingly. 'Time for the
sermons. The old devil won't let me get a word in!' And, from
outside, he added, 'Wait for me, lads, I won't be long . . .'

'What a fellow!' the mechanic said, watching him leave, and
raising a finger solemnly. 'We flew together, we fell together, we
escaped from encirclement together. What am I saying, escaped,
he carried me out on his back. I'd follow him with my eyes closed,
wherever you like, through hell or high water. There are only a
couple left like him. They're like mammoths, they're dying out –
soon there won't be any of them left. We should know their worth,
dear comrades.'

'What can you say?' Nosov hastened to agree. As far as one
could see he was ready to agree with everyone and anyone, as long
as it didn't require any duties or efforts on his part. 'The lieutenant
isn't to be trifled with – he's got a head on his shoulders.'

The mechanic grimaced with distaste, narrowed his eyes, and
looked at the soldier as if he were something tiny and almost
invisible.

'You walk around the earth, Nosov, and I ask myself, why?
What is all this about trifles and heads on shoulders? I talk to you
about lofty matters, about life and death, about kindred souls, and
you throw in your clichés. Peasant!' But immediately he softened:
'All right, sit down and listen, though you don't deserve to . . .
Once they shot us down just outside Lvov . . .'

It was a story that was exactly like and totally unlike dozens of
others out of the hundreds which it had been Fyodor's lot to hear
that bitter summer of war. Fact and fiction were closely mixed in
it, with the harsh after-taste of fear, secret shame and elation. In
the story two men made their way towards the rising sun, hiding,
losing their way, retracing their steps, avoiding habitations and

roads as if they had the plague, and the sun shone in their path, scorching, interminable, pitiless. The mourning sun of the start of the war . . .

When Konashevich returned, the field and the wood outside were dissolving slowly in the thickening shadows, the warmth of the earth was rising to the frozen heights already decked in stars: two seasons clashed on the border of day and night, and winter was noticeably the victor.

'He wore me out, the cop,' Konashevich spat in rage. 'He doesn't have anything to do, the pig. Get up, lads, duty calls, in an hour or so we can take off, the bosses are already on the spot . . .'

They walked silently to the plane: the particular gravity of what was taking place made them somewhat solemn. Before their eyes and with their participation a mystery, a secret ceremony, a forbidden rite was taking place. And this rite required of each of the participants a degree of self-restraint and sacrifice, which gave them the sense of taking part in something far more significant than they themselves were.

They were already waiting for them. The major stepped out of the darkness and mumbled: 'It's time, we shouldn't delay. Comrade lieutenant of the air force, are you ready to execute your military duty? Privates Nosov, Samokhin, prepare the fires for landing: in two hours fifteen minutes exactly the plane will be back. Is that understood?'

'Understood,' barked Konashevich, and plunged into the darkness, towards the plane. 'We're not children, and as for the return, the timetable's in the hands of the Almighty.' He then turned to the mechanic: 'Take care, Lyonya, I'm taking off blind.'

And he blended into the winged silhouette.

'Dig out some drier hay,' Nosov whispered to Fyodor. 'I'll get some brushwood, we'll spread it around the edges, sprinkle it with petrol, and we'll get a good blaze. Go on, go on,' he chuckled quietly and with what struck Fyodor as special significance, 'don't be afraid.'

But no sooner had he distinguished the scattered patch of hay in the dark of the forest than two intermingled voices swam out towards him.

'It was the first time for me, Polya, I swear it . . .'

'I know.'

'Can one know such things?'

'Yes. I'm old, I know everything.'

'What do you mean, old? Ten years is nothing.'

'Oh yes it is! It's only now you think it's nothing, while you're still young. When you get older, it'll be the first thing you notice.'

'I still won't forget you, Polya.'

'Thank you, my dear.'

'I'll come back to you.'

'Come back, I'll wait for you, come back without fail, who else would I wait for . . .'

'Is that true, Polya?'

'It's true, it's true, Misha, it's the absolute truth . . .'

The major's voice rang out in the night: 'Lieutenant Gurevich, are you ready? It's time.'

There was a rustling of hay in the dark: 'Ready, comrade major! . . . Goodbye, Polya, it'll be a long time this time, till the end of the war.'

'Goodbye, Misha, take care. You only live once.'

'Only for you, Polya, only for you. Wait for me . . .'

At first Fyodor froze, then something in him broke and a burning sensation strangled his throat. Even yesterday, vaguely sensing what had just happened, he had still not expected that it would happen so suddenly, so close at hand, with such humiliating banality. 'So that's how these things happen,' thought Fyodor, feeling as if he was suffocating. 'So it really can happen that easily!'

He heard the rest through a furious noise in his ears and a slight dizziness.

'Propeller!'

'Engine!'

'We're off!'

To a whistling of air and the whirring of the propeller, the winged shadow shot out over the glade, lit by the new moon. It sped away, getting smaller and smaller, and the next moment, juddering, it disappeared over the ridged edge of the wood. Soon unmitigated silence reigned again over the night.

And only after this an indulgent note entered the dull voice of the major: 'All right, lads, meet the plane when it comes back and you're free. Sleep till lunchtime if you want.' And suddenly his voice became thin, almost plaintive: 'Comrade Demidova, where are you going, wait for me! . . . Polina Vasilevna! . . . Polina Vasilevna! . . .' His voice became duller as he walked away. 'Polina! . . .'

Standing near Fyodor, Nosov rustled the hay, puffing, spitting, muttering; finally he blurted out: 'She's gone off with Lyalin, much good may it do her. All he's interested in is drinking. That's the way it happens every time. The major chases after her – she runs away from him. She's not a woman – she's a witch. She twists our lads round her little finger, she captures them with her potions, but she's not that special, the one good thing about her is her figure. There's a lot of flesh on her, that's all. She takes up with anyone you like, but with the major she's a wild animal. I reckon she does it all to spite him. What happened between them to set it all off I don't know, but it's been going on for some time, that's definite.'

He was silent for a moment, breathing heavily. 'I tell you, Samokhin, don't you swim in her pool – you won't come out of it alive.' And he added quickly, 'Let's go and prepare the beacons. All we'll have to do later is set fire to them.'

But even the work didn't break the obsessive spell for Fyodor: he could still think of nothing else. Throughout his life, he was sure of it, nothing like this had ever happened. Of course he didn't have much experience of life, and so, apart from a few notes passed at school and occasional embraces at parties, he had nothing to look back on in that area. Yet now he felt as if he'd suffered a long and furious beating: his whole body ached, stung, smarted from the hairs on his head to the soles of his feet. Fyodor was shaking from the very thought that someone else could be with her before him . . .

Suddenly the noise rang out of nothing, and then began to hang in the air and grow louder over the forest.

'Light it up,' came Nosov's whispered cry. 'I'll start this end, you start that.'

And off he went. A minute later the glade was illuminated by the dancing flames of several bonfires. In their flickering light the mechanic danced his way obliquely across the field: 'Sound the assembly, brothers, we're going to drink! Konashevich won't let us down. We'll clean out the canteen!'

The sound grew louder and closer, coming down towards them, and finally, lit up from in front and below, the bird appeared over the wood.

Rumbling merrily, it sped towards them, falling sharply on the edge of the clearing; it rocked and its wheels bumped lightly along the grass. Wheezing and spluttering, it taxied towards its parking place and fell peacefully silent.

'Cover up this petrol-can, lads, and let's have a drink!' In two jumps Konashevich was on the ground, wriggling in the mechanic's bear-hug. 'You've probably got frozen waiting for our little drinking-bout.'

Camouflaging the plane took no more than half an hour, after which the whole bunch of them bundled into the guard-post, where the lieutenant took the promised goodies from the rucksack he'd brought that morning: three bottles of pure spirit and a fat jar of stewed meat.

'Organize it, Nosov, that's your job,' Konashevich said tiredly. 'We'll baptize my latest godson and wish him good luck.'

They began quietly, without toasts, as if they were carrying out a duty. After the third drink their souls felt cramped in their chests, their hearts melted, they felt the need to talk. The first to give way to it was Konashevich.

'You might say I'm irrelevant here,' he began. 'I get my orders and I carry them out, but here,' he punched his heart with his fist, 'here I feel pain, as if I'd sent this nestling to his death myself. I can't take it any more, I'm going to stop flying. Let them put me before a court-martial. They can't do more than shoot me. They can't send me further than the front. I'm not a cop – I'm a fighter-pilot. I've had enough! . . .'

But by this time his speech was a waste of time. Each of them was overwhelmed by his own ills. The mechanic, again prey to his drunken visions, returned to his theme: 'I remember my old dead mother – she worked as a secretary in the cleansing department – saying to me . . .'

What precisely she said to him nobody wanted to know, but the amenable Nosov nodded sympathetically each time: 'Of course . . . That goes without saying . . . No question about it! . . . You don't say! . . .'

What was going on around him seemed to have no effect on Fyodor. He drank as fast as the others but without getting drunk, the alcohol only making his imagination more feverish. Some sort of destructive force dragged him there, to the window that shone out in the cold night. And no longer capable of resisting this force, he got up while everyone was talking at once and walked across to the guard-post, across the wood, across the field towards the light that glimmered from the black abyss. And, taking a deep breath, he knocked. And she opened. And letting him in, she ran her hand across his head as if he were a child.

And the world and memory ceased to exist.

6

It lasted until the first snows, until the sharp frosts, until the bitter winter covered everything around with lengthy cold. In the mornings, when after a sleepless night Fyodor dozed in the guard-post, Nosov, busy at his tasks, droned unmaliciously in his ear: 'I told you, you crank, don't get involved. Such fruit is not for your table. In the village there are loads of girls – they throw themselves at you. You can have a new one every day, but ones like her are not for the likes of us – they use us like toys. The bitch is on heat, doesn't know what to do with her body. And if the major finds out you'll be off to the front, and you won't see anything there you haven't seen before. Haven't you had enough of fighting? Give it up, lad, I'm telling you straight, give it up! . . .'

Fyodor realized himself that Nosov was right, that he'd taken on a load that was beyond his strength and would end up crushing him. But as soon as night fell and there, in the house on the other side of the landing-strip, the light went on in the window, he got up like a sleepwalker and made his way there stealthily, to start the whole thing again.

It stopped only with the appearance of the new 'boy', who spent longer than usual at the objective: there was some hitch with the normally well-oiled mechanism of the airlift. Fyodor wandered around in a daze, hanging about in corners, watching with a sinking heart as the light went on and then off at her window, cursing himself for his whim and his weakness, and tormented by jealousy: 'The bitch, the bitch,' he muttered in jealous frenzy, 'the snake in the grass!'

Every time they met, the mechanic, feeling indolent after a drinking-bout, would say to him in a lazy, doleful voice: 'You're not a survivor, Samokhin. You're doomed, you might say. It's like a slow-acting mine with you: sooner or later you'll be blown to pieces. She's pulverized better men than you. You'd do better to drown your sorrows, have another drink tomorrow morning and forget. Tie yourself a sailor's knot in your handkerchief in blessed memory. I nearly got caught myself, I only just escaped her. Listen to your uncle, dear comrade, your old uncle. If you carry on with this it'll be the end of you . . .'

And of course it had to happen that one morning he met them – her and him, the new boy – on the path leading from the woods. Skirting the field, they crossed his path at the edge of the wood; their elbows were touching and from the indulgent trustfulness with which Polina turned towards her companion when she spoke to him, Fyodor realized with a tremor that everything he had heard from her during their most intimate moments was now being repeated word for word to this lad. And the agonizing despair of the last few days suddenly gave way to cold fury: he'd kill her, shoot her like a dog, come what might, he didn't care any more! 'They can't do more than shoot you' – for some reason he remembered the pilot's words. 'They can't send you further than the front!'

After lunch Konashevich finally appeared, and events took their normal course: a meeting, a conversation over tea in the guard-post, preparations for take-off. Fyodor walked off somewhere, had a discussion with someone, looked at someone, but the world around him seemed to exist despite him and what was happening in him. The resolution that now directed him had no need of support or confirmation from outside – it lived of its own accord, purposefully and separate from the rest of life.

Only Konashevich realized his state. Following him out of the guard-post late in the evening, the lieutenant murmured: 'Your eyes are white, soldier, white as anthracite ash. Don't go mad, soldier, why make a delayed drop without a parachute? Your whole life is ahead of you, if you get through the war, of course. Look at yourself in a mirror, your face has turned to shale . . .'

But by now Fyodor was not listening to anyone or anything around him. He had no time left for reflection or discussion: a will far more powerful than reason now ruled his every moment and thought. Above all, as soon as Konashevich had taken off, he had to slip off into the darkness unnoticed, get to the big house before Polina, wait for her there behind the partition which separated the doctor's office from her living quarters, and, as soon as she came in, pull the trigger. The main thing, he told himself, was not to give her a chance to open her mouth: he was afraid that the very sound of her voice might disarm him. 'We have nothing to say to each other,' he kept repeating to himself as he got used to the darkness behind the partition, 'nothing. We've done enough talking – it's too late now!'

Every corner of the room, every object was familiar to him. Whenever he touched anything, some memory wounded him: too much here was associated with her. Groping his way from object to object he reached the belt with the holster fixed to it, hanging above the bed. The touch of the cold steel of the pistol against his palm increased his resolve. 'As long as she doesn't speak,' he felt another tremor, 'as long as she doesn't speak!'

The first thing he heard was the voice of the major, calling her pleadingly; then the rapid and light steps of a woman, which were immediately joined by other tramping steps: 'Polina, stop, it's time we talked.'

'Aren't you fed up of talking, Viktor?' he heard on the porch steps. 'We've been talking for ten years.'

The steps creaked again, but more heavily and assertively: 'This'll be the last time, Polina, I give you my word. This has got to stop sometime.'

The door squeaked briefly. Polina came into the room and called out with malevolent provocation: 'All right, then, come in, Viktor, if it really is the last time. But it had better be, Viktor, because I'm sick to death of hearing it.'

'All right, Polya, all right.' The major was breathing jerkily, with difficulty, behind the partition. 'But let's take it point by point, we're not children!'

'You can say that again! The children, Viktor Nikolayevich, are the ones you're sending to their deaths.' She made no attempt to conceal her fury. 'You've got no kids of your own, so you send off other people's!'

'Think of what you're saying, Polya, I am carrying out duties of importance for the whole state; the motherland has placed its lofty trust in these lads. The party has entrusted me . . .'

'Stop it, Viktor, you're not at a meeting. Your didactic talents are wasted on me. You're full of ideology, Pashin, but you never forget your own advantage. You sent my Borka to his death not for the party but for your own pleasure: you wanted to get your hands on Polka Demidova. Well, you did, Pashin, you got your hands on her, Viktor Nikolayevich. I slept with you because I thought I could plead for Borka's life; but are people like you capable of pity?'

'But, Polya, he admitted his guilt on all counts.' The major clearly had difficulty remaining calm. 'The links with Kosarev's group, the sabotage.'

'He admitted it! As if you didn't know how your people come by their confessions, getting people to admit all sorts of nonsense.'

'Polina Vasilevna, do not forget that you too work for the Organs. Walls have ears, the enemy is on the lookout, and such talk can have very severe consequences.' But he could not keep it up, and admitted guiltily, 'Polya, you know as well as I do that the Revolution demands victims – you can't make an omelette without breaking eggs. He's not the first and he won't be the last.'

'Maybe not for you, but for me he was the first and the last!' She almost moaned. 'And don't try to frighten me, Viktor Niko-layevich. After Boris I fear nothing – there's nothing left in my life and no reason for me to live.'

'All right, Polya, all right,' the major conceded without a murmur, 'I understand, Polya, calm down.'

'Just stop hanging about my feet, Pashin. It won't get you anywhere. Your friends in high places won't keep me near you, I'll get away somewhere or other. I'd rather go with the first man to come along than with you.'

'You're your own mistress, Polya, but why be so ostentatious about it? People can see what you're doing, there's talk.' The major almost begged her. 'It'll pass, Polya, it's just your hurt pride. I can wait, Polya, I can wait.'

'No, Viktor, don't wait, it won't pass! For me any one of them is like Borya: greenhorns whom you're sending to their deaths. There's been no joy in their lives – they've known no love, no women. So let them have an easier end of it. Their deaths will be less painful, and I shan't feel any worse. And stop pestering me. Tomorrow I'll request a transfer to the front, I shan't stay here; and if they don't let me go, I'll lay hands on myself, I'll shoot myself. I can't breathe when you're around.'

'All right, calm down, Polina, lie down. It'll all seem clearer in the morning. Tomorrow we'll talk more calmly.'

'Go away, Viktor, and don't let me ever set eyes on you again.' Her voice had become a frenzied whisper. 'Don't push me too far. If my own life is unimportant to me, then so much the more so is yours; I wouldn't hesitate. Go away!'

The door shut almost inaudibly, and afterwards, in the darkness, Fyodor heard a stifled sob from behind the partition. Polina was clearly trying hard not to burst into tears. His earlier resolve had given way to devastating tiredness and shame. Shame for himself, shame for her, shame for the major, and also for something which as yet he could neither define nor express through a specific concept or word. 'That's all it is, then,' he thought, 'that's all there is to love.'

A light went on behind the partition, swung, and moved closer, illuminating the aperture of the connecting door. Polina appeared in the doorway holding a kerosene lamp in front of her, and the moment she saw Fyodor sitting on the bed with the pistol in his lowered hand, she understood everything. Her tear-stained face immediately sank, became sharp and furrowed.

'Oh, Fedya, Fedya,' she sighed, scarcely audibly, 'what have you done, what is your sin to merit such a burden? Can you support it? . . .'

There was nothing he could say to her. There was no longer any need for words. His throat was stifled by such piercing pity for her at that moment, for her misfortune and her vulnerability, that silently walking past her, he could not stop himself gently running his hand over her hair.

Back in the guard-post, Fyodor found the others out like lights, still sitting at the table covered with the remains of their meal. In the morning he knocked at the major's door with a written request for a transfer to the jurisdiction of the local commandant's office. And the haste with which the major, without looking at him, wrote out a note expressing his agreement made him realize that he had long known all about Fyodor and Polina. 'Nosov,' he realized too late, 'the double-crossing traitor!'

The same truck with the same sergeant-major at the wheel drove Fyodor back across the bare copses. Hemming him into the corner of the cab, the sergeant-major raged, spat furiously and cursed, just like the last time: 'I'm sick to death of it, fuck it, they send you backwards and forwards like a lorry-driver; the moment anything happens they threaten you with the front, the bastards. What do I care about the front? I've seen worse when I drove black Marias. My hair's still standing on end – all marshals and People's Commissars, packed in like sardines. They crapped in their pants as they stood there, fuck them!'

The road led out into a stretch of meadows and there, between the woods and the fields, Fyodor saw Polina for the last time. She was standing among the leafless birches and was watching them intently, screwing up her eyes in the sun. Intercepting her gaze, Fyodor felt a sudden illumination, and stretching out, he said, 'Farewell, Polya, Polina, Polina Vasilevna, comrade Demidova. May God give you what you desire!'

'Hallo, Polina Vasilevna.' He immediately corrected himself, timidly: 'Hallo, Polya . . .'

The windows shook barely perceptibly as far away there was a dull rumbling.

Chapter Ten

1

From above the island looked like a ship, or rather like a large fish which had raised its fins and tail out of the water. As the plane descended the land under its wing grew, spread out, revealing the different shades and colours of its surface, the details of its terrain, the scattered sprinklings of houses and work buildings. Rocking smoothly from side to side, Sakhalin sped towards Zolotarev.

The island greeted him with fine damp rain. From the direction of the sea there was a cloying smell of seaweed. The grass, the leaves, the spikes of the conifers, the roofs – all were covered in sticky drizzle, and everything around looked clammy, damp, swollen.

He was met by a whole band of local big-wigs, among whom a tall, well-built, relatively young fellow had the bearing of a man used to leading others. He introduced himself as Prikhodko, head of the island's civil authorities.

They packed into two old jeeps and set off, as one of the reception committee put it, to 'taste the bread and salt of Russian hospitality'. The road led alongside low buildings that, apart from their flat roofs, looked like barracks. They seemed relatively well maintained, with kitchen-gardens fenced in in front of them.

Looking through the windscreen at this Japanese idyll, Zolotarev grinned involuntarily to himself at the thought of the muddy wasteland it would turn into when the swarm of recruits made up of Central Russian peasants and cut-throats recently released from the disciplinary battalions swooped down on it like drunken locusts.

Prikhodko, who was sitting at the back, seemed to guess his thoughts: 'We're going to destroy these card-houses bit by bit. They're not fit habitations for Russians: they don't have proper stoves and they're not solid enough. You feel as if you're living in a matchbox! Right, we've arrived!'

The tea-room they arrived at was in a little old wooden house which had been darkened by winds and damp. It stood on a hill from which you could see the sea, and had a side entrance for important guests.

During the several years in which he had occupied important posts, Zolotarev had had time to study the ritual of these sessions at table down to the finest detail; but since he did not take particular pleasure in them, he always managed to withdraw from the game in time. It was especially easy for him to do so here, since he was surrounded by subordinates. When, therefore, the solemn toasts were over and the banquet was showing signs of turning into an ordinary drinking-bout, he got up: 'Time for business, as they say. We have a great deal to do, comrades. Let's get down to it. Comrade Prikhodko, explain the situation to me.'

Prikhodko got up obediently: 'As you wish,' he had the sense to reply in the same tone. 'It's time, comrades. Please come to my office, comrade Zolotarev.'

Zolotarev knew from experience what was going through the heads of the drinkers at this moment, but he was not in the habit of taking the moods of his subordinates seriously: they'd survive it, just as he himself sometimes had to: once you'd climbed into the *nomenklatura* you had to put up with whatever entered your superior's head, but you made up for it by crushing your inferiors, and they could compensate for wounded self-esteem in the same way; they weren't children after all. They should know the score!

In Prikhodko's office he immediately sat down behind the boss's desk.

'Well, tell me what's going on here.'

Zolotarev was not interested in hearing about the situation on the islands – he had received all the necessary information before his departure – but it was a rule in such circumstances, an obligation, which he never flouted, to assert one's position by this display of authority, so as to keep one's subordinate in place. And Prikhodko accepted his role in the proceedings without irritation, knowing that in his visitor's place he would have acted in exactly the same way.

'The main problem at present is the resettling of the Japanese. Their presence here is demoralizing for the new arrivals. Then it will be a question of the accommodation, but we'll make do with things as they are for the time being; our people are survivors, those who don't get a place to live will winter in dug-outs. Then there's the food, of course. Deliveries aren't regular, but there too if we have to, we'll survive . . .'

Prikhodko's large body was swaying from side to side, the eyes in his fat face staring obsequiously at Zolotarev. All his serious 'on the one hand's and 'on the other hand's were intended to outwit his visitor, but in fact Zolotarev was hardly aware of what he was saying. Zolotarev was thinking of his youth, of that unique time in every man's life, the visions and dreams, smells and colours, faces and voices of which come back to him for the rest of his days.

The path he had followed from his bitter village beginnings now seemed to him to be utterly inconceivable. How, by whose will, had this lad from Sychovka managed to tread this path without perishing, and without ending up among those milliions who had vanished in the rotting huts of the camps? What, when it came to it, had determined his fate? . . .

'Oh yes, there's something else,' the voice of the local boss pierced his reverie, 'there's a paper come from Moscow, some crazy scheme. By God, you'd think we had nothing better to do with our time here than set up parishes! Take a look at it . . .'

What Zolotarev saw and read stabbed his heart and his head began to spin: so this was his fate; he'd hardly had time to ask the question and here was the reply!

In the paper which Prikhodko had handed him the All Union Council for Church Affairs had instructed the civil authorities to set up a parish in Yuzhno-Sakhalinsk (and whatever the appearances Zolotarev knew that this could not have happened without instructions from the very top), and recommended that priestly functions be carried out by a man already on the island, a certain Matvei Ivanovich Zagladin.

So that was it, that was why life had led him through it all, had caused him so many years of anguish! Just in order to bring him here, to these God-forsaken islands, so that he could meet the witness of his shame, his weakness, his unhappiness, throwing in a meeting with another witness on the way.

He had great difficulty in maintaining his self-control, but he did not betray himself and immediately steered the conversation towards a safe subject.

'The first thing for me to do is to take a look at the town. I can get to know some of the people and take some air at the same time.'

Prikhodko's face lengthened noticeably. With a sensitivity trained in the same sphere as Zolotarev's, and only one rung lower, he realized that he had made a mistake but couldn't for the life of him think what it was, which only added to his misery.

Later, trailing Zolotarev along the town's wooden paving-blocks, he tried to smooth over the awkwardness that had arisen between them with the breath of servility.

'We do make mistakes, of course. Only those who do nothing make no mistakes, as Lenin said. But we learn from our mistakes. Criticism and self-criticism have an honoured part to play here; we make our conclusions and turn to new methods.'

But Zolotarev had no time for him now; his brain was concentrating on a single name – Matvei Zagladin – and everything else had disappeared into a past to which there was no return.

Yet Prikhodko went muttering on at his shoulder: 'We're up to our necks in work; sometimes you work so hard you can't think straight – that's what it means to be a leader of men!' When they were already back at the hotel, he almost shouted at the back of Zolotarev's retreating head, 'Comrade Zolotarev, put yourself in my place – I'm a human being too, you know!'

But Zolotarev slammed the door in his face without a word. Left alone, he lapsed into a dull, almost dreamless sleep.

2

And suddenly he felt as if someone was calling him: quietly, insistently, with sympathy: 'Ilyusha, Ilya, Ilya Nikanorych!'

The voice was very familiar, but somehow listless, like a dead man's. Zolotarev opened his eyes and glanced around the empty room, but seeing no one there he tried to go back to sleep. Yet as soon as he shut his eyes, the voice called out again: 'Ilyusha, Ilya, Ilya Nikanorych!'

By now he was frightened. Trying to shake off the delusion, he dressed quickly and walked out of the building into the night, into the town, no matter where.

A damp starless night hung over the town, a few lights shone in the houses, even the barking of the dogs seemed dull and stifled in the darkness, as if they were lying under wadding.

Only here on the street did Zolotarev realize that the voice he was hearing came not from outside, but from within him. And suddenly in his bursting heart a name arose, a name which belonged to that voice, and its sound was Mariya! As soon as he realized this he was ready for anything.

Sleepwalking his way towards the smell of the seaweed, Zolotarev had no sense of the road beneath him; he walked without a single thought, without aim or direction. A force without name or designation led him, and it was only this force to which he now submitted.

Consciousness began to return to him when, straight ahead of him, at the edge of land and sea, he made out the red patch of a small bonfire. As he walked towards it, he gradually recovered his bearings. 'Amazing,' he thought, 'just like a sleepwalker!'

The dying flames of the bonfire, which turned out to be at a little mooring-stage, lit up the faces of a group of men – geologists perhaps, or fishermen – and the edge of a large boat.

'Good evening, comrades! Enjoy your food.' Zolotarev went up and crouched beside them.

Nobody replied, nobody even turned to look at him. They all went on eating without paying him any attention. Only the one woman among them silently held out a spoon to him.

Deciding that it would be rude to refuse, he moved a bit closer and politely swallowed a couple of spoonfuls of fairly thin fish soup.

They ate carefully, savouring the taste, almost religiously, keeping a hand under their spoons so as not to lose a single drop. The proximity of the sea made Zolotarev find this almost funny.

Only when they had finished, one of them, the oldest, with a narrow pockmarked face, asked him: 'Where are you from?'

'From Moscow.'

'Ah,' the man replied, without particular interest. 'They say there are a lot of people there, isn't that right?'

'Quite a lot.'

'Are you on a visit here or what?'

'On business.'

'Ah,' the man said again, with absolutely no interest, and fell silent.

'Why is your fish soup so thin? You live right by the sea!'

This time nobody replied. Their silent faces swayed in and out of the shadows of the dying bonfire in front of him, and he had no place in this silent rocking; he didn't exist for them, he wasn't there, he wasn't alive.

And once again, with some inner vision which he himself did not understand and which lasted no more than an instant, he suddenly realized that this had happened to him before; yet his memory immediately erased the apparition and he moved off again from the bonfire into the night, into the town, no matter where.

But at the last moment he could stand it no longer: he turned round and choked on his own breathing. The woman at the bonfire was watching him with a long and sympathetic gaze, as if she wanted to see him off with the words: 'Ilyusha! Ilya! Ilya Nikanorovich!'

It was approximately at this time that a new star shone out above the earth. It was difficult at the time to imagine what it portended: maybe the end of the world, maybe the Second Coming. Neither the one nor the other happened. But soon after it was remarked that throughout the country boys and girls were being born who, to the enormous horror of their parents, began to ask questions.

And towards the end of the fifties and at the beginning of the sixties, these boys and girls moved from questions to direct action. So the boys and girls were sent in groups or individually to places not so far away and places in which they tried to turn them into mumbling invalids who would then be registered at their local psychiatric clinics.

But as a rule these measures against them were carried out by other boys and girls, only ones who had been brought up in the best tradition of the eternal principle of 'it's no concern of mine'.

They were extremely civilized people, unlike their parents, who had gone through their drill in very different times. They did not shout during interrogation sessions, and they never – God forbid! – resorted to physical violence; they just asked questions of an official nature, and were particularly fond of heart-to-heart talks.

And one day one of them, tormented by his detective's conscience, in the course of an interrogation asked a girl who had gone out into a square in support of a people who were absolutely remote from her and of whom she knew little: 'But just tell me, why did you do it, why, it's an absolutely useless gesture!'

And the girl replied: 'I did it for myself, or I couldn't have gone on living. That's all I have to say.'

There was a star, and though there were no Wise Men, we now know that that star portended the Coming to us of Conscience.

Chapter Eleven

1

Mid-ocean. Midnight. A sinking steamer. Amid the cries on the rapidly emptying deck, a man is alone with himself. A conversation.
'Who are you?'
'Your fate.'
'What will you tell me?'
'Are you amazed?'
'No, I knew in advance that I was condemned.'
'Do you have any questions?'
'Only one.'
'I am listening.'
'You have taken care to put me precisely on this floating coffin, forewarning me in my youth of the end which awaited me, but tell me, please, why, for what sins, must so many innocent people perish with me?'
'Calm down, I spent twenty years gathering you together from the entire world to put you on this vessel. It was no easy task, believe me!'

2

Fyodor's fragile little launch was chugging along the Kurile chain on the way back to its mooring-stage. The water was calm, with hardly a wrinkle on its grey-blue surface. The sky above was of newly washed blue freshness, the horizon ahead promised clear and fine weather, and only to the side, above the black chain of the islands, were there occasional tufts of smoke. Everything around was fresh, windless, calm.

Fyodor had got used to his new work quickly; his brief experience as a driver had come in useful. In his hands the launch carried out its simple duties efficiently and punctually, taking the post to the isolated settlements, occasionally carrying freight if it was going his way; but most of the time it was at the disposal of the

163

authorities, satisfying the transport needs of local labour camp officials.

Fyodor's island life gradually settled down into a rut and became ordinary, mundane. Seen from here, from the heights of time and space, his village past seemed so distant and illusory that sometimes it seemed as if it had never happened. And only on rare occasions, at night, he would wake up and a delightful vision would suddenly flash past him: the cold night outside on the eve of the Epiphany, the coals turning to ashes in the open hearth, the sour smell of dough throughout the hut, and above it all, through it all, reaching him here through the years and the miles, the intermittent chirp of the cricket. Lord, calm his grief, console his sinful soul!

Behind Fyodor's back, in the dark of the passenger cabin, the carousel of voices was gathering momentum as a drinking-bout began. The island's ruling trinity, Ponomarev, the head of department of the civil authorities, Krasyuk, his deputy for political affairs, and Pekarev, the head of personnel, were returning from a pre-holiday banquet at Paramushir and judging by appearances, didn't intend to stop celebrating for a few days yet. In fact, though, only two of them had been drinking; the third, a hunchback from the special section whose hair was always untidy, was taking no part in the revelry. He had a reputation on the island for never getting drunk, he was omnipresent and all-knowing, and consequently equally hated by everyone.

As usual the bass voice of Ponomarev, hoarse with alcohol, rang out in the drunken din: 'Listen to me Krasyuk, when I started working for the Organs you could still walk under tables without bending over. During Collectivization I boxed the ears of those kulaks almost all over the Ukraine – they won't forget Ponomarev in a hurry, the suckers of peasant blood! I personally shook the hand of the boss of the whole Union himself, comrade Kalinin, Mikhail Ivanych. I held out my hand to him just like I'm doing to you now, only then it was still whole. It felled enemies of the people without mercy and without pity! When I worked in the mobile obstacle construction detachments I saved entire fronts from panic, and General Serov himself pinned a medal on my chest. If it wasn't for that damned mine, who knows what rank I'd have reached by now. And you try to tell me! . . .'

His political deputy, a Ukrainian with a head on his shoulders, kept a cunning grin on his taut face. Without letting the drink make him unduly familiar, he obligingly echoed his boss's tone: 'Experienced cadres are like a stone wall in front of us, Vasily

Kondratych, we do not advance into battle without the old man's orders. We have much to learn from the old guard, we remember Stalin's precepts well, and we cannot survive without you and your experience. We are still young, we must study . . .'

The chief of personnel occasionally righted the conversation, putting in a word or two, without, however, showing any particular excitment or interest: 'What order can there be among the personnel without discipline? Unity of command is our law; without it we are lost, like blind puppies. Everyone must know his place. What would we have done in the war without iron discipline? Thanks to our Leader, who directed our minds and taught us to live.'

Sometimes the conversation died away only to pick up again, soon merging into a general din from which in the end Ponomarev's voice again emerged: 'What's the hurry, special section? Or maybe you don't like our company? It's true what they say – a goose is no friend for a pig. Go on, go on, old man, get some air in your grey cells – they seem to be running on empty at the moment . . .'

A minute later the hunchback appeared at the wheel-house and stood next to Fyodor. He looked straight ahead, huffing angrily: 'They stuff themselves, the devils. They talk the devil knows what, and there's no way of stopping them. A very good example they give to the men! They never do a stroke of work – it's round-the-clock drinking.' He bit his lips and looked at his companion piercingly. 'You, Samokhin, listen if you like, but keep it to yourself, yours not to reason why. Whatever you see or hear is a military secret. Keep your trap shut, as they say, is that clear?'

'It's nothing to do with me,' Fyodor replied in the same tone, only hoping to be rid of him. 'We don't do the drinking, so we won't get the hangover.'

The launch obediently turned towards the shore, the island grew larger, took on different shades; the plume of smoke above the cone of the volcano was making the sky darker and darker, spreading a veil of shadow over the surrounding area, broken only by the occasional flash of light.

'Somehow I haven't liked the look of that stove recently,' the personnel officer muttered as if to himself, quietly, pensively, slowly. 'There's a hell of a lot of soot. Can it really be going to erupt? If it goes up properly we've had it – at least that's its reputation.' A mocking smile flashed across the sharp, stubbly face of the hunchback. 'You're not afraid, are you, Samokhin?'

'If you're afraid of wolves, stay out of the forest.' Fyodor tried again to put an end to the conversation. 'As we used to say at the front: Moscow is behind us, there's nowhere for us to retreat, the order was to stand here till the death!' He slowed the launch down, steering it smoothly to the jetty. 'What will be will be.'

'Well, Samokhin, I see you're not at a loss for words!' He had clearly lost his desire to continue their conversation. 'Everyone's become very garrulous lately. The war's spoiled them. We're going to have to shorten their leads.' The personnel officer watched with particular attention as Fyodor moored the boat, fastened it and switched off the engine. 'You know your job, Samokhin. Well done!' Before stepping off on to the jetty the hunchback turned round once more, stared at him with his stubborn eyes and ordered, 'Lock them in. Let them sleep it off on board, and don't let them appear in public looking like that. It's on your head, Samokhin, do you understand me?'

And without waiting for a reply, he tramped off along the wooden planking of the jetty as if he'd spent his entire life giving orders in all directions.

Fyodor didn't even have to look into the cabin – the sound of snoring spoke for itself. Carefully, so as not to awaken the sleepers, he battened down the hatch, and without waiting any longer he went ashore.

3

Fyodor found nobody at home. He looked in at the Ovsyannikovs, but their door was locked too. Since it was not a working day and there was nobody else whom they could have gone visiting, Fyodor didn't take long guessing where they were: 'Another gathering at Matvei's,' he decided. 'What a way to spend their time!'

Soon after their first meeting in the tea-room, Fyodor had begun to notice that his old folk had taken to making extended visits to Zagladin's pastures, taking their neighbours along with them. At first he had merely laughed at the old couple's whim: anything that keeps them happy! But as time passed he felt more and more often a vague presentiment of crisis in his life, linked in some as yet unfathomable way precisely with his parents' vigils at Matvei's. Sometimes Fyodor even felt the urge to go there himself, to taste the forbidden fruit, to look down into the abyss, but each time he was on the point of going, something inevitably came up which saved him from the frightening temptation.

Now, walking down the spiral path to the coastal meadows,

Fyodor was stil internally resisting, still trying to put down his sudden resolve to simple curiosity, but a will far stronger than his self-justifications told him that the path he was taking today had been predetermined by someone long ago.

In the light of the fine day there was no portent of bad weather or catastrophe. The water along the shore was calm. The usual cloud hung over the volcano, already, it had to be admitted, streaked with black. A light smoke hung over the fields by the shore, over the alder-grove, over the roofs of the houses. Everything was quiet, fresh and festive.

Fyodor's spiritual state as he descended the path made the world seem simple and pliant, his own body almost weightless, his life long and full of promise. 'As long as my old folk keep healthy, I can take care of all the rest!' Even the rats which poked about his feet aroused none of the previous squeamishness or repulsion: 'They too are living creatures – they have their own desires!'

He was still some distance away when he noticed the people gathered round the pastor's dug-out, and going up closer he heard Matvei's voice from inside: '. . . And Moses stretched his hand over the sea and towards morning the sea returned to its place, and the Egyptians ran towards it, so the Lord drowned the Egyptians in the midst of the sea . . .'

In front of him, in the dug-out, lit only by an oil-lamp, Fyodor immediately saw the faces of his parents, Ovsyannikov and, something he had not been expecting at all, Lyuba. The timid flame cast light and shadows upon them, which made them seem not the ordinary faces he was used to seeing in his daily life, but suffused with a sort of special solemnity, as if they were at a cemetery or an important meeting.

'. . . And the Israelites saw the mighty hand which the Lord had raised against the Egyptians, and the people feared the Lord, and believed in the Lord and in Moses, His servant. Then Moses and the sons of Israel sang to the Lord this song . . .'

Matvei stood facing everyone with a large book in his hands and glasses on his nose. There was an unexpected catch in his deep bass voice.

' . . .And they left Elim, and the whole company of the sons of Israel came to the desert of Sin, which is between Elim and Sinai, on the fifteenth day of the second month since they had left the land of Egypt. And the whole company of the sons of Israel murmured against Moses and Aaron in the desert . . .'

Even one day earlier Fyodor would hardly have been able to take these fairy-tales seriously, but the more he heard, the more strongly he imagined this unfamiliar and incomprehensible people who strove with such difficulty where – towards the desert! – and the more he was penetrated by their torment and by their fate, by their misfortune and by their endeavour.

When Matvei finished Fyodor started the climb back, without waiting for his parents, and on the way he kept imagining these men walking and walking, round in a circle, walking and walking.

And so – without end.

'Maybe we too are like that,' he repeated to himself endlessly as he climbed. 'We wander and wander, but maybe one day we'll reach our destination.'

Chapter Twelve

1

One of them was an ordinary Jew from Riga who was allowed to move outside the camp, with the nickname 'Thirty-three misfortunes', and the other was the boss of the camp, a small difference but a significant one, as they say. The Jew had just got through the first five years of his ten-year sentence, and the boss was being promoted to a job somewhere else, also a sort of distance between them. Then again, the boss ate and drank, and the Jew just cleared up after him, but for the rest they were almost friends.

Before he left, the colonel called the Jew to him for a final heart-to-heart.

'Here, have a drink.' He poured the Jew a glass of brandy. 'Don't play the fool, you've earned it: five years and not a single penalty.'

'Thank you, citizen colonel.'

'Tell me honestly – I promise there'll be no consequences – have you ever noticed anything particular about me?'

'If I'm to speak honestly, then yes, citizen colonel.'

'What is it, tell me?'

'You've got one glass eye, citizen colonel.'

'Which one?'

'The left one, citizen colonel.'

'You mangy devil, it's so well-made, I ordered it from the best oculist in Moscow. How did you guess?'

'Well, it looks vaguely human, citizen colonel.'

2

The voice of the Minister of Fisheries was tremulous and humble in the receiver, choking on a torrent of words: 'Comrade Stalin . . . As a Communist . . . As a true soldier of the party, I take it upon myself to liquidate the breach . . . I shall personally fly out to the scene of the disaster.' His voice became a plaintive wheeze. 'I shall risk my life, comrade Stalin . . .'

169

He put the receiver down without bothering to hear the end of it: let him try to get off the hook, the old hog! He knew that after such a telephone conversation the lout would dig the ground with his snout if he had to, but he'd put things right. To hell with them, these natural disasters. The war had hardly finished when they started attacking the country one after the other. It was as if they were in league: drought in the Ukraine, then in Moldavia, and now this *tsunami* or whatever in the Kuriles. And every time he had to fill in more and more expensive holes, which meant readjusting the budget and finding and punishing those responsible. He never managed to get the country securely back on to its feet, so as to take his former allies by the scruff of the neck again. They were naïve enough to believe that he would end up being satisfied by the fat portion he'd got out of the division of the spoils at the end of the war. Think what you like, kind sirs, think what you like, he hadn't spent years fine-tuning this enormous machine, tempting fate and violating all the commandments, so as to be satisfied with a part: all or nothing, and, as the Gospel says, let the dead bury their dead!

He had another cautious look at the Tass report lying at his side: 'From the 10th to the 14th November there was a large-scale eruption of one of the active volcanoes of the Kurile chain. Subterranean tremors . . .' Then there were details which interested him little since he saw no particular point in them: it was too late to stop anything and too late to put anything right. All that remained to be done was to find those responsible, and then start again from scratch. The guilty men would be found, it went without saying. He was never prepared to consider the elements as extenuating circumstances. He knew from experience that you only had to loosen the grip a bit for everyone to start excusing his own carelessness through various subjective and objective causes: the country would drown in a sea of talk. 'If you've said you'll do it, then do it,' he thought, suddenly remembering Zolotarev. His only small regret was that he hadn't had time to see the Tulan at work, to be convinced yet again of his own perspicacity and knowledge of human nature.

He had long ago perfected an instinct for self-preservation which saved him from pointless reflection on any concrete issue. This helped him to take decisions without getting bogged down in details, which in turn facilitated the rapid execution of his decisions: Zolotarev, with his cornflower eyes and his dog-like fidelity, immediately wafted into non-existence, giving way to a new subject, a new name.

170

This name was mentioned in a decree which had been lying on his desk since morning waiting for his approval. This decree, or rather this name, was connected to a story which went back almost forty years and which he felt should now be brought to a suitable conclusion. Adopting with relief a playful tone, he picked up the receiver, dialled a one-digit number and said: 'Come in here, Lavrenty.' For once even his guttural accent seemed appropriate. 'There's business – it's time to have Sergo baptized . . .'

He'd disliked his Georgian accent from childhood – it reminded him too sharply of his plebeian background. He had listened with envy to the fluent speech of his fellows from noble backgrounds for whom Russian was an everyday language. He had noted the ease with which they moved from the rolling Georgian 'e' to the almost silent Russian 'e', pronouncing the alien 'sh' and 'ch' without a single whistling sound. His childish envy of them, of their appearance, of their air of superiority, although almost all of them had the same penurious existence he had – in Georgia, as is well-known, there are three noblemen for every beggar – had developed with the years into a burning, almost insuperable hatred which long after, after the victorious march of the eleventh army through Transcaucasia, he had attempted to assuage. But he had not managed to do so, only gradually cooling it down with the years. And therefore, when the ambitious Kutaisian, David Rondeli, clearly attempting to flatter him, had shot an inane but malicious comedy about two penniless princes from Eristavi, he had showered the quick-witted director with gifts, and he had the film reshown periodically, each time shaking with satisfied laughter. For all his deep-rooted Caucasian contempt for Russians and everything Russian, he still wanted outsiders to take him for a full-blooded Russian, so as to have the right to look down on foreigners and their pitiable attempts to imitate a grandeur that was alien to them . . .

Beria came in, or rather slipped in without knocking, as usual, the lenses of his pince-nez shining merrily at him in anticipation of the coming amusements. Without taking his understanding eyes from his leader, he walked up to the desk and stood by it, but did not sit down, his whole body silently exuding frankness and complicity.

This had long been a favourite game of theirs, which they played from time to time at the expense of members of their close entourage. Keeping strictly to a scenario that had been carefully worked out long ago, he nodded silently to his visitor to pick up the telephone.

Beria carefully took hold of the receiver, his eyes still shining conspiratorially, a wave of amused satisfaction slightly shaking his body, but as soon as he began to speak his voice took on its usual peremptory tone.

'Ready your end? . . . Put me through then.' (He gave a serious cough to settle himself.) 'Good day, may I speak to Sergei Ivanovich, please? . . . Who is this? Really, what curiosity, citizeness! An old friend wishes to speak to him . . . Citizen Kavtaradze doesn't pay for his calls? Dear oh dear, would you credit it. A party member since before the Revolution, a professional diplomat, a man of transparent honesty who adores children, and it turns out that he is a malicious non-payer! We shall punish him, you have my word of honour as a party member, we shall punish him, or at least, citizeness, the central committee of the All Union Communist Party (Bolshevik) will pay his bills.' His tone of voice changed abruptly. 'And now go and get Kavtaradze and look sharp about it. It's the Organs speaking!' Sure that the lady subscriber would fulfil his instruction, he grinned victoriously. 'Sergo! Hallo, Sergo! Who's speaking? No, it's not about the flat, it's the self-education circle. You can send an indent with an order straight away. It's Lavrusha. Don't you recognize me? . . . Now why are you calling me "Comrade Beria"? Lavrusha, Lavrenty, call me what you like, only please, cut the formality. We made the Revolution shoulder to shoulder, and now you're being formal. Stop it! I only found out today – you know how it is – my lads told me, that you've been in Moscow for a whole year. A whole year, Sergo, and you show no sign of life. My dear fellow, you should be ashamed. You're too young to forget your old friends. Soso keeps asking after you: how's Sergo, he says, what's become of Sergo, where is he? Come over today if you're not busy . . . Rubbish! What do you mean, "I've got nothing to wear"? Come as you are. Oh yes, I almost forgot. Soso is embarrassed to ask you himself, but can he come along too? He'd like to see you too – he misses you. The three of us can sit down, without any women, have a drink and a song, simply, man to man. Agreed? Listen carefully, Sergo, at twenty-one hours precisely Sarkisov will call for you . . .'

He did not listen to the rest of the conversation, his thoughts taking him back to the distant past when fate had first introduced him to this lad from Zestafoni. And though he was a scion of a noble family he behaved simply and even with a measure of servility, like an inferior with a superior, missing no chance to emphasize his respect for the experience and the achievements of his elder. The lad was six years younger than he was, and wrote a few verses, but then who didn't in his adolescence? He was eager for work, didn't stop to argue, didn't hesitate, wasn't fastidious and did as he was told, which was why, in the end, he was useful. And so he had used the neophyte skilfully where he hadn't wanted to get involved himself; training him, gradually building up his experience in small things, even taking him with him when later on he moved to *Pravda*. But the intoxication of the successes of October went to many people's heads, including the lad from Zestafoni, who in the excitement of the talk at meetings turned out suddenly to be on the side of Trotsky, hung around Ioffe, hobnobbed with Larin, rubbed shoulders with Shlyapnikov, and after the exiling of his idol ended up, as he might have expected, being put off ship. For years he hadn't touched the foolish fellow, occasionally reminding him of his existence either by a politely discreet notice from the police concerning the legality of the registration permitting him to live in Moscow, or by a chance invitation to 'come down to the station' over an alleged infraction of the traffic laws, or even – this was his harshest measure – by the mention of his name in the latest article on the history of the struggle of the party against oppositionist factions. And so, blowing hot and cold on the poor fellow for almost thirteen years, he had reduced him to a complete human nonentity, after which, acceding to Lavrenty's request, he had readmitted him to the party and got him a job in the Ministry of External Affairs, with occasional brief errands to do abroad. But then he had again changed the temperature: he had kept the obdurate fellow without work or food for a whole year, living in a communal hen-house on the edge of town. And now it was time for his final trial . . .

'Listen, Lavrenty.' Changing the subject totally, he returned to the question of the Kuriles. 'Your Zolotarev was not up to the task. He has made errors. He wasn't able to tame the elements.'

Beria understood his hint, his half-glance, his half-expressed thought; he immediately stood to attention: 'It was my fault, Soso.' Speaking in Georgian, the semantics of which allowed a certain familiarity, Beria cautiously tested his mood. 'I haven't been able to trace the idiot, but don't worry, the scoundrel will answer for all he has done. He won't get off the hook.'

'You can do that later . . .' He stopped him with a condescending gesture, returning to his previous mood. 'You'd do better to think about our baptism. Arrange it so that he'll never forget it and tell his grandchildren and great-grandchildren about it. If we're going to baptize him, we may as well do it properly!' And he immediately interrupted his visitor's feeble attempt to continue the conversation. 'Go on. I'll come over later . . .'

Then once again he retreated into himself, into his solitude, into his old man's visions. He couldn't come to terms with the idea that his life was rushing down a slope, that the end was near and that the chimeras of the past, which had plagued him so much in recent years, were rising from the ashes of his own disintegration. Because it seemed such a short time ago, only yesterday perhaps, that he had been sitting with that very same Sergo Kavtaradze in the airy cellar of a Batumi tavern, talking to him about women, Kakhetian wine, foreign countries and many, many other things, which it was impossible to recall after so many years. Drunk with wine and youth, his moist eyes flashing in the half-darkness, Sergo stretched his whole body towards him across the table and insisted with passion: 'Because we won't die, Soso, we won't die. That's not for us, you'll see, Soso, we won't die!'

And laughing happily he had retreated into the semi-darkness and his eyes, moist with drink and youth, had flashed once more . . .

Outside, the shadows of winter were getting stronger and colder, increasing the number of the city's lights in the distance. His gaze again chanced upon the white *Tass* announcement at his side, and lingered upon it involuntarily. 'What the hell!' Such was his irritation, he almost muttered something really obscene. 'I'm sick of the sight of it!'

He jerked open the top drawer of the desk, violently swept the miserable piece of paper into it with his sleeve, and slammed the drawer shut. The decree, which was still lying in front of him, he folded carefully in four and stuck in the side pocket of his field-jacket.

3

Late that evening his car silently entered the courtyard of a faceless apartment house on Insurrection Square. From inside, the house looked just as faceless, but smaller, though the convenient arrangement of flats and service buildings was attractive. On his rare visits here he noticed every time the house's similarity to a small fortress: all the windows looked out on to narrow passages; along the Sadovoye ring-road, where it was possible to set up a cordon of fire, there was an unbroken brick wall; at the rear of the courtyard there was another unbroken wall six storeys high, but the most important thing of all, which he had noticed immediately on his first visit, was the Radio Committee building straight opposite, at the end of a narrow alleyway. 'He's dug himself in, the son of a bitch,' – as usual caution scorched him – 'it's as plain as the nose on your face that he's waiting for his time to come, the jackal. He's found himself a cosy place right near the microphones!'

Clearly illuminated by the light of the open door, Beria was already rushing down the steps of the low porch to greet him.

'He's waiting. Our dear friend is waiting for his godfather.' His host took him carefully by the elbow and, trotting alongside, led him towards the house. 'He just can't wait to see you, believe me, his cheeks even look a bit pinched.' He took his visitor's uniform coat and then caught him up, squinting merrily at him from the side through his pince-nez. 'As they say, the baby's ready, all we need now is to immerse him. This way . . .'

The table was laid for three; it flashed and glowed with crystal, nickel, food. The starched white of the table-cloth and napkins bristled severely. The windowless room was plunged into the warm glow of a fringed lampshade hanging low over the table, and in consequence everything in the room – the furniture, the pictures, the door-curtains – seemed hazy and unsteady, as if seen through misted glass.

'There he is, there he is, the little godchild, trembling like a schoolboy who's just done something naughty.'

The host nimbly overtook his guest, sped across the room and pulled back the door-curtain. 'Come through, Sergo. Don't be shy! Soso's here – he wants to see you.'

A faceless hunched figure appeared in the doorway opposite, started to rush towards him but suddenly stopped, bending almost double in greeting.

'Good evening, Iosif Vissarionovich . . .'

'Stop these formalities, Sergo.' His host was already nudging him forward, grinning, his pince-nez flashing. 'Soso has come to see you as a friend and you address him officially – it's not right. Go on, go on, don't be afraid, he won't bite.'

And the nearer Sergo got to him, the less comfortable the visitor felt: suddenly he recognized in this hunchbacked old man, who was, moreover, six years his junior, his own reflection. And though thoughts of old age had dogged him for years, it had never occurred to him that things had gone this far and that age had already played such a foul trick on him. He needed a certain effort of imagination to recognize in this gelatinous ruin the smart young fellow in Batumi with the broad white-toothed smile and the moistly flickering glance. 'No, he clearly spares no one, the reaper.' In his thoughts he concluded their conversation in the tavern all those years ago. 'He sweeps up everyone without exception.'

Sergo approached him as if walking on thin ice: before each footfall he instinctively tested the floor under his feet with his sole. His woollen suit, which had gone shiny from being cleaned too many times, was so ill-fitting that he might have borrowed it from someone else, his old-fashioned tie hung outside his ancient shirt like a noose, and his carefully cut but thinning hair scarcely hid his balding skull – a dull approximation of a man, a careless copy taken from a ruined gambler, a yellowing negative from their common past.

'*Gamardzhoba* Soso!' the man looked at him with a hunted air, obviously trying to tell from the expression on his face what distance it was essential to maintain between them during conversation. 'Hallo, old friend!'

'*Gagimardzhes, gagimardzhes*, Sergo.' He opened his arms in an embrace and patted him lightly on the back to calm him down. 'Come on, now, Sergo, come on, be a man . . .'

The woollen jacket was thickly spattered with dandruff, and he stepped back fastidiously, suddenly recalling with a sullen malice the French proverb about the guillotine as the best remedy for such a problem.

No, he felt no pity for this exalted chatterer, who had dared at a difficult moment to join the camp of his political enemy, but he considered that every rule can be maintained for a long time only by admitting exceptions, through which it acquires even greater and more consistent ineluctability. And let the man who gets the lucky ticket rejoice, especially if he's a former friend.

But the host was already busy at the table, shaking with mischief, his hands hospitably outstretched: 'Dinner is served, dinner is served, dear guests. As the old Russian proverb says, a nightingale cannot be fed on fables . . .'

'Pour us a drink, Lavrenty.' He was in a hurry, eager to reach as quickly as possible that unfettered state in which words become confident and easy, and listeners compliant. 'I'll have some Isabella.'

Then, throughout the meal he watched attentively as the guest grew more and more helplessly drunk. On the basis of uncon-nected, almost imperceptible, details of his behaviour he tried to create a complete picture of this man who was linked to his youth, but the moment the familiar traits seemed to be fusing into a whole they immediately crumbled, revealing again the approximate carcass, the skeleton, the outline of a face covered in flabby senile skin.

'Do you remember, Sergo,' he was swept along by malicious curiosity, 'do you remember our tavern in Batumi?'

Caught in the attention of two pairs of eyes as if in two interlocking beams of light, he darted imploring glances at each of them in turn, prattling with drunken emotion: 'Of course, Soso, of course I remember, how could I ever forget. Oh youth, youth, golden time! . . .'

But in the guest's sclerotic eyes, where fear lurked only slightly weakened by drunkenness, he unerringly read something different: he doesn't remember, he doesn't remember anything, but he'll agree with everything in advance so as to save his skin one more time. Good God, to think that this breed of humanoid hares once threatened to overturn the whole world and put in charge of the resulting bedlam an orphan Jew from Kherson!'

All of a sudden he again remembered the frank ardour in the blue eyes of Zolotarev. He compared the visitor with the fair-haired Tulan, and the comparison was not to the advantage of his old friend. 'Perhaps I should test him one more time.' He vacillated for a moment. 'Who knows, maybe he'll come good. Once bitten, twice shy, they say.' But aloud he said, sweeping away his doubts and paying no attention to the logic of the conversation: 'Your Zolotarev has made a mess of the Kuriles, Lavrenty. Whipping is too good for him.' And after a short pause he added, 'There are crowds of men, but there's no one any good. Sing us a song, Lavrenty.'

The host coughed obediently and, half-closing his eyes, began in a soft little tenor voice: '*Chemo tsitsi*, Natella . . .' The guests took up the second line in harmony, and for a while the song united them in shared languor and yearning. They were not remotely interested in the Georgian girl Natella, in her love and her cares, but in this girl they now mourned their own fate, their own past, present and future, the ghosts of their vain hopes, their own smallness, their homelessness, their loneliness. Where are you, where are you, Natella, longed-for spectre, unattainable horizon, unquenchable thirst?

The moment was approaching for which the whole performance had been arranged. Almost imperceptibly, he gave the host a meaningful nod. The host winked affirmatively and turned expansively to his other guest: 'Listen, Sergo, Soso is embarrassed to ask you, but can he pay you a visit? Soso wants to see how you live, meet your wife. Be a good fellow and invite him. How about it?'

'Yes, yes, I'd be happy to . . . And my wife will be happy.' He was rapidly sobering up, everything within him turned over and went grey. 'Only, well as you know, it's a communal flat – it's crowded with people. We have a single room – there isn't really anywhere to receive guests . . .'

But his host was no longer interested in the guest and his pitiable prattled excuses: 'What are you talking about, Sergo? We're simple people – we didn't grow up in princely mansions. It would not suit us to lose contact with the people. We'll go now.' Advancing rapidly towards the door, he shouted into the dark corridor, 'Sarkisov, get the car!'

4

In the gaps between the curtains at the car's window he saw nocturnal Moscow spread before them, covered in the first frost, decked with occasional lights. He had long since grown accustomed, even attached, to this clumsy city where, with the help of Russian accomplices, he had managed to cherish and effect vengeance against his haughty fellow-countrymen who had once not wished to accept him into their company, and then to return to Georgia in triumph. But even after that he felt more secure and invulnerable here, in Moscow, behind the protective wall of huge masses of people and vast spaces, than in his own country. Consequently he had no love for the land of his childhood: he visited it rarely, in passing, against his will, preferring the solid bulk of the streets that were now swimming out to meet him.

Moscow still bore some traces of the terrible years gone by: there were still the tatters of paper crosses on the darkened windows, and the once solid wooden fences had been reduced to the gnawed stumps of the supports, but the numbered lamp-posts still shone behind their blue panes. He could hardly believe now that exactly five years earlier, at this time of year, Moscow had been drained of blood and was seriously considering throwing herself upon the mercy of her conqueror, while he himself, locked in his study, waited anxiously for news from the Volokolamsk sector: the destiny of the country and his own destiny had then depended on this news. Could he really have imagined during those November days that in no more than four years capricious fortune would place almost half Europe at his feet, forcing the

178

weakened allies to bend their haughty necks before him?

Perching directly opposite him on a collapsible seat, Kavtaradze was breathing with great difficulty, fidgeting, muttering intermittently in his direction: 'Of course my wife will be pleased . . . And how! . . . Only we don't really have anywhere decent to receive guests . . . It's a communal flat – there's scarcely room to swing a cat . . . Of course, the more the merrier . . . I'm not complaining, Soso, I live no worse than others. It's sufficient for me – only there's nowhere to receive guests. It's very cramped . . .'

'Stop playing the beggar, Sergo,' the lenses of the pince-nez flashed in the darkness beside them. 'You are a member of one of our healthy communal collectives, among the people, at its very bosom, you might say. You should rejoice – you're in constant contact with ordinary people . . .'

The car turned off the main road and began to weave its way smoothly through a labyrinth of low alleys: soon it turned into a small courtyard and stopped at the entrance to a wooden wing.

'Be careful, Soso.' Kavtaradze had got out of the car before him and stretched out a hand to support him. 'It's absolutely pitch-black around here. We still live without light like in the war.'

His experienced ear immediately heard the whispered calls and stifled rustles in the nocturnal darkness: the guard was forming a chain around the house. As usual, this anxious bustle provoked in him a sharp sense of his own vulnerability, putting him on his guard at every step, and at the same time reminding him of the fragility and vanity of human existence. 'They encircle me on all sides,' he thought with sudden fury, 'like a wild beast!'

The fan-like light of a torch, held somewhere behind his back, obligingly lit up the ground beneath his feet; heavily he followed its path into the dark abyss of the entrance. A dense bouquet of smells assailed him: the stale odour of the building, the stuffiness of homely decrepitude, a mixture of accumulated dust and rotting sewage. The fan of light under his feet slid up the chipped staircase, climbing from step to step, rushing round corners, until it stopped in front of a grubby door and immediately sought out the rosette of the entrance bell.

'Just a minute, just a minute.' Kavtaradze tried to fumble for the bell, but it seemed to take life and slip from his fingers. 'They're all asleep . . . They'll open up in a moment . . .'

For a long time there was silence, then a door slammed, footsteps were heard shuffling along and a sleepy female voice asked: 'Who's there?'

'Rakhil Grigorevna, please forgive me, it's me, Sergei Ivanovich. Be so kind as to open up,' he implored hastily. 'My wife has a temperature – she probably finds it difficult to get up. Please forgive me.' Then, obviously remembering his companions, he came to his senses and raised his voice: 'Get a move on, Rakhil Grigorevna, what are you up to?'

There was an obvious defiance in the clank of the furiously drawn bolts. The door burst open to reveal the figure of a woman lit by the dull light in the corridor. Her ample body was scarcely covered by a shiny old dressing-gown.

'It's disgraceful!' Her already opulent flesh was swelling with frenzied indignation. 'Your wife has a temperature, so I have to have a headache! You roll up drunk in the middle of the night, you wake up the whole house, and still you have the gall to raise your voice to me. This isn't the end of it, in the morning I'll . . .' Then she stopped short in terror, and growing smaller, huddling up, wasting away, she retreated somewhere to one side, melted away in the depths of the corridor. 'Forgive me, Sergo Ivanovich, I didn't notice the portrait behind you . . .'

Rushing down the corridor after her, he said to her tensely: 'Calm down, Rakhil Grigorevna, calm down! Go to your room and lock yourself in. Don't make a sound.' Before disappearing through a door at the end of the corridor, he turned sheepishly to his guests: 'I'll tell my wife to get dressed. She'll only be a minute . . .'

As he crossed the threshold the guest even felt a moment of timidity, so clumsy did he feel himself to be in his marshal's greatcoat in the middle of this communal kingdom with its bicycles and tubs hanging on the walls and the clutter of trunks and useless rubbish. 'These people live like cavemen!' he shuddered, imagining himself in their place.

At first hardly audible, the voices behind the door at the end of the corridor grew gradually louder and more tense. Finally one of them – the woman's – rang out distinctly: ' . . . Calm down, Seryozha, these things happen. You're overwrought, you've had too much to put up with, but it'll pass. I'll get up now and make us some tea. Have a cup of tea and you'll feel much better . . . You're imagining it . . . Please, Sergei, calm down!'

Winking fawningly at him, his companion tiptoed off in the direction of the voices, opened the door without knocking, stuck his head in the gap and said loudly, but less for the owners than for the man standing behind him in the corridor: 'Just look who's come to visit you! Receive your dear guest, citizeness!' And he turned to him: 'Come in, Soso, we're all friends here.'

The table was laid with lightning speed and a minimum of fuss: Major Sarkisov knew how his superiors liked it. In the chaotic and noisy drinking-bout that followed he didn't get a proper look at Sergo's wife as she fussed helplessly around them and then melted quietly away into a corner of the room between the bed and the cupboard, giving no sign of life until the very end. All that impressed itself upon his memory was her almost birdlike timidity and the jet-black lock of hair with its touches of grey that hung over her forehead.

He hardly got drunk at all, and though rumour had it that he used to swallow special spices before these sessions, he drank on an equal footing with the others, like an honest man, although for the most part only wine. The only sign of inebriation in him was a certain relaxation of his emotional tension and a tendency towards crude jokes. As soon as he felt a slight light-headedness therefore, he took the opportunity to egg on his host: 'Listen, Sergo, I remember you were a brilliant dancer. Bring us back the old days! Dance the *lezginka*!

Already in his shirt-sleeves, with his collar undone and his tie loosened, the man smiled with drunken embarrassment, his rabbit eyes darting guiltily from side to side; nevertheless he did not dare disobey, so he got up, left the table, and circled falteringly round them to his own accompaniment. But even now, after so many years, the elegance, innate musicality, the perfect sense of rhythm and gesture that are inherent in almost all southerners were apparent in his uncertain old man's movements. He floated around in a circle, oblivious to anything but the dance, and dull tears coursed over the swollen bags under his eyes and down his wrinkled cheeks. What was he mourning now, this wretch who was decrepit beyond his years? His fate, his youth, his present humiliation? God knows! 'All right,' the guest made a final decision, 'to hell with him! Let him live!'

Only before dawn, when the faces of the carousers had started swimming vaguely before his eyes against the palisade of bottles of various sizes, did he suddenly recall the purpose of the entire enterprise, and negligently taking the piece of paper folded in four from the side pocket of his uniform jacket, he concluded tiredly: 'Thank you for the evening, Sergo. It's time to go home. But just one thing before I go: will you go to Romania as ambassador?' And shrugging off all possible expressions of gratitude before they happened, he yawned prosaically. 'Do you have a pencil on you?' He waited indifferently while his host rushed around the room in search of a pencil. 'Don't hurry, my dear fellow. Speed, as you

181

well know, is necessary only when catching fleas. Take your time.'
Taking the miserable stub of pencil, he made a show of wetting the
point like a child, signed the paper with a flourish and handed it to
his host. 'Give it to Vyshinsky and he'll put it into operation.' And
immediately he turned to his companion. 'Let's go, Lavrenty, we
mustn't outstay our welcome . . .'

By now he could see and hear almost nothing; he had managed
almost effortlessly to cut himself off from his surroundings. It was
only after getting into the car that he cast a brief glance at his host,
standing at the porch in his shirt-sleeves with his tie loosened, and
gave him a languid, melancholy wave of farewell.

When the car had found its way out of the labyrinth of twisting
alleyways and was making its way noiselessly along the main road,
he suddenly said with sleepy indolence: 'Listen, Lavrenty, you'll
have to get rid of that Zolotarev of yours. It's all very well talking
about the elements, but someone must take responsibility.'

And he leaned back in relief against the seat.

Chapter Thirteen

1

The path which now separated these men from the land of their birth, from the villages, the suburbs and the slums of the settlements which they had left was no longer measured by days and miles but by History and Time. By now this road was thirty, or perhaps three hundred, or more probably three thousand years old.

The stream of the migration to the Kuriles flowed silently into the humming whirlpool of the general Russian Black Days, dissolved into it without trace, like rust in alkali. Furiously torn from her axis, from her foundations, from her pivot, Russia was pouring her human masses into a spiral of year after year of misfortune, following war with famine and famine with war.

Stretching along the roads and paths of a devastated country, they moved off in all directions in search of bread and happiness, stopping occasionally, hastily establishing something resembling a family or a home, only to move on, setting off on their journey again as if in response to someone's call.

On the way, in families, in clans, in whole generations, they forgot about the past and about themselves, noticing nothing around except the earth beneath them; their desert was within them, and they were fated to wander within it to the end of time. And they wandered through it without aim or direction, in the blind hope of sometime stopping for ever and at last finding peace and vision. But the years passed and their mad procession went on and on, with no promise of halt or rest ahead, and the prophet who led them was so far away that it did not even occur to them to attempt to turn to him with the question: until when? And was there really someone ahead of them? It is quite possible that they were walking in a closed circle and among them there were neither sheep nor goats, neither victors nor vanquished, neither leaders nor led, only blind men, each of them unhappy in his own way.

'Vanya, God has brought you happiness.'

'What are you saying?'

'Vanya, do you want to look at your happiness?'

'That is nothing extraordinary, let me rather look at God himself.'

2

The German booty passenger launch, rolling smoothly from wave to wave, was advancing along the Kurile chain . . . Over the straits between the islands there was thick fog, and above it the truncated cones of the low volcanoes seemed to hang in the air. One of them, with particularly gentle slopes, was smoking heavily, darkening the high cloudless sky which was criss-crossed by voracious gulls.

'Now old Sarychev has started to smoke, he'll go on for some time,' Yarygin sighed timidly, following Zolotarev's gaze. 'He hasn't started smoking by chance, mark my words. It's serious this time – it'll have consequences!'

The head of the political section of the regional civil authorities, who never failed to accompany him on his trips round the islands, struck him as a man who had been so terrified by something that he would never get over it. The rumour was that he had been one of the victims of Ezhov, and had had time to drink his fill of labour-camp soup; that just before the war, by some unexplained miracle, he had surfaced and been readmitted to the party, but so as not to tempt fate he had settled down permanently here in the back of beyond. On his perpetually alarmed face, with its sharp wrinkles, there was always a guilty half-smile, or rather the approximation of one, which for some reason made Zolotarev uneasy. 'I can't make him out,' he grumbled to himself. 'Either he's about to kiss your hands, or he's about to bite them off.'

From the very first day he'd arrived on the island Yarygin had dogged his heels, not leaving him for a moment, openly trying to be of use; yet at the same time, for all his terrified caution, there was a certain obviously intentional tenacity in the way he stuck to him, as if he was carrying out some obligatory but extremely unpleasant duty. Zolotarev didn't bother to ask himself whether he was being protected or followed, reasonably concluding that both conditions were the price he must pay for his present situation: if he's been told to protect me, let him protect me, and if they want him to follow me, good luck to him! I wish him well of it!

In fact Zolotarev had no particular duties on the islands: the running of the department that had been entrusted to him was effected through the numerous state and party institutions in Yuzhno-Sakhalinsk itself, but this time he had a special reason to take advantage of a handy pretext – the coming celebration of the anniversary of the Revolution – to come out here. And that reason was Matvei. He had found out somehow that Zagladin was working as a herdsman on this island.

Once again, just as in his dream over Baikal, Zolotarev remembered everything in the minutest detail, and the whole scene passed through his mind and impressed itself on it in a split second. There were two Zagladins at the sidings then – Ivan and Matvei – and they both disappeared the night before Ivan Khokhlushkin was arrested. Matvei was always secretive and he'd evidently got wind of something being up, for he had gone off, taking his brother with him, so as to keep him out of trouble.

Zolotarev had become obsessed with the idea of seeing Matvei again. He was drawn to the island of Matua, where Matvei lived, as a sinner is drawn to the witness of his fall. And although he was aware of the danger such an adventure held for him, especially in the presence of such a watchdog, he still decided, on the pretext that it was essential to visit the new arrivals on the occasion of the revolutionary festivities, to set off for the islands.

Now they were returning from a meeting at Yuzhno-Kurilsk, skirting island after island approaching Matua. The sea ahead of the prow of the launch was calm, the weather on the islands showed no sign of anything unexpected, and everything led him to assume that their time on land would be uneventful.

'What are you saying, they all smoke around here!' He tapped his companion condescendingly on the shoulder. 'If you're afraid of wolves, stay out of the forest.'

'But look, Ilya Nikanorych.' His familiarity had unnerved Yarygin, but he was not prepared to agree with him. 'The smoke has traces of black.'

'They all have traces of black,' Zolotarev retorted. 'We'll get through the winter!' Yet he listened cautiously to the imperturbable silence of the island as it sped towards them.

The island fell away towards the sea in smooth terraces thick with alder, and the settlement seemed to be clambering up it to storm the smoking peak of the volcano. Most of the buildings were still of the local Eastern type, light little flat-roofed structures that looked like starling-boxes surrounded by neat fences, but in places this fragile, almost cardboard, kingdom had already been invaded by the first of the five-walled huts of central Russia; the heavy tread of Russia was slowly crushing the airy ornament of the Japanese architecture.

But, strange to relate, the nearer the launch got to the coast, the more the surroundings seemed bleak and inhospitable: a swirling opaque fog, getting thicker and thicker, was crawling over the water, veiling the portholes. And soon, through this wadding, through the silence that was settling in around the launch, through the planking, from the direction of the island, Zolotarev heard a sort of muted, sleepy rumble, which for the first time really alarmed him. 'You never can tell – maybe it really is about to erupt!'

'Do you hear?' Yarygin stood stock still, tense and alarmed. 'I'm telling you, there's a reason for it snorting like that!'

'It's too early to sound the alarm,' Zolotarev snapped angrily, venting his own irritation on his companion, 'it hasn't erupted yet – if it does, we'll take measures.'

'Oh, Ilya Nikanorych, dear comrade Zolotarev!' his companion suddenly blurted out, 'It's as if you didn't know our customs. If something happens they'll find a guilty man – it doesn't matter that it's a natural disaster. And once again they'll begin with the pointsman. Once again Yarygin will have to pay . . .'

'Life has clearly crushed the fellow – he's a broken man!' thought Zolotarev, his heart sinking. 'Only who'll be asked to pay is not yet clear; maybe it'll be him, and maybe it'll be you, Ilya Nikanorych!'

Zolotarev had long since got used to the idea that his life was like a sapper's, that his every step could be his last; there were too many fatal traps scattered about the field in which he had once decided to seek a favourable wind, and besides, he had now walked so far in that there was no longer any sense in turning round. And yet every time a new danger loomed his heart began to sink in his chest.

'It'll pass,' he said recklessly, more to calm himself than Yarygin, 'and if it doesn't, then we'll be responsible. We won't be the first and we won't be the last.'

The sailor on watch looked down into the cabin and without bothering to conceal his mischievous scorn, he grinned: 'It's too rough along the coast, comrade Yarygin.' Despite this he was for some reason looking at Zolotarev. 'We can't get near the jetty, you'll have to take a little rock in the dinghy, get some air . . .'

And then he disappeared, leaving the hatch wide open. Cursing silently, Zolotarev walked towards it, Yarygin speaking hurriedly and pleadingly at his shoulder: 'It's close by, Ilya Nikanorych, only a stone's throw. Of course if you're not used to it, it does rock a little . . .'

On deck they had to grope their way about: damp darkness had swaddled everything around and the sticky, slightly sulphurous air made breathing difficult. It was as if some force were slowly dragging them through an enormous smoky aperture, at the end of which a furnace grumbled and bubbled with lava. 'Just my orphan's luck,' he muttered irritably while the strong hands of the watchman helped him into the dinghy which kept slipping away, 'to have all my disasters at once!'

The surge, which in the open sea was scarcely perceptible, reared like a mighty wave as they approached the bay, its lacy foam slapping against the sides of the small boat. The silhouettes of the oarsmen were hardly visible, the helmsman's voice sounded long and hollow, as if from the bottom of a well.

'Starboard, row, port, lift oars! . . . Starboard, row, port, back the oars! . . . Sinkov, back the oars! . . .'

At first they couldn't moor and the little boat bounced past the jetty several times, almost crashing against its tarry piles. After three failed attempts they finally made fast, and immediately someone's obliging hand loomed down to help the bosses disembark: 'Comrade Zolotarev, hold on tight! Don't be embarrassed – we Kurilites are a tough lot!'

Sensing the firm planking of the jetty beneath him, Zolotarev was about to give a sigh of relief, but almost simultaneously he felt a brief tremor beneath his feet: the earth was responding to a dull rumbling within the island. 'It goes from bad to worse,' he thought, weakly gripping the arms stretched out to him, hardly distinguishing faces and voices – 'out of the frying-pan into the fire.'

The last one to appear, right by his elbow, was a dishevelled hunchback in a semi-military cap, and staring at the visitor with his piercing eyes and sharp, stubbly chin, he looked him up and down: 'We've been waiting for you for some time, comrade Zolotarev. There are a number of urgent problems. You know as well as I do: everything comes down to the quality of the men, and that's just where we have problems. All sorts of seekers after easy money and a good life have rushed to the islands like moths to a flame, but they're no use at all – they're just eating-machines on two feet, but what we need, comrade Zolotarev, is a few more demobbed soldiers – then we'd move mountains!' The hunchback wouldn't leave him alone, angrily panting alongside him. 'I've been in charge of men for twenty years, so you might say I'm familiar with the problem. You can't pull the wool over my eyes – I know more about my workers than they know themselves . . .'

Fate itself had sent this gnome to get Zolotarev off the hook:

187

now he could find out all about Matvei without attracting the attention of the others. Zolotarev would have been incapable now of explaining properly even to himself why, for what reason, to what end he had been so determined to take at look at this distant acquaintance, but this need of his was so much stronger than the arguments of logic or reason that he no longer had the strength, the capacity to stop himself in his risky enterprise.

'You pose the question correctly, and we'll work it out together, before leaving the cash-desk, as they say.' He was eager not to miss the chance that had been presented to him. 'We'll put our heads together and find a way out of the situation, comrade . . . Forgive me, what's your name?'

'My name is Pekarev, . . . Mikhail Faddeyevich.' The hunch-back's sharp voice even broke with mortification, so absurd did it evidently seem to him that there were still people in the world who did not know who he was. 'I've been in the Organs since 1925, always in the special section.'

'Oh yes, I've been told about you,' Zolotarev had the wit to reply immediately, soothing the hunchback's hurt pride. 'Very pleased to meet you. If it's urgent, I am ready to take a look at your problem straight away.'

The man turned his stubbly chin towards him again and, pushing open a door marked 'Civil Authorities,' he pierced him with his probing eyes: 'As you wish, comrade Zolotarev, as you wish. My files are always completely up to date – I can give you any information you need instantly. Only it is our custom to start by welcoming our guests, especially since it's a holiday. I think you're going to have to accept our bread and salt.'

And walking round Zolotarev, the hunchback went off along a wide corridor, signalling to him to follow.

3

In a separate corner of the café where the local labour camp administration ate, things began almost officially: they drank small measures and spoke with restrained solemnity. The order of the toasts went strictly according to rank, from the most senior to the most junior; this was appropriate to the content of the speeches, which were strictly monitored by the man who was presiding, a peasant of about forty with one arm longer than the other, dressed in a uniform jacket without badges of rank but with a shining row of medals.

'Quite correct, Krasyuk, you have shed light on the situation. You have gone straight to the nub of the issue, the very essence, you have explained the position correctly, but you have slightly exaggerated the difficulties and thus underestimated the role of the masses. When the time comes we shall trim that Sarychev's horns – we've done harder things in our time!'

He shook his shaggy greying head imperiously towards the other end of the table. 'Now you, Golovachev, it's your turn. A young man can always make his way here. Tell the comrade from Moscow, in the name of the Komsomol, about our successes in our work. Tell him with feeling, with good sense and without haste – after all you write poetry, so all the cards are in your hands, and then we'll have a song . . . Listen to Ponomarev, my lad, Ponomarev will always give you sound advice . . .'

Gradually the normal course of an official banquet was punctuated by more and more drunken voices, and eventually it turned into an ordinary drinking-bout. And although Zolotarev's position had periodically required him to take part in similar orgies at the most various levels, this pointless waste of time always oppressed him. He was instinctively afraid of crossing the barrier beyond which one ceased to distinguish between ranks, titles, ages, and where there always lurked the dangerous possibility of a trick or a trap. Though it was never possible for him to get out of it, he always contrived to keep a clear head and a vigilant memory: he drank with the others, but he drank little and only wine, usually on the pretext that it had long been his habit not to drink spirits.

Getting used to the muddled carousel of the drunken revellers, Zolotarev noticed every now and then that the hunchback personnel officer was staring at him intently. Sitting at an angle to him he would glance at him surreptitiously, obviously eager to continue the conversation they had begun on the way there. You might almost have thought that the hunchback knew exactly why, to what end, he had come here, to this hole in the back of beyond, and what torment was gnawing at his innards. 'The sooner they get completely drunk the better, I suppose,' Zolotarev felt irritably, turning away from the hunchback's probing glance. 'They're certainly taking their time about it!'

The hunchback was pouring himself another glass and seemed to be drinking as much as the others, yet he hardly seemed drunk at all, and only his harsh face, under its week's stubble, grew paler and sharper all the time. When they started singing, and the revellers became completely oblivious, he leaned towards him across the table and asked in a businesslike tone: 'Perhaps we

189

shouldn't get in the comrades' way?' And signing to Zolotarev to follow him, he immediately began to make his way towards the exit: 'There's a time for work and a time for play,' he grinned censoriously, as he led Zolotarev into the corridor, 'only we don't know how to play – all we know is how to get drunk . . .'

Once he was back in the silence of the corridor, Zolotarev heard outside and felt under his feet the muffled rumbling of the bowels of the earth. It was as if the earth's fragile crust could hardly contain the slowly but stubbornly growing power of the awakened lava. Fearing the worst, he felt another quiver of unease, and he said hurriedly, trying to shake off the anguished languor that had seized him: 'Unfortunately I'm extremely pressed. I shan't have time for a detailed examination, but I'll try to get to grips with the basic situation.' He took a deep breath and came decisively to the point. 'By the way, there is one file I'm particularly interested in. Moscow has instructed me to set up an Orthodox parish on the Kuriles, and recommends one of your men as priest. He lives somewhere here, on Matua – I think he's a herdsman by profession.'

'We've already been consulted, comrade Zolotarev, we've already been consulted.' His face expressed neither surprise nor suspicion, as if he had been expecting this sudden curiosity. 'I know this Zagladin like the back of my hand. He's a declassed element – what kind of profession is herding cattle?' The hunchback pushed open a door in front of him. 'Here is my domain, my diocese, so to speak. Go in and make yourself comfortable – it's rather cramped, it's true, but we'll be close but comfortable as they say.'

They crossed an empty waiting-room with benches along its walls and found themselves in a little square cell, cut off from the rest of the room by a flimsy plywood partition with glass at the top. As soon as the hunchback sat down at the desk he seemed to blend into this tiny kingdom of cupboards, shelves and dusty papers just like a rapacious little spider at the centre of its web.

'One moment.' His busy fingers ran through a row of folders, pulled one out with a practised gesture and handed it to Zolotarev. 'May I present citizen Zagladin, Matvei Ivanovich, in person. Year of birth 1901, place of birth village of Kondrovo, region of Tula.' The personnel officer looked at him closely with his piercing eyes. 'The same region as you come from isn't it, comrade Zolotarev?'

The spectre of the abyss at the edge of which he was now standing loomed into sight before Zolotarev's eyes, but it was too late to retreat. Deprived of will and strength, he blundered on: 'Not quite, but near enough . . . The name seems to ring a bell, and besides he must be an interesting type if they know about him in Moscow . . .'

Leafing through Matvei's personal file, Zolotarev felt as if he was examining his own life, reflected in that of his former subordinate. It turned out that the higher and steeper the ascendant spiral of his successful destiny, the more sheer and ineluctable were the zigzags of Matvei's descent into beggary and misery: arrested as a tramp just before the war, evacuated to famine-torn Kazakhstan, then in administrative exile. He didn't need to guess what this meant for an ordinary mortal during those terrible years: having tasted orphaned hunger once in his childhood and youth, he would retain the chilly memory of it for the rest of his life. 'You've had a hard life, Matvei Ivanych,' he thought bitterly, 'a cart-horse wouldn't survive all that!'

'Perhaps he does come from the same place, after all.' The personnel officer seemed to have become convinced that he was right, and had begun to fidget on his chair. 'Maybe he's even an acquaintance, or a relative?'

'Not exactly, but something seems to fit.' Zolotarev made a fitful attempt to resist the interrogation, to get off the hook of the hunchback's meticulous tenacity. 'Does he live far from here?'

The man jumped up immediately and rushed towards him as if he was afraid that his guest would change his mind and decide not to go: 'It's no distance at all, comrade Zolotarev! Just down the slope from here we're setting up a subsidiary enterprise and your Zagladin has settled in there. He occupies a whole dug-out on his own. We can be back here within the hour . . .'

He rushed off to the exit with such headlong enthusiasm that Zolotarev had trouble keeping up with him. 'Here goes, then,' he thought, shrugging off all vestige of uncertainty, 'I might as well be hanged for a sheep as for a lamb!'

The fog was clearly lifting. As the milky haze dissolved he could make out the shapes of buildings, trees, the gentle slope of the volcano. The acrid smell of sulphur in the air was becoming stronger still, the submerged rumbling was occasionally interrupted by peals of thunder, and the first powdery ash was mixing with the misty drizzle.

The lower they walked, the more bands of rats began to dart out from under their feet. There were so many that the very earth beneath them seemed to be teeming. A sense of purpose that normal reason could not restrain seemed to guide their panicked

191

movements. 'You'd think they'd come from the ends of the earth.' Zolotarev winced. 'How nervous they are – maybe they sense danger.'

For a long time they followed a spiral path down through thick alder and damp tall grasses, until they came out almost at the edge of the ocean, which was breathing noisily close by. Only then did the hunchback stop, whispering for some reason: 'He lives just close to here. He spends his time praying for his sins, or maybe he's printing counterfeit notes or anti-Soviet propaganda, the devil only knows! In short, not a gift for the personnel officer! Look, over there, that dug-out with the chimney over it, that's his. Meanwhile I'll drop in on the local Japanese – they're a difficult crowd, always asking to be resettled. I'll go and calm them down. We'll let them go soon, what use are they to us, never anything but trouble, but we don't know how to get rid of them.' And just as quietly, he added with a parting chuckle, as he melted into mist, 'Have a good chat!'

The throbbing in Zolotarev's throat had become unbearable: now, any minute, any moment, he would have to lay eyes on yet another witness of the guilt he could never forget. The damp grass parted before him and he walked across it as if across moving waters. At the entrance to the dug-out he took a deep breath and knocked: 'Is anyone in there?'

For a while total silence reigned in the dug-out, then there was the sound of someone bustling about, and a low, hoarse voice asked, 'Whom has God brought here?'

'A friend.' Zolotarev felt that he would suffocate. 'You'll recognize me when you see me.'

'I have many friends,' said the voice from inside, 'but they are all strangers to me.'

Nevertheless, the door was opened with a slow creak, and there in the doorway Zolotarev saw a bearded, heavily pockmarked peasant. There could be no doubt that this was Matvei Zagladin, and besides, not so long had passed since the time they both remembered.

'Do you recognize me?' Zolotarev was recovering his usual calm as if all he had needed was this meeting with Matvei face to face. 'We once worked together.'

The man looked him over expressionlessly from head to toe, and then said calmly and slowly, 'I never worked with you, Ilya Nikanorych, because *I* was working, but you, well, we know what you were doing. But come in anyhow. Be my guest, although, to tell the truth, you'd do better to continue your walk.'

'All right, Matvei.' Zolotarev felt it would be pointless getting offended – that wasn't why he'd come here, and he'd known in advance what it would be like. 'I have business with you. Then we'll see how things stand between us.'

Without saying a word Matvei retreated into the murk of the dug-out, and Zolotarev stepped inside. At first all he could make out was the icon in the upper left-hand corner with the tiny lamp beneath it, its yellow tongue of flame the only light in the place. But when, after the grey light outside, his eyes began to get used to it, he distinguished the furniture, if you can call furniture the scanty accoutrements of a temporary settlement: the plank-bed, covered in rags, the temporary iron stove, a rudimentary shelf with a pot, a tea-pot, a basin and a mug, standing in a row on it. But the unpretentious tidiness of this meagre habitation seemed appropriate to the man.

'Sit down there, there's nowhere else.' Matvei indicated the corner of the plank-bed. He also settled down on the planks, but nearer the door. 'Explain to me, in my foolishness, what business you can have with me.'

'It's Moscow itself that is trying to get in touch with you – they want you to run a parish in Yuzhno-Kurilsk.'

Matvei laughed, shook his head in amazement, but said nothing, keeping his visitor waiting. Then he sighed: 'No, Ilya Nikanorych, it's too great an honour. Let them find someone else – I'm not going to connive with you.'

'You're a bold one, Matvei, only what's the point? They've broken stronger men than you.'

'Maybe, but not everyone.' His voice suddenly hardened. 'You didn't manage to break our brigade leader. He turned out to be too tough for you.'

Zolotarev's voice became almost hoarse.

'How do you know? Things like that aren't done in the market-place.'

'You think you're the only ones with men everywhere. Your power's been in existence thirty years, and how long it'll survive we'll have to wait and see, but our faith has lasted for two thousand years, and it will never wear out, remember that. So we always know more than you do, and we see everything.'

Zolotarev realized that his companion had guessed long ago what was passing through his soul, and therefore hadn't bothered beating about the bush but had come straight to the point. Sensing that he was completely defeated, he said in a lower, even more stifled voice, 'Tell me.'

'If you wish, Ilya Nikanorych, if you wish,' the man replied, looking straight at him. 'They tortured him for a long time, they put their heart and soul into it. They kept on asking him what plots he'd hatched against the state. They were desperate to know what he was going to blow up and with whom, whom he was going to kill, whom he was going to poison with gases he'd got from abroad. And he just' – at this point Matvei's voice broke – 'he just pitied them: why were they wasting their time on such nonsense? So they just got angrier and angrier; they became like wild beasts – what they did is too horrible to relate. When they took him off to be killed, he still wasn't angry with them; he just asked them to leave us alone, because he said we were completely innocent.' At this point he lowered his head for the first time, staring down at his feet. 'One sin I shall never forgive myself is leaving that night with my brother: I'd chanced to overhear your conversation with that boss from Uzlovaya and I was too scared to stay.'

Matvei fell silent and Zolotarev was overwhelmed by an anguish he had never previously experienced, or rather by painful burning spasms in his heart. Only now, here, on the edge of the world, did he realize bitterly: everything he had gone through – the district party committee, working for the Organs, the front, Kira, even Stalin – was just a path, leading him to this miserable dug-out where the spectre of the heavy weight of his distant youth had finally tracked him down.

In these few short minutes he had come to the firm and irrevocable conclusion that there was no guilt in a man's life for which he would not eventually have to pay. And the fact that this expiation was to be demanded of him in a place where his own land finished and alien skies began seemed to him to have some special, as yet unfathomable significance. 'It's your turn now, Ilya Nikanorych,' he concluded. 'Outside with your belongings!'

'Well, forgive me for disturbing you, Matvei,' he said as he got up. 'As the saying goes, I came for the wedding and arrived for the funeral.'

'God will forgive you,' the man replied without expression, and turned away, seemingly cutting himself off both from Zolotarev and from everything that stood behind him.

For a moment Zolotarev was tempted to tell Matvei about his meeting with Ivan on Baikal, and to help the brothers to meet, or at least to write to each other, but catching Matvei's motionless gaze he realized that he had already decided not to listen to him any longer. 'As you wish,' he thought sullenly as he went out, 'nobody's forcing you.'

194

The personnel officer immediately appeared out of the fog to meet him as if he had been waiting there all the time, which anyway was perhaps the case.

'I see you've had a good chat!' he winked understandingly as they hurried back. 'I told you he was an odd fish – they should shoot him now. That's the men I have to work with: thieves and vagabonds, with a few counter-revolutionaries for good measure. Put yourself in my position, comrade Zolotarev – it's not a job, it's hard labour. I'm desperately in need of some demobbed soldiers, then we could quickly get things sorted out . . .'

Now that it had emerged from the morning mist, he could see the whole of the volcano. In the train of black smoke over its smoothly truncated summit he could already see tongues of red flame. The smooth rumbling was broken by occasional tremors. Their spiralling progress up the narrow terraces of the hill led them gradually further from the shore. They finally reached the local administration building, where the hunchback stood waiting for Zolotarev by a door marked 'Infirmary'.

'You can stay here,' he announced, and for some reason he winked knowingly. 'We have a room for special guests here, with all mod cons, as they say.'

At first glance there was nothing special about the woman who greeted them. She was quite pretty, a fairly large woman of thirty or so in a white medical coat. It was only when he'd had a good look at her that her gaze and bearing convinced him that she was someone out of the ordinary, clearly confident of her own authority, but with an admixture of hidden but harsh grief.

'Come in, I've already prepared the room.' Her manner of speaking was also unusual: she behaved as if they were old friends. 'D'you want to rest straight away, or will you have supper first?'

'No, no,' he tried to avoid her calmly insistent eyes. 'I want to sleep, I want to sleep now, I'm dead beat.'

'Yes, yes,' the hunchback intervened fussily, his eyes darting in all directions. 'Comrade Zolotarev absolutely must get a good night's sleep, we've got a very full day tomorrow.'

But she didn't so much as glance at him, it was as if he didn't exist. She turned to Zolotarev again: 'In that case go through to your room, the bed's already made. If you need anything, don't hesitate. Just call me – I'm always here.'

With this 'if you need anything' in his troubled heart, Zolotarev went to his room, to the next refuge on his forced march. Only when he was finally alone did he really sense what viscous heaviness had filled him in these seemingly short hours. As soon as he lay down he fell into a dreamlike stupor, and therefore he took the half-dressed woman, who came in soon after and quietly got into the bed next to him as if it were her own, for a hallucination.

Thus the night passed, in hallucination, between waking and sleeping. Convulsive embraces alternated with a seemingly endless tale, and someone's entire life passed before him, a life of such pain and tension that it was difficult to imagine one person surviving it. And, perhaps for the first time in his life, the sweet poison of pity entered him: for her, for himself, for everyone who had left and everyone who was still to come, for everything that existed in this vale of tears. Dissolved in this pity, he fell into a deep sleep only towards morning, with a single name, new to him, on his lips:

'Polya . . .'

4

Zolotarev awoke to the sound of an intermittent cannonade. It sounded like a lengthy artillery barrage before a major offensive. The room was shaking slightly; the window-panes, covered in powdery ash, were tinkling quietly, the floor beneath his feet was unsteady and precarious. 'It's started!' he muttered, dressing hastily. 'Hold tight!'

Polina, already dressed, looked into the room and reported in a businesslike voice, as if nothing had happened between them: 'The fires have started, Ilya Nikanorych. We'll have to evacuate the women and children, and as for our bosses, we'll have to spoon them up off the floor – they're in no fit state to do anything after yesterday's celebrations.'

The feeling of embarrassment, for himself and for her, which he first experienced was immediately replaced by cold fury. He suddenly sensed within him that elation, that exaltation which always heralded risk, action, power. At such moments no obstacles or restraints existed for him.

'I'll shoot them all like dogs!' His imperious fury carried him victoriously forward. 'They will answer according to the laws of wartime!' By now he was outside. He turned to Polina: 'Everyone must stay at his post!'

He rushed into the administration office at the height of the panic. People were rushing senselessly around the corridor and the offices, all shouting at once, not hearing, or perhaps not understanding each other: the uproar reminded him of a station

during a bombing raid. From the radio-cabin Yarygin's almost
tearful voice cut through the babble: 'We need vesséls urgently' –
that was the way he said it, 'vesséls'. 'How are we going to get the
people out? . . . Try to understand, everything is on fire . . .'
Stopped in mid-sentence by the appearance of Zolotarev, he
instantly shrivelled up, trying ingratiatingly to catch his superior's
eye. 'Here is comrade Zolotarev himself. I'll hand you over.'
Ceding him his place at the transmitter, he did not even bother to
hide his relief and gratitude: he was no longer in charge. 'Please,
comrade Zolotarev.'

Zolotarev was in his element and he abandoned all pretence of
standing on ceremony: he immediately switched over from
reception to uninterrupted transmission: 'This is Zolotarev speaking. I take full responsibility. I am declaring the island to be in a
state of martial law. I am beginning the evacuation of women and
children. I consider the entire male population to be mobilized. I
order the entire fleet of the neighbouring islands to arrive off
Matua within the hour. Immediate implementation!' He cut the
radio-link and turning to Ponomarev, who was sitting next to him,
he ordered: 'Place guards at the storehouses and the shops. In case
of looting shoot without warning. You are personally responsible
for the extinction of the fires. Is that clear?' Not sensing an
adequate response from the man's sullenly drunken face, he
grabbed him by the collar of his field-shirt and, lifting him up,
pulled him towards him. 'Listen, philosopher, it's not going to take
me very long to knock your shell-shock out of you. If you don't
know anything about life yet, then I'll teach you, and each lesson
will have nine grams of lead in it, is that clear?'

Ponomarev sobered up instantly at these words, and cautiously
detaching himself from Zolotarev's grip, he stood to attention: 'I
shall carry out any task entrusted me by the party and government,
comrade commander.' His drunken hoarseness took on a solemn
tone. 'Through fire and water, comrade Zolotarev!'

'Precisely,' said Zolotarev calmly, and went out into the
corridor. 'Listen to my orders. All the women and children must
be grouped within the hour in the safety zone by the water. I make
the head of the political section of the civil authorities, comrade
Yarygin, responsible for the evacuation.' Catching the look of a
beast at bay in Yarygin's eyes he repeated, almost voluptuously:
'Comrade Yarygin. That is all, carry out the orders . . .'

A minute later the headquarters building was empty; the
machine which he had set in motion, and which worked upon the
inertia of fear, was functioning without a hitch. All he had to do

now was to make a few minor adjustments from time to time, to stop it slowing down or veering to one side. He had long known by heart the art of managing such processes.

As the confusion in the corridor steadily diminished, the hunchback suddenly reappeared.

'You are responsible for all our lives, comrade Zolotarev,' he said confidingly, 'but I am responsible for yours. Your security must be guaranteed. This man,' he pushed forward a young fellow with a wide forehead, wearing a military padded jacket and a cap pushed to the back of his head, 'has a small launch, small but sturdy. He even,' at this point the personnel officer grinned mockingly, 'has a crew. He'll stand waiting specially for you, just in case.' And hastily sweeping away all objections, he concluded, 'You might need it at the very end.'

The lad reminded Zolotarev of someone: the likeness was so astonishingly strong, so clear, that he couldn't stop himself asking: 'Where are you from?'

'He comes from where you do, comrade Zolotarev,' the hunchback blurted out before the lad could reply. 'Yet another one! And not just from Tula, from Sychovka itself. Samokhin, Fyodor Tikhonovich, in person. I'll tell you straight, he's a first-class man: he's been at the front, he's got a profession, he's a worker – with men like him we can build communism in no time at all. Maybe you even remember him?'

How could Zolotarev forget the Samokhins! There wasn't a more evil and quarrelsome peasant in the village than old uncle Tikhon. He never let the chance go by to pick on Zolotarev's father and play some trick on him. Zolotarev's mother cried many tears over Tikhon's favours! It's true he remembered the younger Samokhin only vaguely – there was a big age difference between them – but even if he had remembered him, he would not have felt any particular enthusiasm at seeing him now: everything connected with Sychovka was still too sensitive for him.

'Yes, yes, I remember him,' he said drily, fending off in advance any attempts at familiarity on the part of his unwanted fellow-villager. 'You'd do better telling me how you think you're going to keep your launch in place. Have you seen what the sea's like?'

The lad had obviously guessed the state Zolotarev was in, but he turned out to be intelligent enough not to take offence: 'I'll put it bow to the waves, give it full throttle, drop anchor, and we'll hold our place somehow or other, comrade commander.'

The tact and restraint of Fyodor's reply pleased Zolotarev, but he still preferred to keep his distance; it was safer: 'All right, go on board your launch, stand on watch, but bear in mind that I'll be the last one to leave.' But finally he softened and shouted after the lad as he went off: 'Keep up Sychovka's reputation!'

The personnel officer positively beamed in Fyodor's wake; you'd have thought he was admiring the work of his own hands: 'He's a good lad, and no mistake!' And getting in step with Zolotarev, he added in a businesslike voice: 'I'll come with you.'

'You'd do better smoothing out any possible misunderstandings with the Japanese.' Zolotarev would have been glad to be rid of the clinging hunchback. 'Find out if they want to be evacuated or not.'

'Let them work things out for themselves, and we'll concentrate on our people,' the hunchback began, but catching Zolotarev's impatient look, he did not dare to disobey. 'As you wish, comrade Zolotarev, as you wish, only why should you bother about them?' Turning to leave, he screwed up his eyes and said tauntingly: 'Maybe you've found some fellow-villagers there too?'

His very gait as he walked away betokened threat and warning, but Zolotarev was no longer bothered. Standing on the step outside the administration building, he observed the whole scene: the smoky flame above the roaring volcano, the stones shrapnelling the roofs of the settlements, the human streams flowing along the roads and paths down towards the jetty. But in this apparent chaos there were already signs of order and discipline. The mechanism of power was working slowly but unswervingly: the fires were not lasting so long, the babble of voices was becoming calmer, the lines of people more coherent. 'If I let them,' he reflected in calm satisfaction, 'they'd strangle each other without noticing.'

Suddenly Polina appeared at his side, a medicine bag slung across her shoulder, her autumn coat buttoned from top to bottom, the white collar of her doctor's smock visible above it.

'I'll have to go. I've been called out – a woman down there,' Polina nodded in the direction of the shore, 'has started her contractions. What a time for it!' She gave him a sidelong glance, expecting him to say something, but he avoided her gaze. 'You ought to go down as well. You can't keep a watch on all this stuff.'

'I can't go down till everything's been loaded, Polina. You know as well as I do that I can't rely on your local louts – I'll have to supervise the whole operation.' He nudged her gently and affectionately towards the road. 'Go on, they're waiting for you – I shan't be long.'

With a grateful tenderness that surprised him Zolotarev

watched her set off obediently but uncertainly towards the road, occasionally looking back at him as if she was hoping that he would change his mind and call her back, but since he said nothing she continued on her way. And for a long time the white collar of her smock, sticking out from under her coat, continued to flash in front of him until she disappeared down the slope.

Scarcely was she lost from view when Zolotarev was suddenly taken aback by a thought that was searing in its simplicity: what, what force makes people born so different, unites and divides them, invisibly guides their actions, revealing to them love and hatred, fear and courage, cruelty and mercy? He was discovering in all this some special law, some logic, some meaning. Before his very eyes, in the chaotic motion of seemingly undirected elemental forces, the network of human relations, though apparently distorted, did not lose its inner, almost geometrical, order. But what was the secret of all this?

The thought was so childishly obvious that for a while Zolotarev's mind went blank and everything around him ceased to exist. Circling time after time around the same spiral of questions, he tried to make the tortuous ascent to their summit, from which the essential would be revealed; but it kept taunting him with the phantom of revelation and then slipping away, sending Zolotarev tumbling back towards the base.

When he came to, silhouettes of ships had appeared offshore and people were beginning to be helped aboard. It was only then that he went into the office for the last time and turned on the transmitter: 'This is Zolotarev. I'm cutting radio contact! I'm cutting radio contact! I am the last to leave! I repeat, I am the last to leave!'

Zolotarev cut the radio-link decisively and left the building. The volcano was in a frenzy, showering its surroundings with a hot flour of grey ash. The tail of fire and smoke above it rose high into the firmament, and occasionally a rain of white-hot stones would thunder down. The smell of sulphur in the air was becoming so strong that he could hardly breathe. There was not another living soul around. 'Thank God, it seems they've all got away,' he sighed, making towards the beach. 'That's one load off my back!'

But he had hardly reached the first turn of the slope when he was almost knocked off his feet by an old Japanese who was hurrying purposefully uphill. He was astonished to see Zolotarev and jabbered out, pointing at the volcano: 'Must crime mountain . . . Bad, bad thing come. Big water come . . . Must mountain . . .'

'Where are you going, you old devil!' Zolotarev shook with fury. 'Are you out of your mind? Can't you see what's going on?'

'Must crime mountain,' the man reiterated, walking round him. 'Big water come . . .'

Zolotarev no longer had either the strength or the will to chase after this old man whom fear had obviously deranged. He had suddenly been seized by the profoundest indifference towards everything around him. The fury which had guided him these last hours had evaporated, leaving him alone with himself in his devastation. It was the end for him. The end of everything: of the present and the future, of wishes and hopes, perhaps of life itself. He knew in advance that nothing would now be forgiven him: neither Kira, nor his link with Matvei, nor, above all, this earthquake. The man who had elevated him did not know how to forgive.

Its engine spluttering, the launch loomed enticingly just offshore, but he hardly noticed it waiting for him as he made his way down on legs turned to jelly. He was looking somewhere further off, over the horizon, where the sky fused with the ocean and the light began again.

Only when he was at the water's edge did he hear Fyodor begging him to hurry: 'Comrade Zolotarev, Ilya Nikanorych, hurry up! We'll capsize and then you'll have to stay! . . . Grab hold of the end! . . .'

Zolotarev was about to step into the troubled water, but Fyodor's call reminded him once again that even the village he had been running from in panic all his life had caught up with him in the shape of one of the Samokhins, here in this back of beyond, bubbling with fire and foam, so as to return him to his accursed origins. After all he had gone through in the last two days this turned out to be too much for him, this he could not endure.

And Zolotarev turned back in a final attempt to escape his past, even if it cost him his life. But he was not to step on to dry land: the earth beneath him shuddered and fell away, a huge wall of water covered him from behind, seized him up and, bearing him along in its centrifugal vortex, hurled him down on to its flowing surface. Resisting no longer, he was carried along by its stubborn current.

When the first stupor had passed after the dizzying watery font, and his eyes had penetrated their salty shroud, his soul felt a final, mortal tremor. Not far from him the roof of a house was floating by, and clinging to its chimney, which by some miracle had remained in place, was the hunchbacked personnel officer, his

unshaven face for some reason suffused by a beatific smile.
And that was the last thing Zolotarev saw in his life.

5

'Hail, my brother Ivan! I have received your letter safely and whole.
It was delivered into my hands, I have read it with humility, and I
write in answer. Thanks to your prayers I arrived safely. I found a
dry hut, I equipped it as well as I was able; I live in it, I am my own
master, I look after the cattle, and I do not forget the Lord. In these
times, brother, it it better to be with beasts than with men; the people
here are all noisy vagabonds and beggars, eaten by misfortune as if
by mites. There is nobody I can speak to – they stick in the slime of
their hungry deafness. The main boss here is a devil with one arm
longer than the other, drunk from morning till night. All he does is
curse and swear, and his side-kick, though sober, is even worse. He
rushes about the mountain, shaking his hump, always sniffing
things out, always spying things out, making little notes – he's the
devil incarnate, may the Lord forgive me. And the workers take
after their bosses, stealing anything they can lay their hands on,
drinking and fighting; the people have gone completely off their
heads, yet you say they are awakening. How can they awaken when
they are being herded who knows where, with never a chance to
come to their senses? They have no time for God now, and their
heads are full of the pestilence of foolish ideas, which lure them
towards the fiery abyss. Here the sacred Word is not sufficient – you
need the knout. We must follow the precept of Christ and drive the
band of money-lenders out of the Temple of God before they
become as wild beasts. But it is sinful to despair. I have met a
family here – we came over together on the steamer – who come
from our own region of Tula, and they give me some reason for
hope that, given sufficient sustenance, something will come of them,
and they will come to grace. I console myself with the hope that
gradually, blade of grass by blade of grass, branch by branch, I
shall gather my flock and we shall sing the praise of Our Lord, the
Almighty. The earth here is very fluid and moves at the slightest
thing; the mountain above us smokes day and night, sometimes
even spitting fire. Today it has become completely unstrapped, and
is flowing uncontrollably in all directions; there is a rumbling that is
out of this world, and outside there is a smell of sulphur like in hell
before the Last Judgement. Ilya, whom you mention in your letter,
was here just now and proposed that I set up a parish. He

questioned me about Ivan; forgive me, brother, I did not take your counsel to heart. Instead I told that murderer all that I think of him. Let him suffer – Ivan's sufferings were worse. As for him, you are right, brother, he has the brand on him, the mark of Cain; he is not long for this world, he is rotting from within. I refused the parish, though the paper had come from Moscow itself: the Patriarch's eye is clearly sharp – he tries everywhere to lead us into temptation. But I do not want this favour; like their mitre it is the devil's charm, and the Patriarch's cowl is only falsehood. With God's help we shall resurrect the Body of the true Church of Christ, and our Mother will rise from the ashes in her former beauty and strength. I remain your elder brother, Matvei, the son of Zagladin, and may Christ be with you.'

Chapter Fourteen

1

Above the darkness and the light, above sleeping and waking, above all the doomed earth the two voices continue the same conversation.

    'Send me to them again.'

    'Will you have enough strength to endure it again?'

    'You will help me.'

    'The last time your spirit grew weak and you implored me.'

    'Just for one moment.'

    'Were you asking for deliverance?'

    'No – for love: I was ready to begin to hate them . . .'

2

Fyodor dreamt that he was lying in a trench, shaken from all sides by the thunder of artillery, seeing nothing, hearing nothing around him, with an animal desire to squeeze into the earth, to merge with it as much as was possible. At first everything above him seemed a continuous rumbling, punctuated by explosions, and he himself felt part of that rumbling, but then through his oblivious deafness came the voice of his father: 'Fedya, Fedyok, you must get up! They're calling for you! Look what's happening outside – it's the end of the world!'

The day before, celebrating the holiday, Fyodor had had a skinful in the company of the local port-workers, and he had returned home almost unconscious, so that now, through the rainbow of his hangover, he tried painfully to concentrate on working out the significance of what was happening.

The hut was shaking and swaying like a matchbox in the drum of a winnowing machine. Outside the ash-stained windows, crimson lightning flashes alternated with the fractured thunder of lengthy eruptions. The things in the room seemed to have taken on a life of their own, jumping and moving of their own accord. The hubbub and the stamping of feet in the corridor became continually louder, spreading outside the hut, where they were soon submerged in the general uproar.

Fyodor finally realized that the worst thing of all that he had been unconsciously preparing for, since the very day of his arrival, had happened. A tremor had occasionally shaken the island earlier, and the train of smoke never stopped weaving over Sarychev; but in time they had got used to that, as people get used to any unavoidable elemental force, resignedly supposing that all evil brings good in its wake, that you cannot avoid your fate and that sooner or later this horror must abate. Even when, on the eve of the Revolution holiday, the smoke over the volcano had turned black, and inside the crater the lava had begun to bubble, people did not see anything particularly abnormal about it: it would calm down! But now the earth had been set in motion irrevocably, spreading uncontrollably in all directions. Every living creature made instinctively for the shore, to what now seemed the saving water of the ocean.

His mother rushed helplessly around the room, indiscriminately tying their various belongings into bundles.

'What horrors!' she kept exclaiming, crossing herself. 'Protect us and have mercy on us, our Mother, Heavenly Patroness! . . . What have we done to earn such a punishment! . . . I shan't be long, Tikhon, I shan't be long . . . I'm almost ready . . . it won't take a minute . . . Lord Jesus, don't abandon us sinners!'

Fyodor was already in full possession of his faculties – the habit acquired at the front of coming to immediately in moments of danger was having its effect. He dressed quickly and to the sound of his mother's lamentations he made his way to the door, where the personnel officer suddenly appeared in his path.

'Taking a breath of fresh air are we, Samokhin, waiting for a personal invitation?' he said venomously, boring into him with his unmoving eyes. 'Martial law has been declared over the island, so this is no time for practical jokes, Samokhin. You are required to present yourself upon receiving the first order, and if you fail to do so, you will go before a tribunal. Is that clear?' The hunchback bit his soft lips, and said more calmly: 'In short, jump to it! Get your old battleship working! You are being given a position of trust – you are being attached to the responsible comrade from Moscow. Keep your wits about you, for if anything happens to him, it'll be our heads. The task is to get him off the island safe and sound, and to keep me informed, is that clear?' Then, watching Fyodor's mother rushing about the room, he winced with disgust: 'Why the hurry, Samokhina? Nobody dies before their time. Our transport doesn't have to keep to a timetable – you won't miss it.'

Then he turned sharply on his heels and disappeared into the noisy hubbub of the corridor.

What a meddler that man is!' Tikhon spat furiously after he had left. 'He has to put a stopper in every barrel, and turns up everywhere to make sure things are in order even during the Last Judgement, the cursed devil!' Then he turned with mournful anger to his son. 'Run along, Fedyok, or else that worm really might court-martial you. Your mother and I will sort things out here . . .'

But when the raucous crowd had carried Fyodor out on to the road, a voice called to him from lower down, over their heads.

'There's trouble, Fedyok,' Ovsyannikov was rushing towards him through the crowd, waving his hands in confusion, 'the girl's labour seems to have started – she's in terrible pain – I can't think where to take her.' His guilty eyes looked hopefully at Fyodor. 'Maybe you could help us, Fedyok?'

Ever since that memorable night outside Irkutsk Fyodor had felt a strong attachment towards Lyuba; in his thoughts he had already bound her fate to his. Throughout the rest of the journey he had made scrupulously sure that she got to bed in time, had enough to eat and, God forbid, did not carry any heavy burdens. The other people in the wagon had mocked him on the sly; his parents had frowned blackly, evidently considering that their beloved son was worthy of something better than covering up the sins of others. But nobody was bold enough to speak openly; they all sensed timidly that though Fyodor seemed placid and easy-going it would be a foolish man who got on the wrong side of him. And only his dead grandmother would sign to him to come to her corner and lisp toothlessly into his ear, 'Hold on to Lyuba, Fedya. With a wife like her, no ill can come to you. The girl is a real treasure – she'll get you through.' Fyodor had long since got used to the idea that she was going to have a baby and already considered it to be his own. He did not torment himself with guesses as to who the father might be and felt no jealousy at all about the expectant mother's past. For Fyodor everything connected with Lyuba was an inseparable part of her, and therefore a part of him too. And now, running along behind Ovsyannikov, he felt a burning fear stifle him: if only everything was all right, if only nothing happened!

Lyuba, half-lying on an unmade bed, surrounded by parcels and bundles, greeted Fyodor with a tortured half-smile: 'Look at me, Fyodor Tikhonych, I do everything at the wrong time,' her swollen face was dripping sweat. 'I'm so clumsy.'

'Just stay there, Lyuba, don't move.'

Fyodor hovered feverishly on the doorstep trying to think what to do. 'The main thing is to stay lying down, and we'll think of something. Everything will be all right.' Three pairs of eyes watched him with increasing hope. 'I tell you what, Uncle Kolya, she absolutely can't go down on the beach. You've seen what's going on down there yourself – they'll trample her. The best thing would be to get her on to my launch. They've assigned me to the chief from Moscow, so while I'm waiting for him she can lie down there for a bit.' He turned to her mother. 'Aunt Klanya, you'd better go to the infirmary and ask Polina Vasilevna to come. Tell her to go straight down to the creek and we'll wait for her there.' And he stretched out his hands towards her father. 'Grab hold, Uncle Kolya . . .'

Lifting the girl on their criss-crossed hands, they carried her outside and, with an anxious look over their shoulders, began to carry her down, cautiously feeling for the path beneath their feet.

The cannonade over the island had merged into almost uninterrupted firing. The summit of the volcano, like the red-hot muzzle of a piece of artillery, kept spitting out a firework display of fiery shrapnel which, as it fell, bounced against the slopes like little crimson balls. In many places round the foot of the mountain there were tongues of flame: the dwarf-alder thickets were ablaze. And to cap it all, through the shower of ash there was a sudden storm, with lightning zig-zagging all along the coast, although the sound of the thunder was drowned in the rumble of the eruption. 'We're definitely going to need Polina,' thought Fyodor, and every time he glanced at Lyuba he was more convinced of it: her face was even more strained, the sweat was pouring off her; 'the girl's time has come!'

Grabbing at them convulsively, she kept falling back again and muttering semi-deliriously: 'Lord, what's happening . . . Can it always be like this? . . . I can't take any more . . . Lord!'

The damp ash had made the path beneath slippery, as if they were walking through soap, and they kept losing their footing; the sticky rain was getting in their eyes, turning the horizon in front of them into a dark curtain; the fumes of sulphur were making it difficult to breathe. They were completely exhausted by the time they caught sight of Fyodor's solitary launch in the quiet waters of the creek.

'You can lie down now, Lyuba, you'll feel better,' and sensing the firm support of the jetty beneath his feet, Fyodor relaxed. 'All right, Uncle Kolya, I can manage on my own now.' He cautiously took her in his arms, negotiated the narrow gangway and stepped on deck.

'Hold on, Lyuba, just hold on. Your mother's gone for the doctor – she'll be here any minute . . .'

'I'll hold on, Fedya, I'll hold on,' she answered, scarcely moving her swollen lips, 'I'm a patient person . . .'

Racked by pity for her, and dizzy at the thought that she might die, he laid her on a bench in the cabin: 'You should try to sleep, Lyuba.' He found a sleeping-bag in a chest and slid it under her head. Then he took an old sheepskin coat from its hanger. 'Let me cover you up a bit . . . That's it. Try to sleep, Lyuba, try to sleep, you'll feel better, you must try, and then the doctor will come and give you some medicine.'

Lyuba shut her eyes obediently and her anxious bloodless face relaxed into a smile: 'It really does seem to be better, Fedya,' she breathed rather than said, 'maybe it isn't time yet.'

The flashes of red and the cannonade outside were growing steadily worse. The steam that the rain formed over the lava was rising up the volcano's slopes and covering the summit in a swirling turban. The island was shaking and rocking in the middle of the bubbling ocean like a boat caught in a storm. 'When will it end, Lord?' thought Fyodor in anguish, peering through the porthole, 'and will it end?'

Klavdiya's face, cocooned in a winter kerchief, appeared inquiringly from on deck: 'Thank God, I found her! She's just coming.' Grabbing on to anything she could find, she made her way awkwardly down the steps. 'She just had to get her things together.' Leaning exhaustedly against the wall at her daughter's feet, she tried to get her breath back. 'The earth's moving around everywhere, the people have gone off their heads, they're rushig down the hill like men possessed, and shouting like at the destruction of Sodom.' Catching her breath, she turned to her daughter. 'Thank God, she seems to be asleep!'

Fyodor was becoming his usual calm self. 'She seems to have warmed up. Let her sleep now – it'll do her good.' And quite reassured about her, he began to climb back upstairs. 'There's time. By the time the authorities get this little lot sorted out she can have a couple of nights' sleep if she wants!'

Ovsyannikov was tramping up and down the deck waiting for news from down below, puffing gloomily at his cigarette.

'Well?' He rushed towards Fyodor. 'What's happening?' And with added confidence, 'Was it a false alarm?'

'I think so,' Fyodor tried to reassure him. 'The doctor's coming –

she'll take a look at her.' He opened the wheel-house door, carefully checked the levels of water, oil and fuel, and with a practised gesture switched on the engine and let it idle: the engine motored calmly, without a single false note. 'The repair lads haven't let us down – it's purring like new!' He turned purposefully to Ovsyannikov. 'I'll go and report, Uncle Kolya. The bosses like order.' The wooden jetty was slightly springy under his feet. 'I shan't be long. I'll be back before you know it.'

Damp light-brown ash was covering the grass, the leaves of the trees and the roofs of the buildings with glossy scales. The rain had put out the fires, but they went on smoking, making it even harder to breathe. With every step, the slope became steeper and more difficult. He tried vainly to get a foothold but the path kept slipping out from under his feet like a grass-snake.

About halfway up Fyodor saw, on his left, almost directly above the creek, a zig-zag crack suddenly forming in the side of the volcano, which began to crumble slowly, throwing out fountains of steam and red-hot stones. Then a stream of lava snaked out, and began to cross the trough of a coastal hollow, making its way towards the sea, which immediately began to boil and grow cloudy. 'We should move out to sea as soon as possible,' Fyodor felt with a shudder. 'If we stay here, we'll be boiled like lobsters – they can serve us up with beer!'

In the building of the civil directorate, the plywood corner of the personnel officer looked like a quiet haven in the maelstrom of the general hubbub.

'There you are, Samokhin!' Pekarev said briskly, looking him over from head to foot. 'Hold on a minute.' The hunchback examined the labyrinth of folders, tied into large bundles, checking with eyes and fingers that none of the wax seals at the knots of the bundles had been broken. 'In cases like this you have to keep your eyes open, brother. A man without a personal file is a zero – it's as if he didn't exist. On the other hand a personal file in the hands of the enemy is a weapon raised against our State.' His hump floated above the files like the fin of a shark stalking its prey. 'Everything seems to be in order.' He straightened up and nodded imperiously in the direction of the noisy corridor. 'Take these out, Teteryatnikov, they're all ready.' And darting round Fyodor, he added, 'Follow me, Samokhin, we'd better go and see the boss.'

They caught up with Zolotarev at the exit, where Pekarev barred his way and nudged Fyodor forward. Then they walked on, having a brief conversation from which it emerged that the commander had decided to be the last to leave the island, and that he was quite satisfied with the small launch that was to wait for him, though the news that Samokhin came from his village did not seem to fill him with particular enthusiasm.

'The goose is not companion for the pig,' Fyodor thought, stung. 'But it wasn't my idea – I'm no worse than he is.'

'Good luck, Samokhin,' the hunchback said to him in parting. 'Stick to it and carry out your duty. See you soon.' He gave him a piercing look and suddenly winked with a conspiratorial grin. 'While there's life there's hope, eh, Samokhin?'

And he disappeared into the murk of the corridor which by now was almost calm, as if cutting all communication with his surroundings.

Fyodor's return was like a winter toboggan ride; he slithered down, hardly managing to brake at the turns. The inertia of falling dragged him through the tussocks on the clammy path, through the ashy curtain of swelling chaos, towards the mirror of the creek, gleaming at the foot of the volcano. When his feet finally settled on the firm planking of the jetty, he was unrecognizable: he was covered from head to foot in a sticky rust-coloured slime.

He had hardly got his foot on the gangway when he came up against Polina, who was emerging from the hatch to meet him. 'Well, you're a sight for sore eyes, and no mistake!' she exclaimed with her normal good-natured mockery. 'What's the hurry? Are you afraid someone'll steal your lady love?' She skirted round him and stepped down on to the jetty. 'Calm down, nothing's happened to her. She's sleeping the sleep of the just, though how she manages it in this bedlam is difficult to believe!' But evidently touched by his anxiety, she hastened to reassure him. 'I gave her a sleeping-pill and an injection. She should hold on for a day or two, and then we'll see – this chaos can't go on for ever. I forbid anyone to move her, you can tell your boss from me. It's my order. One more passenger probably won't sink the boat. I've already sent her parents off – they can be evacuated along with everyone else.' Suddenly her whole expression darkened: standing half-turned away from him, she stared blindly into space. 'Farewell, Fedya, anything may happen. If you survive, don't forget old Polina – she gave you too a bit of her heart . . .'

'Thank you, Polya,' Fyodor wished her well as he watched her silhouette disappear along the shore, 'I shan't forget you. Women like you are not forgotten!'

His movements immediately became mechanically precise: he stepped on deck, removed the gang-plank, went into the wheel-house, switched on the engine, and skirting round the sharp curve of the creek, he headed the launch out into the open sea.

The first wave lifted the boat and began to toss it smoothly up and down on its watery swing. The storm clouds hung so low over the water that from the crest of the waves it seemed as if you could touch them. The island behind them was steaming and smoking, furiously disgorging the excess of its innards. Far away in the sea-roads was the beacon of the rescue flotilla, and the fragile shells of launches and dinghies were speeding towards it from all directions. 'I don't think we'll sink,' Fyodor calculated, steering his boat straight into the waves and the wind, 'but I don't see how I'm going to get my fellow-villager on board – it looks as if he's going to have to take a swim!'

Everything that followed was imprinted on Fyodor's memory like a colourful kaleidoscope of individual shots: the appearance of Zolotarev on the beach, his strange silence, his sudden disappearance, his own voice shouting after him and, finally, the water surging out of the creek, taking the boat with it out into the open sea, and then with a single crash engulfing everything around in a flashing bewitched abyss.

A few moments earlier Fyodor had rushed to the wheel to alter course, and this was what saved him from incipient disaster.

3

When Fyodor came to, the launch had been carried between water and sky into the boiling abyss of the ocean night. Icy rain was drumming on the glass, and the wind had gusted it into the wheel-house where it flowed across the deck in time with the rocking, from the stern to the bows and back again. The launch was creaking in the pincers of the storm like the shell of a cracked nut, the wheel was turning helplessly this way and that, and the engine, which was on full throttle, showed no sign of life. Outside everything was noise, wind and darkness.

The first thought that came into his head, even before he had realized what had happened, was of Lyuba: what had happened to her, how was she, was she alive? Despite his sickly weakness and the shivers that shook his body, he somehow managed to jam the wheel, and crawled out of the wheel-house. After a tortuous struggle against the helpless rolling of the boat he reached the hatch and, curling into a ball, with a final effort of will he fell almost headlong into the squelching darkness below.

Here the water was ankle-deep and it slopped into all the corners of the cabin, like a jar of preserves hung on a pendulum. Holding on to corners and protuberances, he reached the bench and with a thump of relief in his heart felt beside him the warm breath of his companion: she had survivied!

It was inconceivable to him what miracle had prevented the rocking from throwing her from the bench, but he now had neither the time nor the desire to think about it: the little strength that remained in him was sufficient only for him to collapse on to the bench opposite her and fall into a fevered sleep . . .

And Fyodor dreamed of haymaking in the fields beyond Sychovka, in the heady odours of high summer. He and his father were lying on top of an unfinished stack looking into the white heat-haze of the sky. His father was winking mischievously at him and teasing him: 'They say you haven't found yourself a girl yet, Fedyok. That's bad, son. At your age I was already a great expert in that area. You'd better get a move on, lad, these days people don't hang about. Before you've had time to sneeze you'll find they've grabbed them all, and you'll be a lonely bachelor all your life. Get on with it, Fedya, any girl'd marry a fine fellow like you . . .'

Then the white sky turned into white snow on the window-pane by which his mother sat squinting shortsightedly at her sewing: 'Oh, Fedya, the things that happened then, it terrifies me even thinking about it. Only my prayers saved you; there was nothing at all in the hut, not a leaf, not a grain, all that was left was the dust in the corners. Just think of it, half the village died that year; and it's all thanks to Aleksei Samsonov who got your father fixed up on the railways, and they used to give the men oil-cake, and it's thanks to that oil-cake that we survived . . .'

And immediately after that he saw, as clearly as if he could reach out and touch him, Mozgovoy saying goodbye to them in the buffet in the port in Vladivostok. He was leaning confidently across the table towards Fyodor, his metal teeth flashing like a beast of prey: 'You listen to me, soldier, my word is my law. If I say something, I do it. I'm sending you in the first ship. Grab your fortune tight by the throat, soldier, and don't let go. They're crying out for lads like you there now. Just name your price – they'll pay you anything you ask.'

'Does that mean the others won't get there till the show is over?'

'Don't worry about them, soldier. You must have realized yourself on the way out here. They're dregs, riff-raff. They're just ballast for the journey – they're all talk and nothing else. The whole convoy's only got a couple of real workers, and that's you and me. Let them wait – nothing'll happen to them.' He leaned even closer to Fyodor and his motionless eyes, veiled by drink, grew larger and wider. 'You're a man, soldier. I've got a nose for people, I can tell a man by his scent. Don't think badly of me, soldier. The mountain won't go to Mahommed, but you and me, you mark my words, will meet again . . .'

Faces, faces, faces danced slowly round in frot of him: the hunchback, his grandmother, Polina, Zolotarev, Konashevich, Ovsyannikov and other faces, half-forgotten, washed away by time. They circled round before him, constantly repeating the same thing, one after the other, in every possible tone:

'Fedya!'

'Fedyok? . . .'

'Fedenka . . .'

'Fyodor Tikhonych . . .'

'Comrade Samokhin!'

'Fedya–a–a . . .'

Fyodor forced open his eyes. Beyond the portholes in the dull dawn, the dark grey waves were still lashing the sky. But the rocking had become calmer, less violent, the cold less keen, more bearable, and the water in the cabin had hardly increased. Through the creaking of the beams and the splashing outside, he made out Lyuba's voice: 'Fedya–a–a!' She was huddled in the corner, clinging convulsively to the edge of the bench, with the sheepskin coat over her head. 'What will happen now, Fedya, we're going to die!'

Shaking off the last vestiges of sleep, Fyodor moved over to reassure her: 'God willing, we'll survive, Lyuba. He'll get us out of it.' Realizing she couldn't stay in this position for very long, he suddenly rememberd the chest where he kept his tools at the back of the cabin. 'Hold on, Lyuba!' A minute later he had thrown all the junk out of it. 'Just a minute, Lyuba, and you can sleep like in a cradle.' His hands were functioning of their own accord, way ahead of his consciousness: he carefully pulled out the sleeping-bag from under her, stretched it out along the bottom of the chest, and then helped her to get up. Holding one arm round her shoulders and using the other to find his way, he led her over to the chest. 'Lie down, Lyuba, it's more comfortable here.' He stretched out the fragile body with its swollen stomach in the spacious refuge of the chest and covered her with the sheepskin. 'Go to sleep, Lyuba. Time goes faster when you're asleep.'

'I'm frightened, Fedya!'

'I know, Lyuba, I know.'
'It all seems like a dream.'
'Maybe it is a dream, Lyuba.'
'We're so unlucky, Fedya.'
'Who can say, Lyuba, who can say?'
'But isn't it obvious?'
'Sleep, my darling, sleep . . .'

Soon she calmed down, her sunken, blotchy face relaxed, swaying smoothly with the boat in the light of stormy dawning.

'What will be will be,' thought Fyodor, resigned to their lot, stretching out to sleep again. 'We'll die when we're fated to!'

4

Blazing sunshine, beating straight into his eyes, woke Fyodor. The deafening silence flowed into him, melting away the leaden heaviness of his body. He even blinked to try to gather his wits about him, so inconceivable was this radiant vision. 'Can it really be over?' he thought with dizzy triumph. 'Have we really survived?'

Stretching out with difficulty, he got up and stared out of the porthole: outside, as far as the eye could see, the polished mirror of the sea was steaming smoothly, with a fragile contour of shore over to one side. Thirstily drinking in this unexpected blessing, he finally concluded with relief, 'We've survived!'

In excitement, he rushed over to Lyuba. She was lying in the chest sleeping like a child, with her arm under her head. Her freckled face was suffused by the bliss of oblivion. You might have thought that the tempest and the mortal despair of the last few days had happened somewhere above her, above this dream of hers, away from her chance refuge.

Trying not to wake her unnecessarily, he clambered up on deck, and the expanse that opened up before him left him gasping for breath. Stern-first for some reason, the launch had run firmly aground on a sandbank in the middle of a horseshoe-shaped bay dominated on all sides by bluish volcanoes in the haze of early morning. Beneath them ran a band of vivid yellow sand.

'Fedya,' he heard the faint voice from below, 'eh, Fed!' He turned round with a start: screwing up her eyes in the sun, Lyuba was looking up towards him, her voice trembling slightly. 'Where are we?'

Fyodor burst out laughing and only afterwards exclaimed:

'We're here, Lyubanya, Berezan Station, anyone for Berezan get off here . . . Don't forget your cases, citizens!'

'Where are we though, Fedya?' She was gradually coming to. 'Where have we stopped?'

'Over the hills and far away,' He teased her again. 'Don't you like it?'

'All you think of is making jokes.' Emerging from the warm shade of the cabin, she moved, swam towards him. 'Tell me the truth.' As she moved she kept her eyes screwed up, but when she was on the level of the deck and had got used to the light, she opened them in astonishment and her voice broke. 'Lord, where is this place?'

'Don't ask where, Lyubanya.' He helped her on to the deck and she nestled trustingly against him, looking around expectantly. 'The main thing is, we're here now,' said Fyodor. 'God willing, we'll be all right.'

'I'm afraid, Fedya.'

'We've survived far worse, we'll survive this too.'

'You know best.'

'Right then, there's no point hanging about waiting for something to happen, we'd better get moving; you never know, there might be another storm, the water's very treacherous round here.' He carefully loosened her grip and slowly began to disembark. 'Hold on, Lyubanya!'

The shock of the water burnt him, but it turned out to be only waist-deep, and he soon got used to it as he tested the smooth, almost flat bottom beneath his feet.

'Maybe we should wait a bit longer?' She looked down imploringly at him. 'Maybe we could call someone?'

Fyodor silently stretched out his arms towards her and she obediently leant towards him, clumsily swung her body over the low rail and fell straight into his embrace. He carried her ashore like this, looking into her eyes and smiling uncontrollably: 'Have you got your breath back?'

'Uh-huh,' she replied, smiling. 'Uh-huh.'

'Are you frozen?'

'No, no, Fedya, I'm fine!'

'We'll soon be there.'

'Am I heavy, Fedya?'

'You can say that again,' he chuckled. 'There are two of you now, after all.'

Then they both laughed: quietly, conspiratorially, trustingly.

The water was getting lower and lower, revealing the sandy

ripples beneath his feet. Finally they stepped out on to the already burning sand of the coastal strip. And only then did he put her down. And he sighed. And looked around him.

The beach stretched in a fragile half-loop around the bay. The place was studded with volcanoes and on the top of the highest one of all he made out a tower with a bright width of flag hanging over it: rising sun on a white field. He realized with heart-stopping poignancy – this was foreign soil!

But they had to go on living. And he said to her: 'Let's go, Lyuba.'

5

'And the Lord smelled a sweet savour, and the Lord said in His heart: I will not curse the earth any longer because of man, for the imagination of man's heart is evil from his youth; neither will I again smite every living thing, as I have done. While the earth remains, sowing and harvest, cold and heat, summer and winter, day and night will not cease.'

Paris – La Baule
1976–8

Glossary

Ataman – Cossack chief

Baty – Baty, or more precisely, Batu Khan (1208?–55), Mongol conqueror of north-east and southern Russia (1237–41) and founder of the Golden Horde

Brokgaus and Efron – major pre-revolutionary encyclopaedia

Chaldons – native inhabitants of Siberia

Chapaev – legendary leader of the Red Army during the Civil War

Chekist – member of the post-revolutionary security police

Chemo tsitsi, Natella – Georgian folksong

Denikin – White Army general

Dzerzhinsky – founder and first head of the Soviet security services

Furmanov – Political Commissar of Chapaev (qv). He wrote a novel about him of the same name

Gamardzhoba . . . gagimardzhes – Georgian greeting and its reply

Gendarme – member of the pre-revolutionary political police

Girei – Sultan Kilech Girei, Georgian émigré, who had fought with the Whites during the Civil War

GPU – secret police

Great Hold-up – during and after the 1905 revolution, the Bolshevik Party effected a number of hold-ups, of which the most famous is the so-called 'Great Hold-up', on the State Bank in Tiflis in 1907

Guiliaks – Siberian people, present-day Mivkhs

Kalinin – Mikhail Ivanovich Kalinin, President of the Soviet Union 1922–46

Kherson – birthplace of Trotsky

Kolyma – in eastern Siberia, site of some of the harshest Soviet labour camps

Komsomol – Young Communist League

Komsomolets – Member of the Young Communist League

Krasnov – Pyotr Nikolayevich Krasnov, 1869–1947. Cossack general, commander of one of the White armies during the Civil War, émigré. Fought with the Germans in the Second World War, surrendered to the British. Handed back by them to the Soviets in May 1945, he was condemned to death and executed

Kureika – in March 1914 Stalin was moved from Turukhansk (qv) to this settlement on the lower reaches of the river Yenisei

Kuriles – islands in the Pacific off the eastern coast of Siberia. The closeness of their name to the Russian verb *kurit* (to smoke), is noted by the author

Kutia – traditional food at a Russian funeral

Lapti – bast sandals, traditional dress of the Russian peasant

Lezginka – Georgian dance

Lyubyanka – Moscow headquarters of the security police since the Revolution

Malyuta – man employed by Ivan the Terrible to do his dirty deeds

Manilov – character in Gogol's *Dead Souls*, the embodiment of sentimental unctuousness

MGB – Ministry of State Security

Monomakh – Vladimir Monomakh, 1053–1125, Grand Prince of Kiev 1113–25, a time of the strengthening of Kievan Russia. The words 'you are heavy, crown of Monomakh', spoken by Boris Godunov in Pushkin's play of the same name, have become proverbial

MVD – Ministry of the Interior

Nechaev – revolutionary nihilist of the mid–nineteenth century, author of the *Catechism of a Revolutionary*, with its slogan 'the end justifies the means'.

NKVD – security police

Nomenklatura – higher ranks of the party and state apparatus

Novodevichy – famous Moscow cemetery

Okhrana – Tsarist political police

Organs – popular name for the organs of the security services

Pimen – chronicler monk in Pushkin's historical drama *Boris Godunov*

Pyatidesyatnik – chief of fifty Cossacks

Sermyaga – coarse woollen-cloth coat, traditional dress of the Russian peasant

Shkuro – Andrei Grigorevich Shkuro, 1887–1947, Cossack chief, emigrated after fighting in the army of Denikin (qv) during the Civil War. Handed over to the Soviets by the British after collaborating with the Germans in the Second World War

Stolypin – Pyotr Arkadevich Stolypin, 1862–1911, Tsarist Minister of the Interior and Prime Minister 1906–11. Assassinated

Stundists – sect, influenced by German Protestantism, in southern Russia and the Ukraine

Tolstoy, Lyoshka – Count Aleksei Tolstoy, 1883–1945, the so-called 'Red Count', Soviet writer noted for his cynicism

Turukhansk – province in northern Siberia, first place of exile of Stalin after his arrest in 1913

Tyubiteika – Central Asian embroidered skull-cap

Verst – pre-revolutionary measure of length, approximately two-thirds of a mile

Zek – labour-camp prisoner